There was no way back to the Compact. A single communication from House Hiritsu had made it clear that the Warrior House would accept nothing less than unconditional surrender. Major Smithson thought to relocate what was left of the Lancers and their mercenary support to the mountains, the better to remain isolated until Duchess Liao negotiated for their return or possibly sent a retrieval force. But after four attempts, Doles doubted they would ever make it out of Qingliu.

A Gauss slug slammed into his right arm at the wrist, crushing the medium laser and ripping the *Grasshopper*'s right hand clean off. Two Hiritsu BattleMechs pressed forward, identified by his computer as a *Yu Huang* assault 'Mech and a medium-weight *Huron Warrior*. His HUD showed that the *Wraith* had joined with two other 'Mechs to now threaten Major Smithson's *Victor*.

That Yu Huang *will eat me alive,* he thought. . . .

BATTLETECH®

Threads of Ambition

Book One of *The Capellan Solution*

Loren L. Coleman

A ROC BOOK

ROC
Published by the Penguin Group
Penguin Putnam Inc., 375 Hudson Street,
New York, New York 10014, U.S.A.
Penguin Books Ltd, 27 Wrights Lane,
London W8 5TZ, England
Penguin Books Australia Ltd, Ringwood,
Victoria, Australia
Penguin Books Canada Ltd, 10 Alcorn Avenue,
Toronto, Ontario, Canada M4V 3B2
Penguin Books (N.Z.) Ltd, 182–190 Wairau Road,
Auckland 10, New Zealand

Penguin Books Ltd, Registered Offices:
Harmondsworth, Middlesex, England

First published by Roc, an imprint of Dutton NAL,
a member of Penguin Putnam Inc.

First Printing, May, 1999
10 9 8 7 6 5 4 3 2 1

Series Editor: Donna Ippolito
Mechanical Drawings: Duane Loose and the FASA art department
Cover art by Bruce Jensen

 REGISTERED TRADEMARK — MARCA REGISTRADA

This book is dedicated to Mike Stackpole
—one of my *Sifu,* and a good friend.

I would like to offer my appreciation to the following people who, each in their own way, made this novel possible.

Jim LeMonds, for his teaching and continued friendship. My parents, who have (more or less) stopped asking me to get a "real job." The *Orlando Group*—with special notice to Matt and Tim, computer gurus, and Russell Loveday, resident expert on weapons of mass destruction.

Mike Stackpole, who helped me realize the scope of the story I wanted to tell here, and has helped to keep me sane during my exile. Or relatively so.

Always, Dean Wesley Smith and Kristine Kathryn Rusch, whose continued support and friendship mean so much.

The FASA BattleTech team of Bryan Nystul and Randall Bills, who continue to guide the universe forward. Chris Hartford, Chris Hussey, Chris Trossen—for their comments. The FASA editorial staff—especially Donna Ippolito, who lets me get away with murder. Literally, that is.

BattleTech fans Maurice Fitagerald and Warner Doles, who contributed to charity for their appearances.

My agent, Don Maass, for taking a chance.

My family—Heather, Talon, Conner, and our newest addition, Alexia Joy, without whom this all would mean nothing.

Position in relation to the Inner Sphere

Coreward

Anti-spinward

Spinward

Rimward

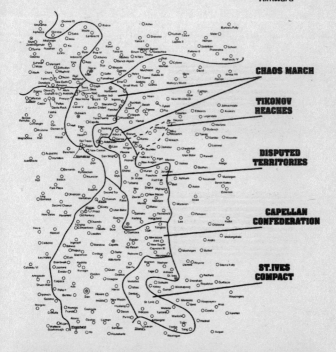

CHAOS MARCH

TIKONOV REACHES

DISPUTED TERRITORIES

CAPELLAN CONFEDERATION

ST. IVES COMPACT

CENTRAL INNER SPHERE

· CIRCA 3060 ·

Prologue

Celestial Palace
Zi-jin Cheng (Forbidden City), Sian
Sian Commonality, Capellan Confederation
3 March 3060

The elevator doors opened onto the palace's Strategic Command Center with barely a sound. Sun-Tzu Liao, Chancellor of the Capellan Confederation and current First Lord of the resurrected Star League, stepped into his war room, the folds of his dark green, heavy silk robes whispering softly. Despite his quiet entrance all activity ceased. His three top advisors turned and stood waiting attentively, among the computers and holographic maps. Not one of them would expect to enjoy the Chancellor's good will. Not today.

One of them, Sun-Tzu felt sure, *expects to be shot.*

Sun-Tzu stared back, saying nothing. Behind him the elevator doors, disguised to seem part of the room's teakwood paneling, slid shut. He slowly ran one hand down his robe to straighten the deep collar with its fine embroidery—black-threaded tigers chasing golden *darndao* swords—and permitted himself to enjoy the smooth touch of the silk. He managed a very thin smile that he knew would only heighten the tension in the room. The Liao family was not known for its humor.

The rage his aides would be expecting was there, to be sure, and it burned down in the core of his being, warming him. But to blind rage he refused to succumb. His grandfather, even before Hanse Davion drove him insane, might have indulged in such rages. His mother, Romano Liao, in her time as Chancellor, certainly had; the purges had been frequent and bloody. Sun-Tzu refused to be his mother. He controlled his emotions, studied them, then directed any anger toward more constructive ends.

"Six months," he said, voice barely a whisper. "Victor Davion has been absent from the Inner Sphere for six months, and I am just informed today?"

He stalked forward, angling to the left of the small group to see what they had been studying on his arrival. A two-dimensional holographic projection stretched floor to ceiling in the middle of the room, but arriving from the elevator had placed him end-on to it. Sun-Tzu noted the light sweat beading the forehead of Sasha Wanli, the aging Maskirovka Intelligence Director, who stepped back a nervous pace to allow him an unobstructed view.

The Inner Sphere, a globular area roughly a thousand light years in diameter, was displayed in its common, compressed two-dimensional format but at only half the size capable by the projection field. Still, large enough to make out the outlines of the various Great Houses that controlled most of the star systems humanity had come to occupy since leaving the safety of Terra so many centuries ago. At this scale Sun-Tzu's Capellan Confederation looked a thin, truncated slice of space. Tiny next to the mammoth Federated Commonwealth, which bordered the Confederation on one side, or Thomas Marik's Free Worlds League, which flanked the other. Even the wedge of space conquered by the Clans, carved from the Lyran Alliance and the Draconis Combine, occupied more space.

And the Clans were the reason for the shrunken scale of the map, as well as the absence of Sun-Tzu's most dangerous enemy, Victor Steiner-Davion. "So where is he?" he demanded.

Not needing to be told who *he* was, Sasha Wanli stepped forward nervously and brushed her hand over the long trail of stars known as the Exodus Road. "We assume Victor Davion's task force is within this area. Not quite to the Clan home-worlds, but close." The Exodus Road was a chain of stars hooking out spinward and coreward from the Draconis Combine border. The path by which Alexandr Kerensky had originally led the ancient Star League Defense Force to a new home, three centuries prior, and the path that had brought them back just ten years ago as the invading Clans.

Sun-Tzu estimated the distance remaining to Victor. "It was to take Morgan Hasek-Davion nine months to a year to make that trip with Task Force Serpent. How does Victor do it in seven?"

Colonel Talon Zahn, Strategic Director of the Confederation Armed Forces, calmly took the question. The man's cold, dark eyes belied his youth, revealing a shrewdness far beyond his years. "Serpent moved on a course parallel to and longer than the Exodus Road, approaching Clan Smoke Jaguar's homeworld unawares."

With a laser-pointer, he flashed an arc over the map to indicate a rough course. "But no one expected the Jaguars' Inner Sphere occupation force to be routed so easily." Zahn gave his master a steady gaze, showing respect but no fear. "Victor moves quickly because he now chases the remnants of that occupation force along the shortest distance to their homeworld."

"Which means he can return just as quickly," Sun-Tzu said, his voice hard as he considered the time lost to faulty intelligence. He watched Sasha Wanli pale. *Compared to Zahn, her incompetence is as obvious as her age.* "Victor has Star League units under his command, " Sun-Tzu said. "As First Lord I should have been informed of their departure for the Clan homeworlds, not fed the public story about clean-up operations in the nearby Periphery. Can he justify that?"

"Almost certainly," Zahn said. "As I read the Maskirovka reports, everyone expects the First Lord position to be largely ceremonial." Slight pause there, which Sun-Tzu read as being more for emphasis than nervousness. Zahn's blunt, straight-forward style was a quality Sun-Tzu tolerated, even appreciated at times, and was what had originally drawn the man to his attention. So long as the senior colonel continued to operate at a high level of competency.

"Though you officially bestowed the SLDF colors on every participating unit," Zahn was saying, "all units were then given into the command of Victor, who apparently made the decision to pursue based on operational security." Zahn glanced over to Sasha Wanli, who reluctantly nodded agreement.

Sun-Tzu didn't like what he was hearing, but he also needed to get the whole story. He glared at Wanli to remind her that he hadn't forgotten her, then turned back to Zahn. "You have estimated Victor's chances for surviving this trip to Clan space?" The question was unanswerable and he knew it. But he wasn't yet ready to deal with the Maskirovka failure, and he wished to gauge his Strategic Director's response.

Talon Zahn never missed a beat. "It would be foolish, for me, to assume anything less than one hundred percent, Chancellor. Victor Davion has shown himself tenacious in the most extreme circumstances. He has survived a decade of battle with the Clans, and now has driven the Smoke Jaguars from the Inner Sphere."

Sun-Tzu nodded curtly, impressed by the quick response but feeling his anger threatening to explode. Zahn was young for his post, barely thirty-six, but he possessed one of the sharpest military minds in the Confederation. Though his appointment to the realm's highest military position threatened older, more complacent colonels, no one dared comment on his age, with Sun-Tzu himself just twenty-nine. Of the Inner Sphere royals, only Katrina Steiner-Davion was younger.

Of course, Yvonne Steiner-Davion was even younger, but Sun-Tzu didn't count her, for Yvonne only sat on the throne of the Federated Commonwealth as Victor's regent. And Arthur, youngest of the Steiner-Davion brood, was four times removed from power by older siblings so he hardly mattered at all. Katrina, though, deserved recognition as a near equal. Three years ago she had wrested the Lyran Commonwealth away from her brother—half his realm, which she blithely announced would henceforth be known as the Lyran Alliance under her rule. Yes, Katrina had proved herself a force to be reckoned with.

"And what of your thoughts, Ion?" Sun-Tzu turned to the final member present. Ion Rush, Master of Warrior House Imarra and Grand Master of all eight Warrior Houses, stood behind Zahn, arms clasped behind his back and affecting an air of stoic acceptance. A large man with Slavic features, he wore a simple field uniform of ivory and what was commonly called Liao green. Sun-Tzu valued the man's counsel, though it often had to be solicited. *As with his loyalty,* Sun–Tzu thought.

"You have been very quiet, Master Rush."

"*Dui,* Chancellor," the large man said, "I have." Rush frowned slightly in concentration, as if evaluating which of his recent thoughts were worth bringing to the attention of his Chancellor, and then merely shrugged. "There is nothing more to add."

"Ah, but there is." Sun-Tzu rounded on his Maskirovka Directress, narrowing his jade green eyes. "A matter of six months during which the implied threat of Victor Davion in command of a multi-national army should not have been looming over my head."

Sasha clasped age-wrinkled hands together behind her back. She had assumed command of the Maskirovka upon the death of Tsen Shang, Sun-Tzu's father who had died alongside Romano. Health reasons had forced her to retire once, but Sun-Tzu had called her back when the interim director had proven intractable to the point of meriting execution for conducting rogue operations. Sun-Tzu knew Sasha would be considering the fact that few were the Maskirovka directors who died of natural causes, and wondering if her time had finally come.

"As I attempted to explain earlier, Celestial Wisdom, the secrecy that shielded Victor's movements in the Draconis Combine from the Clans also hid him from our surveillance. The Mask has few highly placed agents anywhere near the Combine's upper political levels. And when Victor set out after the fleeing Jaguar forces, Theodore Kurita's security net prevented our agents learning of it until just recently when one of them managed to infiltrate the lower levels of the Combine's ISF."

Sun-Tzu resisted the urge to lash out at his intelligence director. *Physical violence will not give me back the six months we've lost.* He worked through a relaxation technique, calming his tight muscles. "So what can be done, now that we *do* know?"

Sasha answered quickly, no doubt in an attempt to mirror Zahn's earlier decisiveness. "I have orders drawn up for the termination of the field agents who failed to discover Victor's absence. They only require—"

Now Sun-Tzu did strike her. His left arm flashed out in a vicious backhand slap. The last three fingernails on each hand had been grown out ten centimeters in an affectation favored by his father, carbon-reinforced and razor sharp. They left three bloody slices across Sasha's cheek. Not a disabling blow, though he certainly could have killed her, and not out of rage for her earlier failure. It was a stinging slap, meant to chastise and shame her.

"You tell me of our depleted intelligence sources in the Combine, and now you want to kill those we do have?" he hissed in a mocking whisper. "Did you learn nothing from my father?"

To her credit, Sasha stood mute and did not raise a hand to wipe away the blood that beaded and ran down her neck. Sun-Tzu's green eyes flashed as he took in all three of his advisors. "I want to know what we do *now* to take advantage of Victor's absence."

Talon Zahn spoke first, always ready. "We have plans underway for reclaiming much of the Disputed Territories." He reached down to punch up a request on a nearby console. The holographic map changed to display only the Capellan Confederation and its immediately surrounding space. The two worlds that remained of the old Sarna Supremacy nestled against the Confederation's coreward border, and beyond that lay the unclaimed but pro-Liao region of the Chaos March to which Zahn referred. Hanse Davion had taken those systems and many more during the Fourth Succession War over thirty years ago. Sun-Tzu's efforts in the Marik-Liao offensive of 3057 had freed them from the Federated Commonwealth but failed to bring them completely back into the Confederation. The situation worsened where the map stretched up toward the ceiling, displaying the Chaos March proper, where dominance by any Great House had been thrown off, and the planets themselves claiming complete independence.

"If we rely on mercenaries," Zahn continued, "and perhaps Magistracy troops, we can step up our operations there. Nothing major, but a place to start and easily incorporated into your Xin Sheng efforts."

The Chancellor nodded. Wringing the First Lord office for every ounce of prestige, Sun-Tzu had instigated sweeping economic, social, and military reforms within the Confederation under the call of *Xin Sheng*. Meaning rebirth or new birth, it was nothing less than a renewed Capellan effort to rebuild the internal strength of the realm. Most significant among the reforms had been the strengthening of the fledging alliance with the Magistracy of Canopus, begun just before his election to the post of First Lord.

Sun-Tzu traced the edge of his chin with his right forefinger. "How *are* the Magistracy units doing?" he asked. In return for technological aid, the Magistracy provided military support in a relationship very similar to the Confederation's Warrior Houses. The Magestrix' two eldest daughters currently commanded several regiments' worth of BattleMechs and infantry either within Confederation borders or as part of Sun-Tzu's contribution to the Star League forces.

"No major incidents to report," Sasha said in a subdued voice, obviously choosing her words with great care. "Danai Centrella has apparently accompanied Prince Victor's task force to Clan space. Naomi Centrella, commanding the bulk of the Magistracy forces, is working very hard to help integrate her troops with yours." This news was significant; Danai was the Magestrix' eldest daughter and heir.

"They are enthusiastic," Colonel Zahn said. "I would not mind testing them."

Sun-Tzu was thinking of doing just that. "What of the Detroit Conference? Can we move that up?"

The world of Detroit lay near the floor of the holographic map. Located in the New Colony Region between the Magistracy and the Taurian Concordat, just rimward of the Confederation border, it was the site of a minor 'Mech production facility that Capellan engineers were renovating to incorporate newer technology. BattleMechs, two-story war machines often constructed on a humanoid model, might reign supreme on the field in general, but the Periphery still lacked much of the rediscovered technology. Again, Sasha Wanli answered carefully. "Not if you want the factory back on-line for the public relations boost that would give you, Chancellor Liao. My analysts recommend you allow it to produce at least one full company of 'Mechs before you travel there to meet with Emma Centrella and Jeffrey Calderon."

Sun-Tzu's forehead tightened in frustration. Meeting with Emma Centrella would do little more than strengthen the ties already existing between Confederation and Magistracy. Jeffrey Calderon, ruler of the nearby Taurian Concordat, was the key to further support.

Support I must have, Sun-Tzu thought. *With no significant old business to be advanced, new plans are in order.*

He typed his own request into a nearby console. On the map, a light outline of the old Confederation border sketched itself around star systems to include the Sarna Supremacy, most of the Chaos March and the Federated Commonwealth worlds that had once been the Tikonov Commonality. Another ethereal line enfolded the nearby St. Ives Compact—once the St. Ives Commonality. His aunt, Candace Liao, ruled the Compact. She had deserted the Confederation in the Fourth Succession War, taking her realm with her. It still remained lost to the Confederation, a recognized member of the new Star League, but not forgotten.

"You are thinking of Sarna again?" Ion Rush asked, nodding toward the tiny two-world alliance that sat on the coreward border. In 3058 Sun-Tzu had given him the task of hurting the Sarna Supremacy, which he had performed admirably.

"Two years ago you and Zahn both assured me that Sarna was ours to control through its food supply." Sun-Tzu raised a delicate eyebrow at them both. "Has the situation changed?"

Both shook their heads, and then realization dawned as they studied the old border lines for a second time. Again, Rush was a touch faster. "St. Ives? Forgive me Chancellor, but the Star League member states would never stand for that. Candace . . ." He paused, careful in selecting his next words. ". . . Candace would turn the others against you."

Sun-Tzu neither confirmed or denied the House Master's speculation. He simply stared at the map. "Sasha, what are the current projections for Katrina Steiner-Davion?"

"There are reports of civil unrest originating across the entire Federated Commonwealth. Yvonne Steiner-Davion is flustered and out of her depth." Before Sun-Tzu could ask, she added, "We do not know, yet, if these reports are real or engineered by Katrina. Regardless, our profile of her, incorporating the data you provided from your meeting at the Star League conference on Tharkad, suggests that she will make an attempt to claim the rest of her brother's realm while he is away."

Also privileged with the information from that meeting, Ion Rush spoke up, following his earlier train of thought. "But in the meantime Yvonne, Theodore Kurita, Magnusson, and Candace herself form an unassailable power bloc within the Star League. Hypothetically," he continued, no doubt hedging to preserve some form of respect for his master, "as First Lord of the new Star League you could be doubly damned, Chancellor, if you were seen as abandoning your responsibilities for nationalistic efforts."

Noting Talon Zahn's silence, Sun-Tzu looked to his senior colonel, who stared back evenly for several long seconds and then shrugged. "Militarily the Compact is no match for the Confederation, though even with Magistracy troops that will be stretching our resources thin if we are to continue our other efforts. St. Ives would not be easy to hold." He shrugged again. "By your will, of course, Chancellor."

Reaching out, Sun-Tzu brushed the fingers of one hand over the Chaos March worlds. "We still support irregulars and professional resistance cells within the Chaos March, correct?" He waited for Zahn's nod of assent. "Replace them with line units and begin an organized push to reclaim as much of the Chaos March as possible," he said. "Move the resistance effort to the Tikonov worlds controlled by the Federated Commonwealth."

Zahn blinked, a fair display of surprise for him. "Tikonov? You expect to hold the Tikonov worlds without a secure border stretching that far coreward?"

"I never said I would try to hold those worlds for myself,"

Sun-Tzu said evenly, the plans meshing together in his mind. He would have to rely heavily on his Maskirovka intelligence people, but that would at least give Sasha a chance to redeem herself. "I simply want them causing trouble for whomever sits on the FedCom throne of New Avalon." His gaze sharpened. "And I want those people in place by *zhong-qiu-jie,* the Autumn Festival. They can use it to help rebuild traditional Capellan sentiments."

His advisors glanced at each other, none of them able to read his intentions. "What of St. Ives?" Ion Rush finally asked for the three of them. "You spoke of—"

Sun-Tzu shook his head, cutting off his Warrior House Master. "*You* spoke of," he said, his jade gaze taking in all three.

More glances. Sasha Wanli appeared confused and frustrated, her normally sharp mind unable to piece together the picture that was becoming ever clearer to Sun-Tzu. Ion Rush lapsed back into his usual stoicism, silently contemplating his master. Only Talon Zahn appeared unconcerned with understanding Sun-Tzu's train of thought. "So what, if any, are your plans for St. Ives?" he asked bluntly.

Sun-Tzu—Chancellor, First Lord and, above all else, Liao—merely smiled disarmingly. "I believe I shall arrange a tour."

Path of Shadows

Nothing is more difficult than the art of maneuver. What is difficult is to make the devious route the most direct and turn misfortune to advantage.

Thus, march by an indirect route and divert the enemy by enticing him with a bait.

—Sun-Tzu, *The Art of War*

The art of misdirection has its purposes; for what leader does not rely on it on a daily basis? But such deceptions, political or military, can carry a realm only so far toward victory. After that, it remains in the purview of the warriors.

—Sun-Tzu Liao, journal entry, 21 February 3058, Sian

1

Shen-cai Amphitheater
Gao Shan Province, Sarna
Sarna Supremacy
25 June 3060

Sarna's bright afternoon sunlight beat down on the carved gray rock of the amphitheater, picking out the dark cracks that had formed naturally over time and bringing out the rich grain of the redwood stage. Carefully trimmed pines ringed the upper rim, and cultivated fern, ivy, and jade plants grew in redwood boxes set strategically within the immense bowl. No flowering plants, full of perfume, and no trees whose colors would turn with the seasons. Only green and a fresh woodsy scent to the air; nature's most basic forms.

A good choice for the induction ceremony, Company Leader Aris Sung thought grudgingly.

Aris stood at proud attention on the redwood stage, a light summer breeze running soft fingers through his short-cropped black hair. He flanked House Master Ty Wu Non on the left, while Infantry Commander Jessup stood a similar post on Master Non's right. Only a small section of the theater's seating was occupied; the first five rows fronting the stage, five warriors deep to either side of the main aisle. Slightly better than half of House Hiritsu's infantry battalion. Aris and Ty Wu Non were the only MechWarriors present—Ty Wu Non in his capacity as House Master, Aris as the aspirant's sponsor. All present wore the black and green dress uniforms of House Hiritsu, cloaks pinned open as was custom in a House ceremony.

All wore the uniform save the aspiring House warrior, Li Wynn.

Li knelt at the foot of the main aisle, hands resting on his thighs and head bent forward in supplication. The young man wore a simple, dark green silk robe, the closest yet he had ever been allowed to formal House Hiritsu colors. Though he'd never been in Li's position—Aris' own initiation into the Warrior House had been very atypical—he knew Li would be mentally rehearsing prepared responses to the formal questions that Aris and Jessup would put to him.

As the aspirant's sponsor, Aris recognized the duty that demanded his presence. And it was unfair to Li Wynn that Aris begrudged him the entry ceremony he himself had never received. All things being equal, however, Aris would rather be strapped into the cockpit of his *Wraith* and leading his 'Mech company through today's exercise maneuvers.

So long as I am wishing, why not hope that we receive assignment soon to the Disputed Territories or even the Chaos March? The Sarna Supremacy might be considered a high-tension post, but it is also decidedly low-action.

Sarna, dependent on the Capellan Confederation for steady food supplies ever since they had recently lost their agricultural world of Kaifeng to House Hiritsu, was now forced to sell at reduced value their entire military production to the Confederation, which then brokered it to the Star League. The Star League member states, the same nations that had once recognized the Supremacy as a legitimate independent government, had turned a blind eye to the situation so long as Sun-Tzu Liao kept military supplies flowing to the offensive against Clan Smoke Jaguar, and even now continued to ignore the Supremacy's situation.

The "deal" also called for one Confederation unit to act as observers, ensuring that the Sarnese carried through on their part. House Hiritsu had drawn that honor for the past six months, largely in reward for their earlier service. But to Aris and most of the House the post was standard garrison duty, to be endured until the state called them forward again. All House warriors wanted to take an active part in strengthening the

Confederation. Even Li Wynn, who had confided to Aris that it was the Chancellor's Xin Sheng call for a "renewed Capellan effort" that had prompted him to petition for membership in House Hiritsu. "When the House is called forward again," Li had said, "I want to be a part of it."

Aris appreciated such sentiment and, remembering Li Wynn's assistance on Kaifeng, had backed the young man's request to join the Warrior House. *When the fighting comes, he will do well. But how much longer will it be?*

Aris could never have guessed how quickly he would receive an answer to his question.

Warrior-aspirant Li Wynn felt the ceremony of the moment weighing on him. The period of reflection, waiting for the House Master to call him forward, was harder than any of his time spent on the streets of Kaifeng, dodging authorities or, under the Capellan occupation, BattleMechs. But for the first time in his twenty-one years, Li actually felt as if he could belong somewhere. And that, more than anything, carried him through.

"The aspirant may approach," House Master Non called out, his voice devoid of any emotion.

Li Wynn rose fluidly, the braid of his long dark hair brushing against his neck and upper back. He noticed that Ty Wu Non kept his eyes focused on the theater's rim to signify that Li Wynn was beneath his notice and would very likely remain so. Aris had explained that tradition demanded that new students be accepted by the House Master at age twelve, not age twenty-one. But the House Master *could* make exceptions. And though he had finally decided to make one in Li's case, that meant the aspirant could only expect his true acceptance to be a long time in coming.

With his future comrades looking on, Li Wynn mounted the stage and approached Aris Sung. His sponsor drew a simple *gim* dagger from beneath his cloak, holding it out edge-on to Li. "For services rendered to House Hiritsu and by extension the Capellan state," Aris said, speaking for the benefit of the audience rather than Li, "on the worlds of Kaifeng, Randar, and Sarna, the aspirant has been granted Capellan citizenship."

No small honor, that. And Li Wynn knew it. Even someone native-born to the Confederation was required to perform a service that somehow benefited the state. To come from outside required a significant contribution. Li remembered the arguments Aris had faced just so the younger man would be allowed to accompany House Hiritsu as a servant and occasional contact to street-bred news.

Aris looked down into Li Wynn's fierce dark eyes. "How will you continue to serve the Capellan nation?"

"In any way I can," Li said with utter conviction. "As a producing member of society, and I hope as a defender of the realm. So I do swear myself."

Awarding Li a thin smile, Aris nodded. Li placed the flat of his hand along the sharpened edge of the *gim,* breaking the skin and allowing blood to well up in his palm. Aris sheathed the blade. "Infantry Commander, I sponsor citizen Li Wynn for your consideration," he said, naming Li for the first time as a citizen and potential House warrior.

Stooping so as to not cross Ty Wu Non's line of sight, Li passed along to the commander of House Hiritsu's infantry battalion. The tall, well-built man stared down at the smaller Li Wynn. Jessup did not care for Li, the aspirant knew, but House Master Non had already allowed for his acceptance. *And the will of the House Master is the will of the House.* "To serve in a Warrior House is to serve both the state and the person of the Chancellor," Jessup stated. "What do you pledge to this service?"

The question was slightly misstated, and Li knew that Aris had arranged the slight deviation. Within tradition, to be sure, but giving the aspirant pause before answering and forcing him to alter his planned response. Li Wynn hesitated only a second, drawing sudden strength from the tranquility of the amphitheater's natural surroundings. "I pledge all that I am now and all that I am capable of becoming," he said, paraphrasing a House Hiritsu adage. "My honor, my service, my life."

The infantry commander unrolled Li's pledge scroll, on which the vows of House Hiritsu were inscribed in Chinese pictorial characters. In an open area near the bottom of the scroll, Li smeared his blood onto the vellum. No dainty mark, the blood slashed across in a wide, bold splash of color. Li noted that the blood neither ran over any vows nor off the edge of the vellum, favorable omens for long and honorable service, he hoped.

"House Master Non," Jessup said, "I have a potential warrior in need of guidance."

Half-turned toward the House Master, Li was able to read the faces of all three men and quickly realized by a tightening around the eyes and half-formed smile that Ty Wu Non had readied a surprise. The House Master turned his gaze on Aris. "Company Leader Aris Sung, by sponsoring this warrior, you have made yourself responsible for his conduct. I name you *Sifu*, his Mentor, so long as Infantry Commander Jessup has no objection, and relieve you of your other responsibilities."

"It would be a pleasure to have Aris Sung under my command again," Jessup responded immediately. So quickly, Li knew that he had been warned beforehand.

Aris stood dumbstruck for a few long seconds, and Li read the indecision there. A House *Sifu* was an honored position, carrying with it the prestige of inculcating younger warriors into House traditions and skills. But to be placed back within the ranks of infantry, relieved of his BattleMech company, seemed a demotion in itself. Then, realizing that his House Master awaited some response, Aris nodded his understanding. "I am honored by your trust, House Master."

Li nodded to Aris when his sponsor's gaze fell on him, hoping that Aris was now not regretting his decision. *I will not fail your trust,* he thought, willing Aris to read his mind.

Aris gave him back no answering expression.

Aris Sung and Infantry Commander Jessup waited with House Master Non while the House infantry filed out of the amphitheater. Infantryman Li Wynn trailed behind, last to disappear over the rim and doing so with only a single glance back at his new Mentor.

Aris waited patiently. He hoped for—indeed expected—an explanation from Ty Wu Non, but was not about to demand it. Central to Hiritsu intra-House relations were the teachings of K'ung-fu-tzu, and courtesy foremost among those. Ty Wu Non would broach the subject, or he would not and the matter would remain closed. A light summer breeze brought to Aris the scent of fresh pine, and he attempted to enjoy the moment while awaiting his House Master's opening remarks. It almost worked. The natural surroundings were ones Aris had learned to enjoy for their own sake, though they could not quite force his attention from the apparent loss of his company.

"You must be upset, but your appearance is one of tranquillity. You hide it well, Aris Sung."

Ty Wu Non's voice was speculative, but Aris doubted the House Master expected a confirming response. "Or it means I am not upset, House Master." Aris looked to Jessup for support, but found only stony silence. "I am confident that your reasons will make sense to me."

The House Master laughed, something he did seldom. "Well done, Aris. You prompt me to explain myself, without being impertinent enough to ask directly." His mirth quickly died, however. "You are being placed back within the infantry because I need you there. Our new orders have arrived."

That captured the attention of both Aris and Jessup. Chancellor Liao's recent expansion into the Disputed Territories and harder fighting in the coreward Chaos March region had left most House Hiritsu warriors hoping for combat assignment. Certainly their success in liberating Kaifeng argued for it. Aris frowned. But if the House was heading into combat, why would Master Non pull him from his company?

"We did not receive assignment to the Disputed Territories," Ty said, anticipating the question. "We have been selected as honor guard to Chancellor Liao himself. He is making a 'goodwill' tour of the Confederation side of our border with the St. Ives Compact. Isis Marik will accompany him." He paused, apparently marshaling his facts. "On Necromo and Capricorn III we are the main guard, supplemented by local militia. But with

Relevow and several worlds after we can also rely on McCarron's Armored Cavalry."

The Chancellor! Aris' head swam with the implications. No chance for combat, not if Sun-Tzu thought it safe enough for his presence and that of his fiancée, but the honor being shown House Hiritsu was nothing short of incredible. "And after the tour . . . ?"

Ty Wu Non deigned to pick up on the trailing question. "We are slated to accompany Chancellor Liao to the Detroit Conference. But after *that,* he promises us all the combat duty we can handle."

It was a lack of combat assignment that had once instigated unrest among the Hiritsu warriors, then almost ruined the Kaifeng operation. *Like owning a Liao stallion, and then forbidding it to race.* Aris shivered with anticipation, just as he knew his company would. Then he remembered that he had been relieved of his company, and the apparent reasoning behind House Master Non's pulling him from his command hit him full force. "I am on the honor squad?" he asked cautiously.

Ty Wu Non looked to Jessup, who smiled thinly and nodded his agreement with the House Master's unspoken endorsement. Jessup had obviously known a few of the details, but not all. The older infantryman gave Aris a good visual bracing, and then caught the younger warrior with a weighty gaze.

"You are *in charge* of the honor squad," he told Aris.

2

The simulator pod was the next best thing to being there, Cadet Maurice Fitzgerald decided, relishing the realism as a simulated head-hit bucked him hard against his four-point restraining harness. Hazlet's Home Guard training facility was the best on Nashuar, and Fitzgerald always looked forward to his class' sim time. It also had the added bonus of making up for his average academic status, placing him in the front-running for a MechWarrior position.

The enemy *Dasher* that had scored the hit against him attempted to disengage, its thin humanoid frame running off the side of Fitz' main screen and angling back out away from his position. A Clan OmniMech of impressive speed but very light armor, the *Dasher* was trying to use hit-and-run tactics against his larger *Blackjack*.

"*Bù zhè cì,*" he murmured, falling back on the Chinese his mother had taught him as his primary language. *Not this time.* He tracked left with a torso twist, working the foot pedals for a tight turn. As lead element for a lance, simulated or not, he wasn't about to allow a Clan scout 'Mech to report back on their position.

As his targeting reticule caught up with the *Dasher* and burned the deep gold of hard lock, Fitzgerald triggered both his *Blackjack*'s extended-range large lasers. From the ends of his

'Mech's barrel-like arms, ruby lances of coherent light stabbed across the field and into the fleeing enemy 'Mech. One lance of energy cored into the rear torso, carving away engine shielding. The second sliced through armor and the endo-steel skeleton beneath to amputate the right leg at the knee.

The lasers' energy demand pulled a spike from the fusion reactor that powered Fitz' BattleMech, and even as the *Dasher* toppled over a wave of heat slammed through the cockpit of the forty-five-ton *Blackjack*. Fitzgerald's vision swam and he gasped for breath, his ragged breathing loud in the confines of his neurohelmet. Only the cooling vest he wore alleviated some measure of the distress. Heat sinks installed around the engine quickly bled off the excess, though it left him well into the yellow band on his heat monitor.

And no time to cool down, he realized, as his head's up display painted a new threat coming in from his forward-left quarter. The HUD compressed 360 degrees of scanning ability into 120 degrees of vision, projected across the top of the *Blackjack*'s main viewscreen, and Fitz was ahead of the other Nashuar Home Guard trainees in learning to read it. He could tell from the HUD coding that he faced a medium-weight Clan Omni-Mech even before glancing to the auxiliary screen to find a fifty-ton Clan *Black Hawk* profiled.

The *Blackjack* rocked violently as the incoming *Black Hawk* sniped at him from medium range and scored several hits with its medium-bore autocannon. Fitz could picture armor raining down around the *Blackjack*'s feet, his protection becoming so much litter on the ground. Slamming down on his pedals, he engaged jump jets. The *Blackjack* lifted out of the *Hawk*'s line of fire on superheated jets of plasma, and the young MechWarrior angled his machine in toward the Clan Omni.

He landed rough, not yet accustomed to skywalking, and missed with a single laser attempt. Fortunately the neurohelmet linked his own sense of balance to that of the massive gyro that kept the *Blackjack* upright, and he held his footing with only the lightest adjustment on the control sticks. The *Hawk*, meanwhile, had run in across a patch of clear field, closing the gap, and while Fitz dealt with a new heat surge from his failed laser shot the Clanner rose on its own jump jets and sailed completely over the *Blackjack*.

Leapfrog maneuver! Too late Fitz worked the BattleMech into a turn, his muscles straining to pull the control sticks past their limit. The *Black Hawk* carved into his thin rear armor with everything it had, its large pulse laser and autocannon chewing through his torso and left-side protection, leaving it open for smaller weapons. Ironically it was a machine gun, mounted on the *Hawk* more for protection from unarmored infantry than engaging another 'Mech, that found the ammo supply for his short-ranged missile systems. The magazine ruptured and blew through his internals as the *Blackjack* effectively disintegrated.

The cockpit shook violently in the BattleMech's simulated death throes, the edges of the restraining straps digging into Fitzgerald's chest. Fortunately he was spared the neural feedback through his helmet that would accompany a normal ammunition explosion. His screens grayed out and then faded to black, with a simple message queued to one auxiliary monitor.

Report to simulation debriefing at once.

"Ma de dan!" Fitz cursed, slamming one fist down against his thigh. He unhooked his harness and safety equipment, shoved his neurohelmet up onto the ledge above the main viewscreen, and then climbed out of the simulator pod, still muttering over his bad fortune.

Fitz walked into the empty briefing room still clad only in the T-shirt, shorts, and combat boots that was normal garb for MechWarriors because of the high levels of heat buildup common in a 'Mech cockpit. He grabbed the first metal fold-down chair inside the small room and sat, tipping it back against the wall. The air-conditioned space felt good after the simulator's heat, though he knew that soon enough his sweat-damp clothes would turn chill to the skin. He swallowed dryly, mouth still parched from gasping the hot air. Part of him reveled in his spent condition, despite his performance, while another, more practical side worried over the effect today's performance would have on his scores.

"You could have showered," was Commander Nevarr's greeting as he entered the room.

Tall and muscular without running to heavy bulk, Nevarr looked every bit the Nordic hero with this tousled, white-blond hair and washed-out blue eyes. Soft-spoken and a bit hoarse, but able to make his voice carry, he habitually talked in short, easy speech, as if in practice for the battlefield, where all communication was clipped and to the point. Certainly he wasn't the average recruitment-poster soldier for the St. Ives Compact, which tended more toward Fitz' slender build, with or without the touch of Asian features that bespoke a Capellan heritage. Nevarr commanded the BattleMech company attached to Nashuar's Home Guard battalion, and personally oversaw the militia's training program. Somehow he got away with not wearing a uniform, dressing in a simple cut of black clothing that reminded Fitzgerald of a much older time.

"The message said at once, Commander," Fitz said, straightening up in his chair.

Nevarr grunted noncommittally, then grabbed a chair for himself. He sat, slouching forward as if some great weight rode on his shoulders. "What were you trying to do in there?" His voice was weary with frustration.

"Engaging the enemy, sir." Fitzgerald knew the answer would not be accepted, but from his point of view it was the least-damaging thing he could offer.

"Committing suicide was more like it." Nevarr leaned back, clasping black-gloved hands behind his head. "I expected you to take on the *Dasher,* though it tied you up longer than it should have. It was no match for your *Blackjack.* And its reconnaissance abilities presented a threat to the unit. The *Black Hawk,* though . . ." He paused, shaking his head. "That's a typical Clan support 'Mech. It rarely ranges out very far from its Starmates. If you see one, expect company soon. Another minute in the sim and two *Mad Cat*s would've popped into your rear quarter." Nevarr frowned. "You were point man for a lance. You should've fallen back."

Fitzgerald bristled at the advice, given to him as if it were holy writ, though he knew it was nothing personal. The commander talked to all cadets that way. "I felt I could take the *Black Hawk* and then pull back. I made one mistake, slipping into its jumping radius. If the two *Mad Cat*s had shown up, I would've pulled back. Clanners don't use concentrated fire anyway."

Nevarr rocked forward again. "That's playing by the old rules. Many of the Clans have adopted a more liberal attitude these days. These were programmed to open fire at once." He caught Fitz' attention in a gaze of blue ice. "You made the wrong choice."

Fists clenched but held to his sides, Fitz also felt the muscles tightening along the back of his neck and a warm flush creeping up to his collar. Nevarr knew how to cut into a cadet, without ever raising his voice or using profanity. What made it worse, he knew that Nevarr was right.

When Fitzgerald held his silence, Nevarr nodded once and continued. "You aren't much of a team player, Fitzgerald. You take risks without hope of backup. That will get you killed out there. And worse, it will get lancemates killed. Now just what are you trying to prove? And don't tell me 'nothing' because I know better. I see it in the way you pilot your 'Mech."

Fitz' muscles ached and his thirst left a metallic taste at the back of his throat, and now he began to regret not grabbing a shower before the debrief. Exhaling slowly, he dismissed the discomfort and organized his thoughts. "Just trying to prove that I'm good enough," he said finally. "You're testing eight of us from the Home Guard armor corps for two open MechWarrior billets. I want one of them." He paused for the briefest moment, then surged ahead. "Commander, I want a billet in the St. Ives Lancers of even the Cheveux Legers, someday. I *know* I'm good enough. Or at least I could be. But I don't have the credentials to make the St. Ives Academy, and so distinguishing myself in Home Guard 'Mech duty is my only chance. From there, I could request transfer directly into the Academy Training Group." Fitz sighed. "I don't want to go back to the rolling pillboxes."

Nevarr stared long and hard at Fitzgerald, rarely blinking,

until the cadet began to grow uncomfortable. "I've reviewed your files. Your aptitude is high enough to qualify for the Training Group on St. Ives, yes. I also know that your maverick performance would have you at the bottom of your class. Or bounced back to Nashuar's Home Guard by now, to stay."

Fitz felt his earlier flush spreading up and over his face. Nevarr had hit on just the right attack, shredding the cadet's armor. Being bounced from the Training Group, given that he ever made it there to begin with, *would* be worse than never joining it. It would send his career prospects straight into an administrative black hole—he'd be lucky to hold onto a simple MechWarrior billet then. *If the commander is willing to cut me some slack here, maybe I should be a bit more appreciative.* "All right. What do you want from me?"

"Try working with the group," Nevarr said at once, offering a thin but encouraging smile. "Play it safe for a while. Learn how good you are in a unit, then *maybe* you can learn how good you are by yourself."

Fitzgerald nodded wearily, resigned. "Okay. I'll try to do it your way."

"Good." Nevarr nodded sharply, then held Fitz fast with an icy stare. "And make no mistake," he said. "You'll learn it my way first, or you won't learn your way at all."

3

***DropShip* Pearl of True Wisdom**
Castle Sands Spaceport, Relevow
Capella Commonality, Capellan Confederation
8 August 3060

Isis Marik found Sun-Tzu in the *Lung Wang* Class DropShip's small gymnasium, cooling down from his daily workout with some tai chi exercises. The room smelled of neoleather-covered mats and the sweat of honest exertion; a pleasant, masculine mix. Not wishing to break his concentration she waited in the doorway, straightening the green-trimmed tan nehru jacket which she thought lent her a paramilitary Capellan look. Her chestnut brown hair cascaded over her shoulders, finally free from the bands that tied it back during spaceflight.

Planetfall on Relevow, the third world on Sun-Tzu's tour of the Compact border, placed them back into full contact with the rest of the Inner Sphere. Isis had spent the morning involved with her own concerns, answering the dozens of HPG communications that had finally caught up with her. They included only a brief message from her father, Captain-General of the Free Worlds League. There was also a brief note from Omi Kurita, extending good wishes for the health of her father's new family. *Hard to think of either Sherryl or Janos as my own family, after all, considering I've spent all of perhaps two months in their company.* No pity, not for her, but a touch of unavoidable regret.

"Yes, beloved?" Sun-Tzu said, straightening up from his final stretch and shaking sweat from his dark hair. He grabbed the towel he'd hung on a nearby post and mopped at his face, smiling warmly as he waited for her to speak.

Where other people might fear Sun-Tzu as Maximilian Liao reborn, Isis had found in her fiancé a strength of character and clarity of thought that she had grown to respect and even to love, and which most people did not see. *That he does not* allow *most people to see,* she amended. Sun-Tzu was not raised a warrior, as were most Inner Sphere leaders, but Isis recognized him as a master of appearances and manipulation—survival traits learned growing up in the madness of the Sian court under his mother.

"Word of Blake delivered a batch of messages," she informed him, working to keep the sadness from her voice that thoughts of Sun-Tzu's younger years always brought to her. "My father wished to inform us that little Janos' pneumonia appears to have run its course. He is out of danger."

Only a slight narrowing of his green eyes gave away the mask Sun-Tzu firmly settled in place. "Indeed," he said in carefully controlled tones. "Then you should draft a response to Thomas, from the both of us, expressing our happiness for him and his consort."

"Sherryl," Isis said, "his wife." She knew Sun-Tzu did not require the reminder. Thomas Marik's marriage to Sherryl Halas, and naming their new son as legitimate heir over Isis, should have removed any final obstacles to Isis marrying Sun-Tzu. That her father continued to stall on their wedding after an eight-year engagement was a source of constant frustration for them both. "I shall send a message at once," she promised.

When she did not retire immediately, Sun-Tzu draped the towel about his neck and regarded her now with neutral interest. "There is more?"

That his passions often ran hot and cold did not surprise or offend Isis, especially of late. In her opinion, Sun-Tzu had performed admirably as the initial First Lord, never flagging in his duty to the Star League but also working extremely hard to bring his own nation up to par with the rest of the Great Houses. This tour of worlds bordering the St. Ives Compact was important with respect to the latter effort, and many future decisions hung in the balance of its success. She smiled, hoping to offer him some support. "I thought you might wish to talk about your speech for this afternoon."

Sun-Tzu returned her smile, though she noticed that it did not quite reach his eyes. A cold, empty expression. "What was your opinion of our reception in the Necromo and Capricorn systems?" he asked, not bothering to smooth over the change in subject.

Isis could not be sure if she were being tested or consulted, though she preferred to assume the latter. "The people were very enthusiastic, especially on Necromo where the success of your economic reforms is easy to see. Capricorn III does not yet enjoy such a successful economy, but they receive a healthy subsidy from nearby Ares, which raises their standard of living." Isis' eyebrows knitted together as she worked to unravel a minor point. "Capricorn III has had a stronger resurgence of Capellan nationalism, though, judging by the latest fashions all based on Asian cuts and the swell in numbers for Capellan Armed Forces recruitment."

This time his smile reached his eyes. "You've been talking with Zahn."

"And Sasha," she said, then frowned, "though they will only discuss generalities with me." Sun-Tzu waved off her pique at being left in the dark on some matters, and she let the irritation fade. "If you are wanting evidence that your Xin Sheng effort is working, I would say you have it."

Sun-Tzu appeared to stare right through her. "Yes, but to what extent?" he asked, obviously a rhetorical question. His voice hardened. "There is so much more to accomplish."

Isis shivered internally. Sun-Tzu could be deathly patient, but in matters concerning the Confederation he could also be incredibly ruthless. "You have accomplished so much already," she said by way of easing into a touchy subject. "Even the recent surge of pro-Capellan nationalism in the old Tikonov Region attests to your efforts." He did not hide his hard glare, and she continued quickly. "No, no one has said anything. But it does not take much to see your hand behind it. I'm only surprised no other Star League member state has voiced protest."

"Only two would care," Sun-Tzu stated flatly. "Yvonne has her hands full dealing with reports of unrest from all across the Federated Commonwealth—Tikonov is one voice in a multitude. And Katrina," he paused, obviously deciding how much he wished to disclose, "she will not complain loudly so long as I do not threaten any of the older Davion-ruled worlds."

A bargain, struck at the Star League conference on Tharkad? It was difficult for Isis to imagine Katrina Steiner-Davion as anything but a social creature, though Sun-Tzu certainly thought otherwise and his acumen was seldom in error. She reached out and laid her hand on his sweat-damp arm. "Step carefully, beloved—"

Sun-Tzu recoiled from her light touch, cutting off the well-intended word of warning. Isis read the sudden coldness in his eyes and felt it in the tensing of his muscles. She allowed her hand to drop down to her side. He studied her for a few long seconds, then just as suddenly awarded her a bright smile that almost, but not quite, convinced her she'd been imagining his coldness. *He desired or expected support,* Isis thought, reasoning out his brief agitation, *and I advocated caution.*

"Prepare our message to your father," Sun-Tzu said as if the awkward moment had not existed. "I must clean up and prepare for the speech. If my people are ready to follow, as you suggest, then it is time for me to lead them further toward where I wish to go." He stepped by her and into the passage, then turned to give her another warm smile. Reaching out, he lightly brushed her cheek with his forefinger. "With your help, my love, I will make the Confederation strong again."

Aris Sung stood at the foot of the steps leading up to the stage. The black silk cloak of his dress uniform billowed as the wind rose again, its damp touch carrying a hint of salt from the ocean only a few kilometers distant. Beneath the cloak, hidden from sight, his right hand rested on a Nakjama laser pistol. Brown eyes narrowed, he swept his gaze across the stands, the high windows and rooftops of buildings overlooking the Castle Sands Staging Grounds, and the media islands where newspeople clustered with their holocams and recorders.

Applause washed the grounds as Sun-Tzu Liao finished praising the local garrison force, in this case a regiment of Mc-Carron's Armored Cavalry. The sound reminded Aris of rain thundering against ferrocrete, and though the sky remained clear of clouds he could not shake the feeling that a storm brewed. He brought his left hand from beneath his cloak. In it was a small microphone whose wiring trailed through his sleeve and then down to the remote unit on his belt. Bringing the unit close to his mouth, he whispered, "All posts check."

His earpiece, also trailing a thin black wire back into his clothing, whispered tinny voices in his ear as posts one through nine all checked in clear. He then called for a check of the remote teams, the ones driving around in security vans, piloting BattleMechs along the perimeter, or monitoring activity at important areas such as hospitals and the spaceport. The contact for each remote team relayed back an all-clear as well. "Main stage, all clear," Aris reported back, then dropped his hand to his side.

Though meticulous in the performance of his duties, Aris couldn't imagine a safer location. Relevow was as safe a world as one could hope for, with no history of insurrection or even a vocal minority. The staging grounds were directly controlled by McCarron's Armored Cavalry, a mercenary command that had faithfully served the Capellan Confederation for over fifty years. Each of the command's five regiments guarded a world bordering the St. Ives Compact, a position of enormous responsibility that bespoke the Chancellor's high regard for the unit. All media personnel and attendees to the Chancellor's speech had been thoroughly checked out—Aris and his people had reviewed the files themselves and monitored the security equipment. And on stage, four of the Chancellor's Death Commandos stood their own vigil. Large, muscular men who appeared carved from solid marble, they were like impressive statues draped in black uniforms. Two backed Sun-Tzu Liao and two stood behind Isis Marik.

It appeared that everything was to run smoothly. No surprises. Sun-Tzu, however, smiling and nodding to the crowds as the applause finally died away, was apparently of another mind.

"I have commended the garrison forces of the two worlds we visited before coming here," he said, the words catching Aris' attention. "The difference was that in those remarks I praised Capellan *citizens* for the sterling performance of their duties. And citizenship is never to be taken for granted, because in the Confederation each generation must earn it as their mothers and fathers did before them. Such garrison troops continue to prove they are worthy of their citizenship, by placing themselves in continued service to the vital interests of our nation."

Sun-Tzu gestured to Colonel Marcus Baxter, commanding officer of all five mercenary regiments, who stood to his left alongside Isis Marik. "Has McCarron's Armored Cavalry done any less?"

Sun-Tzu paused, allowing the implications to sink in and anticipation to build. Aris Sung found himself holding his breath, though he continued to dutifully scan the crowds while awaiting the Chancellor's next words.

"Few mercenary commands have served the Confederation with such distinction," Sun-Tzu continued after drawing the moment out to heighten the drama. "I would say that fewer still, in this nation or any other, are even capable of such service. But the fact does remain that the Cavalry"—he turned again to Baxter—"your Cavalry, has shown that such ability does exist. You and your people have shown an even greater loyalty than some regular units from the Capellan Confederation's past. In our darkest hour of the Fourth Succession War, you remained at the Confederation's side when other regiments, when entire worlds, when even an entire Commonality, deserted it."

Thundering applause, dwarfing any previously given Sun-Tzu during this speech, drowned out the rest of the world for a moment. Aris felt a swell of pride for his nation and even some small measure of justice at the Chancellor's words. In one sentence Sun-Tzu berated units such as the Northwind Highlander regiments, who had deserted their posts in the Fourth Succession War, and worlds that then had failed to put up even token resistance to Davion aggression, and even now in the Disputed

Territories might oppose being reclaimed by the Confederation. And, of course, Candace Liao and her St. Ives Compact, with their ultimate treachery in abandoning the Confederation in favor of the Davions and their damnable Federated Commonwealth. Aris realized that he was witness to a speech that would shake worlds throughout the Inner Sphere, and would certainly be recorded for Capellan history books. *Especially if Sun-Tzu Liao follows through on this line of reasoning.*

Sun-Tzu waved down the applause as Aris performed a quick check of all posts. "My mother," Sun-Tzu said slowly, sure in the knowledge that he held his audience captive with every word, "named McCarron's Armored Cavalry a regular Confederation unit with regard to preferential treatment by our logistics corps and with regard to contract payments. I would take this further, awarding the warriors of the Cavalry and their families full citizenship on behalf of the Capellan Confederation. It is within my power, yes, though I have decided not to usurp that honor from your new lord."

Aris blinked his surprise. Until that point, he had read Sun-Tzu's intentions. An unnatural silence fell over the parade grounds as everyone waited for what was certain to be Sun-Tzu's most dramatic proclamation.

The Chancellor did not disappoint as he continued in a still-quiet, matter-of-fact tone. "Before today's speech, I privately offered Colonel Marcus Baxter the Barduc title of Lord of the Realm. And he did accept. As a new and valued member of the sword nobility, and following proper ceremony on the world of Sian, we will agree on a Warren of no less than two star systems that he will rule in the name of Liao and that McCarron's Armored Cavalry will now and forever more call their home. It shall be *his* honor to name any of you who desire it as Capellan citizens, and of course under his direction that the Cavalry will eventually take to the field in the Xin Sheng effort to reclaim what was once ours." The Chancellor waved Marcus forward to the front of the stage. "May I present to you, Lord Marcus Baxter."

Aris refrained from the applause he wished to give. Not to Colonel—no, Lord—Baxter, though the man certainly deserved accolades for his appointment to the sword nobility of the Confederation. But to Sun-Tzu Liao, who had in one speech reaffirmed the loyalty of a most important military unit, which in turn strengthened the border with St. Ives *and* would strengthen Capellan national pride. And, of course, to the Xin Sheng effort that promised a stronger nation as the Capellan Confederation reclaimed what was once theirs.

Aris pitied any worlds that failed to acknowledge the Confederation's manifest destiny. His only wish was for the glory of BattleMech assignment when the call finally sounded.

4

Royal Compound
Tian-tan, St. Ives
St. Ives Compact
10 August 3060

Cassandra Allard-Liao watched her mother stab down on the remote control button that shut off the huge tri-d display on the wall. Immediately, the image of her cousin Sun-Tzu basking in an enthusiastic ovation on Relevow faded to black and white just before winking out altogether. The applause and cheers seemed to wash over Candace Liao's private sitting room for an extra moment before giving way to the normal stillness of the St. Ives Royal Compound. Cassandra had to admit that her cousin certainly knew how to put on a show. Only his security detail had shown signs of trying not to be moved by the rousing pro-Confederation rhetoric, though Cassandra had read their positive response in the way they grew taller even while remaining at a parade rest. The holocams had almost picked up the cracks of their straining vertebrae.

"It's impressive," Cassandra said.

Candace Liao frowned at the dead screen where Sun-Tzu's face had faded away to nothingness, as if wishing it could be so easy. She glanced sidelong at her daughter. "It's trouble."

Cassandra returned her mother's frown, and for a moment the two women seemed to share the same face, one just slightly older. Though pushing into her mid-seventies, Candace Liao still retained the same timeless Asian beauty she had passed along to both of her daughters. As yet few gray hairs lightened her shiny, jet black tresses. Her skin retained a healthy glow, with only some tiny laugh-lines near the Asian folds of her eyes. Cassandra could only hope she aged half as well.

"I don't understand, Mother. I've heard you give similar speeches, reaffirming to the people of the Compact that we made the right choice in the Fourth Succession War by leaving the Confederation. How is this any different?"

The Duchess turned in her high-backed chair and settled herself more comfortably to be able to face her daughter. Her expression lightened as she looked into this mirror of her own youth, but the concern was still there. "It is hard to explain to one who did not live through the courts of Sian under my father," the Duchess said, speaking slowly. "Symbolism was important, both to our Chinese heritage and also because symbolic victories were often the only ones open to us. My sister Romano, for all her madness, learned to integrate true victories with the symbolic. I *know* Sun-Tzu to be capable of this as well. He does not make empty gestures, or empty threats."

Glancing briefly at the dark screen, as if her cousin might again be peering out from its depths, Cassandra considered her mother's words before replying. She drew a deep breath, drawing in the light scent of incense Candace occasionally burned. "You think he is threatening the St. Ives Compact? How can he?"

"I think he is trying to provoke us. Exactly how I cannot say. But my nephew understands one thing very well: the St. Ives Compact is a house of cards built on a foundation of quicksand." The Duchess steepled her fingers together. Eyes narrowed in thought, she suddenly looked very Liao. "The Confederation *does* have a claim against the St. Ives Compact," she said. "And our people share too much history, too much culture. It would be difficult to resist assimilation."

Shaking her head, Cassandra refused to acknowledge that point. "We would fight," she said with conviction.

Smiling, Candace regarded her daughter with eyes no less sharp for their age. "Justin's fire burns in your spirit," she said, naming her late husband. "The same fire that burns within your brother Kai, though tempered by careful insight."

Was that a rebuke? Cassandra was a fine MechWarrior in her own right, and eager to prove her ability. But if her mother was trying to tell her that she could not hold a candle to her brother, that Cassandra already knew only too well. Kai was one of the best MechWarriors the Inner Sphere had ever seen. *That does not mean, however, that I cannot make my own contribution.*

Candace folded her hands into her lap, then returned to the subject at hand. "Yes, we would fight." The Duchess hardened her voice. "And we will. But in a military engagement, we would be hard pressed to hold the Confederation forces off for long without aid. You know that as well as I. We must, of necessity, rely on the Federated Commonwealth to supplement our defensive posture."

"But we cannot count on that protection," Cassandra said. "Not with the Clan threat. Not with Katherine already dividing the realm and in all likelihood just waiting for a chance to cause trouble for Yvonne." She paused to think, grateful to her mother for giving her the time to work though this herself. "So we must avoid the fighting," she finally said, as if the solution were simple. She was sure that was the answer her mother wanted, though personally she believed the Compact strong enough to defend itself.

Candace nodded again. "We have somehow gained Sun-Tzu's notice. He looks for an excuse, and that we mustn't give him. Eventually, another project will occupy his attention, one with more immediate gains." Candace took a moment and drew in a deep breath of the perfumed air. "In reviewing our border defenses, I have noticed a potential problem. We have a large mercenary command, two regiments, sitting on Indicass that might take this opportunity to go after Sun-Tzu. Their fanatical hatred of the Chancellor is too well-known not to have reached his ears, and his comments from the Relevow speech do call into question the loyalties of most mercenaries."

"He said as much about the average St. Ives citizen," Cassandra noted, "but yes, with the elevation of McCarron's Cavalry he does seem to be trying to diminish other mercenary commands."

Candace smiled her approval of Cassandra's evaluation. "I

have ordered one of those mercenary regiments back to St. Loris, the worse of the two with regard to self-control."

Cassandra performed some quick math in her head, spotting an opportunity and wanting to slip into her mother's train of thought before she moved on to other matters. "I could mobilize a battalion of the Second St. Ives Lancers and be on Indicass in three to four weeks. Providing I can use Kittery as a lay-over to recharge my JumpShip at their recharge station. That should be well before Sun-Tzu reaches either Hustaing or Purvo," she said, naming the two Confederation worlds closest to Indicass. "I will reinforce the garrison regiment and keep them heeled."

The idea gave Candace pause, and she reluctantly nodded her permission. "Justin's fire. Very well, take your people out there and monitor the situation. In the meantime, I will order garrison units on other border worlds to conduct military exercises. That should allow them to flex their muscles enough to not feel threatened by Sun-Tzu's actions. I will also release letters to my regimental commanders, reaffirming my faith that no danger is forthcoming." Candace Liao allowed some steel to creep into her voice. "We *will* hold the peace."

Admiring the strength in her mother, at that moment Cassandra held no doubts. Let Sun-Tzu come if he dared. The St. Ives Compact could hold its own.

Pinedale, Denbar
St. Ives Compact

Standing against the back wall of Denbar's Whiteriver Base recreation hall, sipping ice water and trying not to choke on the room's smoke-filled air, Major Trisha Smithson quietly conferred with her executive officer in between outbursts from the rest of their unit. For the fourth time the Blackwind Lancers' second battalion watched Sun-Tzu Liao's Relevow speech, knowing it so well that they began their growls and shouts of objection before an offending statement was even made.

"What do you think?" Warner asked, gesturing to the Mech-Warriors who flung oaths and obscene gestures at the giant holovid wallscreen.

Trisha surveyed the rabble her unit had become in a few short hours. In light of the hard, anti-Sun-Tzu sentiments she had cultivated in them in her six years as battalion commander, she expected no less a reaction. Though, in truth, she still thought them fairly tame. *But they will have to do.*

She glared at the image of Sun-Tzu Liao, for good form if nothing else, as he first presented Marcus Baxter as a Lord of the Confederation and then, after the applause finally died away, launched into some more vague slurs against the St. Ives Compact. "I think they're ready to start a low-grade riot," she said, pitching her voice low and covering her pleasure with a note of concern. "But we can't allow that." *Yet.* "Colonel Perrin might just relieve me of command if that happened."

Captain Warner Doles merely nodded, though Trisha read his understanding in that simple gesture. Despite some private dressing-downs the Blackwind Lancer CO had given her, and once Doles, Colonel Perrin had kept her record clean. At times it seemed that Perrin tried to forget that Second Battalion, or even the entire world of Denbar, even existed. He spent his time on Milos or Texlos, with First and Third. When one of Second's warriors, more often than not Trisha herself, did step out of line, he preferred to handle it within the unit and not send reports up the chain.

His three-dimensional image cloaked in green and red silk, Sun-Tzu Liao continued his verbal barrage. "McCarron's Armored Cavalry will always be one of the premier Capellan units. We shall rely on it to defend the nation against all enemies, foreign *and* domestic. With your help, what once was ours, will be ours again."

A domestic target. Pieces of the Chancellor's speech continued to narrow her choices down. "Comment?" Trisha Smithson asked of Warner as her warriors shouted denials and more disparaging genetic remarks at Sun-Tzu.

Warner brought his pipe out, long-stemmed with a clay bowl. Very traditional, but also a not-so-subtle dodge to give him time to think. Noticing Trisha's look of distaste he nodded an apology and slipped it back into his pocket. The powerfully built man ran fingers through his light brown hair, then folded large arms over his chest and leaned back against the wall. "Liao could simply be talking about the Disputed Territories," he said finally.

"But you do not believe that?" *Or if you do, I'll have to change your mind.*

He shook his head. "No, I don't. Too many of his comments have hit too close to the mark. The fact that he recently referred to the formation of the Compact as a military coup staged by units too cowardly to meet the Davion threat tells you his opinion of us. And let's face it, if he wants the Compact he can take it. Only the reformed Star League stands in his way. That, and a reluctance to attack the FedCom units that Duchess Liao has allowed inside the borders."

Trisha nodded, her XO's thoughts mirroring her own. *The Chancellor is obviously looking for an excuse. He's coming, one way or another.* She sipped at the ice water, letting it cool her smoke-burned throat. "Sunny-boy and his psycho mother before him have never formally relinquished their claim to the Compact. But does he have the *qiu* to try and take it?"

To that rude remark, Warner only shrugged. For such a large man, he was decidedly soft-spoken. After a moment, he added, "The Duchess certainly doesn't think so. We've heard no comment out of St. Ives proper."

Trisha chose her words carefully, not wanting to alienate her exec. "Duchess Liao does well enough in political circles, but she's sitting back on St. Ives while Denbar and worlds will be hit, and hit hard." She nodded to the screen. "He's threatening us with McCarron's Cav, and we just sit here like a fat quail waiting to be shot in the quillar fields."

"What else can we do?" Warner asked, looking at her with a mixture of interest and concern.

Trisha leaned over, not wanting her words to carry any further. She also told herself to keep her words professional and above board. "Pull in the company commanders and start some planning sessions. I want several defense, evacuation, and assault plans contingent on what Sunny-boy might try, ready to fly at a second's notice." She noticed the speculative look that crossed Warner's face, fading to acceptance, and she nodded. "He caught the Sarna Supremacy sleeping in '58. This time he won't get off so easy."

5

A light drizzle fell from the dark gray skies over the city of Yushui and thunder rumbled in the distance. A dramatic backdrop for Sun-Tzu Liao's speech, Aris thought. Despite the weather, a crowd had gathered in the riverside park, with umbrellas and foul-weather gear shielding them from the elements. Gei-Fu knew one of the heaviest annual rainfalls in the entire Confederation, and a little moisture was not about to deter these people.

The Chancellor's speech ran mostly along the lines of Relevow's, allowing Aris Sung to concentrate more on the security of the area. He wiped at the rainwater that streamed down from the hair plastered against his head to drip from his jaw and runnel down his neck. A poncho worn over his uniform helped keep him somewhat dry, though he refused to raise the hood. Covering his ears and blocking some of his peripheral vision was no way to keep the Chancellor safe, and Gei-Fu was not a world that endeared itself to Aris' heart as a safe zone.

House Hiritsu had been ordered to Gei-Fu before, in 3051, to put down a rebellion in which the world attempted to secede from the Confederation and join the nearby St. Ives Compact. Aris expected some comments about that to surface in Sun-Tzu's speech, eventually. Back then, a BattleMech had traveled secretly into the city under the Nunya River, rising up next to this same park like a leviathan bent on destruction. Only quick thinking on Aris' part had saved House Master Virginia York, and by extension the situation on Gei-Fu. Infantry Commander Jessup had privately let Aris know that it was that incident above all that had prompted him and Ty Wu Non to select Aris as head of the honor squad.

Aris couldn't help believing that history would somehow find a way to repeat itself.

He'd had similar thoughts on Relevow, though of a much less dire nature. Now, on Gei-Fu, he felt the impressions clearer, though a regiment of McCarron's Armored Cavalry remained to supplement House Hiritsu's security. A storm was building. Not of rainfall and lightning, but of men and 'Mechs. Aris knew it. He felt it—just like some people had a feel for the weather. He read the certainty in the warm flush on his skin, the tightness in his muscles, and the itch to have his *Wraith*'s control sticks in hand. But whether or not it would happen here, exactly, he could not say. *Or it could just be the old memories plaguing me.*

The Nunya River, coursing along the ferrocrete bed laid through the city's heart, swelled up against the top of the levee. This time Aris had ordered sensors strung into the river, several kilometers up and down stream. He had a 'Mech lance from his own company and a small infantry detachment holding the Bisn'z Dam further up the Nunya, just in case someone hit on the clever idea of trying to flood out Yushui to get at the Chancellor. He'd left nothing to chance.

Aris shook his head, shaking the excess water from his short-cropped dark hair, and surveyed the crowd as he called for a post check. The grass had been trampled to mud in several spots, making footing treacherous. He noticed Li Wynn, dressed in civilian clothes and circulating with a camera as if a local photographer out to catch some film on the historic visit. The camera had no film, Aris knew, but its telephoto lens still made for a good spotting device.

"And in the last nine years," Sun-Tzu Liao was saying, his address rolling over the park in the man-made thunder of a state-of-the-art P.A. system, "not one disharmonious voice has been raised on Gei-Fu, which makes me believe its people are truly repentant for the crimes of the previous Refrector and his ill-fated rebellion. In fact, Gei-Fu boasts one of the highest percentiles for enrollment in the Capellan Armed Forces, a truly noteworthy contribution to the Xin Sheng effort."

Probably just trying to escape the rain. Aris wiped a sheet of water from his forehead, listening as the final, "all clears," came in from the remote posts. The Chancellor was being very kind, he thought.

"A pity more once-rebellious worlds have not followed your example," the Chancellor continued, then paused so everyone could draw their own conclusions as to whom he referred. "Terrible, that they continue to ignore the call of their Capellan heritage or that unjust governments continue to suppress their people's natural desire to rejoin with their brothers and sisters. There was never a more appropriate time than now, during this rebirth of the Confederation."

Ouch. Aris winced in partial sympathy, partial humor, as Sun-Tzu's easy words ripped long, bloody furrows in the sovereignty of the St. Ives Compact, the tiny Chaos March alliances, and the supposedly independent worlds of the Disputed Territories and Chaos March. Even further, he considered, if news of unrest among old Tikonov Commonality worlds was true. Chancellor Liao had a MechWarrior's gift for inflicting the maximum damage with minimal weapons fire, even if his battlefield was political.

Waiting for the applause to stop, Sun-Tzu leaned away from the microphone to speak privately with Isis Marik and then Lord Marcus Baxter, who flanked him at either side. Isis awarded him a brief kiss on the cheek, whether for the private comment or just for show, and Lord Baxter nodded.

Sun-Tzu returned to the microphone. "Such worlds will once again know the Confederation's comfortable embrace," he continued. "*That* I promise. The same promise I made on Relevow, and will make again as I continue my tour on through Overton, Harloc, and Hustaing."

Aris knew a second's confusion as the Chancellor left Purvo off his touring list, the world after Hustaing, but then dismissed it as he felt the pro-Capellan charge swelling within him, cresting over and threatening to sweep him away on the ideals of Sun-Tzu's Xin Sheng movement. Xin Sheng—new birth, and that was just what the Chancellor was offering.

"This is *our* time," Sun-Tzu Liao said, obviously easing into what would be his closing remarks, "where all Capellan citizens can once again take pride in their nation and their heritage. With worlds such as Gei-Fu, and military units such as McCarron's Armored Cavalry, the Confederation will once again know its former greatness."

This time a roll of thunder underscored the applause with a bass rumble, reminding Aris of battlefield noise. He glanced apprehensively at the raging waters of the Nunya, half-expecting the appearance of an enemy 'Mech, and then ordered another check of all posts, though one had just been completed. Yes, there was a storm building. But a glorious confrontation, in which Aris pictured himself reclaiming words for the Confederation.

He just couldn't be sure when, or where, it would break.

For form's sake, Li Wynn snapped a few non-pictures of the Chancellor and of the Yushui crowd. The shutter clicked and the automatic winder spun. It didn't matter that there was no film. Anyone who paid him the least attention would hear the noise and be satisfied.

He trod carefully over the muddy ground, the foul-smelling muck sour and growing stronger as the people continued to churn it up with their feet. He heard Aris' request for a post check, the second in almost as many minutes, but waited for post-three command to pass along the request. Li squeezed the small hand-held microphone he cradled in the palm of his left hand. "Crowd-seven, clear," he reported, then snapped a few faked pictures as he scanned the crowd again, ever more thoroughly.

Something has Aris on edge.

Li could not find it. And though he trusted Aris' instincts, he couldn't help but wonder for the briefest second if his sponsor and *Sifu* might not be mistaken. From his viewpoint, the speech was proceeding without a hitch. Li felt the call of the Confederation's Xin Sheng. And more important, the crowd was firmly behind Sun-Tzu Liao, the more so when he held them up as a positive example when he could just have easily done the opposite. Li Wynn knew something about the fervor that could be aroused when a person was elevated from their previous station.

On Kaifeng, before House Hiritsu had come, he'd been little more than a strèet kid, and that was a charitable description. Petty thief was another term that came to mind. He remembered the night he had crouched in a storm drain, the air dank and rotten, while 'Mechs fought in the streets overhead, hoping that one of the metal monsters would kick in the side of a jewelry store or possibly a bank before passing on to other fights. Aris Sung had befriended him, and given him the opportunity to be a part of something bigger. *To belong.* Li Wynn could not remember ever belonging before. That was the magic that had drawn him after House Hiritsu, to Randar and then Sarna, proving day after day that he was worthy of admission, until House Master Ty Wu Non finally agreed to give him the chance. And now, Li had direction—duty, as a Capellan citizen and member of a Warrior House.

And more?

Li Wynn politely shouldered his way through a small knot of people, camera clenched in his cold fingers as he listened to Sun-Tzu Liao. Li could not shake the feelings of enthusiasm that welled within him. Nor did he try. Though not native-born to the Confederation, he was Capellan nonetheless. And while duty had called him to the Confederation's service, his building self-respect and pride promised that the future could perhaps hold something even more enticing than a feeling of belonging. Something he could not yet define, that remained just beyond his reach but occasionally tempted him with a light touch like the brush of a butterfly's wing against his cheek.

For almost his entire life, Li Wynn had struggled to survive in a world without direction, without purpose, and for the most part had succeeded. Now that he possessed direction, he would see just how far and how strong he could run.

And the entire time, he felt the Chancellor's eyes upon him, urging him onward—ever forward.

6

Home Guard Training Facility
Hazlet, Nashuar
St. Ives Compact
28 August 3060

Tracers chewed up the darkness, small streaks of light that strobed against the simulated terrain and that the eye followed back to a wash of orange flame wreathing autocannon muzzles. Heat suffused the simulator, pumped into the tight confines in response to the constant discharge of weapons. Blinking stinging sweat from his eyes, Cadet Maurice Fitzgerald floated his targeting reticule over the distant, dim silhouette of an enemy *JagerMech,* with its keg-like torso and distinctive autocannon barrel arms. He chanced a single laser shot as soon as he read partial lock in the reticule's golden aura. The ruby lance missed wide as the *JagerMech* walked backward out of his line of fire.

The scenario was a familiar one. Fitzgerald felt fairly certain that it was an adaptation from a scenario the training lance had run not three weeks prior. Only instead of Clan 'Mechs the Nashuar Home Guard cadets faced designs common to the Capellan Confederation, each enemy machine bearing the Confederation's infamous gauntlet-and-sword insignia, a testament to recent tensions mounting along the Compact's border. The *JagerMech* and one of the new *Snake* designs were shielding an enemy *Catapult* armed with Arrow IV homing missiles, while a lighter *Raven* scout 'Mech tried to sneak in from the east flank to TAG one of the Compact BattleMechs with a spotting laser. The *Raven* was the wild card. If it could be contained, the Compact cadets would win.

That puts a lot of trust in our own light 'Mech pilot.

Fitz cut loose with another long-range laser shot at the distant *JagerMech,* missing again. He wanted to shout his frustration, holding back because he knew an internal simulator pod microphone would record the outburst for Nevarr's later review. Sparring at range in the dark did not make for an easy battle. It forced MechWarriors to rely more on sensors, missing out on some telltale signs in an enemy's movement or the lay of terrain that could make all the difference. He also devoted too much attention to the tactical feed of his head's up display, he knew. But he trusted his own analysis over that of his three lancemates, and so worked to keep tabs on all aspects of the battle.

What was most difficult for Fitzgerald was that this time around Nevarr had assigned him a supporting role, relegated to the backfield to protect against the *Raven* should it slip by their own light 'Mech or against any attempt at a flanking maneuver. *Pinning me in place.* The sim pilot of the *JagerMech* was good, riding the optimum range for his light autocannon and picking away at the *Blackjack,* which had trouble responding.

A light tremor shook the cockpit as thirty-millimeter slugs chewed into more of the *Blackjack*'s armor. A glance at his damage schematic showed the loss of roughly another quarter-ton of protection, this time from his 'Mech's lower left leg and left arm. He fought the urge to throttle up into a run and close with the enemy machine. *If I break formation, Nevarr might toss me back into the armor corps—no more chances.* Jaw clenched and his grip knuckle-white on the control sticks, Fitz throttled into a backward walk and took some cover within a light stand of fir and hickory. Another hastily targeted laser burned into intervening trees, saving the *JagerMech* again.

"Guard One, this is Guard Four. The *Raven* is loose." The voice of Cadet Rastecht, the lance's *Jenner* pilot, whispered into Fitz' ear through the neurohelmet's built-in speaker, the air waves unable to fully rob her voice of her frantic excitement. The *Raven* had slipped by her, and could now threaten their flank. Just one of the *Catapult*'s homing missiles brought down by the light 'Mech's spotting laser could spell ruin for any member of the lance. "I'm in pursuit," she informed them.

Fitz dropped his jaw down to activate his own commline. "Guard Three, breaking off to intercept," he said, maneuvering the *Blackjack* around into a tight turn to the east. *Taking out the* Raven *will save the scenario and bump my standing*.

His thoughts of personal victory were short-lived as acting lance commander Danielle Singh ordered him back. "Negative, Guard Three. Hold position." Her voice came across strong and confident. "We almost have the *Snake* boxed. Keep that *Jag* off us. Guard Four, you stop that *Raven*!"

The head's up tactical showed the *Raven* coming in fast from the east, followed at a distance by the slightly faster *Jenner*. It was going to be a close race, and the *Blackjack* stood right in its path. If Rastecht lost, Fitz would be the first to know. "Request release to engage *JagerMech*," he said. If he could slip into better range for his lasers, he could at least hope to put down one enemy 'Mech.

"Negative, Guard Three. Keep between us and the *Raven*."

Nán-rén fù-kuan! Human sacrifice! Fitzgerald's teeth ground together as tracers once again tracked in on his position and small-caliber autocannon slugs bit into his 'Mech. He switched his primary monitor from magres over to infrared scanners, but could improve little on visual sighting. *JagerMech*s simply ran too cool, relying on their autocannon rather than heavy, heat-generating energy weapons. Damning his own heat curve, he triggered off both of the *Blackjack*'s large lasers. He got lucky on one, skimming it in between a pair of tall pines to score the *JagerMech*'s right torso. Alarms sounded as his heat build-up threatened to shut down his engine, and Fitz slapped the override while gasping against a hard wave of near-scorching air. Still, it felt good to have finally scored some damage.

Though not enough by far to bring the heavy BattleMech down. The *JagerMech* simply walked back out of range while peppering Fitzgerald's location with a continuous barrage of thirty-millimeter armor-piercing slugs. Fitz almost broke formation then to pursue, urged on by his own success. He held his position only through the greatest of self-control.

"*Raven* is down."

Restecht crowed over the comm frequencies, her announcement barely preceding the fading of the *Raven*'s symbol on the *Blackjack*'s HUD. Her final word blurred with the first of Danielle's, who spoke with a quieter strength. "*Snake* is down." And then before Fitz could request it, "Guard Three and Four, released to engage *JagerMech*."

About time. Fitzgerald throttled forward, bringing his *Blackjack* into a run that would close quickly. Victory was fairly assured for the lance. Now it was time to claim a piece of it for himself.

No one seemed to notice Fitz' silence as the four trainees walked in a group from debriefing to the mess hall. The others were in high spirits, having won the scenario with no losses. The second training lance was up for the same mission now, and they had set a hard score to follow. Danielle Singh was in especially good spirits, and with reason. Besides commanding the win, she claimed the killing shots against both the *Snake* and the *Catapult*. Freya Restecht claimed sole credit for the *Raven*, and the fourth lance member, Cameron Lee, could at least claim partials for both of Danielle's kills.

Fitz had zeroed out.

The *JagerMech* had kept him from closing, and once the *Catapult* went down it had disengaged and escaped. *Released too late,* he kept telling himself. *I could've taken it down with just one more minute.*

Cameron grabbed the door to the cafeteria and held it open for the others. The mixed scent of food and spray cleaners used on the tables assailed them. Fitzgerald barely noticed when Cameron glad-handed him on the shoulder as he passed. The noise level dropped considerably for a moment as the four MechWarrior trainees entered. Their comrades in the Home Guard armor corps glanced their way, some with looks of envy and others with shrugs of indifference. Conversations quickly resumed, and the four of them grabbed trays of food and found seats together.

"I really thought I'd bought it," Danielle said after her first few bites. "*Catapult*s don't usually carry their own TAG laser. Nevarr set me up good. And then it missed! I mean, I know that can happen to anyone out there. But when you hear that warning for missile lock and you know it's an Arrow IV, you're already tensing against the hit."

Fitzgerald scooped up some rice and teriyaki chicken, using eating as his excuse not to contribute much to the discussion. Freya talked about her running down the *Raven*, and Cameron was more impressed with the sticking power of the *Snake*. "If Fitz hadn't kept the *Jag* off us," he said, "there's no way we could have taken it down so fast." The comment was seconded by Danielle, and Fitzgerald smiled and nodded his acceptance of the praise though inwardly he still regretted losing the *JagerMech*.

Kills weren't everything. In fact, in the end they technically meant relatively little. Scores were based on multiple variables, and in lance engagements the points for enemy kills were divided fairly evenly. What no one could predict was Nevarr. The commander always added his own little modifiers into the final scores, and in the end he would simply choose two cadets of the eight. Nevarr had made it clear that high scores did not necessarily mean selection. But then again, he'd also indicated that they helped. And having a good kill ratio had to make a difference.

That was how MechWarriors were always judged, wasn't it?

7

DropShip *Pearl of True Wisdom*
Aht'raplar Spaceport, Harloc
Sian Commonality, Capellan Confederation
11 September 3060

Only the lightest of tremors betrayed the *Pearl of True Wisdom*'s landing on Harloc. An aerodyne DropShip, its horizontal approach called for more space but made for a lighter touch-down. And although twenty-five hundred tons of space vessel meeting earth is not conducive to feather-soft landings, the pilot's deft touch certainly made it seem within reach. If one were preoccupied, the landing might actually have gone unnoticed until the braking maneuvers began.

Sun-Tzu Liao noticed, however. Seated behind the metal and glass desk in his private shipboard office, he had been waiting for it, gauging his pilot's mastery of the *Lung Wang* Class DropShip's controls just as he always tested, gauged, and considered the loyalty and skills of those around him. Survival traits, bred into him with twenty-one years of living in the Celestial Palace before he ever became Chancellor. He felt the slight bump and noticed the rippling across the surface of the fresh glass of light plum wine that sat on the desk's safety-glass top.

All things considered, not a bad landing at all. Sun-Tzu raised his glass in a light toast to the pilot's ability, but took only the barest of sips. Enough to savor the sweet nectar, but not enough to make him thirst too badly for the next drink. *Everything in moderation. Everything consumed in its own time.* An exercise in patience, like so many of the small rituals that filled his day.

Patience.

Something Lord Colonel Marcus Baxter could use more of, Sun-Tzu thought, noticing his guest's discomfort through half-lidded eyes. The older man sat in a chair mounted to the ship bulkhead and facing the desk, its plush cushion comfortable enough for hours of sitting, though the back of ridged hardwood did force people to lean forward, paying attention to whomever sat at the desk. The new Lord Colonel leaned forward, toying with the campaign ribbons of his dress uniform and occasionally tugging at the hem of his jacket. His dark hair shot through with iron-gray, his crag-like features, and parade-ground formality in most every action showed him as a man not prone to restless movement.

The Chancellor did not believe that Baxter's impatience stemmed from nervousness or a lack of comfort. Baxter was *janshi.* A warrior. And like a dog bred for hunting he wished to slip his leash and be away to where skill in a BattleMech, not political maneuvering, decided the outcome and the accolades. But the presence of a Cavalry regiment on Harloc demanded the presence of the newly made Capellan lord. "All good things to those who wait," Sun-Tzu murmured. It was one of his favorite maxims.

Baxter glanced up. "Did you say something, Chancellor Liao?"

Sun-Tzu smiled thinly. "When the strike of a hawk breaks the body of its prey, it is because of timing."

Baxter's smile showed a mix of amusement and puzzlement. "You have not begun quoting Jerome Blake, have you, Chancellor Liao?"

Now the Chancellor frowned, though lightly. "Wisdom does come from other sources, though the Word of Blake might want us to believe otherwise," he said, only a bit unsure if Baxter was attempting humor. "I shall have to send you a copy of the *Art of War*."

"Ah, yes." Baxter nodded. "Strike the enemy as swiftly as a falcon strikes its target. It surely breaks the back of its prey for the reason that it awaits the right moment to strike." The Lord Colonel spread his hands in apology. "I'm afraid my translation slightly differs from your copy."

"Under either translation," Sun-Tzu said, once again at ease, "I was advocating patience." He waited for Baxter's nod of understanding, then gestured toward the office's small dry bar that was kept shut up in the event of zero-gravity conditions. "Help yourself to some refreshment, Lord Baxter. I have a small matter that requires my attention now that we are on-planet."

The Chancellor pressed against one corner of his desk. A touch-sensitive keyboard came alive under the glass in front of him, and he typed in a few simple commands that would activate his message-recording programs. A muted red light appeared near the desk's upper rim, to indicate that the holocamera, also hidden beneath the glass, was recording.

"To Archon Katrina Steiner-Davion of the Lyran Alliance from First Lord Sun-Tzu Liao," he said formally, pausing to lend his title its full weight and then allowing some measure of cordiality to seep into his voice, "I bid both you and your nation greetings." With Katrina, at least, based on their meeting on Tharkad two years prior, he could drop many of the pretenses he usually affected others. *But of course not all.*

"I was most upset," he lied, "to receive your message of September tenth, in which you made clear your strong feelings toward events taking place in the old Tikonov Free Republic." He purposely refrained from naming it the old Tikonov Commonality, which Hanse Davion had stolen from the Confederation during the Fourth Succession War. "Though I would have expected to hear such complaints from your sister, Yvonne, whom I believe still sits the throne on New Avalon, I can understand your own"—he paused, mouth rigid but eyes smiling—"*proprietary* interests."

Sun-Tzu yielded to a longer pause now, allowing Katrina to calm down after what—he was certain—would be a near-violent reaction to his reminder that she did not *yet* rule the whole of the Federated Commonwealth. He picked up his glass, allowed himself another small sip of the fruity wine before replacing it, and then straightened with great deliberation the wide silk sleeves of his robes.

He began again. "Now let me assure you, for the record, that this Free Tikonov Movement that has made the newsnets of late is in no way a coordinated effort on the part of my Confederation to reclaim the very old Tikonov Commonality. Even though it does lie within the pre-3025 border of the Confederation, my attentions are better turned elsewhere. You will not see Capellan units making planetfall there anytime soon. So, if you are seeking the advice from the Star League's current First Lord, I would recommend that you lend no more credibility to the Free Tikonov Movement than you would the other stories of political unrest that have surfaced on any number of other Federated Commonwealth worlds."

And that, Katrina, is my answer to your barely veiled order for me to redirect my efforts away from Tikonov. Yes, I will unbalance the area, but it is an instability that we can both use to our advantage. Sun-Tzu felt certain that she would leave it at that, providing he did nothing overt to reclaim the Tikonov worlds at this time. And the reference to the little conversation the two of them had on Tharkad, one in which Katrina had, in effect, relinquished her own claim to worlds on the Capellan side of the pre-3025 border, should also serve as a reminder of their *understanding*.

But with every subtle message, applied with the politician's silver tongue, Sun-Tzu knew that he must also remind her that he also had teeth, or he might lose even the grudging respect he'd won from her on Tharkad. "Now I have matters which *do* require my immediate attention, Archon, and so I will bid you farewell. I know you will use the Tikonov incidents to your benefit. After all, it was your noble father who pledged that the Federated Commonwealth"—Sun-Tzu smiled lightly as he quoted from memory—" 'is dedicated to the support of political freedom and each individual's right to pursue his or her destiny.' "

With that, Sun-Tzu brushed the glass over the End Recording control. Katrina Steiner-Davion, if she did not throw something through the screen, would not have listened further once he used Hanse Davion's own words against her. And worse, once she realized that he, as First Lord, could make public such sentiments and turn Hanse's quote to a pro-Capellan rallying cry. *And eventually, that might not be such a bad idea.*

Lord Colonel Baxter, who had remained silent, now nodded with some measure of admiration. He might prefer the battlefield to political circles, but apparently he could acknowledge a game well-played on either side of the fence. "Enough to make her think, that," Baxter said. He took a healthy pull at a bottle of Timbiqui Dark. "So long as it keeps her out of our hair."

Sun-Tzu allowed himself a healthy draught of the sweet, dark liquid from his own glass, then set it aside and vowed not to touch it again until after he had dismissed Baxter from the room. He sank back into his chair, hands clasped over his middle and staring toward the ceiling. "I was never worried about her interference," he admitted. "Tikonov is a long game, waiting to be played out, and I merely advanced my own position there. Katrina will respond soon enough. And so long as she makes life difficult for Yvonne, that can only help our cause."

Both men allowed the silence to stretch out then, Sun-Tzu forcing on himself a calm by which he hoped to stave off any rash or irrational judgment that could doom his grand design. *Plans are proceeding well, but the cost has yet to be paid. Soon there will be no turning back.* Then Baxter began to fidget again. The Chancellor sighed to himself and refocused his eyes on his guest. "Do you have some concerns," he asked, "regarding your latest orders?"

Baxter shook his head, rolling another drink of ale around in his mouth. "No, Chancellor Liao. My Nightriders regiment will readjust to garrison duty on Kaifeng quite well, and so long as they receive orders to make a few battalion-strength assaults into the Disputed Territory, they will remain content. I plan to set them after Wei, with your permission, of course."

"Do so," Sun-Tzu said with a curt nod. "The Disputed Territories are sapping too much strength that will soon be needed within the Chaos March, and elsewhere." He paused, considering the newest lord of his realm. "We are entering a volatile time, Lord Colonel, and I must know that you have control of your people. They must be held in check until we direct their energy toward the right goal."

Baxter set aside his Timbiqui and smiled grimly. "Have no fear, Chancellor. The Nightriders will deliver Wei for you, and the rest shall prepare. And when we strike, it shall break our prey's back."

Xin Singapore Spaceport, Indicass
St. Ives Compact

Planetfall on Indicass was routine, though Cassandra found the ride across Xin Singapore Spaceport's extensive grounds interesting. Rubinsky's Light Horse—according to her mother, the more stable regiment of Khorsakhov's Cossacks—had commandeered the old control tower and administrative buildings as their support base. Located at the far southern edge of the landing fields, as opposed to the new buildings along the west, it kept them plugged into the planetary defense network and close to their DropShips, two strategic concerns she admired. To make the drive over memorable, though, Colonel Rubinsky had also arranged a little welcoming ceremony.

From the ramp of the *Overlord* that had brought her battalion down from their JumpShip, she had been met by the first of Rubinsky's outriders. It was a brand new *Cossack* painted a flat rust red and sporting the mercenary unit's insignia on the right torso, a Russian Cossack horseman riding out of a golden circular field and wielding a flaming saber. The *Cossack* was a new light 'Mech design that had only this year begun rolling off the assembly lines of Ceres Metals Industries on Warlock. To honor Khorsakhov's Cossacks' integrity and commitment to the freedom of the St. Ives Compact, her mother had christened the new design *Cossack* and ordered a lance of the new model delivered to Rubinsky's Light Horse. Cassandra was sure that the Light Horse was using this opportunity to thank the Compact for this singular honor.

The *Cossack* paced her bullet-proofed Avanti luxury sedan

for a half-kilometer, peeling off with parade-ground precision as an old but still-worthy *Phoenix Hawk* took up the chase for the next half a klick. The next hand-off placed her in the company of a new *Clint,* complete with the 3U package that replaced the old autocannon and medium lasers with a particle projection cannon and pulse technology.

The BattleMech pulled ahead as they approached the main building, taking up a port arms stance next to the door to the admin building. Two MechWarriors dressed in Cossack costume opened Cassandra's door for her and escorted her into the building. The entire display left her feeling very secure but more than a bit out of touch with the thirty-first century.

Colonel Marko Rubinsky met her at the door to his command center, which had once been a DropShip crew's lounge.

"Major Allard-Liao," he said formally with a stiff nod, hands clasped behind his back. The colonel had iron-gray hair and a short beard kept well-trimmed. His blue eyes were piercingly alert and his body trim for a man pushing into his late fifties.

"Colonel," she said. "An interesting display out there."

"Old Cossack custom." Rubinsky gave her a tight-lipped smile, his Slavic accent heavy but cordial. "A relay of picket riders would always escort a visitor into camp."

The colonel ushered her through the door and into a relaxed atmosphere. The tactical consoles and computer screens were dark. Off to one side were several couches and chairs arranged around a low, broad table where two other men sat comfortably. "My executive officer," Rubinsky said, gesturing to the older man with jet black hair and almond-shaped eyes. "Lieutenant Colonel Raymond Li Tran."

He waited for both men to rise, and for Tran to give Cassandra his hand, then nodded toward the younger man, who possessed Rubinsky's hard-worn but pleasant features. "My son, Tamas. Captain, Second Company." Tamas gave her a bow, one arm behind his back and the other arm pressed across his stomach.

Cassandra smiled, then laughed as she sat down. "I'm sorry, but you've caught me off guard. I'm afraid I expected . . ." She trailed off, suddenly feeling out of place. She had expected to come in and take immediate charge of a dangerous situation. Instead, she found herself pleasantly charmed by this courtly man and his companions.

"What?" the senior Rubinsky asked, one eyebrow raised in humor. "Expected to find us frothing at the mouth? Ready to start a riot?" The three men sat and Tamas began pouring a clear liquid into four shot glasses. A wisp of frosty smoke rose from each.

"I'm afraid so," Cassandra admitted, regaining her composure. Well-received or not, she was still here to take charge. "Tensions have risen along the border, and I'm to coordinate my battalion with your regiment for the time being."

"Vodka?" Tamas asked, pushing a shot glass in front of her.

Cassandra snatched it up. "Please." She waited for the other three men to raise their glasses in salute, then quickly downed hers. The vodka was ice cold, chilling her throat and then burning down into her stomach. "What . . ." she began, then had to clear her throat before trying again. "What is the state of Indicass' defenses?"

Colonel Rubinsky nodded to Li Tran, who answered. "Duchess Liao transferred our first regiment to St. Loris, but the Light Horse remains and there are still two battalions of Home Guard armor and the militia infantry. More than enough to garrison this planet. Even," he added, after a few seconds, "providing a continuous guard at Ceres Metals."

The Ceres Metals factory on-planet manufactured several different armored vehicles, as Cassandra recalled. *A very important concern for the St. Ives military, and of course they would be very vocal in demanding protection.* "Nothing else?" she asked.

Tamas poured another round of shots. "We were informed two days ago that the St. Ives Cheveux Legers, Third Battalion, are en route." His accent was not so hard as his father's and very pleasant to the ear. "Indicass was their garrison post for some time before they were added to the SLDF assault on the Smoke Jaguars." He paused, then added quietly, "I understand the Legers are the only St. Ives unit to return, so far."

Awarding Tamas a smile for his tact, Cassandra nodded. "I'm sure the First St. Ives Lancers under my brother are fine," she said, never doubting it. "The Clans have tried their best to kill Kai, and he always pulls through." *Though it's the first time he's tried to beard them in their own den,* she thought. From the nods the men gave her, Cassandra was sure she'd let some of her concern show. She dialed for a light smile and a more assured tone. "He always pulls through," she restated.

Colonel Rubinsky raised his shot glass, blue eyes hard and jaw set. "Here's hoping," he toasted, "that it runs in the family." He tossed his drink back with a practiced flick of the wrist. "Major Allard-Liao, the Light Horse are at your disposal."

Cassandra joined them in the toast, then settled in for a more detailed survey of Light Horse assets. No fancy ceremony or political dances here. No reading the fine print of the mercenaries' contract. Command had been assumed with a simple toast between warriors. Despite any regular line officer's concerns about mercenary troops, Cassandra had to admit that she liked the way Rubinsky's Light Horse did business.

8

In the freedom of null-gravity, Aris Sung drifted along one of the horizontal transship passages that ran through officer's country of the *Overlord* Class DropShip *Dainwu,* House Master Ty Wu Non's command vessel. Capable of transporting the Warrior House's entire 'Mech battalion, it currently carried only the command company, while the two *Union*s also docked along the spine of the JumpShip *Tao-te* carried the rest. Aris' company, still under the command of Raven Clearwater as Aris pursued his security duties, traveled in the *Union* Class *Lao-tzu.*

Drifting up to the door of House Master Non's stateroom, Aris caught one of the many handholds recessed into the right-hand bulkhead and anchored himself. A klaxon further along the main corridor sounded three times just then, harsh, grinding peals that warned of the impending jump from Harloc to the Hustaing system. Aris paused briefly, staring at the klaxon as if it were somehow claiming credit for that impressive event.

Despite a DropShip's apparent strength—well armored, heavy weapon bays, and the ability to shuttle BattleMechs planetside— they were still dependent on the slender, almost effeminate-looking JumpShips that rarely ventured into star systems but whose Kearny-Fuchida engines could tear a hole in space and transport themselves up to thirty light years in an instant.

Deploying solar sails or, if available, accepting the faster microwave feed from a system's recharge station, JumpShips could recharge for the next jump in anywhere from three days to a week. The *Tao-te,* meaning the Way of Power, was one of the newer designs equipped with lithium-fusion batteries that allowed it to jump twice on the same recharge. It was a feat that still often boggled the mind of Aris Sung.

He rapped on the teak knocking panel set into the steel bulkhead next to the door. A faint "Enter" sounded from within, the door opened with a soft hiss, and Aris went in.

"Company Leader Aris Sung, reporting to the House Master," he said. He held himself at some semblance of attention in the null gravity by keeping one hand behind his back to grasp a handhold welded next to the door.

Ty Wu Non glanced up from his work. Efficiency reports, by the look of the data displayed across his hand-held noteputer. "Please take a seat, Aris Sung." He waited while Aris buckled himself into one of the two empty chairs.

"Your duties are being amended," Master Non said flatly, omitting all the usual pleasantries.

Blinking his surprise, Aris nodded once. "The will of the House Master, or course," he said, hiding his disappointment. House Master Non would never *add* to his duties while Aris was assigned to a mission as important as safeguarding Chancellor Liao, so that meant he was completely off the assignment. He consoled himself with the honor he had known as the squad leader on six worlds already. "Would you like my recommendation for security replacement?" he asked in a carefully neutral voice.

The House Master shook his head, his dark hair whipping back and forth with no gravity to weight it down. "You have not been removed from security. Only your assignment has changed. You will now be directly responsible for the safety of Isis Marik. Chancellor Liao is no longer your concern."

"May I ask why my assignment has changed?" Aris chose his words carefully. Questioning the House Master was a tricky process, only to be done under the strictest of protocol. "If there was a failure in my previous work, I should know so as to correct the situation."

Ty Wu Non held Aris under his intense gaze for a few moments, no doubt a caution. But when he spoke, his tone gave away his concern for how Aris might be taking the news. "There was no failure, Aris Sung. Chancellor Liao no longer requires your services, and so has instead entrusted to you the care of his fiancée."

Aris felt a mixture of relief and pride in Ty Wu Non's indirect praise. The possibility of having failed Sun-Tzu Liao had worried him greatly. Another three warning tones from the klaxon, this time alerting everyone that jump procedures had been initiated, cut off his next comment. Though muted through the steel door and bulkhead, the tones still commanded attention.

Tensing, Aris tried to prepare, even knowing there was no real way to do so. One instant everything was normal, and in the next it seemed as if the entire room was being stretched in some fourth-dimensional way. It hurt the brain to look at it, and Aris tried to squeeze his eyes shut. In that frozen instant he could almost sense the firing of his synapses, the emission of the bioelectric command that traveled through his central nervous system like a tiny piece of fire slowly crawling along a fuse, and the final jump to muscular response. Then the instant finally passed, and everything returned to normal.

Aris blinked.

Shaking off the effect of the jump, Aris shivered as if cold. "I will revamp security procedures at once, House Master," he said.

"No, you will not," Ty Wu Non said, voice suddenly hard. "No changes. You will keep the same codes and procedures as when guarding the Chancellor. And you are to tell no one that your assignment has been altered."

That makes no sense. Obviously, there was more going on here than the House Master was telling. Aris read in Ty Wu Non's tone that no further questions would be tolerated. *But to do my job, there are things I must know.* "We will coordinate with McCarron's Armored Cavalry as usual?"

The House Master visibly relaxed, as if he'd been concerned that Aris would press beyond the normal House courtesies.

When he spoke it was still with a forced calm. "You will coordinate with the Hustaing militia. The Nightriders have been relocated."

Aris felt himself groping in the dark for anything familiar. House Master Non had to be aware that radical alteration of preset plans constituted a possible security breach. His team would be operating on incorrect information, and now their main backup force was missing. He sensed hidden plans at work, but did not possess enough information to reason it out for himself. The honor squad suddenly seemed much less glorious. *What else can they throw at me?*

As if in response to his private question, the comm set on Ty Wu Non's desk chimed once and then began to emit the *Dainwu* captain's voice. "House Master Non, the *Celestial Walker* jumped in after us and immediately released its DropShip."

Ty Wu Non pressed down a button to talk. "And why is that a problem, Captain Wan?"

"Sir, it immediately jumped out again. The *Celestial Walker* has left the *Pearl of True Wisdom* behind."

Ty nodded to the disembodied voice. "Thank you, Captain. You will please institute an immediate communication's blackout with Hustaing. No messages without my express permission and then only under my supervision."

Questions burned on Aris' lips. The *Celestial Walker* was the Chancellor's JumpShip and the *Pearl of True Wisdom* the DropShip on which he traveled. Things were happening too fast, impinging on his ability to provide protection. He looked to his House Master, hoping for some explanation, but found only a mask of careful neutrality looking back.

"You are dismissed, Aris Sung."

Aris left, still groping in the dark.

Pinedale, Denbar
St. Ives Compact

Activities buzzed throughout the Whiteriver Base's huge 'Mech hangar as Major Trisha Smithson walked the floor with her executive officer Warner Doles. Black night showed outside the huge, open doors, but inside, banks of glaring floodlights kept the darkness at bay. She smelled the mixed scents of grease, sweat, and hot metalwork. Her hearing protection kept the blaring cacophony of sounds to tolerable levels.

Technicians worked everywhere, some pulled from Denbar Home Guard bases located in other cities around Pinedale. They ran diagnostics and performed last-minute maintenance on BattleMechs and the Blackwind Lancers' armor company vehicles. Flashes of white-blue light occasionally strobed out from behind protective screens as they welded armor into place. Civilian laborers pushed handcarts or drove forklifts as they hauled supplies out of storage bays; mostly foodstuffs and munitions. MechWarriors supervised the work on their own 'Mechs or clustered in tight knots, passing along the latest rumors or predicting the battle to come.

It is a chaotic, savage stage play, and I am the writer, thought Trisha Smithson. She leaned in toward her XO. "They certainly believe we're going somewhere."

Warner Doles shook his head in frustration. "I haven't been able to figure out who exactly is behind the rumors. It has to be one of the company commanders, though none will take credit. Near as I can tell it started with a few MechWarriors dragging techs out of the club to get their machines combat-ready. That, plus the intel from Hustaing."

"What about that intelligence? Is it reliable?" Trisha stepped aside to make more room for a forklift carrying missile reloads. "Sun-Tzu is unprotected?" She watched her exec closely.

"He has been traveling with a Warrior House," Warner reminded her. "I would not call him unprotected. But yes, the Hustaing garrison regiment from McCarron's Armored Cavalry appears to have been relocated from Hustaing to Kaifeng. That gives Sun-Tzu only the Warrior House and the Hustaing Home Guard, which does not include BattleMech forces."

Trisha brushed fingers through her auburn hair, lips pursed in thought as she recalled the speech Chancellor Liao had given on Gei-Fu. *Hustaing—he mentioned ending his tour on Hustaing.* She had no doubt that it was a sign. *But is Captain*

Doles ready to head off in the direction I want to go? "The Home Guard will be spread around the world in company-strength lots," she said, yelling a bit louder as technicians used a nearby cherry-picker to lift themselves up to an *Orion*'s shoulder. "But a Warrior House is nothing to laugh at."

They stopped in front of the berth that held Trisha's *Victor*. Two astechs serviced the assault machine, loading large, nickel-ferrous slugs into the Gauss rifle ammo feeder. Both paid a moment of silent respect to the impressive war machine, before Warner finally spoke. "When you asked me to draw up some assault plans, I talked to a few of the small mercenary units on-planet. We *could* call up two more BattleMech companies. That would give us the edge."

Good. Good. "They have to be inbound by now. Could we make it?" Having spoken several days ago with a JumpShip navigator, Trisha knew that they could. But again, she had to keep Warner involved. *He's borderline. What I'm setting up will run counter to his devotion to the Compact, but then he's also of the old Capellan school where you follow where your commander leads regardless of cost.*

"They have seven days to planetfall," Doles told her. "If we boost hard to the JumpShip, I calculate we can be docked up in three. Two navigators have separately plotted jump calculations for a pirate point that would bring us in on the back side of Hustaing's moon." He hesitated for the briefest second, but then nodded confidently. "Yes, we could make it."

Just as she had figured too. JumpShips usually left and entered a system at the zenith or nadir points well outside a system's elliptic plane, avoiding the gravity well that interfered with the ship's interstellar drive. Pirate points were places inside a system where gravitational effects canceled each other out and allowed for a closer approach. If it were going to be done, that was the way.

Trisha walked along silently for several long minutes, passing her *Victor* and coming now to Warner's *Grasshopper*. It was a gamble, she knew, and at stake would be her career in the St. Ives military forces and the years of preparation to get her this far. But so long as Colonel Perrin kept her bottled up in the

Blackwind Lancers' second battalion, her career path was dead-ended anyway. *So one last roll of the dice to break free.*

Trisha turned to fully face her exec, who met it with equal determination. *Not that it was ever your decision to make,* she thought, *or mine.* "Load them up," she ordered.

9

Aris Sung fought his control sticks, trying to keep his *Wraith* balanced as a hail of twelve-centimeter autocannon slugs chewed into the armor on his left leg, effectively laying it bare to the endo-steel skeleton beneath. The *Wraith*'s tactical computer painted the new threat on his head's up display, a *Hunchback,* which had been hidden behind an overpass to Qingliu's main highway and now stepped down from a grass bank to join Aris' *Wraith* on the pavement. Almost by reflex Aris triggered off one burst from the large pulse laser mounted to his 'Mech's right arm, the scarlet pulses stitching into the *Hunchback*'s torso but failing to penetrate, and then raced outside the reach of the other 'Mech's main weapon.

Can't afford the time to fight it. Not now.

Caught at Qingliu's spaceport, well outside the city proper, Aris had stood in shocked amazement to learn that a battalion of Blackwind Lancers supported by mercenaries had dared to assault a Capellan world. The shock lasted all of ten seconds, giving way quickly to a chill of concern for the welfare of Isis Marik. Having seen her safely ensconced in the city's convention center, with Death Commando guards and a healthy complement of Hiritsu infantry, he had returned to the landing fields to coordinate 'Mech patrols with the Hustaing Home Guard armor forces present. But except for a company's worth of Warrior House 'Mechs already patrolling the outskirts of the city, security wasn't set to handle a full-scale assault by Compact forces.

Separated from his charge by several kilometers and who knew how many hostiles, Aris had ignored his ground car in favor of his *Wraith*. The fifty-five-ton 'Mech, powered by a large extralight fusion engine, was faster than most ground transportation and could stand up to hostile fire. An impressive design, its smooth segmented parts lent it a streamlined appearance, while the turret-style waist allowed it a good range of pivoting motion. Hiritsu techs had given its armor the blued-steel look of a rifle barrel, heightening its deadly appearance. As the *Wraith* ran along the freeway at better than one hundred fifteen kilometers per hour, the few cars remaining on the road had hit the shoulder quickly on seeing the 'Mech moving up from behind.

Aris opened a channel to the rest of his lance, hastily formed at the spaceport and now trailing him by a kilometer in slightly slower BattleMechs. "Enemy *Hunchback* one klick up from you," he informed them. They could take care of a single *Hunchback,* and he had to get into the city.

Gaining the highway's paved surface the *Hunchback* throttled up into a run, trying to keep the *Wraith* in range of its deadly weapon for another few seconds. Aris slammed his feet down on the *Wraith*'s pedals, engaging jump jets and hurling the 'Mech skyward before he had even consciously considered the action. Tactical instincts bred into Aris over years of 'Mech piloting had spotted the opposing MechWarrior's error in committing himself to forward momentum that would place his *Hunchback* within jump range of the *Wraith*. Angling backward and spinning through a slow barrel-roll, Aris brought the *Wraith* right back at the *Hunchback*. As he passed overhead he noticed the Blackwind Lancers' insignia on the *Hunchback*'s shoulder, a blue ax-head set against a yellow circular field. Then he was over, and coming down for a landing not ten meters behind the enemy machine.

His large laser flared with a burst of staccato pulses, melting armor across the opposing machine's wide back and laying it open for the medium lasers on the *Wraith*'s left arm. These stabbed scarlet fire into the *Hunchback*'s internals. The damage missed the autocannon ammunition, which would've turned the fifty-ton war machine into instant scrap, but as the gyro was completely cut away, the enemy 'Mech sprawled forward and continued in an ungainly skid along the pavement until it piled up along the shoulder and remained still. *No way to tell if the pilot is injured or not.* Aris was surprised at the thought. *These people are the enemy!*

The cockpit temperature spiked sharply as the fusion reactor bled waste heat, but Aris hardly noticed except for the salt taste of sweat burning his lips. He reopened the channel to his lance.

"Correction," he said in a flat tone, throttling back up into a full run. "One *Hunchback* down. Proceeding on track toward Capella One." He paused for a moment, then gave in to a slight twinge of conscience. "One 'Mech drop out and check on the downed pilot."

"Don't wait for us," Raven Clearwater transmitted back, her voice robbed of any emotion by the air waves. "And quit wasting time with the visitors. We'll clean up behind you."

Aris raced onward.

At the outskirts of Qingliu he traded hasty shots with a *Cataphract* bearing the blue and yellow of the Lancers. He sacrificed some armor along his right arm before evading, but claimed in exchange a solid head shot against the heavy 'Mech that no doubt left the enemy MechWarrior evaluating his own mortality. A moment later Aris found himself sandwiched between two *UrbanMech*s. Insufferably slow but decently armed and armored for a light 'Mech, the walking trashcans pinned him in a crossfire of autocannon cluster munitions that sanded off armor all over his *Wraith*. A lucky combination of laser hits damaged the autocannon of one, and with their firepower halved, the *Urbie*s withdrew.

And bothering Aris more with each passing encounter was a hollow sense of futility. Part of it was his fighting against machines that were unmistakably Capellan in their original design, bearing colors that had once been familiar to the Confederation. Part may even have been the idea that the face inside the other pilot's neurohelmet might show Asian features speaking of a Capellan heritage. Mostly it was a sense that he had failed Isis Marik, and so failed his Chancellor. He shouldered the doubts aside. He was a warrior in a Capellan Warrior House, and his vows demanded that he always strive for success. No matter the odds or the situation.

Two more blocks. A chill that had nothing to do with the coolant flow to his vest shook Aris as he saw the column of smoke rising above buildings ahead. Only the lack of enemy units in the area bolstered his confidence that he could still find and extract Isis Marik. Then the commline crackled to life with the static-filled background that told of a jamming attempt or long-distance transmission.

"All units, this is House Master Non. Fall back to the spaceport. Repeat, fall back and establish a line of defense at the spaceport. Senior officer on station, take command until relieved. Home Guard units are hereby arrogated by House Hiritsu command and will abandon Qinglui. The city is lost."

As others acknowledged the orders, Aris set his jaw in silent mutiny and continued up the street. It wasn't as if he were directly disobeying. House tactical doctrine suggested that he return by a slightly different path, and so he would circle this block and come down the back side. And if he just happened to find the security force guarding Capella One . . .

His muscles tightened involuntarily, and the *Wraith* nearly stumbled with the brief loss of control. The convention center was in ruins, though no enemy 'Mechs remained in the area. Walls were smashed in and the street littered with bodies. Several bodies wore House Hiritsu uniforms, Aris noted. He even spotted what might once have been a Death Commando, someone in an all-black uniform cut in half by 'Mech-grade weapons. At the sight of Aris' *Wraith,* a few surviving Hiritsu warriors left the shelter of nearby buildings. Aris began to hope for Isis' appearance, but some hand signals from an infantry commander on the ground dispelled that illusion.

"Aris Sung, acknowledge the fall back order!"

Aris opened a comm channel. His tongue felt thick and awkward as he tried to speak. "Company Leader Sung, acknowledging," he said slowly. "Escorting infantry survivors back to spaceport. Capella One is missing, presumed captured. Repeat—"

"Acknowledged," Ty Wu Non cut him off. "You are released to safeguard survivors back to defensive line." A pause. "Get home, Aris."

There is no glory to be had on Hustaing today. Slamming a fist against his thigh, Aris stared down the street and into the depths of Qinglui, wondering what had happened to Isis Marik.

Only six blocks over and several more deeper into the city, Infantryman Li Wynn helped Isis out of the back of the wrecked limousine where it had plowed through the front of a hotel and ended up in the lobby. That the Death Commandos had made it this far, running a gauntlet of enemy 'Mechs and armored vehicles, seemed amazing. A bruise was blossoming on Isis' right cheek, and shards of glass glittered in her chestnut-brown hair, but she seemed fairly whole and healthy.

She looks beautiful.

"The men . . . in the front . . ."

Li shook his head, having already checked out the Death Commandos. "The engine is practically sitting in their laps," he said, brushing glass from the shoulders of her gray, martial-cut outfit and then taking her by the elbow. "I've got to get you out of here."

Isis glanced uncertainly toward the smashed-in front of the car as Li pulled her through a ring of shocked hotel guests and toward a side entrance. "And just who are you?" she asked, regaining a small measure of her composure.

"Hiritsu infantry." Li glanced down, understanding the reason behind the question. He wore a button-down white shirt and slacks, and still carried the empty camera from playing photographer. He threw down the camera and then led her back out onto the street.

"I knew you wouldn't make it far—that vehicle screamed out *V.I.P. inside*—so I followed on foot." He glanced around quickly. A white van was idling at the curb twenty meters down the street, just outside the hotel's service entrance. "That is more what we need."

"A bread truck?" Isis asked, reading the Farm Fresh Breads logo on the side of vehicle.

"Sure. Who would fire on a bread truck?" Li yanked open the door. "Besides, it's already running." He ushered Isis into the cab. "Into the back, Duchess," he ordered, glancing both ways down the street for enemy 'Mechs and then sliding into the driver's seat. Isis moved to the rear, but then leaned halfway into the cab. Li shifted into gear and pulled away from the curb, taking the next corner, which put them back along the hotel's front and heading toward the southern district.

And also straight at an enemy *Crusader,* which fired a burst from its machine gun across the van's path. Several bullets skipped up from the pavement and starred the windshield as Li braked to a fast stop.

"I thought you said they wouldn't fire!" Isis yelled, ducking completely into the back.

"I can be wrong once," Li shot back, forgetting completely whom he was addressing. He was in a race against time and very large machines of destruction; criticism he would take later. He shifted into reverse and cranked the wheel, then floored the accelerator. The truck spun and bounced over the curb in reverse, then smashed through the large glass doors that opened onto the hotel lobby. Behind him he heard Isis shriek. Glancing back, he saw bread loaves raining down from the shelves to half-bury her. "Dig down into them," he ordered, hoping they might give her a bit of cushioning.

Fully inside the lobby and out of the BattleMech's line of sight, Li straightened out the wheel and shifted back to drive. Leaning on the horn, he took off across the lobby and then through a large lounge. The bread truck sideswiped the abandoned limo and then a large piano, smashed aside chairs and sofas, and scattered people just coming off the elevator. Then, faced with a choice between the downstairs café and a real wall, he chose the café. Crushed chairs and splintered tables flew aside, and so far as Li could tell he hit no one, though that was not a big concern at the moment.

"Hang on!" he called back as they approached another glass wall.

Glass shattered and rained down over the white bread truck as it plowed out into the street again, though now around the corner from the BattleMech. Still, the streets would not stay safe long, and so he simply bounced back over the next curb and plowed into a new building, this one a major department store.

"What are you doing?" Isis shouted.

Li slowed, steering around large displays and trying to give people a chance to move. "Browsing the lingerie department, I think." He kept the horn blaring as he gunned the engine, then smashed through the opposite side of the store and back onto the street.

"Okay, let's make a run for it," he said, more to himself, pulling out onto the deserted street and pushing the engine for all it was worth toward Qingliu's southern districts. He had done it; rescued Isis Marik out from under the guns of the enemy. He almost smiled. *It's not everyday I rescue a beautiful princess from threatening dragons. With a bit of luck or a House Hiritsu BattleMech for escort, we just might make this.*

His luck lasted all of four blocks before he raced through an intersection just ahead of an *UrbanMech,* which moved in from a side avenue and cut off any chance of retreat. Approaching the far end, a *JagerMech* stepped out to block their way, firing several quick bursts of autocannon fire down the street to either side of the bread truck. One burst of slugs edged in close and ripped away the sideview mirror.

"I think they want us to stop!" Li yelled back over his shoulder, then checked both sides of the street for a new wall to demolish. Unfortunately he was in an area of small shops, all brick-faced and likely to stop the truck cold. As the slugs tracked inward he braked hard, stopping the truck twenty meters short of the looming *JagerMech.* He dove into the back.

Isis was digging her way out from a mound of smashed bread and plastic wrappers. The aroma of bread filled the truck. "Now what?"

Desperate, Li glanced around for inspiration. What he found was the previous driver's ball cap, with the Farm Fresh Bread name and logo on it, hanging from a peg near the door to the cab. He snatched it off its hook and turned around, then started as if suddenly remembering exactly who Isis was and what he was about to suggest. He almost allowed his modesty to slow him down, but he didn't have the time. *The dragons are closing.* He tossed her the ball cap and began unbuttoning his shirt.

"I hope you aren't shy," he muttered, and then when she did not move, he said most formally, "Duchess Marik, please remove your clothing."

Lance Sergeant Erik Richards pulled his Hetzer wheeled assault gun up into the *JagerMech*'s shadow, training the large-bore autocannon onto it. Was it possible he held the Chancellor of the Capellan Confederation under his weapon? One burst and all the recent slurs and threats were a memory, but common sense reined him in. This was only one possible vehicle, and anyway Major Smithson wanted the Chancellor alive.

He hit some toggles on the communications set, tying his transmitter into the vehicle's P.A. system. "You in the truck. Come out with your hands up," he said. "Make any further attempt to escape and you *will* be fired upon."

The driver's side door opened and a pair of hands showed, followed slowly by a woman wearing a white button-down shirt and ball cap. She stepped onto the street, but did not attempt to move further.

"Move away from the vehicle," the lance sergeant ordered over the P.A.

External mikes picked up her stammered reply. "He—he's got a gun on me."

Richards switched quickly over to his regular comm channel. "We've got a live possibility here," he said. "Checking it out." Grabbing a rifle and hand-held radio, he undogged his vehicle's top hatch and pulled himself up and out.

"Stay calm, miss," he said, approaching the truck carefully and speaking loud enough so anyone inside could hear him. "If he tries anything, that nice big *JagerMech* over my shoulder will chew through that truck in about three seconds flat." Closer now, he could see that she was a mess, her hair partially tucked up into the Farm Fresh Breads ball cap and a bruise forming on her right cheek. "Just step away from the vehicle and walk toward me."

She did as she was told, hesitantly at first and then with a more determined step. The last few paces she fairly threw herself at Richards, arms around his neck and sobbing against his shoulder. "Thank you. Oh, thank you."

Richards was very aware of her figure and the perfume she wore, and allowed himself a second to enjoy the gratitude. "Just keep walking now," he told her. "Get past the *JagerMech* and hide behind its leg." He spoke quickly into his radio, to keep the MechWarrior aware of the situation. *This is one fringe benefit you don't get, stuck up there in that sweatbox.*

He leveled the rifle at the truck as she broke away and hurriedly moved around the giant BattleMech to remove herself from the line of possible fire. "All right. You can come out now or the *Jag* can pick the truck apart one piece at a time. What's it going to be?"

"I'm coming out," a voice called from inside.

Richards knew a momentary thrill when he saw Asian features and the martial cut of the outfit the man wore. But it became quickly obvious that this was not Sun-Tzu Liao, or even any regular line officer. The outfit was not a real uniform, and it fit him awkwardly. He came out of the truck very slowly, with hands laced behind his head, and smiling.

"Name and rank?" Richards barked at the man, watching carefully for any sign of aggression. The man's gaze flicked over Richards' shoulder and then back. He grinned wider. "And what's so funny."

"Infantryman Li Wynn, House Hiritsu," the man said simply. "And I was just thinking that you look nothing like a dragon."

JumpShip Celestial Walker
Sian System
Sian Commonality, Capellan Confederation

Standing at attention within the *Celestial Walker*'s shipboard office of the Chancellor, the Death Commando read aloud the latest release from Associated Stellar Press.

"Today, in an unprovoked surprise assault, forces of the St. Ives military struck at the Capellan Confederation world of Hustaing. Chancellor and First Lord Sun-Tzu Liao is reportedly on-planet as part of his recent tour of the St. Ives border. He is accompanied by his fiancée Isis Marik on this tour. One confirmed sighting was made of Duchess Marik by a reporter of this service before the Word of Blake granted Capellan representatives on Sian a total communication blackout against Hustaing for security purposes.

"The exact composition of the attacking force is, as yet, unknown, though elements of the Blackwind Lancers are certainly involved. No official statement has been released from St. Ives by either Duchess Candace Liao or a representative."

Sun-Tzu Liao, sitting behind his desk with hands clasped before him, smiled secretively. "Thank you. Now please check on my shuttle."

He waited for the warrior to leave the room, then addressed the empty office. "With your help, my love, I shall make the Confederation strong again. As I promised."

Pandemonium

Now war is based on deception. Move when it is advantageous and create changes in the situation by dispersal and concentration of forces.
                                        —Sun-Tzu, *The Art of War*

Turmoil. It is the genesis of both political and military solutions. When my opponents stand confused, out of ignorance or through my designs, then I have been given free rein.
    And someone must bring order.
        —Sun-Tzu Liao, journal entry, 3 March 3060, Sian

10

To Candace Liao, the Gallery Hall of the St. Ives' Royal Compound had a special atmosphere, subtle, yet still tangible. Visiting it always spoke to her strongly of history and heritage, and of responsibility. It smelled of the polishing agents used on the teakwood flooring and the wonderful, old scent of canvas and oils. A museum smell. Sculptures, carvings, paintings; the walls and floor space were tastefully arranged with over three millennia of Chinese art. Some of it priceless, like the Shang dynasty jade tiger sculpture that Elias Jung Liao, founder of the Liao dynasty, had carried away from Terra when he first took to the stars. Some items were deemed relatively worthless, recent pieces picked up by Candace's curator as examples of current Capellan work.

Unlike her estranged brother Tormano, to Candace the cash value of the collection meant nothing. She funded the collection out of respect for her heritage, and she made sure that the pieces constantly rotated out to public museums and touring shows so that her people could come to know and enjoy them as she did. She brushed the tips of her fingers very lightly over the cool, slick jade of the Shang sculpture, marveling at its ancient beauty and inherent strength. *Its endurance.*

The approach of careful footsteps interrupted her reverie. Candace turned to face Senior Colonel Caroline Seng, her top military officer. "A beautiful piece," Seng said, her soft-spoken words loud in the peace of the Gallery Hall. "Does it have a name?"

Caroline Seng had come lately to her Capellan heritage, Candace knew, but her senior colonel understood enough of the Confucian concepts of courteous behavior that she chose a neutral topic for the first of their conversation. Candace smiled at the courtesy, though her sharp eyes picked out traces of Colonel Seng's frustration in the stiffness of her walk and tightness around her narrowed eyes. *The news is not good.* "If it had a name, it was lost to time long ago," the Duchess said. "Elias renamed it *zì-lái-yu,* running jade, when he discovered it on Terra in 2181."

The other woman nodded, then seemed to lose herself in the near-translucence of the light green stone. "Word of Blake has reaffirmed its decision to honor the HPG blackout on Hustaing," she said after a quiet moment, "as requested by Talon Zahn." Her doe-brown eyes sought out Candace's. "Zahn passed word to me that the only message he would allow the Blakists to deliver is one ordering the Lancers to surrender unconditionally to Capellan forces present on-planet. And," she said, swallowing hard, "only after your public apology to the citizens of the Confederation."

Candace began walking along the Gallery Hall, Colonel Seng falling into step with her. Their footsteps echoed hollowly along the passage. "My nephew knew what he was doing when he appointed that one his Strategic Director," Candace said finally, in grudging admiration. "The HPG blackout keeps the scandalvids from claiming any respectable source for their wild suppositions, and also prevents the Blackwind Lancers from receiving any orders but the ones he wants them to have. *And* he knows how to play political hardball."

"It places the Compact in a delicate position," Seng agreed. "His terms mean that we would be admitting we cannot control our own troops, and that the Confederation could hold the Lancers indefinitely. Any other course of action could be construed as our support for the assault."

"Two unacceptable choices," Candace declared with a shake

of her head. "That battalion has never been rated as a completely reliable unit, but I've not seen a prediction that they would go rogue, either. You have been in contact with the Blackwind Lancers' commanding officer?"

Seng nodded. "Colonel Perrin. He admitted that Major Smithson has been a discipline problem, with a fanatical hatred for your nephew, and that he has tried to keep the situation under control without formal measures." She cleared her throat meaningfully. "He tendered his immediate resignation."

Pausing to consider the request, Candace quickly discarded it as wasteful. "Refuse it. Perrin is too valuable to lose right now. If things heat up, we will need him."

"Surely you don't plan to back Major Smithson's actions?" The shock in Colonel Seng's voice was readily apparent. "Zahn is already making good media use of the demonstrations on Denbar, with the populace supporting the Lancers—*their* Lancers, as they are calling them. But if you were to give official support—"

Candace cut off Seng with a placating gesture, quick to assuage the concerns of her military advisor. "Not officially," she said. "Not as such." She paused to collect her thoughts. "The Confederation has its military forces spread thin right now, reclaiming the Disputed Territories and pushing into the Chaos March proper. Still, I am sure Talon Zahn is moving at least one heavy unit in to support the fighting on Hustaing and rescue his Chancellor. A regiment of McCarron's Armored Cavalry, I'd think. If the Lancers can defeat this Warrior House or at least capture Sun-Tzu in the time it takes for that support to arrive, they present us with a fait accompli and I can use that political coup to lessen the damage to the Compact. So we wait, stretching out our decision to the last possible moment and praying that the Lancers rescue themselves from their own stupidity."

Seng stiffened, as if sensing the alternative. "And if they do not?"

"Then we sacrifice the battalion for the good of the Compact," Candace said, voice hard and certain. "I will publicly condemn Major Smithson's actions and leave her to the mercy of the Confederation. The others we *may* be able to repatriate, but the battalion itself will be disbanded. Colonel Perrin's career will be in ruins, and we may even have to disband the other Lancer battalions before they turn sour."

"A heavy price," Seng said, nodding wearily, "but necessary."

Candace felt the weight of the St. Ives Compact pressing, but she'd borne that for over thirty years and so shouldered it easily. She turned toward the end of the Gallery Hall, no longer finding peace among the artifacts and desiring some form of action now.

"I want to review the files on every border unit," she said. "Line unit, mercenary, and Home Guard. I want to *know* that no one will make the situation worse. Then we upgrade their state of readiness in case Zahn thinks to stage a reprisal raid.

"The Compact will suffer from the situation, no way to prevent that," Candace said, moving along with a strength of purpose, "but damned if I will make it easy for them."

Hazlet, Nashuar
St. Ives Compact

All eight of the Nashuar Home Guard MechWarrior trainees had gathered in the on-base apartment that Danielle Singh shared with Freya Restecht. Most clustered around the trivid viewer that Danielle had bought and installed, watching news reports and hoping for some information concerning the fighting on Hustaing. Danielle and Trahn Choya, a member of the other trainee lance, sat at the dining table comparing notes. Sodas were constantly rotated from the closet stockpile to the fridge and out to waiting hands, and the room smelled of delivered pizza.

Maurice Fitzgerald sat away from the group, back against the wall with his legs stretched out comfortably in front of him. *Waste of time watching the news, and sharing tips and insights on 'Mech piloting with my competitors seems just a bit counterproductive.* He closed his eyes and mentally reviewed his performance over the last few weeks, searching for flaws and trying to figure out some new way to stand out from the others.

With all the talking and the others moving about the room, Fitzgerald wasn't aware of a presence until he heard the rasping slide as someone leaned against the wall and then slid down to sit next to him.

"Hey, falling asleep over here?"

He opened his eyes. Danielle sat next to him, staring over toward the trivid viewer. Her Asian ancestry was very pronounced in her features, much more so than the light touch Fitz had inherited from his mother's side. He studied her eyes—windows to the soul, he could remember his mother saying—their rare and intense blue, with lighter blue-green flecks of color imbedded within. *Alive,* that was how he thought of them.

Danielle kept her dark hair cut to medium length, but in MechWarrior fashion had shaved small spots over her temples and near the back of her head in the belief that it facilitated contact with her helmet's neuroreceptors. Fitz doubted that it really made a difference, but then belief could be a powerful thing and he couldn't argue with Danielle's performance in the simulator pods.

Danielle glanced over, saw that his eyes were open now, and then returned her gaze to the viewer. "Not interested in the fight on Hustaing?" she asked.

He shrugged, then played with the cuff on his button-down silk shirt, straightening it. "Rather see the box scores for the latest Solaris matches. At least with those I can be fairly certain of an honest report."

"Yeah, the HPG blackout has given the scandalvids pretty much free rein," Danielle agreed. "Though I doubt anyone believes their claim to independent and secret sources this time. You just can't get around the HPG network. Everyone knows that."

She shrugged, though her eyes remained focused and alert. It was then that Fitzgerald noticed that she studied the other trainees watching the trivid, not the viewer itself. "So do you really follow the Solaris games, Maurice?"

Fitzgerald blinked his surprise at her use of his given name. He tended to avoid it, but her use of it felt good, warm even. Nodding an answer to her question, he continued to observe her as she observed the others. *I'm just studying the competition.* He kept trying to tell himself that. "I've got a hundred C-bills riding on Garrett."

"That's a hefty wager." Danielle pursed her lips, considering. "You didn't bet on Cenotaph?" she asked, naming the Battle-Mech stable owned by Kai Allard-Liao and run in absentia by an old friend of the family.

Fitzgerald shook his head lightly. "Jamie Ferrero is good, but that renegade Clanner is going to the top and Ferrero's just a stepping stone." He paused, suddenly uncomfortable, then pushed ahead. "I'd rather bet on a winner."

Danielle turned to face him, her face carefully set against any show of emotion. "That's pretty cold," she said quietly. "Even for you."

Caught under her unblinking stare, Fitzgerald shifted uneasily. He felt the warmth of a blush rising to his cheeks. "Maybe so," he admitted. "But it's reality." He nodded toward the other trainees, who clustered around the viewer. "Just like them. Every one of them would bet that the Lancers can pull this off. They don't care about the odds or who is in the wrong. And let's be honest, the Lancers are the ones in the wrong."

Something flashed in Danielle's eyes and was gone almost as quickly, leaving Fitzgerald unsure as to what it might have been. Disappointment, or perhaps an undefined pain.

"So have you rated us, Fitz?" she asked, switching back to his regular nickname. "The training cadre? There are *three* open slots instead of two now, with Sub-Commander Pherr's recent transfer to the Second St. Ives Lancers. Who's going to make it?"

Fitzgerald didn't like the shift in Danielle's voice or the tightening around the eyes. He tried to make light of it, but couldn't. Not even to himself. *She's the competition, but she isn't my enemy. Nevarr has been trying to teach me that, among other things, but have I really been listening?* "You will," he said, with just a tinge of envy. "I think you're so far out in front that no one can touch you now."

Danielle blinked heavily, taken aback by his blunt appraisal.

When she spoke again, her voice was softer. "Who would be next?" she asked, drawing her knees up to her chest.

"It gets close between Choya, Freya, and, I hope, me. Nevarr is a hard one to read, but I don't think he's given up on me yet. He's still pushing me. The others . . ." He paused, not wanting to hurt Danielle again, but then not finding it within himself to stop now. "The others," he continued quietly, "I think have already been dropped from consideration. Maybe Cameron, but he hasn't racked up near as many kills."

"Kills aren't everything," she said, mirroring his thoughts from past weeks. "Cameron is as good a back-up man as any MechWarrior could hope to have in a lance. He's . . ." She trailed off, searching for the word. ". . . He's solid. And so are you, Maurice. That's really what I wanted to say when I came over. Nevarr has kept you pinned in supporting roles these last few weeks, and you've held up. Without you, I wouldn't have the success rate I do." She glanced down. "I came over to thank you, and to wish you luck." She uncoiled herself and rose to her feet, then moved back to the table and a new discussion with Choya.

Fitzgerald's gaze followed her, then swept the room self-consciously. Danielle had given him something to think about. Several things, actually, but especially with regard to his standing. Maybe his chances were stronger than he'd thought, and maybe he could better them by applying himself to whatever role Nevarr assigned him. Even a supporting role.

Maybe.

11

Celestial Palace
Zi-jin Cheng (Forbidden City), Sian
Sian Commonality, Capellan Confederation
15 October 3060

On the dais sat the large, hand-carved wooden artifact that was the Celestial Throne, seat of the Capellan Confederation, and on that throne Sun-Tzu Liao leaned back in comfort. He wore a black silk Han jacket, its jade green embroidery matching his eyes. Conspicuously absent were the wide-shouldered silk robes of the Chancellor's office. Sun-Tzu broke with tradition only with purpose, and right now his not wearing the silk robes in the throne room served as a constant reminder to everyone that his very presence on Sian was a carefully guarded secret.

No one, Sun-Tzu was sure, wanted to be the person who let that secret slip before its time.

His gaze traveled from one advisor to the next, lingering on each for only a few seconds. Present were Talon Zahn, forced into full dress uniform with Sun-Tzu's alleged disappearance on Hustang and so now acting as regent, Imarra House Master Ion Rush, and Maskirovka Directress Sasha Wanli, the same three people who had been there seven months ago when he had begun setting his plan in motion. Only one new presence this time, his sister Kali, who stood quietly in the shadow thrown by a display suit of ancient Chinese armor from the Nán Bei Cháo dynasties.

The only slice of darkness in the room and she finds it.

Kali's presence bothered Sun-Tzu, in several ways. He believed her irredeemably lost, heavily afflicted by and now embracing the insanity that had plagued their mother. A member of the Thugee cult of assassins and worshipped by its members, even she believed herself to be the reincarnation of the death goddess for whom she'd been named. It made her one of the most unpredictable forces under Sun-Tzu's rule. But skewed though her reality might seem, the best Maskirovka psychoanalysts vouched for her complete devotion to the Confederation and to Sun-Tzu himself. And because Kali was one of only six people who knew of his return to the palace, he could not afford to dismiss her. She obviously had her *ways* about her, and so he would placate her desire to be present if it might buy her cooperation.

And as for cooperation . . . "Why is my aunt so quiet?" he asked, this first question pressing on his mind. He needed to spark a confrontation with Candace, and it was hard to argue with silence. Unbidden, an old piece of advice rose to mind. *When your actions are hinging on an enemy response, do not forget to inform the enemy.* He thrust the unwanted thought aside. Sooner or later he would force a response from his aunt, but Sun-Tzu would rather it be sooner.

Zahn nodded to Sasha Wanli, deferring Sun-Tzu's question to her. "Candace is playing a waiting game," Sasha said, full of the confidence she had been missing in March. She'd had more than half a year to win herself back into her Chancellor's good graces, and obviously thought she had done so. "Security has held, and she believes you trapped on Hustaing. She's hoping the Lancers can capture you, presenting her with a bargaining chip. We would not be able to claim as many concessions from the Compact if she were to then intervene and see you safely back to Sian." She smoothed a wrinkle from the arm of her black dress. "Her only other choice, per Colonel Zahn's terms, is full capitulation."

She will not capitulate. Candace would see the Blackwind Lancers destroyed rather than invite what were sure to be unreasonable—to her—Confederation demands. He had thought that Candace would find another way, but not silent support.

That was almost too crafty. *Too Liao?* He saw ways to take advantage of that. Bringing his hands together in front of him, fingertip to fingertip, Sun-Tzu looked to his Imarra House Master. "And is that true, Ion? Has security held?"

"The facts seem to suggest so, Chancellor." The large man clasped his hands behind his back. Possibly in support of Talon Zahn's position, Rush had opted for House Imarra's dress uniform. Simpler than the standard Confederation Armed Forces formal dress, it still prevented Zahn from standing out overmuch. "The HPG communications blackout on Hustaing has certainly held, and palace security is as tight as I can make it." He glanced once toward Kali, but said nothing.

Yes, Kali. The proverbial fly in any ointment. Sun-Tzu kept his face studiously neutral. "What of Hustaing? Has Word of Blake relayed to us anything of value?"

Rush nodded. "The Blackwind Lancers technically hold Hustaing's capital city Qingliu, but only because House Hiritsu employs its DropShips to keep the Lancers bottled up inside. Of course, per your request, we have implied to the scandalvids that the Lancers are strongly defending their gains in Qingliu against efforts to retake the city." The House Master smiled without humor. "The fighting has turned desperate since the Lancers learned that their JumpShip abandoned them. They try to make breaks for the nearby mountain range, but when they do House Hiritsu manages to lop off another piece and then drive them back. I estimate they can hold out perhaps another month at best."

Another month of desperate fighting. Good news. Sun-Tzu had been slightly anxious. Having a WarShip scare off the Lancers' transportation back to the Compact had been his idea, but it could have backfired by taking the heart out of them. He knew a moment's concern for warriors and citizens of the Confederation who would suffer and die because of the prolonged fight, but it couldn't be helped. The final result—Sun-Tzu's vision of a strengthened Confederation—required the sacrifice.

Talon Zahn gained his attention with a slight cough. "We also have news of your fiancée, Celestial Wisdom." By Zahn's stiffly formal delivery, Sun-Tzu knew what that news would be. Useless. "Her Death Commando bodyguards and approximately a dozen infantry were killed, but Isis Marik was apparently rescued by an infantryman and is safe. For the moment."

Isis is hardly worth a dozen Capellan lives these days. Not while Thomas Marik has a new heir and continues to refuse our marriage. Sun-Tzu frowned. *Well, not everything can go strictly according to plan.* "Very soon people will begin to wonder why we have not dropped a regiment onto Hustaing," he said. "Colonel Zahn, how do our troop dispositions look?"

"Many of our newest units are still masquerading as Home Guard. Now, because of the assault and the recent upgrade in alert status of all St. Ives military forces, I have placed all regular line units garrisoning our border with the Federated Commonwealth and those on Confederation *core* worlds on full alert. This locks them into place, pending a possible invasion. The vocal support that the Blackwind Lancers are receiving out of Denbar and a few other worlds is not hurting our efforts in this regard. Along with our current efforts in the Disputed Territories and Chaos March, there are few units we can move right now without opening up a supposed hole in our defenses." Zahn paused. "I did send another unit into the Magistracy; garrison support for Naomi Centrella while her mother attends the Detroit Conference. But they were already posted so far away as to be out of consideration for Hustaing."

Sun-Tzu stood and paced slowly along the edge of the dais. Not that he was nervous, but he sensed the subtle yet impressive forces under his control converging and felt the sudden need for movement. Slow pacing was a compromise. It gave him a focus for his physical energies, but did not distract his thoughts. He stopped at a brazier and added a pinch of sandalwood incense to the coals. The scent drifted up, lightly perfumed and soothing.

"I will contact Thomas Marik," he decided aloud. "He should be the first to know that I did not travel to Hustaing, and I can explain that his daughter was continuing on in my place. It will give me the excuse to draft one of his border units, the Second Oriente Hussars, I would think, and place them under SLDF colors. They will be brought in to supplement our defenses so I can rescue my betrothed. Thomas does not need to know that Isis is currently safe and protected, not that I believe he truly cares one way or the other."

Sun-Tzu paused, considering. "Katrina, Theodore Kurita, and Yvonne will be contacted too, in that order and all within the next two weeks with a similar request to place troops under SLDF colors. That will get troops moving this way."

Zahn smiled thinly, his dark eyes impassive. "It also reinforces our inability to divert heavy forces at this time." He nodded. "A useful arrow that brings down two birds."

Three birds, Sun-Tzu corrected his top military commander silently. But it was not yet time to divulge the balance of his plans, so he simply nodded in agreement.

"Katrina Steiner-Davion will likely demand something in return," Sasha noted for the benefit of all present. "Reports of civil unrest are sparking all over the Commonwealth, and with the Tikonov incidents, she has even offered to loan your uncle Tormano's services to Yvonne to help quiet the troubles." The older woman's grin came nowhere close to touching her eyes. "In a most regrettable incident of late, some FedCom soldiers walked into an area of Tikonov's capital where celebrations for the Festival of the Dead had begun. A riot started. The next morning the soldiers were found crucified."

A fine ending, Sun-Tzu thought. Just the kind of efforts he wanted conducted there. But news that Katrina might release his uncle Tormano to interfere with the Free Tikonov Movement troubled him. "My uncle once headed Free Capella. If he were to pick up those reins again he could damage our work." He wrestled with his options, but in the end Tikonov was still a long game and could afford a setback. "I will make Katrina an offer before she requests her own, and allow her to pick the unit I will draft from Yvonne. A trade of minor concessions. Perhaps that will keep her happy for now."

"You intend to allow Candace to discover your presence on Sian through Theodore or Yvonne?" This from Ion Rush. "That gives her the advantage in planning a response."

Sun-Tzu nodded, already having thought that out for himself. "I can trust Theodore not to disclose my presence here if I tell him that it would threaten Isis' safety. Yvonne, however, I cannot trust to be so close-mouthed where my aunt is concerned. The day after I send a message to Yvonne I will make a public address damning the Compact for breaking the peace and threatening the safety of my fiancée. That will steal the thunder of any reply, *and* hurt Candace's credibility with the others for being silent so long."

Then Sun-Tzu fixed his House Master with a cold stare. *And speaking of hurting credibility.* "But since you suggest it, Ion, perhaps on the same day I record Yvonne's message you could leak the news to my aunt as well."

Ion Rush never flinched, having two years before come to terms with Sun-Tzu over his old ties to Candace Liao. Sun-Tzu did notice that Rush missed quick glances of suspicion from both Sasha Wanli and Talon Zahn. He studied a nearby wall hanging for a moment to allow those suspicions to take root. *You are all competent people, and while I do not doubt any of your loyalties at this time it is better for me if you do not get too close to each other. More than one Inner Sphere ruler has been replaced through a conspiracy, but a conspiracy is impossible without complete trust.* When he returned his gaze to the floor the concerns were past, for now, and Kali was just leaving the room.

Sasha brought an end to the awkward moment with a new thought. "Chancellor," she said, glancing at both Rush and Zahn before continuing, "you realize, I'm sure, that this assault has effectively ended the usefulness of a Capellan deep-cover operative? We must arrange an extraction, in case Candace suspects."

Pacing slowly back toward the Celestial Throne, carefully placing each foot with studied precision, Sun-Tzu nodded. "Let's not be obvious. I trust the operative will arrange for the extraction." He glanced up and read the looks of interest on the faces of both military men but did not elaborate.

Talon Zahn merely shrugged and then shifted back toward a previous topic. "From all reports, Qingliu is suffering heavy collateral damage. Do you want me to make preparations for sending in engineers and humanitarian aid?"

That was something to be considered. Every day wasted in getting relief to the world might cost the lives of Capellan citizens, but then it would also increase the moral debt owed by the St. Ives Compact. A hard balance to gauge. "No," Sun-Tzu finally said. "Wait until the Lancers are closer to folding and then arrange for it three weeks—" *No, these are my people.* "Two weeks past the day of liberation."

Sun-Tzu fixed them all with a hard stare as he settled back again into the Celestial Throne and smoothed the front of his silk jacket with a quick brush of his left hand. "Keep on top of things. I want no slips in security and no mistakes. A lot of our people . . . *my* people . . . are going to suffer for the Xin Sheng effort. I refuse to allow their sacrifice to be in vain." He nodded a dismissal, and the others withdrew from the throne room.

Alone, with only his own thoughts for company, Sun-Tzu Liao welcomed the peace as he considered the various threads that tied to his overall plan of Confederation rebirth. Many of those threads still ran together in tangle, but slowly he sorted through each one as he studied them for flaws. The pattern, he trusted, would take care of itself.

Qingliu, Hustaing
Sian Commonality, Capellan Confederation
26 October 3060

Autocannon fire chewed into the *Grasshopper*'s right arm while lasers seared the air around the BattleMech. Despite a heat scale already edging into the red, Captain Warner Doles engaged his jets and rode the 'Mech up into the air on plasma streams, performing a lateral jump that would bring him deep into the cover of a thick stand of alder but do little with regard to regaining the safety of Qingliu. *Not that I expect to make it back this time.* In mutual and unspoken commitment, both he in his *Grasshopper* and Major Smithson in her *Victor* had formed a two-'Mech rearward defense against the forward elements of House Hiritsu, buying precious seconds while the rest of the battalion regained the city's protection.

At the apex of its jump, a new stream of autocannon fire tore into the *Grasshopper*'s left leg. Depleted-uranium slugs cut through the last of its armor and into the internal structure beneath. The 'Mech rocked violently, the destruction of one Leviathan Lifter jump jet throwing it off balance as it dropped down barely under control. Slender, gray-barked trunks splintered and cracked as the seventy-ton 'Mech landed roughly among the alder trees, left leg bowing outward due to a damaged actuator. It stumbled, but managed to straighten itself in time to catch a flurry of scarlet laser pulses that stitched into its chest and left side. Armor melted and ran, leaving dull gray trails down the *Grasshopper*'s left side and leg. Some splattered to the ground, scorching the earth and starting smoldering fires in the drifts of damp leaves.

The Lancer captain fought controls turned sluggish from heat build-up and now a damaged leg actuator. Sweat beaded and ran down his bare arms and legs, and burned at the corners of his eyes. Though the padded shoulders of his cooling vest helped bear the heavy weight of his neurohelmet, his neck still felt stiff and brittle from several hours in the command couch. The battle was beginning to tell in his slowing responses, and he knew it.

But I'll be damned if I don't sell myself as dearly as I can.

Riding out the new damage, Doles torso-twisted his 'Mech to the left in an attempt to return fire. Multiple threats littered his head's up display, but he struggled to float his targeting reticule over the fast-moving House Hiritsu *Wraith* that had just turned another half-ton of his armor into slag. Doles triggered his full complement of energy weapons in a shotgun attempt to score with just one. His large laser burned into the ground near the *Wraith*'s feet, but one of his mediums did manage to tag the enemy machine in the right leg. Though it did little more than cut away at fresh, blued-steel armor, Warner still felt a few seconds' measure of retribution.

Then his heat monitor jumped up further into the red as waves of heat washed through the cockpit, sucking away his breath and hammering at his lungs with fiery blows. A shrill alarm warned of impending reactor shutdown. Gasping for air, his mouth parched and sore from lack of moisture, Doles slapped the shutdown override and quickly studied the HUD for a new target.

Targets there were aplenty. The only good news he read off the tactical display showed the green circles representing the rest of the Blackwind Lancer BattleMechs finally slipping back into the outskirts of Qingliu. The rest, minus MechWarriors Jolles and Birkmeyer. Two more lost on this aborted run to reach the relative safety of the mountains.

An abortion, just what this entire mission had turned out to be. Doles remembered Major Smithson's cold fury when, during interrogation, the captured infantryman proudly confirmed Isis Marik's escape before refusing to cooperate further. The abandonment by their JumpShip had also been a hard blow, but so long as the Lancers thought Sun-Tzu still remained, a hope for victory remained as well. But then came yesterday's public address, which Word of Blake allowed through the blackout—shocking, hard evidence that Sun-Tzu Liao had never been on Hustaing. The whole mission, built on a combination of Smithson's rage and his own misplaced sense of duty, a complete bust. Nothing left but to return to the Compact and accept, at best, quiet retirement.

Only there was no way back to the Compact. A single communication from House Hiritsu had made it clear that the Warrior House would accept nothing less than unconditional surrender. Major Smithson thought to relocate what was left of the Lancers and their mercenary support to the mountains, the better to remain isolated until Duchess Liao negotiated for their return or possibly sent a retrieval force. But after four attempts, Doles doubted they would ever make it out of Qingliu.

A Gauss slug slammed into his right arm at the wrist, crushing the medium laser and ripping the *Grasshopper*'s right hand clean off. Two Hiritsu BattleMechs pressed forward, identified by his computer as a *Yu Huang* assault 'Mech and a medium-weight *Huron Warrior*. His HUD showed that the *Wraith* had joined with two other 'Mechs to now threaten Major Smithson's *Victor*.

That Yu Huang *will eat me alive,* he thought. With a damaged actuator and heat levels still too high, Doles knew that jumping was his only real option. He fired his jump jets, arcing the *Grasshopper* skyward in a low-trajectory bounce back toward the city limits. Laser fire from the *Yu Huang* punched into his armor, carving away large chunks and piercing into the exposed internal structure of his right torso. The large 'Mech shook under the damage, and a grayish-green mist erupted from his right side as another heat sink ruptured.

Doles slammed a fist against his auxiliary console, pain lancing up his right arm as he vented frustration in the only way he could. He *had* to wait until his heat levels dropped before he fired any weapons. Lighting off his jump jets again in an attempt to close on the city, he checked his damage schematic. Another internal hit in the right side had too good a chance of rupturing his missile ammunition storage. *And without cellular ammo storage equipment that would rip me apart.* Cursing the designers who hadn't thought CASE a worthwhile modification, Doles punched the ammunition ejection button for his short-ranged missile system. Specially designed panels fell away at the back of the 'Mech and more than a ton of Streak ammunition rained out to litter the ground.

Whether the loss of the ammunition pushed him too far off balance or the dead leg actuator finally betrayed him, Doles came down too hard and lost control of the *Grasshopper*. Seventy tons of upright metal toppled over. The BattleMech's left shoulder drove into the ground, the impact tearing away the last of the armor protecting the left arm. Thrown mercilessly against his restraints, Doles' vision swam, but he quickly shook off the effect. *If I pass out, I'm done for.*

I'm done for anyway.

Working the controls to regain his feet, Warner Doles noticed that no less than three enemy 'Mechs were closing on him too quickly, including the *Yu Huang*. He would never make it in time. Or at least he shouldn't have.

From his right, Major Smithson's *Victor* came barreling in at a full run. Her Gauss ammunition spent a week ago, she used the large-bore rifle that was her BattleMech's right arm to smash aside an enemy *Snake*. She then took up a position thirty meters in front of Doles, apparently ready to take on all comers. Her *Victor* weathered an intense barrage of laser and autocannon fire that would have been meant for the *Grasshopper*. It staggered, but did not go down, and returned with its two medium lasers. A paltry response but all Smithson had left.

Doles' comm set crackled to life just as he regained his feet. "Back to the city, Captain. You have command."

He might have argued. If nothing else Doles might have refused the order, and stood alongside the major to meet the enemy. There might have been a chance then that both of them would make it back. But she never gave him the chance. Instead of standing to meet the charge, the *Victor* surged forward, firing its lasers and swinging its spent Gauss rifle as it went on the offensive. In the condition the *Victor* was in, Doles knew that Smithson couldn't survive the beating she was about to take. And neither could he if he stayed. That would only leave the unit bereft of command.

He fired his jump jets again. And again. Each low-trajectory hop took him further from the battle that had converged around the struggling *Victor*. Doles saw the *Snake* go down with a crushed cockpit, and a kick from Smithson's assault machine sent the *Wraith* stumbling back, but there were simply too many of them. They tore at the *Victor* like wolves on a wounded bear, and then the *Yu Huang* closed and it was all over. Caught in a barrage of emerald laser fire from the *Yu Huang,* the *Victor* succumbed, falling to its knees and then sprawling out over the ground.

That's how we will all go eventually. Torn down a piece at a time until the battalion is dead. Doles cut out his jump jets and limped into the city where several Lancer 'Mechs waited to provide screening fire if necessary. It wasn't. House Hiritsu was apparently satisfied with its victory, and wouldn't need to claim a new victim until tomorrow or the next day. *Two weeks, Duchess. If you're going to save us, you've got two weeks at best before we can no longer hold.*

"We'll hold, I tell you. And no I won't sit down!"

Aris Sung stood to one side of Ty Wu Non's desk, Nakjama laser pistol out and ready, as the House Master "interviewed" the Blackwind Lancers' commanding officer. Removed from the field to an administrative building at the spaceport, which currently doubled for House Hiritsu's base of operations, she had been spewing venom at least for as long as Aris had been in the room. She paced the floor like a caged animal, alternating between predictions of a Lancer victory and threats of reprisals from the Compact. At first Aris had tried hating her as a representative of the Compact, but even her anti-Confederation rhetoric hadn't been able to stir his hatred. Looking at her, at the obvious signs of her Capellan heritage, Aris felt pity for her more than anything.

House Master Non, for his part, never became upset or reacted in any way to the major's threats. He simply sat behind his desk, trusting to Aris and Senior Company Leader Jason James to handle the prisoner if she grew violent. "Will you not consider surrender?" Master Non asked with inexhaustible patience.

"Like hell," Smithson spat. "Surrender unconditionally and give Sunny-boy carte blanche to try my people and have them shot? Not likely. We have a good month of supplies left. Plenty of time for the Compact to send in a retrieval force."

Aris studiously blanked his face. *That is good information in itself. If Smithson were to settle down, she would see that her fury is only helping us.*

"There will be no retrieval force," Master Non stated clearly. "If you persist in abandoning your unit, the way the Compact has abandoned you here, then you force my House to destroy your Blackwind Lancers battalion. Is this what you desire?"

Smithson snorted her contempt. "Our 'Mechs might be battered, but they still have fight left in them. I counted three Hiritsu 'Mechs down, one pilot dead, and maybe five Home Guard armored vehicles burned out today. What did you get? My *Victor* and a couple of light 'Mechs." She laughed. "Hardly a fair trade."

A cold, impassive mask settled over House Master Non's face, and Aris knew that Smithson had gone too far. "You're right," he said simply, with not a trace of emotion in his voice. Then he called out, "Infantryman Chess!"

The door to the office opened at once and a member of the House infantry looked into the room. "Yes, House Master?"

"Infantryman, Aris Sung is responsible for my safety. You have a new assignment." He glanced at Smithson then back to the soldier. "Take a vehicle over to the *Dainwu*," he said, naming his command DropShip. "Shoot two prisoners from the Blackwind Lancers' battalion that are being kept there. Make sure you get Lancers, no mercenaries. Return straight here from the *Dainwu*."

Horror replaced the contempt on Major Smithson's face, followed by disbelief. "You cannot do that!"

"You have your orders, Infantryman." House Master Non returned his icy gaze to the major as the door was shut. "Who will stop me, Major? Now, I'd say that evens things up a bit for today."

For a brief second, Aris had also been taken in by the House Master's savage ploy. Until he realized that all prisoners were aboard the House's *Condor* Class DropShip, not the *Dainwu,* and Infantryman Chess had been specifically ordered to the *Dainwu* and straight back. *But Major Smithson can't know that.*

The major stood there a moment in silence, hands clenching in anger and obviously held away from the House Master's throat only by Aris' ready weapon. "I'll see you dead," she promised, voice thick with fury. "I swear I will."

Ty Wu Non shrugged his indifference to her threat. "I doubt you will see much but a prison cell," he said calmly. "With First Lord Liao's address to the Confederation and other Star League member states, we've been informed that your actions are under serious attack. *If* you are ever allowed to return to the Compact, I predict a military court martial in your future."

For the first time since Smithson had been brought in, Aris read some sign of concern on her face. A quick darting of the eyes and fingers rubbing together in nervousness. Master Non apparently did not see it, so Aris took it upon himself to push her a bit further. "You led your people here," he said softly, playing off the concern any officer has for the troops under his or her command. "They trusted you. Are you going to let them be destroyed?"

Smithson's unease grew more readily apparent as she glanced from Ty Wu Non to Aris. Then her anger returned, and she shook her head. "Better destroyed on the field than handed over to Capellan butchers," she said. "There is nothing that would ever convince me to surrender unconditionally except a direct order from Duchess Liao. I am sworn to serve the Compact, and it is not my place to give away the Lancers' rights."

Aris almost sympathized with Smithson. Her devotion, however misplaced when she jumped the border, was commendable. So like the Warrior Houses' defining rule that "the will of the House Master is the will of the House." But to Aris' way of thinking, it was still a mistake. The Lancers' days were numbered, and so were the Compact's.

Whatever House Master Non felt, he kept it hidden. "Major, I asked you to help spare the lives of your warriors and of civilians who will be caught by the fighting around Qingliu. But if you are adamant, then I will try no further. We will continue to break down the Lancers, and without your fire to lead them I doubt it will take long. Your fate, however, is sealed in the orders I received last week. You will be placed in solitary confinement until such time as the *Pearl of True Wisdom* can safely travel back to Sian.

"And I very much doubt you will ever leave."

13

Home Guard Staging Grounds
Hazlet, Nashuar
St. Ives Compact
3 November 3060

Maurice Fitzgerald's fifth session in a real BattleMech, and the novelty had yet to wear off. He stepped from the gantry to the small recessed platform at the back of the *Blackjack*'s head, enjoying the grease and hot metalwork scents that mixed in Hazlet's small Home Guard 'Mech bay and the cool touch of armor against his outstretched hand. The small wheeled hatch leading into the cockpit already stood open. He grabbed the handholds, leveraged his feet up and through the opening, and then wormed into the cramped space, pulling the airtight hatch shut behind him and dogging it down with a spin of the wheel.

From the storage compartment beneath the command couch he withdrew a cooling vest and quickly slipped it on, cinching it down over his lean frame by the straps under his right arm. He then crawled around into the couch, pulling the harness straps forward to fasten into a quick-release four-point buckle. He pulled the coolant line for his vest out of a nearby receptacle and snapped it into a twist-lock socket at his left side. A powerful rumble built within the *Blackjack*'s chest as he threw a series of toggles, bringing the fusion plant to life.

You can't wait either, can you? Fitz smiled. *Well, today is a special day. I feel it.* A feeling that had grown in this last week as training was stepped up to a faster pace. No one in authority admitted that the situation on Hustaing was responsible for the increased schedule, but then neither did they deny it. And then there was Commander Nevarr's pre-mission briefing, promising the training lance more challenges today since the race for the second and third slots—now that Danielle was confirmed for the first one—was tight. *One will be mine,* Fitzgerald promised himself. No matter that Nevarr had assigned him a supporting role again. He would find a way to make himself stand out.

Removing the heavy neurohelmet from the shelf above the ferroglass viewscreen, he slipped it over his head and buckled it down. The edges of the helmet rested down on his coolant vest's padded shoulders, helping to support the weight. Five electrical leads dangled from the chin, and he plugged four of them into different biomed sensors pads, which he attached to his inner thighs and upper forearms. The fifth lead, thicker and with a multi-prong plug, he plugged into the main console.

"Computer, initiate voice-recognition check."

"Check completed," the voice of the computer confirmed, its voice lacking any emotion but somehow given a slightly feminine edge. "Operator Maurice Fitzgerald, cross-check with vocal key."

Because voiceprints could be faked, every BattleMech also required a verbal code that only the operator would know. The simulators had duplicated even this feature, and Fitz' security code had been uploaded to the *Blackjack*.

"Wo hen hao," Fitz said proudly. *I will prevail.*

What better way to begin a battle?

"Two. Repeat, still only two enemy 'Mechs." Danielle's voice was excited but in control. *"War Dog* and a *Striker.* Stay sharp, Guard Three. They're fielding newer designs and there's a couple of wild cards out there somewhere."

If there are only two, release me to engage and we'll destroy them. Fitzgerald dropped his jaw down to open a channel, intent on passing along his advice, then gritted his teeth and merely replied, "Copy, Guard One." *Easy for her to make the call. She's been guaranteed an appointment to the Home Guard 'Mech company.*

Fitz' thought was unfair and he knew it. Danielle, with them this one last time as their acting lance commander, had to keep at least one back-up 'Mech ready in the event of a flanking maneuver. And newer designs meant new capabilities to worry about. But it burned that she had called Freya Restecht forward first and not him, no matter that Freya's *Jenner* could circle behind faster to threaten the enemy rear.

A warning flashed on his HUD just before the *Blackjack* rocked from a long-range laser hit to the right side. Of course, it didn't take real damage. Fitzgerald knew that it was all simulated through scanners and special programs loaded into their tactical computers. The weapons were powered down to nonlethal levels or loaded with blanks, and the shudder he had felt merely came from a hitch thrown into the *Blackjack*'s gyro by the program. But the classroom analysis of live-'Mech simulated-fire scenarios meant little when you were fighting for balance and trying to track an enemy at the same time.

Fitz' heart raced and his voice trembled with excitement as he opened communications. "Contact," he reported, swinging his *Blackjack* around but taking initial readings off the tactical display. "*Phoenix Hawk,* bearing one-eight-five relative and closing at five hundred meters." *And you're mine!* An older design, like most Home Guard 'Mechs, but with enough advanced equipment on it to give the *Blackjack* a fight. Then he acquired visual, and a chill washed through him. The *Phoenix Hawk* was painted a brown and gray camouflage pattern, but instead of the usual stripe or patchwork design a lighter touch had been used to suggest feathers.

"Nevarr!" Fitz yelled, then calmed down. "Repeat, Commander Nevarr is fielding his 'Hawk against us." He triggered a hasty pair of large lasers, both of them missing as Nevarr ran into a stand of alder and pine. The *Blackjack*'s heat spiked, driving the cockpit temperature up several degrees. You know better than that, he berated himself. *Save the double-shots for close range.* "Guard Three moving to intercept." Throttling up into a run, he angled the *Blackjack*'s path to keep Nevarr from getting behind the unit.

"Copy." Danielle's voice came back. "Guard Three released

to three hundred meters only. There is still an unknown out there, Three. Don't break away."

As if the Hawk *doesn't have enough of a mobility advantage.* Fitz cut his speed back, leaving himself room to maneuver. *Come on, Nevarr. Taking you down will cinch my spot in the BattleMech corps.*

Nevarr burst from his cover, pushing his *Hawk* toward its maximum speed of over ninety kilometers per hour. Fitzgerald turned for a stand of trees, seeking tactical placement, but didn't make it before the *Hawk* fired. In response, he triggered his own pair of large lasers in a trade of emerald and ruby energy. The *Blackjack* rocked violently as it lost a ton of armor to Nevarr's fire, but not so much as to threaten its stability. Fitz only hit with one of his lasers, peeling away armor over the other BattleMech's heart. *An uneven trade, but then he has an extralight engine to protect, which makes him vulnerable.*

As if concerned about that very same thing, the *Phoenix Hawk* took to the sky and jetted back away. *No way it can afford to fire both lasers after a jump like that!* Fitz raced his *Blackjack* forward, eating up his reserve but eager to seize the advantage when presented. *If I can close to three hundred meters, I can put my short range missiles against his medium pulse lasers. That will give me the edge.*

He couldn't quite make three hundred, though, and so triggered off another pair of shots from his extended-range lasers. Cockpit temperatures soared as the fusion reactor spiked again in an attempt to keep up with the constant power demand. One laser hit, but so did Nevarr. Fitz' damage schematic now showed the cumulative loss of nearly all armor over his center torso and left arm. But likewise, his grouped shots had almost penetrated the *Hawk*'s right torso, leaving Nevarr open to hits against the bulky shielding of an extralight engine.

I need another fifty meters. Fitzgerald knew he could push his envelope to four hundred before Danielle reined him in, and taking Nevarr down would be worth it. The lance would have one less enemy to worry about, and Fitz would have an important kill. He scanned his HUD for any hidden threats, then again pushed forward.

With the slight heat build-up, however, the *Blackjack* was already responding sluggishly and so failed to close quite as fast as he would have liked. Nevarr relied on jump jets again, keeping range against Fitz and burning off another half-ton of armor, this time from the *Blackjack*'s legs.

Danielle's voice bled across the air waves, robbed of emotion but not strength, just as Fitz fired a single laser. "Guard Three, you are ranging out too far. Fitz!"

The ruby lance pinned the *Phoenix Hawk* square in the center torso just as it took to the air again. His flight erratic, Nevarr came down just the other side of a stand of heavy oak and stumbled to a prone position. "Nevarr is down. Finishing off and then regrouping."

"Fitz, pull back now. You are too far out and we can't cover you back there."

Thirty seconds. I only need thirty seconds. He pushed the *Blackjack* forward at nearly sixty kph, free of the heat encumbrance of a moment before and determined to put an end to Nevarr. But just before he moved within range of his Streak missile systems, the *Hawk* swiveled around while remaining prone and a new threat popped on the HUD, less than three hundred meters and at ninety degrees to his path toward Nevarr. A trap!

The *Night Hawk,* a light 'Mech at thirty-five tons but still able to train two more large lasers against the *Blackjack,* fired at almost the same instant as Nevarr. Four shimmering beams of emerald and sapphire energy converged in a savage crossfire, ripping into the *Blackjack* and, according to the computer analysis, shredding armor across its torso and left arm. One of Nevarr's lasers penetrated, and was judged to have struck Fitzgerald's gyro housing. Fitz wrestled with his controls, but in the end lost the fight and abandoned himself to gravity. There was no simulating the effect of forty-five tons meeting earth. Armor plating crunched under the impact, and bouncing hard against the restraining harness and the back of his command couch left Fitz dazed for a moment.

By the time he regained his senses and took stock of his situation, it was all over.

Nevarr and the *Night Hawk* pilot had poured simulated but intense fire into his downed machine. Though he still had power, his damage schematic showed a simulated fusion reactor-meltdown from complete loss of engine shielding. His *Blackjack* was frozen in place, robbed of all ability to move or even warn his lancemates, who were calling for him over the communication channels. His HUD showed the *Night Hawk* moving off to threaten the rear of his former lance, but the *Phoenix Hawk* stood just thirty meters outside the ferroglass viewscreen of his cockpit.

Fitzgerald could not see Nevarr, sitting up in the *'Hawk*'s cockpit, but he could sense the almost sad regret that his instructor must certainly be feeling. Nevarr had made it clear before: Fitz was his own worst enemy. Today, he had baited the young trainee and allowed him to defeat himself. *Make no mistake,* he had said, *you'll learn it my way first or you won't learn your way at all.* The *Phoenix Hawk* turned and walked slowly away, disappearing out of the *Blackjack*'s viewscreen.

Fitzgerald didn't bother following the progress on his HUD. He dampened down his reactor, and slowly shut down everything except the communication channels. Then he sat there, in the dark, and listened to his lancemates die their own simulated deaths.

14

Celestial Palace
Zi-jin Cheng (Forbidden City), Sian
Sian Commonality, Capellan Confederation
9 November 3060

Sasha Wanli had been called on the carpet, again.

The Celestial Palace throne room felt intensely cold, and Sasha wasn't sure if it were due to her nerves or the room's actual temperature. Certainly she did not put it past Sun-Tzu Liao to lower the room's temperature just to increase her discomfort. Goose flesh raised on her arms was fortunately hidden under the sleeves of her tailored black silk suit. Standing a respectful distance away from the dais, waiting to be recognized, she stared at the narrow band of blood-red carpeting that trailed from the foot of the throne back to the bronze-faced doors.

If Sasha had possessed any doubts about Sun-Tzu's dark mood, they were cast aside once she had entered the throne room to see her reception. Noticeably absent were Colonel Zahn and House Master Rush, though of course the latter could hardly expect release from the hospital for at least another week. Two Death Commandos, their musculature enhancements showing beneath their black uniforms like knotted ropes, fronted the dais to the left and right, facing inward so as to watch both her and the Chancellor. A testament to Sun-Tzu's mood, she had no doubt. He was ready to dismiss her as head of the Maskirovka, and the Death Commandos were a not-so-subtle reminder that not one of the last five directors had died of natural causes. Two, in fact, had been put to death specifically at a Chancellor's command.

Maskirovka directors do not long outlive their mistakes, and here I have known two in the same year.

A chill washed through Sasha, though her inner strength kept the tremble from showing. *Tread lightly, Sasha. So long as life breathes, there is still hope. If he had made up his mind to remove you, someone would already be hauling your body away.* Sixty-three years old, over thirty of those in the Maskirovka and seven as its director, she was not quite ready to give up this life yet. It actually surprised her, how strong was her desire to avoid death. She thought she had come to terms with all that years ago.

"Ion Rush was not appointed Grand Master of the Warrior Houses for no reason," Sun Tzu said in opening, his voice only one notch above a cold whisper. "He is an elite warrior, a veteran commander, and a valuable asset to the Confederation." A lengthy pause. "That explosion almost killed him."

Sasha raised her eyes slowly, walking her gaze from the carpet to the hem of Sun-Tzu's dark green silk robe and then only gradually moving up to the hard mask the Chancellor wore. On each breast of the robe was stitched the Capellan gauntlet-and-sword insignia in gold thread. The Chancellor's eyes were jade slits, like those of a hunting tiger.

"Yes, Celestial Wisdom," she said quietly. "Fortunately, all reports indicate recovery." *Though with major loss of physical ability, the damage was too extensive.* But Sasha did not want to dwell on that. "I assure you he will be back at your side quickly."

With a casual wave of the hand, Sun-Tzu dismissed the two guards and then waited for them to leave the room before continuing. "You also assured me, Sasha Wanli, that my sister Kali posed no threat to my rule. Yet according to your own report she somehow managed to smuggle a bomb through House Imarra security and nearly deprived me of a valuable aide." He spitted her with a savage glare. "And if she can do that, she could also do so *within* the palace."

Sasha breathed easier with the dismissal of the Death Commandos, thanking whichever deity had smiled favorably on her karma today. She knew, though, that she had only won a round, not the battle. "An oversight, Chancellor Liao, and one for which I have no excuse. It just was not a contingency we planned for, since there was never any evidence of hostility between Kali and Ion Rush."

"And so what changed?" Sun-Tzu asked, almost casually, as if preparing a trap.

Sasha was ready for that question. She had hoped to turn the conversation in this direction. "Your sister apparently mistook your comment to House Master Rush concerning his leaking information to Candace Liao as an accusation." She paused a moment, to allow her Chancellor to consider this. Carefully, she had to try and shift some responsibility from herself without making it sound as if she were in fact blaming Sun-Tzu. "For Kali," she continued, "that was apparently close enough to a direct charge of treason. She believes her actions to be on behalf of you and the Confederation."

Sun-Tzu's pause gave Sasha some hope, though his voice remained cold and unreadable. "It is easy for Kali to be *apparently mistaken* on any number of things, Sasha." Even in private audience, Sasha noted, the Chancellor refused to name her insanity for what it was. "Why should I feel favored in her eyes?"

"Because of the utter devotion she showed your mother," Sasha said at once, then softened her approach. She clasped her hands in front of her, choosing with care words that would not automatically upset Sun-Tzu. "It's true that Kali feels as if the throne were denied her by your earlier birth, but Romano also instilled in your sister a sense of complete and overriding belief in the sanctity of the Chancellorship. What the Maskirovka uncovered of her meddling in the Kaifeng affair in 3058 proves it. Yes, she works to increase her power base, but only to then do what *she* may to strengthen the Confederation."

Sun-Tzu considered her words for several minutes, his countenance impassive as he stared up toward the ceiling. Finally he exhaled sharply. "Very well," he said casually, as if the conversation were on any normal subject. And then, in a rapid shift of topic. "The Maskirovka has been largely unaffected by the renewed Capellan effort—I expect you to now fully embrace the Xin Sheng movement. There are several directives that I shall have delivered to you, concerning my thoughts on the matter. You will apply them, along with any improvements of your own that you think to make."

His head still facing the ceiling, Sun-Tzu lowered his jade gaze enough to catch Sasha's attention and observe her. "I will not tolerate another mistake from the Maskirovka. The damage can be too far-reaching." He waited for her simple nod of acknowledgment and then continued. "Ion Rush is not to know of the attempt; the Maskirovka cover story of a ruptured gas line should hold. I will speak to Kali myself, but I expect her to be better watched from now on." He now shifted his head to stare evenly at Sasha. "Are we clear on these points?"

One last chance, in other words. And more forgiving than I have any right to expect. But the Chancellor was right. He should not have to tolerate such mistakes from his intelligence service. Sasha would see immediately to an internal overhaul, and possibly to some insurance in case she should be burdened with any more mistakes. "Yes, my lord," she said firmly. "Perfectly understood."

Levering himself from the throne, Sun-Tzu strode forward and off the dais. The gold-threaded insignias glittered in the light. "Find Talon Zahn," he ordered as he drew abreast and passed her. "Have him report to my private office.

"Then go put your house in order."

Thirty years before, Sun-Tzu's private office had once been the seat of the Capellan Confederation's ruin. It was from here that Justin Allard, a double-agent for House Davion, undermined Maximilian Liao's reign and engineered several of the greatest betrayals ever known to the Confederation. Not the least of which was his stealing away Candace Liao, convincing her to betray the realm of her birth for the damnable Federated Commonwealth. Risen to Chancellor, Sun-Tzu had almost ordered the room destroyed, ripped from the very walls of the

Celestial Palace. But instead, he had claimed it as his own and worked to redeem it.

Now it reflected none of its treasonous beginnings, and belonged once again to the Capellan state. Rosewood gleamed darkly throughout the room, the polish used to keep it alive mixing pleasantly with the sandalwood incense Sun-Tzu favored. Charcoal sketches decorated the walls, one of them capturing in a few simple strokes the visage of Elias Jung Liao, founder of the dynasty. The Chancellor's desk was set against the back wall, not far from a set of french doors that opened onto a small balcony.

Sun-Tzu lit a stick of sandalwood incense and left it burning in its holder. The light perfume rose up on a wisp of smoke, drifting into and around the office as he then moved to add several pinches of food to the aquarium that bubbled away in the office corner. *Too fast,* he thought, watching the food spread across the water but thinking of Sasha's interview. *Possibly too fast.*

He had not planned for the Maskirovka review and reorganization until much later, and certainly not during such a critical time as this, but Sasha's lapses in competence allowed no other choice in this matter. The overhaul of the Maskirovka required someone with her field experience and knowledge of the organization to implement any necessary changes, and with her uncertain karma Sun-Tzu could not be sure how much longer she could be retained. But he still could not help wishing for a few more weeks, even a month, before having to implement this stage of the program.

Enough. Once a decision is made, it is unwise to reverse it and even less wise to debate it.

Sun-Tzu moved to his desk, relaxing into the overstuffed leather chair. From his pocket he brought out the data cube of his aunt's latest message, then dropped it into the reader at the desk's corner. The touch-sensitive screen mounted flush in the desktop changed from a display of the Confederation's expanding borders to the visage of his aunt, Candace Liao. The flat, two-dimensional format appeared forced—she had obviously used a holorecorder—but served well enough.

Candace Liao, back straight and features stern, bowed from the screen. "*Wèn-hòu,* First Lord Liao." Sun-Tzu smiled at the formal Chinese greeting, and at how much it must have pained her to defer to him as Lord of the resurrected Star League. "By now I am certain you have seen the many broadcasts from St. Ives. You know, then, that the Blackwind Lancers have not been acting under my authority. That they chose to attack you was a grave error on the part of the battalion commanding officer, and that it happened on your Xin Sheng tour a gross injustice against your efforts for a stronger national pride."

I'm not so sure about that, Sun-Tzu thought in the brief pause that followed. *They have proven my point rather admirably. The Compact, in its de facto state of rebellion, cannot hope to match Confederation honor and dignity, nor can you match us on the field.* Then again, having his own citizens yelling for Capellan blood, even if it would spill from the Compact, was not something that set well with him either. But given the choice, Sun-Tzu believed that any true Capellan citizens would gladly sacrifice their lives for the glory of rebirth for their nation.

"And so," Candace continued, only a slight narrowing of her eyes betraying her anger, "with Word of Blake refusing to pass through any order of mine to Hustaing but an unconditional surrender, and not even that without your express permission, I am hereby requesting such authority. I have already made such announcements to my own realm, condemning the Lancers, in general, and Major Smithson's actions, in specific. I understand you have claimed the right to hold her, and I assume she will spend the rest of her life in the servitor caste, making up in some small way for her actions. I would not presume to challenge you on this."

Because you know you would lose. Sun-Tzu did not buy into Candace's apologetic act, and he doubted that she expected him to. *But form will be served, will it not?*

"The rest of the Lancers, however, I *am* responsible to," Candace said, steel creeping into her voice. "After their surrender, unconditional or not, I will fight for their repatriation in the Star League council as soon as your term as First Lord has expired." That was no less than Sun-Tzu expected. "I am asking you, instead, to demonstrate your goodwill by escorting the Lancers back to the Compact. I will guarantee concessions, not the least of which that the battalion will be disbanded and its personal colors struck."

As Candace's message faded to black, the sharp clicks of Talon Zahn's boots against the tiled hallway outside warned Sun-Tzu of the military coordinator's approach. *So the Lancers are disgraced and Major Smithson offered up as a sacrifice. Cold, dear aunt, but efficient. Your Federated Commonwealth ties have not completely shackled your Liao resolve. Yes, Candace, I will escort your wayward warriors home. But not in the manner you suggest or expect.* Sun-Tzu smiled as he thought of how to use his aunt's exact words against her.

"You sent for me, Chancellor?" Zahn, back in his utility uniform now that the charade of Sun-Tzu's absence from Sian had been dropped, stood respectfully in the doorway.

Sun-Tzu nodded, trailing the flat of one long fingernail carefully along his jaw line. "Order the communications blackout lifted. Allow all St. Ives reports to flood Hustaing, and vice versa." Zahn stood silent, obviously expecting more from the summons, but Sun-Tzu merely stared back. "That is all, Colonel."

Zahn frowned, a very unusual show of emotion for him, but then nodded his acceptance of the order. "At once, Celestial Wisdom."

As the senior colonel departed, Sun-Tzu credited him for being able to keep the doubt from his voice. *Every time you believe you know what I am about, I change the rules. But that is not your concern. It is the ruler's place to handle politics. Your job is to win battles, where and when I tell you but the how left to your own design.*

Sun-Tzu listened as Zahn's steps faded back down the hallway, then sent a silent message after his military commander.

The where and when are coming.

15

Leading Isis Marik's honor squad onto the *Peal of True Wisdom*'s ramp, then escorting her down to the ferrocrete landing pad on which the DropShip sat, Aris raised his left hand up to the corner of his mouth and pressed down on the microphone's thumb-activated operations tab.

"Capella One is moving," he stated in a quick, crisp report. A chill breeze pushed gray clouds across the sky and tugged at the cloak of Aris' dress uniform while he mentally checked off each security post as all came in with messages of clear and secure. It still tugged at his sense of order, using the same codes and procedures now that it was known that Sun-Tzu was safely back on Sian, but the House Master had yet to alter his standing order and so Aris persevered.

Not that Hustaing was any longer considered a hostile zone.

House Master Ty Wu Non awaited them at the foot of the ramp, also dressed in House Hirtisu's formal green and black. With him stood Captain Warner Doles, executive officer of the Blackwind Lancers' second battalion. Unshaven and unkempt, Doles looked a poor contrast to House Master Non's precision appearance, though he dwarfed the House Master in size and bulk.

But after six weeks of combat and repeated failures to achieve anything but disgrace and his own nation's antipathy, how should I expect him to look?

The honor squad split ranks, enveloping House Master Non and his charge and then forming a perimeter around the small confrontation. Only Aris broke off, taking up station within the perimeter to Isis Marik's left. His right hand never strayed far from the butt of his Nakjama. Captain Doles was not manacled, and looked strong enough to cause trouble if he decided to take some kind of vengeance on the Chancellor's fiancée.

Isis did not flinch, staring up at the large man and regarding him with cool neutrality. "As senior prisoner of war, you have been asked to look after your people. You can confirm that they have been treated well?" Having come so close to death or capture at the hands of the Blackwind Lancers, Aris felt that she maintained incredible composure.

"Well enough," Doles admitted. "I have five warriors currently under treatment in the *Condor*'s medical bay, but they should recover. I suppose I should thank you for the excellent care they are receiving."

Five people heavily injured, nine walking wounded, and six dead. Aris had read the final reports. Add in one dead House Hiritsu warrior and another who would never again pilot a BattleMech, no matter how good prosthetics were these days. He still believed the St. Ives Compact to be an unlawful state, yes. But it was a high price in Capellan blood for an engagement that effectively accomplished nothing. At least nothing Aris could see.

Aris had also been on hand to witness the prisoners being loaded and confined on the infantry's *Condor* Class DropShip. They were a beaten unit, even the uninjured having little to look forward to but the formal dissolution of their once-proud command. By Candace's own public order, the Blackwind Lancers would be forevermore limited to their remaining two battalions. And so far as he could tell, only the people of Denbar were raising any amount of objection. *No doubt Candace Liao plans public admissions of responsibility from the Lancers, which should quell any final complaints.*

Isis nodded her acceptance of Captain Doles' less than gracious word of thanks. "Then if you have no pressing concern," she said with formal grace but a coldness that suggested the only answer should be no, "our business is concluded."

Warner Doles stepped forward, and Aris immediately caught him by the shoulder to hold him at a respectable distance as his right hand half-pulled his Nakjama. The captain eased off but said, "I do have two concerns, Duchess Marik, if you will forgive the presumption."

Aris kept one hand on Doles' arm, ready to lead him away. Unfortunately, Isis had left herself open to such a request and so nodded curtly. The Lancers captain cleared his throat. "I did not see our commanding officer, Major Smithson, among the prisoners or wounded, or on the death reports. Nor have I seen any indication that our BattleMechs have been loaded. Will they be traveling back to Denbar on a separate DropShip?" He nodded to the *Dainwu,* its egg-shaped outline easily visible, though at the opposite side of the field. "On the *Overlord* perhaps?"

Isis considered for a moment, a small crease between her eyes the only sign of her internal debate, then she relented. "Major Smithson is aboard the *Pearl of True Wisdom,*" she informed the captain. "She is to be taken back to Sian, where First Lord Liao will stand in judgment of her." She paused to allow this news to settle in.

Warner Doles took it calmly enough, though Aris sensed from his grip on the other man the immediate tension that Isis' announcement had caused. The man still felt some vestige of loyalty to his commanding officer, even though she was in the wrong. Commendable, if misplaced.

"As to the Blackwind Lancers' BattleMechs and other equipment," Isis continued, "they have been seized as spoils of warfare. Including DropShips. Only the mercenary forces whom you persuaded to follow you here will be allowed to retain their equipment as they were technically following a legitimate representative of the Compact; namely, the Lancers and Major Smithson."

Disgraced *and* dispossessed! Aris almost lost his hold on the other man as the very idea shook him. No MechWarrior could bear the thought of losing his 'Mech. It was Chancellor Liao's way of salvaging something from the situation, and an effective method at that, confiscating equipment worth millions of C-bills. No doubt with further reparations to come from the Compact.

Doles did not quite see it that way. "Several of those 'Mechs are personal property," he said, anger and disbelief mixing into a look of shock. "Most of them have never known service outside the Blackwind Lancers." His incredulity quickly wore off. "You can't do that."

Tu Wu Non stepped between Warner Doles and Isis. "Mind your manner when addressing the Duchess," he ordered, not bothering to hide his sneer of contempt, though he kept his voice fairly civil for Isis' sake. "Your unconditional surrender certainly does give Chancellor Liao the right. Feel fortunate that he has offered you the chance to return with your lives to the Compact. What you have left of them, anyway."

"The Lancer BattleMechs will be used to form a new Confederation unit," Isis said, a slight curl playing at the edge of her lips. "In the same tradition with which the Harloc Raiders were raised from a Home Guard militia force, Chancellor Liao will use this incident to create the Hustang Warriors."

Aris read Isis' approval of her fiancée's actions in her tone and delivery. *And it is a brilliant move. A Compact defeat leading to the strengthening of the Confederation military.* Aris felt a small swell of pride for his Chancellor at the idea. If anything glorious was to come of the suffering on Hustaing, then this would have to suffice.

Li Wynn walked proudly as a member of the honor squad.

His captivity under the Blackwind Lancers had not been easy, placed in a cell with no windows, twenty-four hour lights, and the same meal served every eight hours. Nothing incredibly inhumane, but with no concept of night or day and no news of the battle, Li constantly wondered after his adopted House. He bore his fate with the knowledge that he had excelled in his duty, and for one moment had actually served Isis Marik, the Chancellor's betrothed, directly.

And now I serve her again, in the most honor-filled assignment of House Hiritsu infantry.

House Master Ty Wu Non had stopped by medical while Li was being checked over, following his release with the Blackwind Lancers' unconditional surrender. He talked only to the doctor, of course, but his visit still officially recognized Li as a member of the House for the first time since his adoption. Infantry Commander Jessup never said one word either, but quietly changed the duty schedule to put Li on the honor squad.

In fact, only two people directly commented on his actions at all. Aris Sung, in his capacity as Li's *Sifu*, had criticized him. "The bread truck was a wrong move," he'd said. "You should have stayed on foot. Easier to move from building to building and minimizing your time on the street." But however harsh Aris' tone, Li caught the hint of a smile in Aris' eyes—a sign Aris surely could have hidden—and knew that his Mentor was secretly pleased.

The other person had been Isis Marik herself. On his first assignment to the honor guard, she had turned to face him directly. There could have been no conversation—no Hiritsu infantry would dare let down his guard to hold a discussion—but she had quietly and simply said, "Thank you."

Both her thanks and Aris' silent approval more than made up for any discomfort he had borne. Then there was also the newfound respect of his brothers in arms, other infantrymen who now behaved toward Li as if he'd been among their number for years instead of months. Li *belonged*.

Now Li watched as House Master Non and Isis Marik faced off against the *sick* officer. His own private joke, that, referring to the St. Ives Compact by the pronunciation of its initials "SIC." He thought it fitting for the mongrel state; a sick dog that needed putting down. Then, the final words exchanged, Aris led the honor guard protecting Isis Marik back up into the *Pearl of True Wisdom* while House Master Non remained with the Lancers captain to turn him over to guards who would escort the prisoner back to the *Condor*.

That such enemies of the Capellan nation, and of the very philosophy of Xin Sheng, were allowed to exist angered Infantryman Li Wynn. *The forms must be followed, but such people couldn't hide forever. Some day, the Chancellor's justice will come to them.*

Li only hoped that he would be alive to see it, and to be a part of it.

16

Xin Singapore District, Indicass
St. Ives Compact
1 December 3060

Strapped into the command couch of her General Motors *Cestus,* the BattleMech hidden within a heavy stand of cedar and pine several klicks out from Xin Singapore, Cassandra Allard-Liao ran her weapons status for the fifth time. The torso-mounted Gauss rifle checked out fine, as did the paired large and medium lasers in each of the BattleMech's arms. Her skin prickled with the flush of coolant through her vest, though she did not expect that to last much longer once the fireworks started. *A bit early for the Chinese new year, but I'll oblige.*

Her comm unit crackled to life. "There they go!"

Cassandra stared out through the *Cestus'* front viewport and into the predawn sky, watching as the three bright stars that had been falling in perfect formation broke apart. One continued its hard drop onto her position, where her battalion of the Second St. Ives Lancers waited with Tamas' Company of Rubinsky's Light Horse. The other two suddenly split off to the south and north, the bright stars of the drive flares turning to flaming streamers as the angle changed.

A toggle on her comm panel opened a channel through the secure land-line that ran to each company commander and Tamas. "Looks like your father called it right, Captain Rubinsky. The flanking DropShips are fading north and south."

Over the air waves came the Slavic inflection of Tamas' voice. "Of course, Major Liao. Two years we've had to figure out how an assault force would take Indicass' capital. You drop one third of a force near Xin Singapore itself, one third near Ceres Metals, and the rest here, halfway between the two and able to support either one or move against the spaceport."

"Well, the Cheveux Legers battalion can hold Ceres Metals." Cassandra flexed her fingers, then eased them around the *Cestus*' control sticks. "Looks like we'll get first blood here." Which was fine by her. Those were *Overlord*s, which meant a battalion at best. With Tamas' supporting company and the element of surprise, she expected her St. Ives Lancers to easily dominate the field.

"Major Liao, Colonel Rubinsky, this is Light Horse central," an unfamiliar voice whispered heavily in her right ear. "We have received first transmissions from dropping force. They order Light Horse to stand down."

Cassandra switched over to regular transmission, but the colonel beat her to it. "By whose orders?" he asked. Sitting with the bulk of his Light Horse just east of Xin Singapore, Colonel Rubinsky was in prime location to decimate the landing deployment of the northern DropShip.

"First Lord Sun-Tzu Liao." A pause. "They say they are the occupation force for Indicass. Peaceful."

"A *peaceful* occupation force," Cassandra asked no one in particular, "dropping under cover of emissions blackout and with no notification from my mother? I don't think so." The drive flare above Cassandra's position brightened as the *Overlord* engaged its final braking. *Nice try, cousin, but you've played your last trick.*

"We hold to our plan, Colonel Rubinsky, striking at them as they move out from the cover of the *Overlord*s. Have your Pegasii fighter squadrons ready to tie up those DropShips."

"No word yet from St. Ives?" This question from Tamas, referring to the message Cassandra had sent to her mother regarding the approaching force. He was apparently somewhat ignorant of the limitations on HPG communication. Though assigned as her adjutant with Rubinsky's command, Cassandra felt disinclined to correct him in front of his father and the rest of the Light Horse.

Colonel Rubinsky, however, felt no such compunction. "Even at their best, ComStar would require eight hours more before getting a message to St. Ives and back." The colonel growled, deep and guttural, either forgetting to close the channel or not caring who heard his frustration. "Central, get me name of that command. And tell them that without orders from Duchess Liao herself I must oppose their landing."

Cassandra almost jumped in to override that order. Why place the assaulting force on their guard? But the Light Horse were too efficient, and by the time she tried to countermand Rubinsky the request would have been passed along. You want an identification? she thought, watching as the *Overlord* grounded in the bowl of a very shallow valley. She increased magnification on an auxiliary screen, the starlight video filter cutting through the predawn dimness. *I'll get you an I.D.*

The large, egg-shaped DropShip had barely settled when its 'Mech bay door opened and ramps extended to the ground. The first 'Mechs down the ramp were, predictably, lighter scout machines. Even before Cassandra could focus in on the Drop-Ship's registration markings, she knew that the disembarking 'Mechs were wrong. An *Ostscout,* never a Capellan design, and a *Mercury,* rare outside of ComStar or Word of Blake. Then two new *Hammers* for recon support. The lance formed up and headed for the low hills, angling in toward Cassandra just as she saw the eagle stenciled on the *Overlord*'s side.

Thomas Marik's Free Worlds League! And the dark shadows that her passive sensors could barely pick up, leaping around the legs of the second lance to debark, those would have to be the League's new Achileus light battle armor. Shades of the Marik-Liao offensive of 3057 leapt to Cassandra's mind, when Sun-Tzu and Thomas had collaborated to shatter the Sarna March and retake worlds both had lost to the Davions three decades before. She swallowed hard, anger choking her. *Well not here, Thomas. I don't care if Sun-Tzu is calling the tune. My job is to make you pay for it.*

"Command Lance," she said, voice low and quiet, as if the Leaguers might hear, "we have the first recon patrol. Two-three

Lance, the second. Tamas, jump in where you like. Concentrate on the probe-carriers first." She floated a dark reticule over the *Mercury* closing in on her position, one finger poised over the button that would power up her active scanners. "If we can keep their scouts from learning how many we have out here, they just might throw good 'Mechs after bad. Now!"

Her finger stabbed down, and all auxiliary screens lit up with scanner information. Her HUD showed three enemy lances debarked, two within firing range of St. Ives units. As her targeting reticule burned a solid gold, she glanced to one auxiliary screen just long enough to see the Star League crest riding the *Mercury*'s shoulder.

You can't hide behind your office, cousin. She pulled back on both main triggers, lighting off all four of her lasers and also the Gauss rifle. All but one medium laser hit, the lasers slicing through armor to penetrate the internal skeleton beneath. Then the nickel-ferrous Gauss slug slammed into the *Mercury*'s right leg, snapping off the limb just above the knee joint.

One of Cassandra's lancemates added to the misery of the *Mercury,* his autocannon piercing the final shreds of armor and chewing apart the light BattleMech's gyro. Her other two warriors downed the *Ostscout* under intense PPC and missile fire. The *Hammer*s struck back, but pitifully weak against the heavy command lance. Cassandra's *Cestus* took two glancing hits from medium lasers, the large 'Mech shrugging off the damage.

Then Tamas' Company opened up, the scintillating gem-like colors of lasers and the man-made lightning of PPCs all converging in a savage crossfire as missiles arced in to help shred armor and tear apart myomer musculature. Both *Hammer*s dropped. *Yes!* Cassandra thought. *Scratch one recon lance with not one friendly casualty. Kai himself could hardly have done better.* Cassandra checked her HUD and auxiliary screens, evaluating the battle on the far side of the DropShip.

The second Marik recon company had fared slightly better, losing only a second *Mercury* and a *Wraith*. But then they also had the battle armor support that tied up good weapons fire. Cassandra sympathized. No MechWarriors liked armored infantry climbing over their 'Mechs, ripping armor off with mechanized claws. Better to put down the recon unit hard than risk lives. "Two-two Lance, pick up those toads," she ordered, using the Inner Sphere slang for battle armor. "Help Three Lance finish off the recon unit."

"Cancel that order!" Colonel Rubinsky's voice came over the general address frequency loud and strong. "All units ordered to stand down. Major Allard-Liao pull back. Those are Second Oriente Hussars."

Opening her private channel to Rubinsky, Cassandra did not bother to hide her irritation. "So they are Leaguers. So what?" She cut in her command frequency long enough to bark out the order, "Two-two Lance, commit." The Hussars' *Overlord*, bristling with a fair number of weapons for close-in protection, began targeting what units it could. Where a weapons mount could not find an enemy within range or arc, it began to burn down stands of trees where enemy units even *might* be hiding. "Colonel Rubinsky, where are those fighters? The *Overlord* over there is angry with us."

"Breskin's Pegasii squadrons have grounded, on my order," Rubinsky said.

Rubinsky started to say more, but Cassandra overrode the comm circuits with a priority transmission to her Lancers. "We've lost fighter support," she informed them through clenched teeth. "All units pull back out of range from those DropShips guns."

By lance, BattleMechs broke cover and either jumped or walked backward out of range. Those within range of enemy 'Mechs traded another quick volley of shots, but to no great effect. Cassandra consoled herself with her opening victory. *We've hurt the enemy, without losing a single 'Mech and barely running up enough heat for me to break a sweat. I'll take that kind of victory any day.*

Swinging the *Cestus* around in a tight arc, Cassandra searched her firing arc for any Marik BattleMech foolish enough to stick its nose out. "Lancers, prepare for a quick charge and retreat maneuver. We'll slip in under the DropShip's sights, but only for a few seconds. Just long enough to bloody them again."

"Major." Colonel Rubinsky again, this time over the general

address frequency. "These forces are under Star League colors. Do not engage."

Cassandra's grip on her control sticks was knuckle-white. "False colors. Or misuse of the office." *I know what I am doing!* "Lancers, Light Horse—advance!"

Every St. Ives Lancer ignored Rubinsky's repeated commands to hold. Running forward at best speed, they took some scattered fire from the DropShip, which could not bring its full power to bear as could Cassandra's battalion. A flurry of weapons fire cut deeply into the few League BattleMechs still outside their DropShip, bringing down two more machines. Each Lancer 'Mech then walked back out of range. Cassandra noted that Tamas' Company never made a single move.

"Tamas," Cassandra yelled, feeling more betrayed by the younger Rubinsky's inaction than the colonel's meddling. "You are under my command and will follow my orders. Is that clear?"

Tamas' reply came in on a private channel to her. "I am sorry, Major Liao." He sounded frustrated and truly apologetic. "The colonel forbids me to take your orders."

Punching up her secure channel to Rubinsky, Cassandra worked to keep her mounting anger under control. Screaming wouldn't help. "Colonel Rubinsky, you will release Tamas back to my command and you *will* commit your forces to the defense of Indicass. Is that clear?"

"Quite clear," Rubinsky said, his voice raw steel. "That order I will not follow, Major."

How could this be happening? "Need I remind you that you are a *mercenary* colonel, in the employ of my family. My St. Ives rank is irrelevant. I *am* authorized to give you orders."

"That I'd not dispute." The colonel's voice was pitched hard and formal. "But under the Mercenary Accords of Outreach, written into the contract your mother signed, *and* under your own St. Ives Code of Military Responsibilities, I exercise my right to refuse an unjust and *idiotic* order.

"Major Liao, I am relieving you of command."

17

Royal Compound
Tian-tan, St. Ives
St. Ives Compact
9 December 3060

Indicass, Brighton, Vestallas, all occupied.

Candace Liao sat in a comfortable high-backed chair in the middle of the Royal Compound's war room, hands folded calmly in her lap. The war room, rarely used in the last three years except to monitor the Star League assault on Clan Smoke Jaguar's occupation zone, now bustled with energy and activity as junior officers manned the console stations and senior officers stood about and debated the strategic implications of recent events and possible future plans. The largest of the three giant wallscreens—no hologram, just straight video—displayed a map of the St. Ives Compact. The three occupied border worlds flashed between St. Ives ivory and caution-amber, signifying their unsettled state. Candace studied the map with piercing gray eyes, as if it might reveal some hidden clue as to how to salvage the situation.

Senior Colonel Caroline Seng stood behind the Duchess, along with General Simone Devon, a petite—almost delicate—fair-skinned woman and the AFFC liaison to the Compact. These two women currently shared the top level of the St. Ives Compact's military command structure, with Seng in charge of the Compact's military and Devon commanding all Federated Commonwealth units on loan to Candace Liao.

"Other than the small skirmish on Indicass," Caroline Seng

noted aloud, "we have managed to avoid any military incidents. But we cannot expect that to remain. The situation is highly unstable."

Nodding, Candace looked back over her shoulder. "Please display the occupation forces," she said calmly.

Caroline Seng passed the order to a sub-commander sitting at a nearby console, but General Devon pulled up the information faster from her photographic recall. "The Second Oriente Hussars, also known as the Crazy Second, dropped on Indicass. From the Draconis Combine, Sun-Tzu borrowed two battalions of the Second Dieron Regulars, complete with full air wing and infantry support—those are on Vestallas. Brighton he gave to the Raman DMM, a Draconis March unit of the Federated Commonwealth." Even as General Devon completed her recitation, the text appeared on one of the large auxiliary wallscreens to back her up.

"The units are still claiming to be Star League *peacekeepers*?" Candace asked. "No direct claim has been made in the name of the Confederation?"

"None," Seng assured her. "And Sian continues to deny any such allegations. Our best analysts have torn Sun-Tzu's formal statement apart looking for any discrepancy or half-truth, anything we could use to help predict his intentions or prove duplicity." Seng vented her frustration in a sharp exhale. "Unfortunately, it holds up. Not that I believe him, or Zahn's apology that our not initially receiving the statement was an oversight."

Candace recalled the statement to which Caroline Seng referred, sent to all Star League member states except the Compact, though Candace's name *had* appeared on the list. In it Sun-Tzu outlined his intention to place Star League occupation forces along the Compact border until he could be sure, as First Lord, that no further hostilities were forthcoming. He also quoted—she could almost say misquoted—her request for him to see the Lancers back to Denbar, making it appear as if she had invited him into the Compact.

The Blackwind Lancers were returned to Denbar all right, notably lacking over five hundred million C-bills worth of equipment, counting the DropShip, but the "escort" I mentioned ended up on three other worlds. "Masterful," she said in a mixture of anger and very grudging respect, "though I hate to admit it. He effectively undermined my efforts to oppose the occupation weeks before it even happened."

General Devon flushed, displaying more anger and less admiration for the move. "Your nephew has done a remarkable job of painting the Compact as the aggressor and his nation as the victim. He will milk that for all it's worth and, I'm sorry to say, use it to disguise his true intentions."

Nodding her agreement with the general's assessment, Candace felt the last two months of stress pulling as an ache in the muscles of her neck and lower back. All the activity of this crisis had interfered with her regular regime of tai chi exercise, and now she was paying the price.

"Patterns," Candace whispered, more to herself. "There must be patterns." *Sun-Tzu knows what he is about, and if I am to counter him I must know as well. Indicass, Vestallas, and Brighton.* "Why those three worlds?"

"Indicass has Ceres Metals," Seng volunteered. "But Vestallas and Brighton are of no extreme strategic significance. Plus, he bypassed Denbar, homeworld to the Blackwind Lancers second battalion and obviously the most vocal world then supporting the Lancers and now denouncing his actions." She shook her head. "It makes no sense."

"My nephew does nothing that does not make sense," Candace said with conviction. "To forget that is to invite disaster."

Invite disaster. Candace sat up stiffly. *Now that strikes a chord.* "Pull up the St. Ives Military Forces roster for those three worlds." Relayed to the sub-commander at the console, the order was quickly carried out. Of course, Rubinsky's Light Horse regiment of the Cossacks and two line battalions held Indicass. And as the other units were sketched in with text labels, Candace saw it. "There it is," she announced quietly. "Part of it anyway. The garrison forces on each world are potential troublemakers."

General Devon frowned her confusion. "Well, the Cossacks are well-known for their hatred of Sun-Tzu Liao, though Rubinsky's Light Horse is obviously the more moderate regiment on that score. But I was not aware that Aliesha's Mounted Fusiliers or Raymond's Armored Infantry were questionable troops."

"Not questionable," Caroline Seng said, understanding dawning on her face, "but unpredictable, yes. Both units have a history of unsanctioned attacks and heavy-handed tactics." Seng leaned forward, excitement in her voice. "And look at the choices made for occupation troops. The Crazy Second from the Free Worlds League, also unpredictable. And the Second Dieron Regulars, well known for their questionable loyalties and near-brutal methods."

"What of the Raman DMM?" General Devon asked. "They don't fit your theory. Green FedCom troops and utterly reliable. No outstanding feuds or history of recklessness."

Candace stood, feeling the need for movement as more pieces to the puzzle fell into place. "Troops of the Draconis March," she said, "which is already heavily depleted to support the assault against the Smoke Jaguars and where most of Yvonne's trouble has originated of late. I sense Katherine's hand behind that choice." She gave her AFFC liaison a hard stare. "Tell me the March won't scream louder with this further reduction in defense."

Simone Devon looked thoughtful as Candace continued. "And they've been matched up with the Armored Infantry, the only Capellan unit ever to have bounties put on their heads by House Davion." *It all fits. He's coming, and no doubt of it.*

Seng put the thought into words. "So he's trying to provoke further incidents."

"Which Cassandra handed to him," Candace said, shaking her head. "She should've known better, true, but I had hoped to smooth this over with Thomas Marik. Sun-Tzu won't allow me that chance, I'm sure. Thank the deities that Colonel Rubinsky was level-headed enough to recognize the situation for what it was. It could have been much worse." *I have to pull Cassandra out of there. She's out of her depth.* "Order the Second St. Ives Lancers back to the world of St. Loris. Let her sit there with the rest of the Cossacks to think on her action."

General Devon ran her fingers back through her blond hair, a thoughtful expression on her face. "You think your nephew will use the Indicass incident to move in more occupation forces? Press the Compact for outrageous concessions?"

Candace pursed her lips, trying to place herself in Sun-Tzu's position and weighing the advantage versus the risks being taken. "It runs much deeper than that," she finally said. "He already had more occupation troops on the way before the trouble on Indicass, I'm sure of it. And only the very last arrivals will be Capellan troops, though more will come later. It is a self-sustaining pattern. He'll find ways to push at our forces, creating incidents and allowing more troops to be brought in."

Colonel Seng frowned, studying the map as if a Capellan invasion fleet might appear any moment. "He left Denbar alone, for the moment, so they can continue to complain and posture and generally agitate the situation." She nodded. "You paint a bleak picture, Duchess, but I think you have it pegged. And I don't think we can throw back the occupation forces, not militarily anyway."

"Agreed," Candace said. "There isn't much we can do at all." Then her voice hardened as she fixed her senior-most officers with a stern gaze. "But there is much we can *prevent*. No matter what the occupation forces attempt, our units will have strict orders of peaceful noncompliance. They may defend themselves, but only if fired upon. In the meantime, I will see what I can accomplish politically. Perhaps it is not too late to shut this down."

Candace turned to face the map once again. "If Sun-Tzu persists, he will cut his own throat with the Star League and eventually will have all support pulled out from underneath him. So long as Yvonne, Theodore, Magnusson, and I form our power bloc within the council, he can be checked."

She glanced back to her AFFC liaison and her senior colonel. "But make no mistake, he's here to stay."

Sian
Sian Commonality, Capellan Confederation

Very little green was to be found in the Celestial Palace's outdoor gardens so late into Sian's long autumn. Trees thrust naked branches toward a gray sky, and flowers slept in the earth. Talon Zahn, now *Sang Jiang-jun,* or senior general, walked the gardens' flagstone path at the side of Sun-Tzu Liao. Two Death Commandos trailed a dozen paces back. Only the shrubs and a few evergreens hinted at the life that would bloom up again in the spring. *Spring, the rebirth of life. Xin Sheng.*

Almost self-consciously, Zahn reached up to touch the new collar devices that went with his new rank, neither of which had been seen since the time of Jasmine Liao's 2455 decree that limited Capellan officers to the rank of colonel.

Sun-Tzu Liao glanced over, a flicker of amusement playing in his eyes. "What is the status of the Confederation's military forces?"

Zahn dropped his hand back to his side and looked down to lock his gaze to the path. Though secure in his position, he still did not like to bring bad news to the Chancellor. Not that any fault rested on him personally, but it always made him feel as if he had somehow failed his lord and master.

He drew a deep breath, tasting the air. Damp and cold, it carried the slightest hint of pine and the promise of more rain. "Overall," he said, "the Confederation Armed Forces are in high spirits. The change in our ranking conventions has been very well received in the spirit of Xin Sheng, and the release of news from Hustaing demonstrates our strength with House Hiritsu's victory."

"And the Hustaing Warriors?" Sun-Tzu kicked a small rock to the edge of the path.

"Formed up to battalion strength and given the best possible training that House Hiritsu could manage in such a short time." *And with their rapid deployment, any rough edges will soon be beaten off of them.*

"But?" the Chancellor asked, voice flat.

Shoulders only slightly slumped from their usual military attention, Zahn nodded. "But. Our efforts in the Disputed Territories do not hold to initial estimations. We are expanding, but slowly. Worlds such as Wei and Aldebaran are causing problems out of proportion to their actual importance, though Wei I expect to be less of a problem with a battalion of McCarron's

Armored Cavalry dropping onto the world in two weeks." Another deep breath and sharp exhale. Zahn watched the play of steam his breath had caused in the cold air. "And in the Chaos March we are stopped cold."

Sun-Tzu fixed his Strategic Military Director with a hard jade stare. "How is that possible?"

"I do not know," Zahn admitted, "yet. The worlds are too well-armed and organized for it to be the product of independent effort. But Maskirovka agents have yet to pin down which Great House is responsible." *And now to broach the problem.* "I have studied your latest directive, Chancellor. You wish to use Capellan troops as part of the SLDF occupation forces?"

"You promised me the troops would be available."

"And they are," Zahn assured him. "If you gave the order, I would mount a full-scale invasion of the St. Ives Compact tomorrow. Or the Chaos March. Or even the old Tikonov Commonality." *And one of those must be coming, though you do not tell me which.* "But that would cost the reserves you have asked me to hold back."

Sun-Tzu slowed his pace, deep in thought. "Then you are talking about time, not manpower, so long as we can proceed with the troops already allocated. Your estimations—"

"Were based on further help coming from the Periphery," Zahn interrupted in a very soft voice. But as a testament to the importance of the matter, never in disrespect. *It is my duty to the Chancellor and the Confederation to make sure our military position is well understood.* "I have read the reports coming out of the Detroit Conference, Chancellor. Jeffrey Calderon is not going to follow Emma Centrella into an alliance with the Capellan Confederation. I have to conclude that the Taurian Concordat is lost to us, which means that we must pull back on at least one front. For now. Or else we risk taking unnecessary losses."

Stopping, Sun-Tzu focused his attention away from Zahn, his eyes on a low, wide shrub kept trimmed into the form of a prowling tiger. "The Detroit Conference is not over yet," he said. "So we continue. In all areas."

Talon Zahn nodded once. "As you desire, Chancellor." *A*

gamble, certainly. But now that I have voiced my only concerns, my duty is to enforce the Chancellor's will.

Sun-Tzu nodded, as if reading his mind. "All will work out in the end, *Jiang-jun* Zahn." He turned to continue walking the path, voice carefully neutral. "Let us wait, and see what the new year brings."

18

Home Guard Staging Grounds
Hazlet, Nashuar
St. Ives Compact
19 December 3060

Operating under his previous rank and handling the controls of a J. Edgar light hovertank, Lance Sergeant Maurice Fitzgerald led his reconnaissance "prowler" lance out of the Hazlet base's vehicle bay. The J. Edgar was an older vehicle, and despite the spit and polish applied, it smelled of rancid sweat left behind in the stained padding by previous drivers over its fifty years of operating history. Well armored, however, the tank could stand up to a BattleMech—for a few minutes anyway. One reason Fitz had chosen it.

Two Harassers followed to his left and right rear quarters, while a new Centipede scout brought up the rear to complete a standard diamond formation. When the Centipede cleared the threshold, Fitz opened up a comm channel. "Prowler Recon has cleared bays," he radioed in to his company CO.

"Prowler Recon, cleared for independent operation. Good hunting."

Fitzgerald opened the throttles, cruising the hovertank up to one hundred kilometers per hour over the light snow-covered ground. The winter twilight was far too cheery to suit him, with bright stars beginning to peak through in the clear, dimming skies. And somewhere out there, was the Lyran Alliance occupation force they were under orders to locate and observe.

And *avoid,* if any attempts were made to enforce Sun-Tzu Liao's stand-down order. All six border worlds were now under Star League "protection," with a declaration of martial law and an order to disarm. *To defuse the possibility of further hostilities and allow the region to slowly regain control of itself.* Or so the official press release read.

Fitz, among the rest of the Home Guard, bought into that as much as Duchess Liao obviously did, meaning not at all. All Compact units were under direct orders to conduct peaceful noncompliance, a tactic that had stalemated the situation so far.

Sliding through the wide open gate in the cyclone fencing, all that surrounded the Home Guard base of operations in Hazlet, Fitz came around on a north-northeast heading. The presence of new units crept in along the forward edge of his head's up tactical display, blue circles with BattleMech coding attached. It was the Home Guard 'Mech company, out on another practice run.

Finger-joints aching from his crushing grip on the controls, Fitzgerald resisted the urge to swing eastward and slip around the patrolling company. None of them knew what reassignment he'd chosen. Having been a member of the MechWarrior company, even if only as a trainee, he knew that his small armor force was beneath the notice of the pilots strapped into those cockpits.

The BattleMechs, ranging up to ten meters tall, broke the horizon with their bulky, humanoid forms. There was the *Phoenix Hawk,* Nevarr's 'Mech, leading the formation. Fitzgerald wasn't sure exactly who piloted what 'Mech in the regular company, though he'd heard that Danielle had picked up the *Blackjack* he'd trained in and that both Choya and, surprisingly, Cameron had made the selection board.

He bit down on his lip, drawing blood. *Your own fault,* he reminded himself. *Nevarr warned you and Danielle tried to help you, but you didn't listen. Or at least you didn't hear. Nevarr let you defeat yourself. In real combat, you would have been responsible for the loss of four BattleMechs and perhaps the death of friends. You weren't ready.*

Which was part of the reason he'd chosen recon assignment when transferred back to the armor corps following that last combat simulation. He certainly qualified for heavier tanks, but the idea of working in close proximity with others as part of a regular three-man tank crew made him shudder after the solitary freedom of a BattleMech. And by committing himself to the lighter vehicles, he forced himself into a supporting role similar to the one at which he had failed. *I need to learn to rely on others, and in turn be reliable to them.* Fitz wanted to believe that Nevarr would have approved of his choice in assignments.

As if he'd been reading the thoughts of his former commander and instructor, the *Phoenix Hawk* slowed to a walk and then stopped, bringing the 'Mech column to a halt directly alongside the armor lance's intended path. Fitz shook with a preternatural chill. He tried telling himself that Nevarr was just waiting for the vehicles to clear the area so the 'Mechs could rehearse formation changes or something, but the way the *'Hawk* turned to slowly follow the progress of the armored vehicles bothered him. Then, just for a split second, his threat indicators warned of a targeting lock from the *Phoenix Hawk*.

He knows! Fitz' hands shook on the controls, throwing the slightest hitch into the J. Edgar's glide path. He had not seen Nevarr after his last failure, having gone to great pains to avoid the 'Mech commander. But he had no doubts now that Nevarr had taken the time to learn his former cadet's new assignment. Though nervous under the watchful eyes of his former commander, Fitzgerald did feel a small measure of pride as well from Nevarr's brief salute of recognition.

"Prowler Recon," he said over his lance's private channel, "track turrets right. On my mark, douse running lights for three seconds. Mark!" Fitz hit the switch that extinguished all outer lights for the hovertank, his infrared and starlight scanners more than enough for safe travel. "Return," he said, lighting back up and completing the armor corps form of a pass in review salute.

"Good hunting," a strong voice whispered into Fitz' ear over the general frequencies.

"Clear fields," Fitzgerald returned, a standard MechWarrior's good wishes. Then he switched back over to his lance's private channel. "All right, let's crank it up to flank speed and make some distance. I want to tag that Lyran force within two hours."

And as the BattleMechs faded back to the rear horizon, Fitzgerald felt Nevarr's gaze follow him.

Lakeside County, Denbar
St. Ives Compact

Zhong-Shao Ni Tehn Dho had heard of spring-green units before, but this performance was embarrassing. The battalion commander shook his head.

Piloting the *Victor* assault 'Mech that had once belonged to the Blackwind Lancers Major Smithson, Dho stared out through the cockpit viewscreen at the growing confusion of Denbar's Lakeside County Shipping Yard. Half a dozen of his Hustaing Warriors piloting lighter 'Mechs were attempting to contain twice their number in tractor-trailer trucks. And failing, Dho noted with a degree of disbelief as the trucks continued to flee the loading docks with the much-needed food.

He had hoped that this little milk run would help to tighten unit cohesion and build on weak skills, but so far all it had done was promote chaos. Only the *Jenner,* piloted by one of his few warriors with any previous BattleMech experience, kept to any semblance of control. Here an *UrbanMech* shuffled along in ungainly pursuit of a truck, obviously having trouble keeping its balance without arms to use as counterweights. There a *Circada* overshot a fleeing semi, then overcorrected the move and nearly crashed into the back of the trailer, and finally ended up standing in helpless defeat as the truck made one of the gates. The trucker's departing blast of his air horns signaled the long-hauler's contempt.

We'll force the CCAF to invent a new rating, Dho thought. *How about newborn-pink?*

Only eight retired MechWarriors with any real life left in

them had been called up from the general population of Hustaing. Dho had been one of those, at the age of fifty-nine and ten years into his retirement but eagerly accepting command of the new unit in order to serve the Confederation's Xin Sheng effort. Previously a major in the Capellan Reserves, he'd been reinstated at the same level of responsibility but with the new rank of *zong-shao*.

Every Hustaing Home Guard with a gram of aptitude had been drafted to fill out the ranks, and a final four members had been accepted from a local college due to their dedicated attendance and impressive records in the local game arcade, which did feature a scaled-down version of 'Mech simulator pods. Interestingly enough, the four Arcade Rangers—the lance's unofficial name—showed faster improvement than any other rookies in raw skills, though the ex-Home Guard personnel naturally commanded a higher level of tactics and battlefield cooperation.

Time and training, that is all they really needed. Dho scratched his neck, where his wispy gray beard irritated the skin. With the help of House Hiritsu, every warrior had been given just over a month of intense training. Two more months, and they might have amounted to something even resembling a green 'Mech battalion. He hadn't even been able to decide on an executive officer yet, but Chancellor Liao, in his ultimate wisdom, had decreed the unit fit enough and dispatched them as the Capellan contribution to the Star League occupation forces. A position of honor.

Dho had hoped the unit would have time to pull together before facing any serious challenge, to keep from embarrassing the Chancellor's trust. But immediately upon landing they discovered a fairly hostile situation in the making. The standing Denbar garrison—Home Guard armor and a few remaining mercenary units—refused the orders to stand down and disarm. The declaration of martial law, ordered by the Chancellor himself in his capacity as First Lord, went largely ignored by the planetary population. Supplies were denied, and tensions remained extremely high as the remaining St. Ives troops kept a strict but non-violent level of alert.

And of the former second battalion of the Blackwind Lancers, there was no sign. To Dho, that implied trouble for the future.

"Enough of this," came a voice over Dho's comm, drawing his attention back to the greased-pig comedy playing itself out in the shipping yard. Dho had yet to learn his people by voice, but thought it to be *Sang-wei* Evans in the *Jenner,* one of his lance commanders. "We've played at fools long enough. Hugh, since you're about to fall over anyway, lay that *Urbie* down across the back entrance to the loading dock. Lo Chang, do the same at the front side. We have three trucks back there still, and that will at least keep *them* from getting away."

Crude, and maybe beneath the dignity of many MechWarriors, but effective. Zhong-shao Dho's pulse quickened. This is what he had been hoping for. Sort of. Coordinated battlefield action, if a bit unorthodox.

"Shen Kei, jump that *Wasp* outside the yard and uproot some trees. Throw them onto the access road there. Then circle the compound until every trail out of here is blocked. With nowhere to go, the truckers will eventually give up or run out of gas, I don't care which." A pause, then, "*Zongh-shao* Dho, this is *Sang-wei* Evans. With your permission, sir, I think we can call in our own transports."

"You are doing a fine job, *Sao-shao* Evans," Dho said, promoting him in responsibility but not pay or authority. *When we expand the unit, he will move up to company commander at once.* "I will return to our base of operations. I trust you to finish out this assignment." Working his foot pedals and throttle, Ni Tehn Dho maneuvered his *Victor* around and then strode off toward the highway, which he would follow back to the spaceport.

Well, it wasn't inspiring, or even pretty, but the job was done and left Dho with at least some hope for the future of his command. Now it was just a matter of instilling in them a sense of unity and a regard for proper Capellan dignity and battlefield tradition. *We shouldn't have been activated so quickly, and if things heat up we'll pay dearly for it, but with a little time I can turn this group into a real combat battalion.* He glanced at an auxiliary monitor displaying the scene behind him, of 'Mechs laying themselves down as barricades. *If nothing else, though, the Hustaing Warriors will be known for their spirited attempts.* Zhong-shao Dho sighed. *The Chancellor's will be done.*

Point of
No Return

Weigh the situation, then move.
　　　　　　　　　　　　—Sun-Tzu, *The Art of War*

For every action, any effort, there is a cost involved. Economic, political, social—it is paid somewhere. And the proper time to weigh such consequences is before a course is begun, when the cost may be evaluated within a proper frame of reference. For at some point, there is simply no looking back.
　　　　　　　　　　　　—Sun-Tzu Liao, journal entry,
　　　　　　　　　　　　22 November 3058, Tharkad

19

Celestial Palace
Zi-jin Cheng (Forbidden City), Sian
Sian Commonality, Capellan Confederation
5 January 3061

So late into the evening, most of the Celestial Palace was darkened and silent. Sun-Tzu sat at his desk, watching again as Candace Liao's latest address to Star League member states played out over the desktop's inlaid screen. Isis Marik, returned from Hustang but not yet reinstalled in her Zi-jin Cheng mansion, stood behind him, hands resting lightly on his shoulders. Both wore comfortable silk evening robes over bedclothes; hers embroidered along the sleeves with crescent moons and stars, his with the Chinese zodiac wheel across the back.

Alternating between a desire for privacy and an appreciation of Isis' company, Sun-Tzu now reached up with his right hand and covered one of her hands with his own. He would have to get used to having her around again, he decided, then returned his attention to the image of his Aunt Candace very carefully. He'd hoped to see an old woman beginning to wear under the strain of the last several months. Desperation showing in rapid eye movements or perhaps futility in the droop of her shoulders. *At the very least, she could have expressed either resignation or anger in her tone. She gives me nothing to work with.*

Candace sat in a high-backed chair, carved from a rich-grained wood and stained a beautiful cherry red. Her dress, an elegant ivory with only slightly exaggerated shoulders and sleeves that wrapped partly over the back of each hand, hinted at an Asian style without overstating her Chinese origins. Back straight, hands folded demurely in her lap, eyes calm and confident, she was the picture of dignified Asian rule.

Sun-Tzu glowered at the screen.

"And so, fellow council members," his aunt continued, "I find myself forced to call for a formal vote to repeal the First Lord's current action." Candace raised her hands in a cautionary gesture. "Not to suggest that he has acted improperly or outside the bounds of his office. I admit that mistakes have occurred which demanded a response, and I would like to think that First Lord Liao might have taken such hard measures were it the Free Rasalhague Republic or the Federated Commonwealth to feel threatened."

Isis kneaded his shoulders, easing away the sudden tension Sun-Tzu felt building in his muscles. *Beautifully done,* he applauded silently. *That cuts several ways.* Prince Magnusson, the remains of his small state pinched in between the Draconis Combine and Lyran Alliance, would worry about setting precedence should Theodore or Katrina be elected the next First Lord. Yvonne might have worried that Sun-Tzu could apply his occupation troops to FedCom worlds—except for the little-known fact that her worries were over, or just beginning. *And,* he noticed, *my aunt does hint that I abuse my position by raising doubts about how I could feel threatened by the much-smaller St. Ives Compact.*

Instead of letting her hands drop back into her lap, Candace steepled her fingertips. "Any well-meant intentions aside, however, I believe it can be seen how the presence of occupation troops trying to enforce martial law and a disarmament of my border can only lead to escalating tensions. Of course, I cannot permit my border defenses to be compromised, just as no League state would. I feel confident that we can arrive at a diplomatic solution to the terrible tragedy that occurred on Hustaing, once tensions are allowed to subside.

"Duchess Candace Liao," she said formally, "of the St. Ives Compact, votes to repeal the First Lord's occupation edict." And with a last, regal nod, the message ended.

Sun-Tzu found little fault in the entire message. *Her one and*

*only mistake was not returning her hands to her lap. The ges-
ture made her look calculating—Liao.* He doubted the minor
faux pas would change any votes, though. "Your thoughts," he
asked, looking over his shoulder at Isis and then remembering
to add, "dearest?"

Isis moved around the chair to lean against the rosewood
desk as she faced Sun-Tzu. Lips pursed, she regarded him with
sad brown eyes for a moment before speaking. "Candace did
not verbally attack you or your Confederation," she said, speaking slowly and obviously taking great care with each word, "as
you likely hoped she might. She made no excuses for the Compact's mistakes, and has even intimated that you are due further recompense for the tragedy on Hustaing. Though, you
have already raised a new unit from the spoils *and* Kuan Yin
Allard-Liao headed an immediate relief action that brought
much-needed aide to the citizens of Qingliu."

*Yes, four days before my own relief action arrived, depriving
me of the public relations boost.* Sun-Tzu worked to keep the
irritation off his face. Kuan Yin was a player of minor importance, and so did not really threaten him. "And what of Candace's call for a vote of repeal?" If nothing else, Sun-Tzu had
come to respect Isis' political acumen and her calm tempera-
ment, which allowed her to see what he might have overlooked. *Also, I know she has had word from her father.*

"She can expect support from her usual allies," Isis said at
once, her voice assured. Then she grew thoughtful. "My father
will vote against her, because of the incident on Indicass in-
volving Cassandra's firing on the Second Oriente Hussars. He
will force some minor concessions from Candace later over
that, and perhaps even for the danger she subjected me to on
Hustaing." Unspoken was the fact that Thomas Marik had yet
to publicly reproach Candace for the Hustaing incident, though
Sun-Tzu knew how that must pain her.

"Katrina," Isis said, grimacing slightly, as if tasting something bad, "Katrina is the unknown. She might vote with you,
for any number of reasons we could discuss. Or she might vote
against you simply for the trouble you've raised in the old Free
Tikonov Republic."

That should be "the old Tikonov Commonality," Sun-Tzu thought with a touch of bitterness toward Isis, but kept it from his face and merely nodded his approval of her evaluation. "And what would you advise?" he asked, voice carefully neutral so as not to prevent her from saying *exactly* what she thought.

Isis never hesitated. "You should call back the occupation forces before the vote is finalized. At the very least, stop them from trying to impose martial law. Seize the initiative, beloved, and you can wring concessions from Candace that will more than make up for one unit's mistake in attacking Hustaing."

Perhaps seeing something on his face, Isis continued in a more soothing voice. "I know the idea of reclaiming the St. Ives Compact for the Confederation burns within you, Sun-Tzu. Your Xin Sheng efforts have brought about an astounding surge in pro-Capellan nationalism. But examine the facts. Your resources are spread so thin, reclaiming the disputed worlds coreward and trying to make inroads further into the Chaos March. Now the trouble with the Detroit Conference . . ."

"Yes," Sun-Tzu quickly agreed as she trailed off uncertainly, "a tragedy." Word had arrived the week before that Sherman Maltin, president of the New Colony Region lying between the Magistracy and the Concordat, had staged a coup during the Conference's Christmas Eve party. Both Emma Centrella and Jeffrey Calderon, rulers of the two large Periphery states, were taken hostage until the New Colony Region was recognized as an independent realm. "I know I could hardly afford to divert more troops into the area, but I owe that to our Magistracy allies. And if not for the Hustaing incident, I would have been on my way to the Detroit Conference and might be held hostage myself."

"Somehow," Isis said with a touch of bone-dry humor, "I suspect you would not have been quite so unlucky."

That is what is called a fishing expedition, dearest. *Full points for the attempt.* Regarding her with studiously blanked face, Sun-Tzu ignored the comment and returned to the previous topic. "So, in your opinion, I cannot hope to take any of the border worlds and should therefore play to the opinion of other states?"

A touch of hesitation there, as if unsure whether or not she should voice an opinion. Then Isis forged ahead. "I believe you could take a single world, Denbar, *and* find enough support in the council to keep it."

"But you recommend against anything further?" Sun-Tzu said.

Isis nodded. "You are First Lord. If you continue to provoke the situation, it might be seen as gross abuse of your position, and the others will eventually censure you. How would that help your Confederation?" She stood, gazing down at him fondly. "You have always put your state first. You will do the right thing." She moved away, turning toward the door and then glancing back. "Are you coming?"

Sun-Tzu waved her on with a smile. "In a few moments, dearest. I wish to put a few more things in order. You go ahead."

Pausing in the doorway, Isis awarded Sun-Tzu with her best smile, full of promise and encouragement. "Walk wisely, beloved, and history will treat you kindly." Then she moved off, her slippers whispering against the hallway tiles.

That's "tread with wisdom," Sun-Tzu corrected her silently. *If you are going to quote from the works of Lao-tzu, please do so correctly.* He waited until the sounds of her movement faded, to be sure she would not overhear, then inserted a new message into the viewer.

Katrina Steiner-Davion, resplendent in white gown and with her golden tresses knotted into a thick braid that coiled over her left shoulder like a snake, stared back from the two-dimensional screen. Her blue eyes reflected an icy sharpness.

"Greetings, Sun-Tzu Liao. As our *honorable* First Lord," she said with heavily applied sarcasm, "I felt it proper that you be informed first among the Star League council. And personally, by me, though an ambassador will afford you greater detail later this week. At Yvonne's direct request, I have assumed the throne on New Avalon in an effort to deal with the legacy of civilian unrest to which my brother Victor abandoned her."

Though he knew what was to follow, having viewed the message earlier, Sun-Tzu could still not help the satisfied smile that stole over his face for the moment. *Ah, Victor. Once more you have focused on the wrong enemy. What a homecoming you will face, if you return at all.*

"Although the process of reuniting the Federated Commonwealth with the Lyran Alliance consumes much of my time," Katrina continued, "I have devoted some thought toward Duchess Liao's recent call for a repeal of your recent actions." She turned down the false charm, becoming much more businesslike. "I predict that Thomas Marik will support you, if for no other reason than for the trouble Cassandra caused his unit on Indicass. Perhaps the danger Isis was subjected to on Hustaing plays a small part of that as well." False smile. "How unfortunate she was subjected to such a harrowing experience," she said lightly, then returned to the business at hand.

"Theodore and Magnusson will back St. Ives, for reasons I'm sure you've already examined. Candace needs a two-thirds majority to override you, and my assumption of the New Avalon throne brings us down to only six voting members. Which means that I still hold the deciding vote. How fortunate."

Exacting a measure of revenge for the Tikonov troubles? Sun-Tzu read that into the current situation easily enough, though to give Katrina credit she never once mentioned it. Apparently she was satisfied, for now, with taking the second throne.

"As I have said before, I do not believe it my business to interfere in what seems to me to be an internal Capellan matter. So I expect to vote against Duchess Liao's proposal." Her voice grew harder yet. "This would be the second kindness I have done you. So before you begin to think my generosity knows no boundaries, consider this. The Star League member states meet again this year, to elect a new First Lord. I would like to see a tradition begin of the current holder of that office nominating his successor. And I'm sure I can count on you."

The image faded. Sun-Tzu leaned back in his chair, right hand trailing a finger along his jaw while the left drummed against the chair's armrest. *Her analysis is as flawless as Isis'. She wants me to nominate her in return for support now? An easy bargain to make. What do I care who is next in office? I*

am *First Lord, and so long as that lasts I will use every last ves-*
tige of power within the office to revitalize the Confederation
and make it whole once more.

He glanced at the empty doorway, where Isis had stood not
moments before. *History will treat me kindly? The winners*
write the history books, dear Isis, and if my Capellan Confed-
eration is to be that winner, then it must always be put before
my own interests. The situation will escalate as my forces push
for incidents. And if incidents can't be made by pushing, then
more forceful methods will be in order. The cost is going to run
high in Capellan blood before I am through. There is no avoid-
ing that, however much I wish I could. But the simple truth is
that we are all expendable—you, me, everyone—when set next
to the end result. Xin Sheng.

20

Whiteriver Staging Grounds
Pinedale, Denbar
St. Ives Compact
17 January 3061

You are hereby authorized to take any self-defensive actions deemed necessary to protect the integrity of your command and its warriors.

Such were the latest directives out of Sian. So now, at the head of his command lance and a supporting lance of the Hustaing Warriors, *Zhong-shao* Ni Tehn Dho walked his *Victor* through the main gate of Denbar's largest staging area, intending to follow those directives to their fullest extent. *So long as we allow Pinedale's Home Guard base to act as a focus for resistance to the Confederation, we cannot hope to protect ourselves, much less enforce the Chancellor's will.*

The heavy footfalls of Dho's assault 'Mech and its companion machines shook the fencing and rattled the glass in the guard booth windows. Inside the small shack, a guard picked up a phone to call in an alert to the mercenary units and Home Guard militia that made up Pinedale's standing garrison on Denbar. Dho ignored him, intent on reaching the 'Mech bays.

Self-defense, he thought again, running over the directive in his mind. *That can be given a very liberal definition.* A definition Dho was inclined to grant after the last few weeks. Three warriors caught between spaceport administration and the DropShip, beaten unconscious by spaceport workers. Another injured by a lucky rifle shot at long distance, probably a radical-minded civilian, but no way to tell for sure. And then yesterday, when *Sao-shao* Evans' lance attempted to peacefully force a Hetzer wheeled assault gun to pull over in order to confiscate the vehicle, the gunner had turned the Hetzer's one hundred-twenty-millimeter autocannon against Evans' *Jenner* and scrapped the BattleMech's gyro. The Home Guard soldier had later claimed that physical contact between a 'Mech and his vehicle constituted an attack in his book.

You want to play by the book, that works for me. Dho opened a comm channel. "Support Lance, remain on station here to prevent any exit from the staging grounds. Command Lance, we continue on to the 'Mech and vehicle bays." *Chancellor and First Lord Liao ordered Denbar placed under martial law and disarmed. And that is just what we are going to do.*

At five different points around the extensive staging grounds, double lances of the Hustaing Warriors—and the single observer's lance from House Hiritsu—would be closing on the same location. They would box in any Home Guard or St. Ives-employed mercenary and force them to accept the First Lord's ordered stand-down.

A pair of targets edged into his tactical screen and sped across at an angle to the path of the command lance. The computer's coding identified them as a pair of Pegasus scout hovercraft. "Let them go," Dho ordered quickly before his lance got sidetracked. "We can't match their speed. Leave them to someone else."

The Pegasus hovercraft didn't seem to want to let it go at that, and half-circled the command lance, drawing in ever tighter as if to make a stab at the rear armor of one of the BattleMechs. *Trying to bait us.* But when the bait didn't work they sped off in search of others. Dho relaxed his grip on the *Victor*'s control sticks. *They wanted to pull us around, throw us off balance.* A sound tactic, especially considering the still disorganized state of the Hustaing Warriors. He radioed a quick caution to the entire battalion.

"Arcade Rangers, have Command Lance in sight," a voice called cheerfully over the air waves.

Ni Tehn Dho checked his head's up display, finding the

lance of four BattleMechs ahead and to his left, bearing two-nine-five degrees, just past one of the large 'Mech hangars and clustered around a vehicle maintenance bay. Moving in closer and verifying through his viewscreen, he counted three of them walking around the maintenance depot and a fourth hunched down before the depot bay doors. Dho dialed for maximum magnification on an auxiliary monitor. Near as he could tell, the lance's commander was using small bursts from his *Vindicator*'s medium pulse laser to sloppily weld the large armored doors closed.

"It's not pretty, but it works," a new voice offered as a *Wraith* and a *Huron Warrior* walked into view from behind the maintenance depot.

The Hiritsu observers, and out of position. Twenty-three years of previous command experience urged Ni Tehn Dho to exert control over the wayward pair, sending them back to their assigned zone of control, but common sense overrode that impulse. The Warrior Houses were not part of the regular CCAF, and so fell outside his command, regardless of whether or not he technically outranked them. And everything he'd seen about House Hiritsu impressed him enough that if Aris Sung and one of his lancemates had broken from their zone, it was with good reason.

"We get the job done," Dho transmitted over the Hustaing Warrior's general frequencies, allowing his people to hear his confidence in them even though he thought their finesse left something to be desired. "That's what matters."

The *Wraith* planted itself on widespread legs, one arm tight to its side and the other pointing past the Arcade Rangers to the 'Mech hangar. With the blued-steel look to its armor, it reminded Toh more of a large armored knight than a BattleMech. "That *does* matter, *Zhong-shao*. But getting the job done also means proper target selection. And while your inventive lance may have trapped a few armored vehicles, they have allowed at least two BattleMechs to power up within the hangar."

Dho swung around toward the 'Mech hangar. The hangar doors slowly slid open on motorized tracks, and within the dark spaces thermal scanning picked out the heat blooms of two fusion reactors. "Command Lance, block those doors," he ordered, already realizing it would be too late.

Although Aris Sung saw something almost amusing in the situation, it didn't take much imagination to also see the potential for danger and he readied himself for battle. Hands tight on his control sticks, all heat sinks online and weapons ready, he kept his targeting reticule floating over the opening doors of the 'Mech hangar even as he warned the *zhong-shao* of the two 'Mechs powering up inside. *They should have noticed. They should have checked the hangar first.* But Aris also knew that he couldn't expect a newly formed unit to know all the tricks, or a retirement-age commander to remember them. They would learn, the old lessons would come back, or the Hustaing Warriors would die in infancy.

All fairly simple really, if one could keep an emotional distance.

Aris activated a private frequency to Raven Clearwater, his lancemate in the *Huron Warrior*. "Let them handle this, Raven. We lend some firepower only if things heat up out of control." According to House Master Non, it was more important that the Hustaing Warriors be allowed to learn from a few mistakes than to quickly enforce martial law on Denbar. Aris wasn't sure if he agreed—the sooner the situation was brought to heel the fewer casualties, on either side—but one did not argue with the House Master.

As the Hiritsu company leader had expected, *Zhong-shao* Dho was not able to block the door in time with his larger 'Mechs. An antiquated *Blackjack* made it through the two-story doors, followed at close proximity by a newer *Cicada*. Both of them might have made good their escape. The *Blackjack*'s jumping power would keep it from being boxed in, while the *Cicada*'s greater speed could outrun even Aris' *Wraith*.

What no one counted on were the Arcade Rangers.

The coordination left a lot to be desired, but results counted even if they were working more as four individuals than a true team. Led by the *Vindicator*, the four medium-weight 'Mechs attempted to box in the *Blackjack* but could not quite do it.

Spotting the opening, the *Blackjack* went for it rather than attempt a jump. Unfortunately for the Compact pilot, the *Vindicator* also noticed the hole and, timing it just right, moved into the *Blackjack*'s path. The 'Mechs collided, the *Vindicator* stumbling to its knees and then falling prone in what could only be an exaggerated and purposeful fall.

Dho's *Victor* cut loose first, the Gauss rifle that made up the assault machine's right arm ejecting a large slug that crushed armor plates over the back of the *Blackjack*. Two Rangers fired next, lasers and small autocannon gouging more armor from the hapless *Blackjack*, which was knocked off its feet under the intense fire. Then the *Cicada* made its mistake, firing on one of the smaller Ranger machines as it attempted to race past. The remaining Ranger 'Mech and three more in the command lance opened fire, two PPCs gouging into the *Cicada*'s left leg and cutting it away at the hip joint.

Aris grimaced at the brute-force tactics as eight BattleMechs kept the two Compact machines pinned to the earth under a barrage of energy weapons. The *Cicada* gave up quickly, powering down, though the *Blackjack* attempted to regain its feet once before another Gauss slug tunneled through its back to crush its stabilizing gyro.

"By the book," *Zhong-shao* Dho broadcast, not bothering to explain what he meant.

Turning his *Wraith* away from the scene, Aris exhaled heavily, almost a sigh. "Raven, let's get back to the *Lao-tzu* and rejoin our House. We've seen enough." *Sloppy, yes. Inefficient, certainly. But the Hustaing Warriors have performed their duty here, and soon it will be time for House Hiritsu to perform ours.*

Aris only wished he could find a bit of his earlier enthusiasm for the entire mission.

Salt River Canyon, Nashuar
St. Ives Compact

Thin patches of snow, melting down under an unusually warm January sun, blanketed the winter-brown field of grass in Nashuar's Salt River Canyon. 'Mechs moved across the canyon—really a wide valley flanked by steep mountains—trading pulses of brightly colored coherent light and missiles that trailed streamers of smoke. A lance of armored hovercraft wove about the field, sliding around the small stands of trees and avoiding when possible the enemy 'Mechs.

Lance Sergeant Maurice Fitzgerald threw his hovercraft into a hard turn, spilling some of the air from its skirt but managing to avoid dipping down far enough to plow up snow or earth. A Lyran *Battle Hawk* spitted itself on the old-fashioned cross hairs that served as the J. Edgar's targeting reticule, more by accident than design, but a quick finger on the trigger sent two pairs of short-ranged missiles into its back. Fitz recovered full control of his vehicle in time to snake around a thick stand of ponderosa pine, before the *Battle Hawk* could turn and take issue with him.

How did this get started? Even in the midst of battle, Fitzgerald could not help wondering who had fired the first shot. So far as he knew, Prowler Recon and a lance from the Home Guard 'Mech company had been ordered out to flank a company of the Seventh FedCom RCT *just in case there was trouble* with the Lyran force acting as occupation troops. Like Nashuar's militia, the Federated Commonwealth unit had ignored the declaration of martial law and the orders to stand down. Part of the forces on loan to Duchess Liao, they were required to act under her orders. *But I don't think anyone thought Lyran troops would fire on the FedCommers. Especially with Katrina Steiner-Davion sitting on the throne on New Avalon these days. Just one more sign of the chaos that seems to reign lately.*

The fight had started before Fitzgerald's arrival, and the first he knew of it was orders to draw off any Lyran troops he could to protect the Seventh's withdrawal from the area. *Nothing like playing tag with war machines that mass two to four times as much as I do.*

"All units, escape and evade contact. The Seventh is clear." The voice was that of Subcommander Danielle Singh, now commanding a lance in the Home Guard company.

Fitzgerald opened a channel to his lance. "Prowler Recon, break off and regroup half a klick north." He sideswiped a few smaller trees as he skimmed in too close to the edge of a forest, then slowed down now that the immediate danger was past.

"Prowler One, this is Four. Mayday, mayday. I'm grounded, repeat. I'm grounded."

So much for being out of danger. Fitz powered into a hard turn one hundred-eighty degrees away from the path toward safety. "Prowler One, out for pickup. Where away, Four?"

"Half a klick south, with a BattleMech looking for me. I slid into some trees and lost my fans to a stump." A pause, then more worried. "It doesn't look good, Sergeant. Abort pickup."

Danielle had been monitoring the emergency channel, and broke in before Fitzgerald could reply. "Lance Sergeant Fitzgerald, abort pick up. We can't afford to lose another vehicle today. Recon Four is POW. We'll get him back later."

He shook his head, as if Danielle could see him. "Negative. That is my man, Subcommander." *My responsibility.* Fitzgerald ran his speed up to a safe sixty kph, fast enough without courting the same disaster that had befallen his lancemate. "Two and Three, proceed to rendezvous. Prowler One, out for pick-up."

"Prowler Three, dropping out for pick-up."

"Prowler Two, dropping out for pick-up."

All right, we'll face insubordination charges together. Fitzgerald caught sight of Recon Three's Harasser, skimming in from the left. Recon Two was already ahead of them, having been further back to start with.

"Fitz, you get back up here. You've got no 'Mech support. I can't cover you."

"Familiar ground, Subcommander. You could probably talk me out of this, except we're already there." Fitzgerald slid his hovertank through a series of serpentine curves as an enemy *Gallowglas* took a few long-ranged shots with its particle projection cannon. "Recon Four, hey, David! Next time, warn me that it's a heavy beating the brush for you and not the light 'Mech I'm expecting."

"I'm sixty meters up and to the monster's left," Recon Four came back. "Abandoning vehicle. Will meet you at the treeline."

Fitzgerald swallowed against a suddenly dry throat. "Two, you make pickup. Three, you're with me. Get in back of that thing and chew on it. I'll keep it busy."

Barreling straight in at the *Gallowglas*, Fitzgerald was sure the 'Mech pilot would be worried he would get rammed. The seventy-ton BattleMech jumped right ninety meters, almost coming down on top of the Recon Three's Harasser. The J. Edgar tagged it with missiles and medium laser, hardly making a dent in the heavy machine's armor. In turn, the *Gallowglas* exacted a healthy measure of revenge; its pair of large lasers carving away more than half the armor that fronted Fitz' hovercraft. The Harasser made up for it somewhat, slipping behind the BattleMech and using its twin SRM launchers to blast away large chunks of the weaker rear armor.

Caught in between two decently armored vehicles, the *Gallowglas* pilot tried to twist around and prevent a second backshot. Fitz used that to his advantage, throwing the J. Edgar into a series of unpredictable turns and almost losing control before slipping around to join the Harasser in the enemy's rear quarter. The *Gallowglas* managed to torso-twist far enough to tag Fitzgerald with its PPC, the manmade lightning almost coring through the weaker side armor of the J. Edgar, but Fitz rode out the damage. The combined return fire worked at the armor of the *Gallowglas'* left leg and right arm, and savaged the armor all across the rear torso. Two of Fitz' missiles flew into the breaches, chewing away at internal structure and cracking wide the fusion engine's shielding.

Its back mostly devoid of any protection, the *Gallowglas* lit off jump jets and moved quickly for tree cover, where the hovercraft could not follow.

"Break off," Fitzgerald ordered, swinging around to make a fast run to the north. "Prowler Two, you got David?"

"I have him, One. He says thanks."

Fitzgerald smiled, the simple acknowledgment of a job well-done warming him. "He's welcome. But make sure he knows how much trouble he's caused today."

"If you boys are done playing back in the woods," Danielle cut into their conversation, not concealing her irritation, "we would greatly appreciate your company at the rendezvous."

"On our way," Lance Sergeant Fitzgerald replied, with more cheer than he should be showing. If Nevarr didn't come down on him for abandoning Danielle's flank and ignoring her order, his own company CO surely would. *But I got the job done, and didn't lose a single man. And if that doesn't make a difference with them, I don't care.*

It makes a big difference to me.

Ceres Metals Factory
Xin Singapore Province, Indicass
St. Ives Compact
27 January 3061

Parked just off the official property of Ceres Metals' Indicass facility, Tamas Rubinsky sat easy in his *Enforcer*'s command couch. He'd long since turned off coolant flow to his vest, when it became clear that action was not soon forthcoming, and his neurohelmet rested on the shelf above the viewscreen. The fusion plant of the fifty-ton 'Mech stood on hot standby, waste heat easily shunted to its dozen heat sinks. The sun had long since drunk up the morning dew, and now it beamed down from a sapphire sky to wash the Ceres Metals factory complex and four companies' worth of BattleMechs in its late morning warmth.

The standoff was entering its second hour, and the warriors of Tamas' company were merely spectators.

Tamas sipped a tepid orange sports drink that many Mech-Warriors swore by for replacing the fluid loss so common in the high-heat environment of a BattleMech cockpit, but for now he drank just for the sake of doing something. One company of the St. Ives Cheveux Legers' third battalion fronted the main factory building for Ceres Metals, their 'Mechs formed up in a single line facing outward to the north and their backs nearly scraping the building's wall. Four hundred meters out and facing them stood two companies of the Second Oriente

Hussars. The Crazy Second grouped together in three double-lance forces, but made no move to flank the defenders or press them. *Neither unit, it seems, is willing to start the fight.*

Tamas' orders were quite clear, spelled out in insulting detail by his father, who had yet to forgive Tamas for his small part in the initial landing skirmish. *What does he expect? I was assigned to Major Allard-Liao and she gave the order to attack.* A poor excuse, though, and he knew it. *Just following orders* was the fallback position of any officer caught in a questionable engagement. And truth be known, Tamas believed Cassandra right in ordering the attack. The Crazy Second had obviously come in spoiling for trouble, a belief borne out afterward by the Second's heavy-handed treatment of Compact units showing peaceful non-compliance. So far Rubinsky's Light Horse had managed to avoid trading shots again with the Second, but in Tamas' mind that could not hold for much longer. *But we will not be the first either, and so everyone waits.*

The Light Horse company under Tamas' command waited four hundred meters off to the west for now, positioned so they faced roughly the midway point between the two opposing units. They were not even allowed to turn on their targeting scanners today unless the fight started on its own, and *only* if the Crazy Second fired the first shot. Marko Rubinsky had also defined a shot as a weapon discharge aimed in hostile intent and damaging an opponent. *Thank you, Father, for that piece of wisdom.*

An auxiliary monitor, selected to the *Enforcer*'s tactical computer, suddenly lit up four new symbols. Tamas quickly read the coded tags, deciphered them as *Thunder, Cataphract, Snake,* and *Huron Warrior,* and quickly set about putting his neurohelmet back on and restarting his coolant flow. *Capellan 'Mechs, every one.*

"Everyone up and ready," he ordered. To verify his suspicions, he twisted the *Enforcer* enough to get a visual on the new machines and punched up increased magnification on a monitor. No Star League colors, just the usual gauntlet-and-katana insignia of the Capellan Confederation.

"Bring fusion plants fully on-line and run weapon checks.

No targeting computers, but be ready to go weapons-hot any time." He watched the new lance draw in closer, no doubt heading straight for the stalemated confrontation before him.

Father said nothing about Capellans.

Sang-wei Jerry Gossett, lately of the Second Confederation Reserve Cavalry stationed on Purvo, marched his brand new *Thunder* to what he knew could very well be his death. His seventy-ton BattleMech boasted a trio of medium pulse lasers, a small long-ranged missile rack, and a Kali Yama big bore autocannon that replaced its right arm. And he was under orders not to use any of his weapons, until and unless it could be demonstrated quite clearly that the Compact troops had left him with little choice.

Of course, firing first often means firing last. So, by the time I am allowed to use them it could be too late. But if the Chancellor required his death for the greater good of Xin Sheng, he would have it.

The Second Oriente Hussars parted to allow his lance into their midst, and he throttled back to a full stop. He'd been given a secure frequency to the Crazy Second, but dialed up a general channel instead and opened communications. "You were to secure this facility," he said without preamble. "Why has this not been done?"

"Orders," the reply came back brusquely. "First Lord Liao has hamstrung us. We are instructed to use force only when all else has failed or if defending ourselves."

The answer I was told to expect, to the very letter. But at least form has been served and recorded by anyone monitoring. Now he switched to the secure channel. "Wait here," he ordered, and started his *Thunder* walking forward again. His lancemates joined him.

"Where are you going?"

Gossett smile thinly, bent on enjoying what could be his last moments. "I'm going to pick a fight," he answered calmly. *The Chancellor's will be done.*

He almost thought he could hear the other MechWarrior's grin in his response. "We'll be there."

The Cheveux Legers did not move at all as Gossett's lance marched up to directly face the middle four of their line. The four 'Mechs stopped less than ten meters from the Legers. Facing a *War Dog,* Gossett dialed back up the general frequency. "You are ordered to stand down. If you do not, I am authorized to remove you."

"Think you can do it?" came an immediate reply. "I don't notice any Star League markings for you to hide behind."

Gossett did not bother with further conversation. He tried to step through the right-hand gap between the *War Dog* and the neighboring *Cestus.* The *Dog* moved to block him then, and again when he tried to pass along the left. Pulling in on the control sticks, Gossett tucked the *Thunder*'s arms down and tried to shoulder past. The *War Dog* shoved back, hard, almost knocking the *Thunder* to the ground. Gossett wrestled with the control sticks, adding some judicious balancing to the feedback from his own inner ear that the neurohelmet translated to the 'Mech's gyro. The 'Mech barely kept its feet.

That should look convincing enough on any gun-cams. Gossett came in again, only this time with both arms thrust out to shove the *War Dog* out of his way. The large-bore autocannon made for a very ineffective arm, but he managed to connect anyway. The larger 'Mech stumbled back, bounced off the heavily reinforced wall of the factory, and then thrust itself forward to punch at the *Thunder.* Powered by myomer musculature, the *War Dog*'s left fist smashed into the *Thunder*'s right side, crushing armor plates, which rained fragments to the ground below.

Gossett rode out the impact. *Thank you,* he offered in silent salutation. He maneuvered forward, then lashed out with a kick that caught the *War Dog* in the left leg. At almost the same instant, he knew that his lancemates would also be engaging, under orders to shove their own opponents aside in the hopes of starting a chain reaction that could throw the entire Legers line into disarray. Of course, they could always argue later that they were merely coming to their commander's rescue, by nonviolent means. How well it worked Gossett had no way of telling right away, since his entire attention span was taken up in a BattleMech-scale fistfight with the *War Dog*.

Both heavy 'Mechs traded punches and kicks, the *War Dog* surrendering some advantage due to its reliance on punching while Gossett constantly threatened to topple the larger 'Mech with a well-placed kick. An eerie fight, with no radio chatter to distract and no rising heat scale to turn the cockpit into a sauna. *The odds will catch up eventually,* he thought, already tensing for it.

Finally, the blow he'd been waiting for arrived, smashing into the *Thunder*'s head. His right, eye-like viewport shattered inward, spraying the cockpit with shards of ferroglass. Shaking off the stunning effect—what could easily have been a killing blow—Gossett floated his targeting reticule over the *War Dog*'s frame. At point-blank range the commander picked up an easy target lock, pulling back on the main triggers on each control stick. The left trigger fired all three of the *Thunder*'s medium pulse lasers, their ruby darts stitching into the already-damaged armor on the *War Dog*'s right leg and body, laying the leg open to the skeleton beneath. The right activated the Kali Yama autocannon, its twelve-centimeter armor-piercing slugs ripping out of the barrel and slamming into the *War Dog*'s right arm. The slugs tore open armor, pierced myomer flesh, and ate into the skeleton beneath.

Shaken and unbalanced by the loss of over two tons of armor, the *War Dog* lost its footing and toppled backward, slamming into the ground flat on its back. Gossett lashed out with another kick, a destructive attack that caught the *War Dog* in its severely damaged right leg and wrenching it off at the hip. *You won't be getting up again.*

But Gossett was given no time to enjoy his victory. Even as he turned to lend help to one of his lancemates, the *Thunder* rocked forward with a forceful hit from behind.

The Light Horse company! He knew it was a laser hit, just by the way it felt. Then he knew nothing but the mental pain of neural feedback and the violent throes of a 'Mech dying around him as the energy penetrated his rear armor and touched off the ammunition magazine for his LRMs. His vision swam as the neural feedback increased in intensity, and his last coherent thought before the darkness claimed him was of Sun-Tzu Liao, and the knowledge that he had served his Chancellor well today.

Tamas couldn't help but think of the escalating fight as one between two rival street gangs. First the name-calling, followed by a shoving match that quickly turned into a bloody fistfight where shards of armor littered the ground instead of broken teeth and blood. The Capellan lance caused havoc beyond their numbers when one lucky push sent a Legers *Cestus* reeling into his neighbor, setting off a domino-chain that ended up throwing the entire right side of the line into chaos. Then, the slow motion brawl in which raw power took the place of speedy jabs, and armor protected the warrior rather than easily bruised flesh.

And after one gang member took a nasty shot to the head, rupturing an eye, the knives and guns came out.

"Weapons-hot," Tamas had ordered as soon as the *Thunder* cut loose with its large bore autocannon. "Weapons-free against any Capellan that fires on Legers, or any Oriente Hussar that fires on us." With those brief orders given, he triggered an emerald blast from his extended-range large laser, the shaft of light coring into the *Thunder*'s back and rupturing the ammunition magazine. Tamas grinned. *I have just committed my first act of aggression against the Capellan Confederation, and it felt good.*

But just as for the *Thunder*'s pilot, any victory today for Tamas was destined to be short-lived. With three mauling tigers in their midst, the Cheveux Legers were unprepared for the onslaught launched by the Free Worlds League Crazy Second. Lasers and the white-blue crackling energy lances from PPCs stabbed into armor weakened by punches and kicks, gouging deeply into internal structures. Autocannon slugs followed, finding the breaches and exploiting them. The Legers who were able quickly fell back under the press. Just so Tamas wouldn't feel left out, a heavy double-lance of Hussars screened him off from the main battle for Ceres Metals and began to target his lighter-weight 'Mechs.

"Fall back," Tamas ordered, returning fire with a second laser blast and a round of clustering ammunition from the *Enforcer*'s LB-X variant autocannon. Then he opened a channel to Light Horse central.

"Relay to Colonel Rubinsky," he ordered without identifying himself, "Ceres Metals has fallen to the Hussars. Light Horse unit actively engaging enemy. Repeat, actively. Responsible for one confirmed—"

He broke off as a lucky PPC shot from a Light Horse *Vindicator* burned into the head of a Hussar *Tempest,* completely gutting the cockpit and providing the MechWarrior within with a ready-made crematorium. "Make that *two* confirmed kills." He triggered off another salvo of his own, walking his heat scale up toward the yellow band. "Expect number to climb."

Cassandra would be proud, Tamas thought. It was his only measure of consolation, knowing that his father would be very displeased to learn that his Light Horse would now be considered active opposition to the Star League occupation force.

Light Horse central apparently had similar thoughts. "Will be very angry, your father. Is there nothing else you would like me to pass along?"

Tamas smiled, though not pleasantly. "Tell him it was all fun and games, until someone lost an eye."

Hunan, St. Loris
St. Ives Compact

Shifting restlessly in the chair she had pulled over next to a window in her hotel suite, Cassandra finished the final page of the Indicass report as the sun slid over St. Loris' horizon. Half of the priority transmission, handed to her by a ComStar messenger half an hour ago, detailed events of the battle around Ceres Metals and the part played by Rubinsky's Light Horse. The way she read the report, Tamas' Company kept the battle from turning into a total rout, allowing two-thirds of the Cheveux Legers to withdraw in good order. *Good for you, Tamas.*

She stood, carrying the various reports with her as she first moved to a wall switch to turn on lights and then began pacing the large room. The Endeavor Hotel had put her up in their best suite, with plush furniture, cream-colored walls, and deep-pile carpet that muffled her steps. She trod harder, feeling more the caged tigress than the honored guest. *And if I am feeling the strain of being stationed so far off the border, it is no wonder the Cossacks are climbing the walls.*

The Cossacks' First Regiment had welcomed her with a comradeship similar to Rubinsky's Light Horse. A bit wilder perhaps, a bit rougher around the edges, but still the same warm acceptance. And, Cassandra had been able to do what they were denied with their transfer back to St. Loris, taking a piece out of Sun-Tzu's forces, even if a proxy unit. The reception might have buoyed Cassandra's spirits much higher if she did not suspect that her mother had sent her here to learn from the Cossacks what *not* to do.

But I was right. Peaceful occupation force indeed! My cousin intended for them to be an assaulting force all along. We just allowed them to entrench. So my actions and methods were correct, just my timing was considered politically incorrect.

Cassandra realized that her actions had certainly helped her cousin escalate events faster, but could anyone really have prevented the return of the Confederation? Candace herself had implied that once Sun-Tzu made up his mind, nothing would keep him away. *So, if fighting is an inescapable conclusion, isn't it better to strike first?* Well, Tamas Rubinsky's actions on Indicass seemed to somewhat validate her earlier conduct.

Cassandra struck the thin sheaf of reports against the flat of her hand. *And at least my mother continues to send reports, so I can keep up on events. But what further purpose can I serve here?* She frowned at the flimsy sheets, then tossed them onto a nearby table. *I should be on the border.* But instead it was Kuan Yin with free rein to travel the border with her humanitarian relief efforts.

But it was more than news of the fighting on Indicass and of her twin sister's travels that bothered her. She stared back at the pile of papers she had tossed down, willing them to ignite. In the stack were also the reports of welcoming receptions for Capellan troops. Galling, though again her mother had warned her of the prospect. Apparently Sun-Tzu's Xin Sheng efforts had touched the hearts of many St. Ives citizens. Even some military units were now under suspicion of harboring pro-Confederation sentiments, and that Cassandra simply did not want to believe.

Our people share too much history, too much culture. That's what mother said. Is this what she feared? Cassandra shook her head. She couldn't really see her mother fearing anything. *Capellan propaganda, that's all.* Or, at least, most of it. She flung herself into the chair again and stared out into the darkening twilight. *We will fight!* That had been her answer to her mother. *And we will. I will!* Cassandra knew what she was doing on Indicass, and she knew what needed doing now. The St. Ives Compact would prevail.

But this time, the doubts were already in place.

22

Shì-Zhong-Xin Park
Pinedale, Denbar
St. Ives Compact
7 February 3061

Zhong-shao Ni Tehn Dho waded his *Victor* across the shallow reflecting pool of Pinedale's central park, each step splashing up the water and stirring the thin layer of mud off the bottom. He could feel the thinly poured ferrocrete crack and give under his BattleMech's massive eighty tons. Autocannon fire whipped the water into a froth all around the 'Mech. Errant PPC and laser hits steamed away large quantities, the resulting mist adding a reflective shimmer to the air over the pool. It was as if in passing, the *Victor* plunged a normally tranquil scene into chaos.

The BattleMech left pieces of itself behind as well, in melted splashes and shattered fragments of armor. Dho fought for control as a well-placed salvo of long-ranged missiles chewed into the *Victor*'s upper chest and head. *We wished them to stand and fight. Now we must survive our wish.*

As near as the battalion commander could tell, the enemy consisted of two mercenary 'Mech companies, a few battered militia BattleMechs that belonged in a museum, and a full armor battalion. Some still fought along the streets and alleys of Pinedale, defending their final refuge, but most concentrated here in the park. Of his own people, Dho could only account for his command lance, most of Second Company, and the Arcade Rangers lance from Third Company. The rest were scattered to the winds.

Or at least among seventy-eight square miles of cityscape. What the garrison forces failed to accomplish at the staging grounds, trying to divide us up, they managed here quite well.

Dho watched as two SRM carrier vehicles paired up and launched deadly flights of sixty short-ranged missiles each at *Sao-shao* Evans' newly repaired *Jenner*. Better than half found their mark, stripping the *Jenner* of nearly every last kilogram of armor and gouging deep into its internal structure in half a dozen places. Evans punched out, his cockpit canopy blowing away on special charges as his command couch rose on ejection thrusters. A split second later the *Jenner*'s fusion engine erupted in a fireball, consuming the light 'Mech.

Zhong-shao Dho noticed that no Hustaing Warriors would close with the carriers, not after that demonstration of raw destructive power. *Can't say I blame them. Few 'Mechs can take that kind of abuse.* He gained the side of the pool, stepping from the water and tearing up beautifully kept grounds as he sighted in on the nearer SRM carrier. The slow-moving vehicles relied on their implied threat of heavy missile bombardment to force 'Mechs to keep a distance. But Gauss rifles were the BattleMech answer to such close-range death.

Dho squeezed his right trigger, and the *Victor*'s right-arm Gauss rifle pulled power from its charging capacitors to accelerate a nickel-ferrous slug down the rifle barrel. It streaked across the once-beautiful park with a silvery flash to slam into the side of a carrier, bursting armor plates and then smashing through into the crew compartment. Dho could only imagine the devastation caused by so much metal flying around at high velocity in cramped quarters. *Not a nice way to go, but then what is?* Ruthlessness and single-minded devotion in pursuing the Chancellor's will, he reminded himself, were two of the keys to victory.

Or at least, he amended, they were keys to a politically correct attempt. Defensible in the investigations that always followed any defeat—which were much too common in the old days—and always comforting for the warrior whose duty it was to spill so much blood. Even after a decade of retirement, these principles still held true for him. And though it might be Capellan blood on both sides now, it *did* feel good to see them applied in Confederation victories. *Another of which we would like to arrange here.*

He opened communications. "Hustaing Warriors, this is *Zhong-shao* Dho. Converge on Central Park." Not that he expected much in the way of response after three calls and no help. His people suffered blocked communications by buildings and radio jamming, were dead or disabled, were simply too involved in their own fighting to assist, or could not find the park.

There was one thing he could do for them, though. "For those of you without a map, Central Park is the wide open area in the center of the city."

Backing the *Victor* into a small stand of elm, snapping branches and knocking whole trees over, Dho twisted the upper half of his assault machine far enough to answer a threat from a nearby mercenary *Rifleman*. At least three vehicles were chipping away at his armor too, but those he could afford to ignore, for a little while at least. *It helps being the biggest boy on the battlefield.*

"Ranger Two, score another fifteen points."

"Yeah, but you're still behind by twenty."

The *Victor*'s Gauss rifle spat out another missile of silver death. This one smashed into the *Rifleman*'s right leg, lodging in the hip joint and freezing up the entire limb. As the *Rifleman* fell, Dho searched his viewscreen and monitors for the source of the distracting comments, finding the Arcade Rangers holding the southeast corner of the park against all comers.

He opened a channel, intent on some kind of quick lecture, then shook his head. *They don't play well with others, or even each other half the time, but if I'm going to keep this unit alive I'd better not argue with success, no matter what form it comes in.* It rankled against his idea of proper Capellan dignity, but everything in its own time. "If you boys are going to play your games, do it on a private channel," was all he finally said.

His comm unit crackled to life again. Dho was ready this

time to chew some *hòu-miàn* should an Arcade Ranger even try to back-talk to him, when instead he heard, "Does that include us, *Zhong-shao* Dho?"

The voice was familiar, even robbed of so much of its personality by transmission. He tried to place it among his own warriors. *Strong, unassuming but confident—Aris Sung!* He searched his head's up display, locating the arrival of new 'Mechs at three different compass points. Aris Sung's *Wraith* he found near his own position, leading a full company into the park from a nearby street and already skirmishing with the Denbar defenders.

His Gauss capacitors recharged, Dho struck again at the *Rifleman,* which was having trouble getting up from the ground. This time he added his medium pulse lasers to the job, the emerald splashes of light cutting into the enemy machine's chest cavity and scrapping its gyro. "I don't suppose you saw any of my wayward Warriors out in the city, did you?" he asked as the *Rifleman* powered down in surrender.

The *Wraith* shredded the armor on a Hetzer armored vehicle, which immediately spun about to put distance between itself and Aris' pulse lasers. "We did," Aris informed him. "They did not respond to your transmissions because we've been enforcing a comm blackout of our approach."

With the Denbar forces falling back on all sides toward the park's center, Ni Tehn Dho found himself with no enemy at immediate hand. He turned, fired off a long-range Gauss shot toward a fleeing *Cicada,* missed. Aris' *Wraith* landed in the *Cicada*'s rear-left quarter, his pulse lasers striking with greater ease but without the hard, knock-down power of a Gauss slug.

Dho focused in on the *Wraith,* noticing the House Hiritsu crest and Confederation insignia. "You appear to be lacking Star League colors, Aris Sung."

"Everything in its time, *Zhong-shao*. House Master Non will address that concern soon."

The Hustaing Warrior commander, alone in his cockpit, still nodded his response. *In other words, the Chancellor and First Lord has prepared a new surprise for us.*

But as the fight wound down, once again some niggling doubts worked at Ni Tehn Dho's resolve as he glanced around at the park's shattered tranquillity. Playground equipment trampled. Trees set afire by laser hits. Ground chewed up and scorched in several places.

Dho reached up and tugged at the wisps of beard sticking out from under the lip of his neurohelmet. *Ruthlessness and single-minded devotion. Never forget that this is what you wanted to return to, old man. Of course, you could hardly turn down the Chancellor's call to arms, even if retirement had suited you, but perhaps you had better start being very careful what you wish for.*

Once the fighting ended, Aris Sung surveyed the same scene as *Zhong-shao* Dho. He could see where the park might have once been a beautiful place for picnicking and family outings, for relaxation and repose. Now it looked like almost any other battlefield he had ever fought on; blasted and wrecked. The reflecting pool still had an air of tranquillity, but only because water couldn't be as easily destroyed as grass and turf.

And nearby buildings.

All around the park's borders, apartment buildings and some few commercial ones displayed signs of collateral damage. Windows blown out. Walls chewed apart or caved in. Fires. *The people of Denbar are paying a high price for Duchess Liao's order of peaceful noncompliance.*

Aris continued to walk his *Wraith* around the perimeter. From his position, he could easily make out House Master Non's new *Yu Huang* assault 'Mech, towering above even other BattleMechs at nearly thirteen meters. The House Master supervised the securing of all opposing vehicles and Battle-Mechs at the park's center. *Enemy,* Aris tried to convince himself, *enemy* vehicles and BattleMechs.

It was a hard sell. Machines with the Home Guard insignia, common to both St. Ives Compact and the Confederation, fallen under the weapons of Confederation forces. A group of prisoners, under Hiritsu infantry escort—many with the telltale signs of Asian ancestry and all in uniforms of a familiar cut and color. Too much familiarity to make it easy.

"We have been holding just outside the moon's orbit," Ty Wu Non said, continuing to brief *Zhong-shao* Dho over a secure channel. Aris, as company leader, was privy to the conversation. "Once Aris Sung reported that you had secured the maintenance facilities, and that he expected a major battle to take place soon because of it, we dropped into the foothills east of Pinedale to await developments. It was the best way to put down the resistance on Denbar."

"Can't say I like being used as bait, House Master Non. But it did give my Warriors a chance to shake out a lot of their kinks."

Aris walked his *Wraith* past a junked *Rifleman* and what he thought *might* be the remains of a *Jenner*. *You still have a ways to go,* Zhong-shao. *Your people all need to go back into a training cycle. Say for about a year.* He throttled back to avoid a small group of observers. People were beginning to filter carefully into the park, looking to see if the excitement was over and who had won. Aris turned more inward, wanting to avoid them.

Ty Wu Non's voice sounded almost amused at Dho's attitude. "You will be getting more warriors, to shake the kinks out of, as you put it. The Chancellor wishes to convey his continued support for the Hustaing Warriors." His voice grew slightly more serious. "Except for what House Hiritsu requires in the way of immediate salvage—and we will need little—the machines and BattleMechs are yours to begin filling up another battalion."

Ni Tehn Dho's voice grew concerned. "I hope you do not plan to announce that until your infantry have cleaned out every last cockpit." A pause. "That kind of information could turn any MechWarrior or tank driver suicidal."

Aris toggled off that channel, no longer interested in listening. The talk bothered him. The small knots of people edging into the park bothered him. The fire trucks, ambulances, and other emergency vehicles circling the ruined buildings bothered him. But these were factors, not problems. As *janshi,* a warrior, Aris helped to cause situations where such talk and circumstances occurred. *But I no longer fully understand why!*

And that was a problem.

* * *

Under the cover of House Hiritsu BattleMechs, Li Wynn and the rest of the House infantry moved from vehicle to vehicle and 'Mech to 'Mech to place under arrest every enemy who had resisted the Star League occupation forces. Li prodded his current captive with the business end of his assault rifle, urging him along toward the holding area, which was really just a roped-off square under guard by two BattleMechs and a dozen infantrymen. The roped-off area was also near a flagpole, which usually flew the St. Ives standard of the ivory horse's head. Right now the lines hung empty, clanging against the metal pole in the light breeze, which made Li feel good.

"Sooner or later someone is going to hand you Warrior Houses your heads," Li's captive, a Home Guard tank driver with light Asian features, called back over his shoulder. "I just hope I'm there to see it." He shook his head. "Sooner or later," he repeated.

Li prodded him again, none too gently, then brought his rifle to port arms and slammed the stock hard into the tank driver's back, shoving him forward toward the ropes. The St. Ives soldier stumbled and recovered and then spun on Li Wynn, who stood ready with rifle aimed unerringly at the man's chest. Li's finger tightened on the trigger as he read the hatred in the other man's dark Asian eyes. "Better figure it being later, *sick* trash."

The soldier thought better of trying anything, turned slowly and ducked under the restraining ropes. Li grinned at his back.

"You will give me your attention!" The announcement blared out from external speakers mounted to House Master Non's *Yu Huang*.

Li glanced that way, but then returned his attention to the men under guard. *This is for you, not me.* He smiled thinly as he saw a small troop of infantrymen walk over to the flagpole.

"For Denbar's initial assault against the Capellan world of Hustaing, and since military and civilian forces present obviously do not respect the authority of the Star League occupation forces, House Hiritsu now claims Denbar in the name of the Capellan Confederation. This world will be held in such a state indefinitely. From now on, any resistance will be dealt with under the *Capellan* forms of martial law."

Angry shouts of protest and a mass movement on behalf of the prisoners to surge past the roped area were quickly put down by several infantrymen firing into the air in warning. Li kept his rifle leveled, his eyes staring unblinking into those of nearby prisoners. *My first shot will be for effect.* He let his thoughts show on his face, and they backed off.

"The Capellan Confederation flag *will* be raised all over the planet in every city," Ty Wu Non continued. "The St. Ives flag may be flown at half-mast. Violation of this order will be an indication of rebellion. Return to your homes and make it clear to your families and any comrades still in arms that the Capellan Confederation has returned to Denbar, and will no longer tolerate St. Ives-sanctioned resistance. Vehicles will be impounded and reassigned to Capellan units or a loyal Home Guard force. That is all."

The *Yu Huang* turned and walked away slowly, its footfalls sending light tremors through the ground. The ropes fell away and an infantry company leader indicated by which way the prisoners would be allowed to leave. Only a few thought to check the flagpole, but their outbursts soon had everyone looking. Li Wynn allowed himself a second's distraction to glance that way himself.

The Confederation flag had been raised during House Master Non's speech. Not the flag of old, however—subtle changes had been wrought. The katana sword had been replaced with a sword of more obvious Chinese descent—a type of *darndao*—and the arm thrusting from the triangle border was more slender than before, suggesting a strong Asian heredity. It signified that the final stages of Xin Sheng had begun, Li Wynn thought with pride. But of even stronger importance than the changes was a simple fact that not one person on the field could ignore.

For the first time in over thirty years, the flag of the Capellan Confederation flew over a St. Ives Compact world.

23

Celestial Palace
Zi-jin Cheng (Forbidden City), Sian
Sian Commonality, Capellan Confederation
20 February 3061

Silence reigned in Sun-Tzu Liao's palatial office, the quiet undermined only by the low hum of the corner aquarium and the occasional heavy whisper of pages being turned. While his *sang jiang-jun* continued to scan through the top-secret papers, Sun-Tzu sat forward in his chair, elbows on his desk and fingers interlaced. He studied the three outside fingers of each hand, inspecting the razor-sharp edges of the fingernails he had grown out in the same affectation his father had once adopted. Incense burned in a censer—cherry today. A rare smile played at the edges of the First Lord's lips as he glanced at Talon Zahn, who was sitting in the office's only other chair, raptly studying the pages of a hardcopy report.

Zahn finished up the final page of the document and then straightened the thin pile. He rested the papers in his lap and rubbed at his jaw, dark eyes shining with a new intensity. "I have suspected off and on for the last year that our goal was the total reclamation of the St. Ives Compact. The military maneuvers. Your Xin Sheng tour of the border. Misleading troop reports that were sure to leak to Candace." He shrugged. "But always the art of misdirection, using the occupation force and overt political maneuverings." His eyes narrowed slightly. "If you had informed me before now, I might have been even better prepared."

Or you might have made a mistake. "Do you know how many people can keep a secret, Talon?" Sun-Tzu waved off any reply his senior general was about to make. "One," he stated emphatically. "To include anyone else requires discussing it, which means the potential exists for a leak. And almost certainly the secret will be referred to again, in who can tell how many offhand manners that would eventually suggest the nature of the secret to others."

Nodding his understanding, Zahn glanced back down at the secret document. "May I ask how long this has been in the making?"

"Since the Star League Conference of 3058. Since a conversation with Katrina Steiner-Davion." Sun-Tzu smiled in recollection. "I have slowly built up what would be needed. The papers in your lap, compiled by myself and kept in my private vault, are the only copy of my notes and pertinent briefings and reports. The only existing hints of the existence of Operation Tian-é-róng Shou-tào. It was at our meeting of March last year that I decided to proceed."

"Operation Velvet Glove," Zahn translated, voice far-off, speculative. "Concealment behind a mildness of approach. But 3058?" He shook his head. "Surely the Maskirovka has some clue."

"The Mask provided me with information as I requested it, but always for a supposed purpose that was tangential to my real reasons." Sun-Tzu gestured to the pile of papers with an offhand gesture. "You will find several reports in there that you yourself wrote over two years ago."

Talon Zahn stared out the balcony doors a moment, collecting his thoughts. Finally, after another glance at the document he had finally been allowed to read, he shifted his gaze back to the Chancellor. "But the Blackwind Lancers. How could you be so sure they would jump the border?"

"Ah, well that part is not in the report, *Sang Jiang-jun* Zahn." Sun-Tzu leaned back in his chair, steepling his fingers before him and smiling. "But since you will be involved with that area momentarily," he said, "I cheated."

Zahn blinked. "You cheated?"

"I had every intention of baiting the Cossacks off Indicass." Sun-Tzu's eyes glittered dangerously. *And I would have succeeded, if my aunt had not taken certain precautions.* "But I was forced to rely on one of my back-up plans. A deep cover agent, who was activated by certain phrases in my Relevow speech. My Gei-Fu speech gave the agent direction, so I knew to leave before Hustaing."

He leaned forward just far enough to press a button hidden under the lip of his desk. A door to a connecting office opened, and an athletically built woman entered, dressed in regular Capellan uniform. "Talon Zahn, may I present *Zhong-shao* Daqing, lately Major Smithson of the Blackwind Lancers Third Battalion."

Talon Zahn appeared utterly at a loss for words. Finally he found his voice. "We've met, Chancellor. I interviewed the major—sorry, the *zhong-shao*—when she was first brought to Sian. A most convincing performance."

"*Shí-fen gan-xiè, Sang Jiang-jun* Zahn," she said, thanking him in flawless Chinese. At a nod from Sun-Tzu, she retired back into the other office.

"Her initial mission was to gain my aunt's attention with her anti-Confederation stance. Unfortunately, that never happened." *Thanks to an overprotective Lancers colonel.* Sun-Tzu drummed his fingers slowly against the arm of the chair. "I'm telling you this because I'm giving her to you."

"Chancellor?" Zahn asked, more curious than confused. "Giving her to me?"

Sun-Tzu nodded. "Sasha does not believe the *zhong-shao* can be used again as a field agent without a complete makeover. I want you to figure out how to insert her back with her old unit instead. Or, if you can find another way to use the Smithson identity, you may do so at your own discretion."

"This is quite a briefing, Chancellor." Zahn tapped the sheaf of papers on his lap. "Do you intend to bring all this out into the open among your advisory staff?"

"Not just yet. Sasha knows only what she has to with regard to *Zhong-shao* Daqing. And of course the Maskirovka are heading propaganda efforts on the St. Ives border worlds. Ion

Rush, once he is out of physical therapy, will know as much as he needs to in order to command the Warrior Houses effectively. How much that is, I leave to your discretion."

Sun-Tzu fixed Zahn with a hard stare. "You, as my Strategic Coordinator, will know it all. 'He whose generals are able and not interfered with by the sovereign will be victorious,' " he said, citing a line from the *Art of War.* "The time has come for you to take over matters of warfare, while I apply myself to diplomatic endeavors. My question to you is, can you do it?"

"You have my promise, Celestial Wisdom," Zahn answered at once and with conviction, his respect for the plan expressed by the formal address. "The Compact will be yours."

"Even with the draining efforts in the Chaos March?"

Zahn knew a moment of hesitation, then nodded. "Even so," he promised. "Most of the Disputed Worlds are under control, except for a few isolated cases. The Chaos March forces will suffer if I cannot support them completely, but the retaking of the St. Ives Compact is obviously of greater importance."

Sun-Tzu nodded, his face growing very serious. "And what of Wei?" he asked, referring to the troublesome Disputed Territory world. "Lord Marcus Baxter is screaming for blood, and I will need him in St. Ives."

Zahn's own features became grim. "I cannot blame him for his anger. A full Cavalry battalion, lost without so much as a shot fired." He shook his head at the thought. "But we never counted on the planetary defenders uncovering an old cache of nerve agent. A terrible way to go. We will lose good men there."

"Isolate the world if you have to," Sun-Tzu ordered. He had seen the holopics of the deaths. *No Capellan should have to die in such a way.* Then he thought better of that. *No true Capellan, anyway.* "Send in mercenaries and regular units of questionable loyalty first. If they can isolate the problem, fine. If not, make sure you recover their equipment."

"I still do not like losing men in such a manner."

"No one *likes* losing people, *Sang Jiang-jun,*" Sun-Tzu said with a hard edge to his voice. "Remember, every person who dies on Wei or in the St. Ives Compact is also a Capellan." *A son or daughter of the state, even if misguided at the moment.*

Zahn bowed his head, accepting the rebuke. "Of course, Chancellor. I did not mean to imply otherwise."

Sun-Tzu drew in a deep breath, inhaling the cherry-scented incense and allowing the sensation to distract him briefly. *And with that calculated reminder, you will watch carefully the amount of force you bring to bear against the Compact. I want them beaten, not crushed.*

A light knock at the door interrupted further conversation. "Enter," Sun-Tzu commanded.

A Death Commando stepped into the office, his large muscle-heavy build blocking most of the doorway behind him. "Chancellor. The St. Ives Compact representative has begged admission to your presence. He waits in the throne room."

Sun-Tzu easily guessed what Candace's representative wanted to see him about. *Three days later than I had expected.* "Tell him that I cannot be bothered with formalities now, and then show him up here."

The Death Commando saluted and went to do as bid. Talon Zahn also made as if to rise, but Sun-Tzu waved him back into his seat. "No, Zahn, stay. You might find this amusing. Part of the diplomatic endeavors I mentioned earlier. But give me the briefing papers."

"As the Chancellor desires, of course," Zahn said, handing over the bundle of reports and briefs and then settling himself back in.

"Just too bad we have none of that Wei nerve agent," Sun-Tzu said thoughtfully, staring at the open door. "I could find some interesting uses for it right now."

The Death Commando escort made Representative Jonathan Xiam-hu nervous, to say the least. A calculated insult by the Chancellor, he was sure, on top of being forbidden the title and most privileges of a full ambassador. The Capellans had never relinquished their claim to the Compact, denying the sovereignty that every other Great House recognized and honored. That was why the Compact representative to Sian was not allowed permanent facilities on the Capellan capital world and had to put up with such indignities as a military escort at all times.

The near-impossibly muscled warrior led Xiam-hu down a tiled hall to a door that looked like any other, then half stood in the doorway to gesture inside. The representative paused, straightening his suit and fussing with his attaché case while waiting for the warrior to move. The man simply stood there, grinning. A flush warming his cheeks, Xiam-hu squeezed past, careful not to touch the Death Commando.

The office was simple, though tastefully decorated in a Capellan manner. The rosewood used in the shelving, the desk, and other trimming gleamed dark and rich. A few soft-brushed charcoal sketches decorated the walls, and cherry-scented incense lightly perfumed the air. Xiam-hu might have felt comfortable in the room if not for the two men seated before him.

Sun-Tzu was behind the desk, elbows resting on the desktop and idly tapping his fingertips together. On the wall behind him was a small banner of *hàn-yu* ideograms translated into the message *I go to war only when I am ready.* The Chancellor stared silently at Xiam-hu, his jade eyes distant as if looking right through him, giving away nothing of his thoughts or feelings. Sitting in the room's only other chair was Talon Zahn, his unblinking dark eyes just as unsettling.

Determined not to be intimidated, Xiam-hu stood just inside the doorway, hands clasped behind his back in a military manner while waiting to be offered a chair, or at least be officially recognized. He counted five times that his attaché case bumped into the back of his legs before Sun-Tzu finally spoke.

"You wished to see me, Mister Xiam-hu," Sun-Tzu said with impatience. "Do you plan on speaking at all?"

So much for official courtesy. Xiam-hu swallowed past the embarrassed lump in his throat and brought his attaché case forward. He opened it and withdrew a manila folder, which he placed on the Chancellor's desk.

"The folder contains the official transcript of Duchess Liao's call for a repeal," he said most formally, "as well as the verigraphed responses of each Star League member state. The results have been known for a month, four to two against, but the Duchess thought the official papers should be delivered to you, First Lord."

Sun-Tzu made no move to claim the folder. He looked at it with a bored expression, and when he spoke it was with an insulting sneer. "Is that all, Xiam-hu? Or did Candace send you with more whining?"

"No, that is not all," the representative said, dropping the geniality from his own voice but holding carefully to a neutral formality. *He* would not give Sun-Tzu any further excuse to claim difficulty with St. Ives. "*Duchess* Liao, of the St. Ives *Compact*," he said, stressing the titles, in case Sun-Tzu had forgotten that he dealt with an independent and recognized member state of the Star League, "officially protests the Confederation's action on Denbar and the arrival of additional forces on several border worlds. Forces that are flying Capellan colors, First Lord, not those of the Star League Defense Force."

Glancing over at his senior military officer, Sun-Tzu nodded for him to speak. "Obviously," Zahn said, as if lecturing a simple child, "that is because the new forces are sent in Sun-Tzu Liao's capacity as Chancellor of the Confederation, not First Lord of the Star League. One does not preclude the other." He spread his hands in a display of false helplessness. "And you can blame the Capellan occupation on the garrison forces of those worlds, Xiam-hu. They refused to accept Star League peaceful occupation, which means that I must classify those worlds as potentially hostile to our nation."

"No Confederation world will suffer as did Hustaing," Sun-Tzu said simply.

Xiam-hu started to speak, then closed his mouth and counted out five deep breaths as he marshaled his thoughts and his calm. *Careful,* he told himself. *He has to listen to reason. Doesn't he?* "The Blackwind Lancers battalion was disbanded, as per Duchess Liao's promise. She has empowered me to begin negotiations for reparations to the Confederation. But to expect the St. Ives Compact to completely demilitarize its border in the face of your provocation is too much to ask." The representative drew himself up proudly. "We will not submit so easily."

"I see," Sun-Tzu said quietly, his eyes half-lidded as he considered the other man's words. "You are leaving me with no choice."

"I'm glad you see reason, First Lord. Now if—"

"No choice at all," Sun-Tzu interrupted, still quietly but with a razor-sharp edge to his voice. "After all, Denbar does not have to be the only world *totally* pacified."

Representative Xiam-hu stammered a few half-articulated words, cursing his own stupidity for having fallen into so simple a verbal trap and barely able to believe Sun-Tzu Liao could be so blatantly callous about escalating the budding conflict. "You cannot do that," he said finally, his formal speech failing him. "Our people will not stand for it. The *Star League member states* will not stand for it."

Now Sun-Tzu reached forward to pull the manila envelope toward him, completely ignoring Xiam-hu's blustering assertions. Slowly he opened it, so that all three men could see the transcript of Candace's repeal sitting directly on top of the small stack of papers.

"Ah, but they have, Mister Xiam-hu. The member states already have." He tapped one long fingernail on the repeal. "Four to two, I believe, was the final vote."

24

Royal Compound
Tian-tan, St. Ives
St. Ives Compact
26 February 3061

Candace Liao sat at a table in the Royal Compound's southern-front sun room amid several broad-leafed plants, sipping a morning demitasse. She wore workout *ghi* in preparation for her tai chi practice. It was something her late husband had taught her years before and now served in her advancing years to keep her generally fit.

She set her cup on the white-painted wrought iron table, then gestured her AFFC liaison to a chair opposite her. General Simone Devon sat with a weary slump, a fact Candace noted and that did not bode well for their talk. *The general does not carry good news, but then I haven't expected good news for some weeks now.*

"Speak your mind, Simone." Candace smoothed her hair back on the left side. "Since you arrived without Caroline Seng, should I assume that she will not be joining us?"

The general nodded. "She sends her regrets, Duchess, and a message that she will be up to talk with you later. Some new reports were coming in on Nashuar and Indicass, and she thought she had better see to them at once."

"And the news is?" Candace trailed off, encouraging a response.

Simone Devon pushed impatiently at her own dark hair, unruly from a long, sleepless night spent reviewing troop dispositions. "Not good, I'm afraid. Indicass is a mess. The Cheveux Legers are under-strength. Rubinsky's Light Horse does what it can to prevent a quick Confederation victory, but without the Cossacks' heavier First Regiment they can't really hope to dominate the world either. Nashuar . . ."

Simone shook her head lightly. "Nashuar is a disaster waiting to happen. With the Seventh Federated Commonwealth Regimental Combat Team on-planet to support your Home Guard, the occupation force cannot hope to force a disarmament. Sun-Tzu will send in more troops, and soon. And the fact that the current occupation force is Lyran leaves me uneasy."

Candace frowned, then lifted her cup to take another small sip of the sweet beverage. "I had hoped that those units would settle down now that Katrina has assumed the New Avalon throne." *Then again, I had not thought she would support Sun-Tzu so easily. Unless, of course, Katrina hopes to tie up Sun-Tzu by keeping him occupied here. Not a very settling thought.*

"The Fifth Lyran Regulars are very pro-Steiner," Devon said. "They resisted the initial merger of the two states and I would not expect them to ever get along with a decidedly Fed-Com unit like the Seventh RCT." She exhaled sharply. "There have already been skirmishes."

"I understand the position you're in, Simone, if FedCom and Lyran troops come to blows." Candace pursed her lips in thought, setting her cup down on its saucer with a clink of china. "It's the kind of incident that ruins careers. You would like me to re-consider my decision to resist the occupation?"

Simone Devon sat up straighter, suddenly showing a force of character that belied her small frame. "Duchess, my personal situation does not matter. Prince Victor placed me under your authority, and the Archon Princess Katrina has not given me any countermanding orders, yet." She relaxed slightly. "But I do see a problem that Nashuar represents all too well." The general placed both hands flat on the table. "If you continue to resist the SLDF occupation, what happened on Denbar is sure to repeat itself and the situation will spiral out of control."

"We are already there, General." Candace looked up through the glass ceiling and into St. Ives' sapphire blue sky, taking the time to organize her thoughts. *Such a beautiful day for so dreadful a conversation.* "When my nephew's forces claimed Denbar, he stepped past the point of no return. To return the world to the Compact would be a loss of prestige that he cannot afford. It could shatter his renewed Capellan efforts, and that he will not chance. His rude treatment of my ambassador supports that."

Candace looked back at Devon, feeling a firm inner resolve. "And neither will I surrender worlds. I know Caroline Seng advocates that I renounce the Compact's claim to Denbar and any other world in the place of Indicass. And the Star League might even threaten to censure Sun-Tzu then, forcing him to accept the deal. But he'd be back, and the reclamation of two Compact worlds would give him a stronger base next time for a call of Capellan unity."

"Then we need to buy time," Devon said. "Sun-Tzu will find ways to force or manufacture incidents. What we have to do is delay things until the Star League finally takes notice and agrees to do something."

The Duchess finished her sweetened coffee, then pushed the cup and saucer aside. "I have been in contact with my representatives on Outreach," she said. "Several mercenary units are already en route, including Group W, which I've managed to sublet from Katrina. Plus I've been approached by The Arcadians and Burr's Black Cobras."

Simone Devon's eyes glazed over a moment, which Candace knew to be the general's photographic memory in operation. "Good units, the three of them. Group W is a tough outfit. They'd be a big help. And I know the Cobras are still spoiling for a fight and the chance to redeem themselves for their 3057 disaster."

"I'll also pass along the order to step up our resistance efforts," Candace said. *Sun-Tzu will have his incidents no matter what. Might as well take advantage when we can.* "Fighting should be avoided whenever possible, but tactical raids against supplies can be authorized."

"And if I may suggest, Duchess, you might want to release Cassandra from St. Loris."

Candace's eyes narrowed. "By all reports I am receiving she

is still too eager." She held up one hand, to forestall any comment from Simone Devon. "Her actions on Indicass precipitated nothing that would not have happened anyway, I know. But the choices were still wrong and she has yet to fully understand that."

"True," Simone agreed. "But I've known Cassandra for several years now, Duchess. I've talked with her. She has high standards to live up to." The general sighed. "We all have made mistakes in the field, Candace." Her use of informal address was rare but allowable when it came to personal matters. "But that is where we learn. Cassandra will figure it out, and in the meantime we need her."

Candace allowed no personal feelings to show. "I'm listening, Simone. What is your idea?"

"Release her for this tactical raiding you spoke of. Send her to Milos or Vestallas. It would be good for the people of the Compact to see her on the border, fighting in the St. Ives Lancers, just as it helps when Kuan Yin delivers humanitarian aid, as she did on Denbar."

The Duchess could not help a smile of fondness showing through her stern composure. "Yes, one week before Capellan relief arrived. That must have upset my nephew, again."

Simone nodded, but also pressed forward in her cause. "Cassandra's role is no less vital, Candace. Your people could use a Liao hero to root for. Kuan Yin, for all her important work, does not inspire as would a military figure. Young Quintus is nearly forgotten, and well that he is."

Mention of her youngest child gave Candace a twinge, bringing his prolonged absence to mind. But she agreed that it was best that Quintus remained cloaked in the anonymity he had built around himself. *And also good that we still have eyes and ears focused on Katrina. May he continue to be overlooked.*

General Devon leaned forward, elbows resting on the table's edge as she continued with her case. "Kai, of course, would be perfect. But he is not here." She sighed. "And let's face it, your and my days in a 'Mech are over."

"Speak for yourself, General," Candace said, drawing herself up with over-exaggerated pride. But she did give serious thought to Simone's advice. *Have I been too critical of Cassandra? Kai limited himself for so long, until he gained confidence, and in doing so never made too grievous an error. It is not fair to judge her by Kai's successes. And Simone is right in suggesting that I have made graver mistakes than the one Cassandra made on Indicass.* "All right, Simone. I'll send the order."

Devon smiled her support. "Cassandra won't let you down, Duchess."

"Let's just make sure that I do not let *her* down." Candace grew serious once again. "We need some solid plans for keeping Sun-Tzu tied up on the border. Anything," she said, "to keep him from advancing against more worlds."

Hazlet, Nashuar
St. Ives Compact

Working on his tank in Hazlet's main vehicle maintenance facility, Maurice Fitzgerald glanced up from his work and saw Danielle Singh crossing the large bay. *Looking for someone else,* he told himself, though he kept one eye on her progress while continuing to work with a technician on the J. Edgar's turret assembly. She angled his way, obviously searching for someone, and was close enough for Fitz to read the look of surprise when she finally recognized him. Dressed in overalls and up to his elbows in grease for the turret's rotation mechanisms, he doubted he looked the same warrior she'd trained with.

By contrast, her uniform was neat and pressed and displayed the new rank of sub-commander that had come with her advancement to lance leader in the Nashuar Home Guard 'Mech company. "Fitz," she said, stopping at the J. Edgar's front. "You're a mess."

He shrugged. "I'd like to see how you look after helping to replace some myomer bundles." He handed his tool belt over to the technician. *She didn't come here for idle talk. We're traveling.* "Let me get cleaned up."

"Still making predictions?" Danielle's voice was very controlled, but he still caught the hint of interest. "Well, you win your bet this time. Take five minutes."

It only took three. Still wearing the coveralls but with most of the grease cleaned off his hands and arms, he followed her back to the Home Guard training facility and into MechWarrior Hall. A pair of MechWarriors passed them in the corridor, their faces registering a certain amount of surprise to find a greased-up tank jock in their area, but Danielle's frosty glare kept them quiet. "I never really thanked you," she said, once the others were out of earshot. "Without your action, I would've come home with a lost man during the Salt River Canyon battle."

"Forget it," he said, shrugging slightly. "You don't thank soldiers for breaking orders, even if they get lucky."

"I'll remember you said that after your meeting with Nevarr."

Nevarr? Fitzgerald had already caught a stiff lecture from the Home Guard CO himself. Nevarr wanted to bring it up now, after over a month? "This isn't about the raid the Lyrans made, is it? My Prowlers weren't responsible for the northern patrol." And whoever had been would probably have been cashiered if not for the desperate need for all warriors right now. Fitz had heard about the casualties in that one—the Seventh RCT losing three 'Mechs, and the Home Guard company one of their own as well.

Danielle glanced at him sidelong. "Hmmm. I think the appropriate answers would be *sort of,* and *we know.* In that order." Then there was no more time for him to ask her any questions. They stopped in front of one of the doors lining the hall and they entered the office after a quick rap on the door by Danielle.

Nevarr looked as unruffled as ever in his black garb, half sitting against the edge of his desk and with arms folded over his chest. "Lance Sergeant Fitzgerald. Good to see you again."

"And you, sir," Fitz returned the politeness automatically, though remaining on his guard. He was sure Nevarr had not brought him here to inquire after his health.

"Relax, Fitz," Nevarr said. "I didn't drag you here to chew

you out. I want you back in the unit." Just like Nevarr, pulling no punches.

Danielle moved to a nearby chair and seated herself. "Lance Sergeant Mangh was critically injured in the Lyran assault," she said, "so there's a hole in the TO&E." She paused, then fixed him with an unreadable stare. "My lance."

Fitzgerald frowned in confusion, his dark eyebrows knitting together as he studied Danielle. "I disobeyed orders, and you are requesting me in your unit? No offense, Danielle, but that's one of the worst examples of positive reinforcement I've heard lately."

"She requested you," Nevarr said, "but I approved it." He leaned forward, hands on his thighs as he matched Fitz's gaze with an icy-blue stare. "Your insubordination comes from MechWarrior training. You are too used to the independence. But you responded to your lancemates. And more important, in my eyes, your people voluntarily followed you back into a hostile situation without hope of support. You've earned their trust, which means you've learned how to be a part of a team."

That is probably the longest speech I've ever heard Nevarr make. And along with the praise, here the commander is offering me what I've worked toward for so long. Worked toward, and failed. "I'm flattered, Danielle, Commander Nevarr. Really. Your opinion means a lot to me." He took a deep breath. "I decline."

Danielle recoiled in shock, but Nevarr merely blinked once, the only sign of surprise. "You no longer wish to be a Mech-Warrior?"

"More than anything." Fitzgerald clasped his hands behind his back, the hollowness that had opened up inside him when he'd spoken his refusal now fading as he recognized how much it was the right course of action. "That you think I am ready would have been enough for me, once." He shook his head. "No, that is not right. What you thought didn't matter to me, only what I thought. And I was wrong."

Fitz read a mixture of confusion and disappointment in Danielle's eyes. Nevarr, never an easy man to read, gave him a single nod of support for his decision. Accepting without judging.

Fitz turned for the door, then paused and turned before reaching out to open the knob.

"I will let you know," he said, "when I believe I am right."

25

Dansing Resort
Dansing, Nashuar
St. Ives Compact
13 March 3061

The snow-packed slopes of the Dansing ski resort were vacant of skiers and snowboarders. The abandoned lift chairs swung in the stiff breeze, and the parking lot mostly stood empty. All to the better, as a dozen 'Mechs bearing the crescent moon insignia of House Hiritsu played their own winter games against an equal number of the FedCom Seventh RCT on the white slopes. The Seventh had taken the resort as their garrison post a week before and with events on Nashuar heating up, the resort owners had shut down, the history of three centuries and four Succession Wars having taught them a simple fact.

The presence of garrison forces invite an assault.

Aris Sung brought his *Wraith* down within a stand of tall pine, the fifty-five-ton 'Mech finding slippery purchase, but the trees helping him avoid a fall. He twisted around to face the beginner's downhill run, targeting the gray- and black-painted *Stealth* that ended its own jump midway on the slope and not ninety meters distant. Belonging to the Seventh RCT, the *Stealth* gave Aris the first clear target he'd had since leaving Sarna almost a year ago. *No Capellan this. Just one more Davion warrior, of the same kind that stole so many worlds from the Confederation in the Fourth Succession War. We offered them the chance to stand down. They declined. We owe them nothing more than that.*

Of course, House Hiritsu had not expected combat quite so

soon, this being only their second day on Nashuar. The main Compact garrison force on-planet still held onto the capital city of Hazlet, located near the base of the mountains where Aris and the rest of his House currently fought. The Lyran force on planet had contacted them, however, requesting help clearing out several minor support bases that had been created to worry the Lyran rear. The resort was one of those.

Aris waited for a good target lock, riding out a light buffeting as two medium enemy lasers scored his armor over the left leg and torso, then he mashed down both triggers. Scarlet fire from the large pulse laser mounted on the *Wraith*'s right arm splashed over the *Stealth*'s left side, melting armor, which evaporated in a dull gray mist or runneled down into the snow to raise tiny streamers of steam. One of his medium pulse lasers cut along the outside of the FedCommer's left leg, while the second also chewed into the left side.

Combined with the heat wash from his jumping, the temperature in the *Wraith*'s cockpit soared as the fusion reactor bled waste heat. Outside, the snow melted away wherever the *Wraith* stepped, while inside Aris sucked in lungfuls of the scorched air, fighting for oxygen. He blinked burning sweat from his eyes, his vision clearing to find that his gamble had paid off. The *Stealth* was down, far too unbalanced after the loss of so much armor along its left side. It thrashed about in the snow as it tried to rise again, finally doing so and backing off to prevent Aris from jumping into its rear quarter.

Aris gave the other warrior credit for taking the only fair option in a lousy situation. He held to the woods, keeping to cover while the heat scale dropped to a more manageable level. The *Stealth* missed with its lasers, the emerald beams cutting into trees and bursting trunks as the water within the wood flashed instantly to steam and expanded. Aris, with pulse technology at his disposal that allowed him to better track in on an enemy, did not miss. His large pulse laser hammered its darts of damaging light into the other 'Mech. The right arm this time, with almost every ounce of its protective armor sloughing off under his attack.

The *Stealth* began a retreat and Aris gave a second's attention to his tactical screen, just long enough to determine that no one in his company required help. Then he ran his 'Mech out of the woods in pursuit of the *Stealth,* which angled further uphill and toward the more advanced runs. *You do not escape so easily.* Another trade of laser fire cost Aris roughly a half-ton of armor from his right arm, but in return he exacted double that, including the last of the protection that had been shielding the other BattleMech's left side.

The *Stealth* cut uphill, engaged jump jets, and rocketed sky-ward in an attempt to flee Aris' *Wraith.* Aris throttled up into a run, not wishing to spike his heat levels again and knowing the other BattleMech could not hope to gain much on him in the way of distance. The enemy machine fired as it came down, lasers and a full spread of short-ranged missiles this time. One missile exploited a faulty seam in the *Wraith*'s torso area, the explosion cracking the gyro casing and throwing that piece of critical equipment out of alignment.

Wrestling his controls, Aris fought to keep the *Wraith* up-right, but then was forced to abandon himself to gravity. He sprawled forward, right shoulder digging down through snow and frozen ground and costing him more armor. He rode out the jostling, then propped himself up on his right arm. *That was your one chance,* he silently told his opponent. He cut loose with his medium pulse lasers, both of them tracking in on the *Stealth*'s damaged left leg to slice through armor and myomer bundles and cut into the BattleMech's internal structure.

The *Stealth* dropped again, this time over a small ledge de-signed as a ski jump. The 'Mech gouged down through snow and earth, partially crushing in its left side, and then continued a slide down toward the base of the hill. A fireball blossomed in its chest, throwing out streamers of smoke and a few balls of fire that exploded within seconds, kicking the *Stealth* up from the ground and then adding to its momentum as it continued a downward slide.

Ammunition bin! Aris did not know a great deal about the *Stealth*'s design, but he recognized the result well enough as missiles detonated in sympathetic explosions to create one huge destructive force. Then the fire tore back out through the left arm and into the center torso, cartwheeling the shattered BattleMech as it melted away engine shielding and joined with the raw fire of the fusion engine. *It doesn't have cellular ammo storage?* Aris couldn't believe such a new design lacked the saving construction procedure of CASE. The *Stealth* disintegrated right before his eyes, leaving large pieces of itself all over the slope.

Punch out, Aris thought, bringing his *Wraith* back to its feet. Though he knew that there would be no ejecting from such catastrophic destruction. The fall, the explosion, and the hard jostling of the continued slide would likely knock the opposing MechWarrior unconscious. And with the cartwheel roll of its slide, any ejection would likely send the pilot plowing directly into the ground anyway. Aris' white-knuckle grip on his control sticks left an ache in his finger joints as he watched the final few seconds of the *Stealth*'s disintegration. "Scrap one *Stealth,*" he said over his company's combat channel, though the elation he would normally have felt was missing.

"So I noticed," came Raven Clearwater's husky voice in his ear. "If the judges' stand was filled, I'd be reading nine point nines down here."

Aris tried to smile at her humor, but the grin seemed to freeze on his face. It should have been a glorious battle, with a triumphant ending. But, watching the violent death of his opponent, it felt hollow. He blamed the FedCom warrior for robbing him of a clean victory, then pushed the thought from his mind.

You had your chance to deal with a peaceful occupation. You were given a second chance to stand down. We owe you nothing.

And if Aris could keep that idea foremost in his mind, perhaps the Nashuar assignment would not plague him in the way Denbar and even Hustaing had. *I am a warrior in service to the Confederation. This is my task.* He turned his *Wraith* downhill, and rejoined the battle.

Yuling Territory, Denbar
Xin Sheng Commonality, Capellan Confederation

Standing on a small hill that overlooked Denbar's Toutle River Valley, Warner Doles raised his binoculars to his eyes and surveyed the scene below. Two vehicles lay smoking at the river's edge, a Manticore and a very old Ontos, both bearing the insignia of the Hustaing Warriors. They were no more than scrap now, but at least his men had pulled one scout 'Mech into their trap, and that one they could rebuild. It was a minor annoyance that it was a Blackwind Lancers BattleMech, but better that it was back in their hands now.

"Major Doles," a voice interrupted his observation. Doles glanced back to find one of his company commanders, also Dispossessed, waiting for him, radio in hand. "We have a report from the valley. The *Raven* is salvageable, but will need new lasers, which we do not have. The MechWarrior and four members of the vehicle crews are alive and in custody."

The battalion *is effectively dead, but still they hold to our old ways.* Doles had tried to shrug off the field promotion his people had thrust on him, but in the end had accepted it as one more means of holding them together. He had led his Blackwind Lancers into the hills south of Pinedale soon after the various occupations began, realizing that Denbar would be on the list and that his people would again be confined as potential troublemakers. *And right now, that is all we are. But hopefully not for long.*

"Thank you, commander. We'll get lasers soon enough, but I'll take that *Raven* for her recon capabilities, if nothing else." It was a start. With the three militia 'Mechs Doles' warriors were able to bring in, they could field a lance now. He knew they needed to start concentrating on more support personnel and supplies. Then maybe they could start hitting back.

Specters of their past defeat, though, whispered up from the depths of his mind, reminding him of what haste had bought them previously. That would not happen again. *We will take our time, and rebuild. We owe that to the Duchess and to the Compact.*

"No mistakes," he said, raising the field glasses to his eyes once more. "Get those vehicles rendered down for any last useful piece of armor or equipment, and then we move further south. We're going to be getting some attention when that patrol turns up missing."

"Yes, sir," the commander said, then pulled back far enough to use the radio without disturbing his commanding officer.

Surveying the scene below again, Doles found his warriors falling in to help the technicians now, wielding cutting torches and tools. Yes, it was a start. One lance could be turned into two, and two into a company. There were certainly more pockets of resistance out there, including some Denbar Home Guard who might take to the back country if it meant slipping the Confederation's leash and striking back. *And maybe, just maybe we can rebuild. If we are allowed the time.*

But right now, time was not on the Compact's side.

26

Hei-sè Foothills
Milos
St. Ives Compact
23 March 3061

A bright array of stars slashed across the clear midnight sky over Milos, providing plenty of light. Cassandra Allard-Liao stood on the ridge of a small hill, focusing a high-powered Starlight Scope on the horizon. She wore only a simple jump-suit over her MechWarrior gear, but it was more than the chill night air prickling the flesh of her arms and legs.

"Here they come," she said as the Starlight picked up distant motion. "Like we'd hoped."

Captain Julius Scavros, commanding officer of First Company, nodded. "They should pass right between these two hills. We'll be ready for them."

How the Third Canopian Fusiliers discovered so quickly the arrival of the Second St. Ives Lancers, Cassandra could only guess. *Better scanning equipment than we gave them credit for, an infantry patrol that we didn't see*—didn't matter. The increase in patrols over the area had allowed the Lancers to lay a trap. All three companies waited at different spots, and Cassandra had apparently picked the winning location. *Which adds my command lance to the ambush. Two-to-one odds—even without the benefit of surprise we should clear the field.* It bothered her, though, that she didn't believe they could keep the element of surprise. *No reason to expect them to be especially alert; except for a few local farmers whose lands we crossed through no one should know that we're here.* She rubbed at her arms as if trying to warm them. *So why am I suddenly nervous?*

"Let's button back up," Cassandra said, and the two officers began to half-walk half-slide down the backside of the rocky slope to where their 'Mechs waited. She searched for a source to her unease. "You sure we can keep them silent? I don't want reinforcements showing up before our DropShip. We need all the salvage we can lay our hands on."

"So long as we can contain them to within half a klick of Lieutenant Frakes' *Spector*. It's been modified to completely jam all frequencies but our own combat channels." Scavros broke away then, trotting to where his Mark Two *Gallowglas* stood thirty meters distant.

Cassandra scaled back up the chain-link ladder she'd rolled down from her cockpit, then pulled it in after her and locked down the *Cestus*' cockpit hatch. Her jumpsuit unzipped down both legs, allowing her to pull it off over her combat boots, and she quickly strapped herself into the command couch, with cooling vest plugged in and neurohelmet snug. All systems checked out, and she opened a secure channel to her command. "Everyone warm up and check your weapons. We'll have company in about two minutes." *And with just a bit of luck the hills will shield us until it's too late for the Canopian troops. Show them that an alliance with the Confederation has hidden costs.*

"We have company!" someone shouted over the channel. "Coming up from behind."

Cassandra's head's up display read the same thing. Three small circles that denoted vehicles, though her computer could not identify them. The coding kept changing, first suggesting that they were Savannah Masters and then APCs and then lightly armored cargo transports. Lights from one vehicle swept across the side of the hill behind which she hid, pinning the *Cestus*' shadow against it. Then a bullet spanged against the outside of her cockpit, confirming that the newcomers were hostile.

They were attacking with rifles? Irregular infantry? Something within told Cassandra that this new threat was what had been bothering her, even as she turned her *Cestus* to get a view of the vehicles. Another Lancer made it easy, firing a small laser at one that had apparently struck at him with small-arms fire. The ruby bolt sliced through the non-armored truck, which erupted in a fuel explosion that cast an orange glow over the other two vehicles. One was a pickup truck, two men with rifles in the bed firing wildly at the Lancers' BattleMechs. Another was a flatbed with a small tractor chained down to it. Which made sense now of her shifting tactical readout. The computers weren't programmed with civilian vehicles.

"Break off," she ordered. "Those are civilians!" And what they were doing out here, she really had no idea. *Except they just blew our ambush.* "Hit the Fusiliers! They know we're here now. Lieutenant Frakes, you'd better be jamming them." Firing her jump jets, Cassandra lifted the *Cestus* to the top of the hill, where it would have a commanding view of the other side. She came down among some fir trees, the massive weight of her BattleMech crushing them. The two lances of Fusiliers were breaking apart into defensive pairs. Older machines, almost every one.

Just like most of the Home Guard units the Confederation has been engaging. Well, now it's our turn. Hardly a fair fight, but then neither was the Confederation's forced occupation of the Compact.

Cassandra selected a *Whitworth*, close enough that she could target it by eye, and struck out with two large lasers and her Gauss rifle. The lasers flashed brightly in the darkness, cutting deeply into the armor along the *Whitworth*'s right arm and left side. Her Gauss slug smashed into the right side, shattering armor plates and crushing the LRM missile launcher mounted there, robbing it of half its long-ranged firepower. The *Whitworth* never had the chance to return fire, her savage attack throwing it roughly to the ground.

A wave of heat washed through her cockpit, though the *Cestus*' double-strength heat sinks quickly shunted it away. Normally, Cassandra would have pressed forward to finish off the *Whitworth*, which was even now trying to rise, but of greater importance was keeping every Canopian 'Mech within jamming range. While she searched for a new target, a newer *Marshal* design out of the Magistracy made the decision easy for her by striking at the *Cestus* with its own laser and a flight of five missiles. Cassandra's 'Mech shook under the fire but held easily to its feet.

She glanced to the wireframe damage schematic of the *Cestus*, noticing that her left leg had lost a fourth of its protection to the laser but that the missiles had done little more than pockmark her torso. She floated her targeting reticule over the *Marshal*'s silhouette, but had trouble getting a lock as it ran through a stand of trees. She squeezed off the shot anyway, adding in her medium lasers this time in an attempt to work with the law of averages.

The law came down on the *Marshal*'s side. The nickel-ferrous slug from her Gauss rifle shattered the bole of an old elm, and her two larger lasers burned through branches and brush to scorch earth. Only the twin mediums hit, each sloughing away barely a quarter-ton of armor from the *Marshal*'s left arm and center torso. *An embarrassing performance. Cassandra, you can do better!*

"*Commando,* two-nine-five degrees. It's heading for the curtain."

Blinking sweat from her eyes and lining up her next shot, Cassandra almost ignored the warning that a Canopian 'Mech was heading for the effective range on Frakes' jamming capability. Then she realized that the bearing placed the 'Mech behind them, where most units could no longer reach but she could, perched atop the hill. She drove her targeting reticule into the right border of her screen, torso-twisting her 'Mech in an effort to establish a line of sight against the fleeing *Commando*. Figuring a rough range from her HUD readings, and realizing that she would hardly be able to see it, she selected thermal imaging and committed herself to targeting by sensors only.

She caught up to the Canopus 'Mech just before it could flee her weapons, the center of its outline glowing red from the fusion engine output and then fading the spectrum to a cool blue at the ends of its arms and legs. She sent a single long-range

Gauss slug speeding after it. The slug took the *Commando* behind the left knee, smashing armor and snapping the foamed titanium bones of its leg at a point that would have been mid-femur on a human. *Not today, little 'Mech.* "Someone clean up that mess," she ordered, proud of the shot.

Then the world through her viewscreen blurred as the *Cestus* stumbled under intense weapons fire, including a laser shot to her 'Mech's head, which threw her against the restraining harness straps and nearly caused her to black out. The *Marshal,* taking advantage of her distraction, had closed on her to strike at the *Cestus* with everything it had. Fir trees burned around her from an errant flamer shot, but everything else had connected against her BattleMech's upper body for healthy damage.

Cassandra shook off the stunning effects of a head hit quickly, then began her fight with gravity. The neurohelmet she wore fed her own sense of balance into the Cestus' gyro, but that was not enough. She manipulated her arms for leveraging effect and moved one foot to a more stable position. It kept her upright, and she ascertained her damage while tracking back over to engage the *Marshal.* She had twice as many 'Mechs out here. Why didn't someone else pick up the *Marshal*?

The answer, when it came to her, was almost frightening in its simplicity. No one else fired on it, just like no one else had fired on the *Whitworth.* Because *she* had targeted it. She remembered the battle ROMs she'd studied from her brother's fights during the Clan invasion, and even some few older ones of her mother's MechWarrior days. How often had Cassandra noted other MechWarriors refusing to assist either of them, believing that Kai and Candace could handle themselves or might even resent any interference. High praise, she had thought then.

The *Marshal* was circling up the small hill, trying for her back. Cassandra wheeled around, centering her torso as she sidestepped in an effort to catch the *Marshal.* The other 'Mech's having to fight the uphill slope worked in her favor, allowing her to gain a target lock just as the *Marshal* shouldered up to the small ridge on which she stood. Close enough that she could read the Fusiliers insignia, and the markings that identified the *Marshal* pilot as a company CO. *One on one with the*

*most experienced enemy on the field. You wanted to see how
good you were, Cassandra. Here's another chance.*

Emerald light flared from the *Marshal*'s right-arm laser and
torso-mounted medium pulse laser. Both connected. The large
laser evaporated the last of her right-side armor, while the
medium chewed into her undamaged right arm. The Canopus
MechWarrior also swept the BattleMech's left arm in at the
Cestus' legs, trying to use the uneven terrain to force a fall. But
before it could connect, Cassandra struck back, hard.

Her Gauss rifle, suffering at the extreme close range, missed,
but that was all. The *Cestus*' large lasers cored into both sides
of the *Marshal*'s upper chest, while its mediums drilled into the
right arm and leg. The backwash of ruby light flared in the
night as armor melted under the intense energy or was simply
cut away from its supports. Bits of fiery metal dripped down to
the ground. *Did I get your attention?*

Cassandra felt the impact tremor and could hear the crunch
of crushing armor as the *Marshal*'s arm smashed into her right
leg. She easily kept her balance, and then kicked out in her own
physical attack. Myomer muscles capable of supporting the
weight of a sixty-five-ton 'Mech drove the kick forward with
tremendous power. The *Cestus*' slender foot drove into the
Marshal's right side, striking sparks as she crushed through the
last of its armor and into internal structure.

Voices overlapped from the speaker built into her neurohelmet as the Lancers radioed in several enemy 'Mechs crippled
or destroyed. Apparently the Lancers had only lost one of their
own so far, a *Blackjack* OmniMech, to a severed leg. Easily
fixed. Then, as the *Marshal* broke off and lowered its arms, she
caught the static-broken words of a close transmission. ". . . for-
withdrawal-repatriation . . ."

The Fusiliers patrol commander was asking for terms of a
surrender. There wouldn't be one, couldn't be one, and Cassandra almost opened fire on him while he continued to back
away.

"Frakes," she called out on her scrambled command circuit,
"reduce jamming enough to allow me to talk with the *Marshal*."
She gave it a few seconds, then tried an unscrambled broadcast

on a general frequency. "This is Major Cassandra Allard-Liao. Do you copy?"

The reply came back weak and full of static, but intelligible and obviously female. "Barely, but yes. What ransom will you take to allow my unit to withdraw?"

Cassandra knew a few seconds of surprise, having assumed her opponent was male. She had forgotten that in the Magistracy of Canopus women were dominant in the military. She swallowed to clear the dryness from her throat. "I cannot take any ransom," she said clearly. "My mission was to secure material and equipment any way I could to make up for that confiscated by Capellan forces on Hustaing and Denbar. Your people will be held, pending a prisoner exchange."

"Then we will fight to the end, Major Liao. And any deaths will be your responsibility."

Breathing easier now that her cockpit's heat levels had fallen back to a more bearable level, Cassandra bristled at the remark. "You do not lead warriors into battle unless you are willing to risk that," she said brusquely. "Besides, the disappearance of your unit will cause resources to be spent searching for you, instead of against Compact defenses." Even as she spoke, though, Cassandra felt some of her anger melting away and knew that the Fusilier commander might find a way to convince her otherwise.

The other warrior did not disappoint. "If I may," she said, "two of my MechWarriors who were forced to eject were picked up by a civilian truck. There will be no extensive search. I have four operational 'Mechs, if we include a *Commando* with a missing leg. I will surrender my *Marshal*, in return for the other three BattleMechs and freedom for all my warriors. I expect First Lord Liao will make good our losses from your captured equipment, or perhaps some of the newer Confederation designs."

Cassandra, jaw clenched tight at hearing Sun-Tzu referred to in such a respectful manner, almost denied the request out of spite. But then she thought it over. *What would my mother do? What would Kai do?* For the first time, she couldn't be sure that the two of them would have agreed. *Well, Kai would never have taken so long to put down a* Marshal, *so he'd be con-*

cerned with clean-up and salvage by now. *My mother, she would probably refuse or bargain for a much harder deal.*

But I am neither.

I have a victory here today. It is not the complete success I wished for, but it is a start. Cassandra nodded to the darkness outside her cockpit. "I agree to your terms, commander." *Next time I will do better.*

Celestial Palace
Zi-jin Cheng (Forbidden City), Sian
Sian Commonality, Capellan Confederation
1 April 3061

Sun-Tzu had pulled his chair over to sit in front of the aquarium in the corner of his office. The low hum of the pump was barely noticeable against the backdrop of busy footsteps out in the palace halls, most likely court functionaries roaming about on their morning duties. Sun-Tzu ignored the activity, instead letting himself become fascinated by the flame-orange Chinese battling fish that cruised gracefully within the tank among neon tetras and small silver angelfish. "So, Kai," he said to the battling fish as it paused in its watery flight, "have you returned with Victor?"

Naming his pet after his cousin went beyond belittling Kai Allard-Liao, though Sun-Tzu admitted that amused him as well. Like many things in his life, it served a second purpose. The fish was as fierce as it was graceful, just as Kai could be. And its wide, staring eyes were always on Sun-Tzu, cautioning him never to discount its namesake, who certainly looked toward Sian from time to time to judge Sun-Tzu's threat to the Allard-Liaos of the St. Ives Compact. *Fortunately, Kai has always embraced his warrior nature over any grand political impulses.*

Then again, that is more than enough reason to worry over my cousin. He frowned at the fish.

Over the last two years Sun-Tzu had occasionally dropped other named battling fish into the tank with Kai, just to watch them go at it. Eerily enough, Kai had never lost and often won handily. It was *almost* enough to make Sun-Tzu consider the idea of portents, though fortunately Kali's preoccupation with signs and omens and other such religious mania was a constant reminder of the sheer lunacy of such thoughts. However, there was that one time he had placed a "Victor" into the tank. The two fish had avoided each other, dividing up the territory and not fighting. Sun-Tzu had put it down to the coloration of the second fish, then netted Victor out and tossed the fish into the garbage himself. That had not been a good day.

But the one thing he had never done was name a battling fish after himself to set it against the one named for his cousin. Though he did not believe in omens, neither did he believe in tempting fate either. Sun-Tzu traced the flat of a long fingernail down the edge of his jawline. *Kai is the deadliest Mech-Warrior of his generation. Possibly the best ever.* If Kai had remained home, Sun-Tzu honestly doubted he would be making this attempt against the St. Ives Compact right now.

But Kai went off with Victor to fight the Clans, and even if he has returned it is too late.

"Little Victor," Sun-Tzu whispered, his mood lightening as he smiled at his partial reflection in the aquarium glass. "Enjoy your stay on Luthien." He laughed out loud, enjoying the sound of his own voice and almost wishing he'd been there when Yvonne Davion had informed her dethroned brother how she'd lost his realm. According to Maskirovka reports, Victor Steiner-Davion had returned to the Inner Sphere two weeks ago with the remnants of Task Force Serpent and his own forces, only to learn the bad news and then find himself exiled on Luthien. The task force had also returned bearing the body of Morgan Hasek-Davion, now deceased but formerly the leader of the FedCom's Capellan March and certain to have been a strong supporter of Candace.

Life is good today, he thought.

Very little he'd learned in the last twenty-four hours had been unfavorable. Talon Zahn's reports indicated that the Compact was beginning to show strains in its military resources. Candace's recent raids against forward supply bases on the Disputed Worlds hurt, and her employment of several veteran and elite mercenary units would slow things down as the fighting moved to new worlds, but they should not make the difference. *Even Kai, at the head of the First St. Ives Lancers, is impotent at this late stage of the game.*

The Chaos March worlds were still opposing his return far harder than anyone would have thought, but they were a minor concern. Only Wei and possibly the heavily garrisoned world of Pleione presented any real or potentially lasting threat among the Disputed Worlds. And the Free Tikonov Movement was well-established, beyond Katrina's means to quash it. *But I hope she tries. Nothing fuels a civil fire like forced repression. For all the Davion propaganda that it is the Confederation which suppresses freedoms, they are just as guilty, if not more so, of maintaining government control through force of arms.*

So many threads, spreading out from his hand and trailing over the horizon. *So a few are soaked in blood, even Capellan blood. The occasional knot must be pulled free, and the tapestry they make will rival anything ever before known.*

Naomi Centrella—another thread, and one of a few that could pull all final knots loose—was soon arriving on Detroit at the head of the Colonial Marshals and a Cappellan regiment to rescue her mother and put an end to Maltin's laughable attempt at a coup. After that, Sun-Tzu would pass along the news that her older sister was dead, lost to the Clans under Victor's command. *That places Naomi next in line for the throne of the Magistracy. Forces both her and her mother more into my camp as opponents of the Federated Commonwealth—who cares that Victor is no longer its ruler? And, I did not have to arrange for Danai's death myself. Always a bonus, that.*

Sun-Tzu forced himself to the edge of his seat. It was tempting to simply settle back into his chair, relaxing in front of the aquarium and leaving any troubles for the next day. But that was not his way. *What I have right now is a series of minor victories that strengthen my realm and promise greater things. But victories are not absolutes. They must be protected.*

He rose from the chair, lit a new stick of sandalwood incense, and slowly paced the office. Locating a problem before it happened was not an easy feat. So far as he could tell, the plans already set in motion would carry him all the way to the next Star League Conference six months away. *Six more months as First Lord.* In that time he would have to establish a stable presence in the St. Ives Compact, to reinforce his claim to the area. That, and something more.

Since I cannot hope to reclaim the entire Tikonov Commonality by November—not without tipping my hand or making a sacrifice elsewhere—it would help if I arrived on Tharkad with something other than ongoing trouble in St. Ives as a testament to my rule as First Lord. He *had* kept supply lines open throughout the Inner Sphere assault on Clan Smoke Jaguar, and had helped rebuild the shattered armies quickly, but that would be forgotten against Victor's ultimate victory and Candace's current complaints.

I need to force the other members off-balance in some way. Keep them focused where I would have them, and prevent any concerted effort against me. Katrina will offer limited support, but only until I nominate her as my successor and the votes are cast. Win, lose, or draw, she will then discard me as I would her. I might once have counted on Thomas, but with young Janos Marik insufferably healthy and rumors of a second child on the way, I can't even be sure that Isis' endangerment on Hustaing will be a lasting concern with him.

Isis—now *there* was a problem, though not for today. He shook his head. *I need something. Some added prestige or victory that might make others cautious in how they deal with me.*

Whatever that could be, it escaped him for the moment.

But, he would not let it slow down his plans for the Compact. *A stable presence in St. Ives requires pacified worlds.* Sun-Tzu paused near the french doors and stared out at the gray skies hanging over his capital city. "If you had any doubts, Aunt Candace, as to my resolve, you will have no longer."

Royal Compound
Tian-tan, St. Ives
St. Ives Compact

Candace Liao stole quietly into the Royal Compound's war room, not wishing to interrupt the discussion going on between

Colonel Caroline Seng and a number of the St. Ives Compact's senior officers. She waved the guard on duty at the door to silence, passing by him but not venturing far into the room. Her senior colonel was studying a holographic display of clashing BattleMech forces on one of the room's tactical tables. *The results of a recent battle, or a proposed action?*

"On Nashuar we are taking heavy losses now," a major was saying, waving his hand over the small-scale BattleMechs that tore at each other, "as evidenced by the battle ROMs of this latest conflict." *So,* Candace thought, *a recent battle. And more disappointing news.* "The Lyran forces under Star League colors are pressing forward harder, and now they are supported by House Hiritsu. The Seventh RCT is holding, but slowly their support structure is being kicked out from under them."

AFFC General Simone Devon shook her head. "They'll hold for as long as they're needed." She glanced to Caroline Seng, deferring to her when matters concerned Compact policy. "If you would place one of the new mercenary units under their command, though, it would relieve some of the pressure for holding the northern reaches on Nashuar."

Seng nodded absently, listening but still studying the board. "Do you have any unit in mind?" she asked.

"The Arcadians," Devon spoke up at once. "Their command structure consists largely of Federated Commonwealth expatriots, so integration will not be overly stressful. Also their general tactics lend to flanking support actions."

Candace could not help but be impressed, again, with Simone Devon's level of recall. *We are fortunate to have her, but then she is staunchly pro-Victor so Katrina probably does not want her back anytime soon.*

"I will second your request and place it before the Duchess," Seng responded. "I'm sure the order will go out at once."

Candace cleared her throat, breaking into the discussion. "You have my permission, Colonel Seng. I do not argue against common sense." *And if such a move can bring a measure of relief to Simone's forces, that is the least I can do.* "Is there anything else I can do, so long as I am here and have intruded?"

No one dared demand anything from her, though Candace read a hesitation in Seng's eyes. "Yes, Caroline?"

"Our military units are still acting under your call for minimum force," Seng said hesitantly. "In the last week, Sun-Tzu's Confederation forces have stepped up their aggressive drive. It's costing us. I know that it will escalate matters—"

"—but there is no avoiding that anyway," Candace broke in, "and it will give our people more options. I've been expecting that." She gave the tactical holographic display on the table a determined nod. "I've just been hoping we could delay until closer to the time of the next Star League summit. Sun-Tzu apparently does not wish to grant us that time."

"It's not just Nashuar, Duchess," a new voice chimed in. A mere captain from the Second St. Ives Lancers, but if Caroline Seng had invited him into this session he had to be extremely competent. He was certainly sure enough of himself to speak his mind. "Vestallas and Brighton are ready to fold, especially with the arrival of forces from McCarron's Armored Cavalry. They need reinforcements, and they need a freer hand in how to deal with the invaders in order to tie them up on those worlds."

"Tie them up?" Candace asked. "Are you suggesting that they do not intend to remain and secure those worlds?"

The captain shook his head. "I've studied the Cavalry, Duchess. They will leapfrog from these worlds once they've bought other Capellan units some breathing space, and hit Taga and possibly St. Loris. It is the next logical step."

Seng nodded her support for the young officer. "I concur. Sun-Tzu will want to shove us back first, place us on the defensive deeper into the Compact, and then he will pull back and consolidate the first-wave worlds while we are shoring up the defenses of secondary targets."

Candace frowned. *It is a devious enough plan, but is it the right one?* "What about the steamroller offense used in the Marik-Liao offensive of '57?"

"Sun-Tzu had the strength of the Free Worlds League at his back then," Seng answered. "Here he is more limited in resources. Despite his access to Magistracy troops, he has strong commitments to uphold in the New Colony Region and the Chaos March."

"And he will want a solid foothold before the conference on Tharkad," Candace said, spotting a new advantage that her nephew would want to gain. It was holding up nicely to scrutiny, which led Candace to believe that for once they had a chance of thwarting his plans.

"Very well," she said, her tone decisive. "Step up our offensive stance and strengthen the border worlds with mercenary reserves. I had hoped to delay this move, but obviously the time has come to make the territory Sun-Tzu wants more costly."

She was about to turn to the door, but paused for one final word to her senior officers. "One way or another, we will shut this war down."

The Killing Fields

The reason troops slay the enemy is because they are enraged.

> —Sun-Tzu, *The Art of War*

What most generals seem to forget is that this works both ways.

> —Sun-Tzu Liao, journal entry, 28 July 3059, Sian

28

Shì-Zhong-Xin Park
Pinedale, Denbar
Xin Sheng Commonality, Capellan Confederation
18 April 3061

The scent of grass and disturbed earth mingled on the warm breeze in Pinedale's central park, where the Hustaing Warriors and many Pinedale volunteers worked to repair some of the damage caused in February's fighting. Ni Tehn Doh, shovel in hand, paused in his work and wiped one sleeve across his brow, mopping up the sweat that trickled from his matted gray hair. The exertion of simple labor under a warm sun had his old heart pumping in a way that even the thrill of BattleMech combat could not duplicate. Still, before returning to his shovel-work he couldn't help fingering the new collar device of a regimental colonel on his utility uniform.

"Still getting used to them, *Sang-shao?*" *Sao-wei* Hugh Feng offered his CO a hesitant smile, rare on his usually dour face. Apparently Feng was feeling in a fairly good mood as well. Then he dug his shovel into the wheelbarrow of fresh soil, dumping a new spadeful into the blackened scar left by an errant PPC.

The newly promoted Ni Tehn Dho nodded absently at the question. With the material and equipment House Hiritsu had left his battalion, plus the Chancellor's verigraphed order to expand the unit, he had sent a small team back to Hustaing for more recruits. On Dho's authority, and liberal redefinition of the Chancellor's order, the team also commandeered enough

Hustaing Home Guard armor and infantry to fill out a full security and support battalion. Surprisingly, the CCAF's Bureau of Administration and Finance had rubber-stamped his actions and had also pushed through his promotion and their permission for the new *sang-shao* to promote men as necessary to fill out his Table of Organization.

But since when do regimental colonels get their hands dirty doing gruntwork? he asked himself. Since the Xin Sheng, and since *Sang-shao* Dho still had something to prove to his unit, were the answers.

Except for one BattleMech company and some combined armor/infantry security lances patrolling Pinedale or safeguarding their DropShips at the spaceport, the Hustaing Warriors were *all* present for the work. Until this week humanitarian efforts had been a higher priority, sponsored first by Kuan Yin Liao and then later by the Chancellor. The fighting had effectively ceased in and around Pinedale, though malcontent civilians still caused trouble enough that Dho had assigned one BattleMech lance to the park to safeguard against any vigilante aggression. Company-strength units traveled to other cities around Denbar on a routine basis to enforce the occupation and place under arrest any non-complying Home Guard units. From reports and a few lost patrols there seemed to be a growing and organized resistance to the Confederation's return, and *Sang-shao* Dho would have to look into that, but not today.

Today was for building a little goodwill with the newly made Capellan citizens of Denbar.

Dho worked alongside his men as an example to them specifically; a lesson that warriors were just as responsible for the damage they caused as they were for their duty, which required them to inflict it in the first place. They'd shown up in the morning with picks, shovels, and other equipment borrowed from the local Parks Department to repair the damaged grounds. Some worked on the torn-up earth itself, as the *sang-shao* did. Others cleared debris or doctored trees. Even more worked inside the reflecting pool, the water having drained away through the huge cracks Dho's *Victor* had put in its bottom.

Bringing back the reflecting pool would go a long way toward building a little good faith with the locals. It was truly the pride of the park. Barely six hours into the project, the Hustaing Warriors CO already saw improvement. For most of the morning his warriors had labored alone. Around noon Pinedale citizens had begun to trickle in, adding to the workforce. One of those civilians even now wheeled over a fresh load of sod, which she would pack into some nearby gouges where the feet of a 'Mech had cut through the park lawn. Not much, but it was a start.

The radio clipped to Ni Tehn Dho's belt squawked to life with a quick burst of static. *"Sang-shao,* this is *Sao-shao* Evans. Two messages from the spaceport, sir. Would you like the good news, or the better news?"

Dho frowned lightly, sweat beading in the lines on his forehead and then running down into his right eye. He rubbed at the burn and plucked the radio from his belt. At the edge of the park, Evans stood guard in a captured *Blackjack,* an older design but the only available replacement since the destruction of his *Jenner. Think I need a sit-down talk with Evans. He's obviously been hanging around the Arcade Rangers a bit too much of late.* Still, there was no reason to dampen the warrior's obviously good spirits just now. He keyed the transmitter. "Give me the good news, Danny."

"The XO has finished with that armored lance that came in this morning," Evans said. "With your permission, she wants to clear them for reassignment."

Making it the third Denbar Home Guard armor lance that has come in of its own accord since the formal declaration of Capellan occupation. Dho smiled. House Master Non's confiscation of equipment from resisting forces may have engendered some incredibly bad blood with the warriors released back to civilian life, but more units had either taken a neutral stance because of it or even come in to formally pledge to Capellan service. Dho pulled at the wisps of his beard. *Not a bad trade.*

"Tell her to act as she thinks fit," he radioed back. "Though I would prefer that they are put back to duty in the same city they came from."

"I think that was the XO's idea, sir."

Dho nodded to himself, mostly satisfied but still feeling just a twinge of regret over his selection of an executive officer. Not that *Zhong-shao* Ilsa Cappuccio wasn't competent and even worthy of the post, but it was another deviation from the old Capellan ways. *When has a BattleMech regiment ever named its armor support commander as its exec?* It sometimes felt like the Hustaing Warriors were out to break as many of the older CCAF conventions as possible, despite Dho's belief that many of those conventions were critical to running a proper Capellan unit.

He keyed the radio again. "So what is the better news, *sao-shao*?"

"Marshigama's Legionnaires are in orbit. They intend to deliver to us a lance of brand new BattleMechs, as ordered, and then take up station on the eastern continent."

The Legionnaires? Dho grimaced and he heard *Sao-wei* Hugh Feng groan as he eavesdropped. They were an older veteran mercenary outfit with long-standing ties to the Confederation, and one of the units recently "adopted" into the CCAF in a manner similar to McCarron's Armored Cavalry. But they were also infamous for their egotistical bent and extreme difficulty in working with other units. *This is good news?* "They are not integrating with the Warriors, are they?"

Evans' humor was evident, even over the radio. "No, sir. That is the better news, aside from the new BattleMechs. I guess they were fairly clear about keeping the commands separate. They are simply relieving us of responsibility for half of Denbar."

Well, they were welcome to it so far as *Sang-shao* Dho cared. His Hustaing Warriors occupied the capital city and the more important continent. The Legionnaires could chase resisting Home Guards through the southern continent's harsh mountain ranges. *And, of course, four new 'Mechs never hurt.*

"I don't suppose one of the new machines is a *Yu Huang*, is it?" Dho worked to keep the eagerness from his voice, though another hesitant grin from Hugh Feng told him that he had not altogether succeeded. Dho's *Victor* was a good design, for all its Commonwealth origins, but the new assault 'Mech House Master Non had piloted *really* made an impression.

"No, *Sang-shao*. A new *Raven*, *Snake*, and two *Huron Warriors*."

Dho shrugged. Good Capellan designs, every one. "All right, Danny. Thank you for the news. Pass my compliments back to *Sang-shao* Marshigama and then find a relief."

"Sir? You want me to switch out?" At the edge of the grass, Evans' *Blackjack* turned toward Ni Tehn Dho.

Smiling mischievously, Dho waved across the park at the *Blackjack*. "Yes. It sounds like you're having too much fun riding around. Get down here and grab a shovel." He returned the radio to his belt, and then laughed aloud when Evans turned the *Blackjack* around with an almost resigned slump in its shoulders. *Maybe I've been a bit too preoccupied with the past,* he thought, the humor assuaging his concerns for the moment. *The Warriors might just turn out to be a representative unit for the renewed Capellan effort; a true Xin Sheng outfit. We all acknowledge our Capellan heritage, proudly, but we aren't afraid of change. And most of all, we get the job done.*

Admirable sentiments, which lasted all of ten seconds and then were shattered as the civilian working nearby stumbled back with blood gushing out of a hole in her neck, the distant *cra-ack* of a high-powered rifle testament to the cause. Dho barely had time to grab his radio and yell, "Sniper," when Hugh slammed into him hard and drove him to the ground, pinning Dho under his greater weight.

Half-lying in the shallow ditch carved by the old PPC hit, Ni Tehn Dho could still detect the ozone scent that had been burned into the blackened earth and grass. Not three meters away the Denbar native twitched a few last times and then lay still, her life's force staining the nearby grass red and darkening the ground. *Was that shot meant for one of my warriors? Or is that the price she paid for collaborating with the enemy?*

A second rifle shot plowed a tiny furrow through the mound of soil in Hugh's wheelbarrow, and then buried itself in the ground a meter from Dho's head. He traced a line from the point of impact through the wheelbarrow and toward a high floor of an apartment building right across the street from the park. He shoved Hugh aside and keyed his radio. "Apartment building, south side. Fifth floor, maybe higher."

Hugh did not waste time looking. He crabbed over to his wheelbarrow, then rose to his knees long enough to run it side-on to the apartments and dump the whole thing over toward his commanding officer. Ni Tehn Dho dove for the improvised cover, followed only a fraction of a second later by *Sao-wei* Hugh Feng.

Not fast enough, as it turned out. The third bullet took the *sao-wei* high in his chest, directly through the breastbone.

Hugh crashed to the ground without much more than a single sharp cry that echoed the rifle *crack,* and then silence. His blood geysered out for a moment, soaking Dho's sleeve in a warm fountain. "Sixth floor," a voice called out over the radio, its owner apparently having seen the third shot. "Fifth window."

Dho punched the Transmit button, his breathing ragged from the excitement but nothing lacking in his fury. "Take that *wang ba dan* out, now! I don't care how. Just do it."

The answer came in a staccato chain of bursts that sounded almost like cloth tearing. *Light autocannon fire.* Dho rolled out from behind the barrow to find Evans' *Blackjack* standing between his position and the apartment, its right arm with a thirty-millimeter autocannon leveled at the building. Glass and a few shards of brick still rained down from the shattered window and its ledge. Just for good measure, it seemed, Evans ripped off another quick burst that chewed through more of the wall to no doubt shred the room beyond.

Sang-shao Ni Tehn Dho climbed slowly to his feet. He looked from the shattered apartment to his dead warrior to the civilian, who had simply been trying to heal some breaches in her own way. *She'll be buried here,* he decided, peeling off his uniform shirt and draping it over her. *Both of them will be buried here, where their blood stained the ground, and a memorial placed over the site.* Maybe it wouldn't mean much, personalizing the war in this way, but Dho could only hope that it would.

And right now, it was the best he could do.

29

Khingan Foothills
Nashuar
St. Ives Compact
24 April 3061

In the morning shadows of Nashuar's Greater Khingan Mountain Range, among the foothills and shallow valleys where a combined-arms company of the Seventh FedCom RCT had been assigned to patrol against any flanking efforts, Lance Sergeant Maurice Fitzgerald found the battlefield. He coasted the J. Edgar to a stop in the middle of the clearing, right in plain sight, and shut down his fans, which died with a final exhale of air from the hovercraft's skirt. He grabbed an assault rifle and handheld radio, checking to make sure the batteries were good, and then undogged the hatch. Fitz knew better than to exit his vehicle on an unsecured battlefield, but he had to get out and look for himself.

Besides, there's no one left here.

"Fitz, are you crazy?" That from Lance Corporal Chi Kung, Prowler Two, her voice a shocked whisper over the small radio. "Hey, Moe. Button back up."

Standing at the forward edge of his tank, the spring sun warming him through his padded uniform, Fitzgerald swept his gaze about. For as far as he could see, before stands of Ponderosa pine or the rise of a hill blocked his vision, lay a graveyard of 'Mechs, armored vehicles, and the bunched corpses of infantry squads. A good twenty meters from the nearest bodies, he still smelled the ripe, rotten stench of death. Many vehicles were little more than burned-out shells, and a few 'Mechs had suffered such catastrophic damage that only a few parts were even recognizable in a mass of twisted, plasma-scorched metal. The light sound of birdcalls seemed very incongruous with the carnage and destruction.

We figured on this. Two days, no contact. Fitzgerald rubbed a hand roughly against the back of his neck and tried to breathe lightly. *But to see it.*

With the scavenging practices of the Inner Sphere, born over several centuries of the Succession Wars, a battlefield like this was a rare sight. Salvage teams of the victorious side, if not both, were usually on the scene before the flames had completely died away. Bagging their own dead, burying the enemy if necessary, and picking the field over for useful equipment. From where he stood, Fitz saw at least three BattleMechs worth millions of C-bills each that could be piloted off the field if not for a missing leg or scrapped gyro. *Did they fight to the last man? No quarter asked or given?*

That seemed to be the case. Fitzgerald glanced about for any signs of motion. He found none, except the wind pushing around some tall but sparse grasses. He pulled off his helmet, listening for the calls or the moans of wounded but heard only wind in the trees. Tossing the helmet back down through the hatch, he then brought up the radio. "Prowlers Three and Four, recon the area," he said tersely. "Give me an accurate and independent count of vehicles and 'Mechs. Include design and colors, when you can tell." From where he stood he could read the Lyran Alliance insignia on several BattleMechs, as if their powder-blue paint would not have been indication enough. "Let me know right away if you find a survivor, or a Confederation 'Mech."

Why a Confederation 'Mech would mean anything special to him, except that House Hiritsu had forces present when the Lyrans hit the Seventh, Fitz wasn't sure. He jumped down to the ground, and walked toward the nearest bodies. An infantry squad, light rifles only, and by the looks of their mangled corpses ripped apart by heavy autocannon fire. He turned away and moved on to a wrecked Goblin infantry support vehicle.

Maybe I'd rather think that Capellans, even ones who are my enemy right now, were not involved in this slaughter. Because if they could do it, so could we. In his view, this wasn't the way battles were fought. Eventually, one side or the other retreated, or offered terms of surrender. Ransoms were paid or terms of salvage negotiated. As he moved from one vehicle to the next, one dead body to the next, Fitzgerald tried to figure out what had made the difference here.

"Did they kill each other off?" Prowler Two asked once.

Scanning the field, trying to get even a *feel* for what had happened, Fitzgerald shook his head. "Negative," he said. "At least, I don't think so. There will be a few soldiers limping back in at least one direction. Probably both, but neither with any good communication gear left to them." He continued his personal survey.

"Prowler One, this is Three," eventually came the call as Fitzgerald headed back for the J. Edgar. "No survivors and no Confederation units present. Count twenty-three, that is two-three, BattleMechs or pieces and twelve armored vehicles. I think I can confirm that all FedCom 'Mechs are present. And the Lyrans never landed armored support." Prowler Four echoed the results.

So the Seventh's combined-arms scouting force had been hit by a company of Lyran 'Mechs, and lost every unit but managed to at least account for all but one Lyran 'Mech. Considering the edge the Lyran force had in the way of experience, on the tally sheet that wasn't a bad showing. Fitzgerald climbed back up onto the J. Edgar and gave the killing field one last look. *Maybe not, but tally sheets never show this.*

Returning radio and rifle to their racks, Fitz pulled on his helmet and strapped himself back into his seat. "Okay," he said over his regular communications gear, dialing for a strong voice. His people would be feeling rather vulnerable after seeing this slaughter. "We have one Lyran 'Mech probably limping home with a busted radio. That makes it a race, and we need this salvage to stay in the game." His voice cracked a bit on the last bit. *A very deadly game.* "Cruising speeds until we hit the plains, and then it's flank for home." *And with any luck, this is the last time we'll have to make this kind of recon.*

But Fitzgerald didn't believe that. Not even for a moment.

Sitting alone in the mess hall and still not especially hungry, Fitzgerald ignored the buzz of conversation around him and stared at his tray. Breaded fish and rice. A typical meal, and one that the mess rarely ruined. He pushed the food around on his tray, quickly becoming more absorbed with the patterns he could make in his rice than in eating.

"You going to eat that, or frame it when you're done?"

Danielle Singh set her tray on the table and slid in next to him. "Heard about this morning's recon," she said. "Figured you would have led the salvage team back out there."

Fitz continued to play with his food. "They put my lance on a twenty-four-hour standdown. We've been pulling long hours lately." He looked over at her, wondering if Danielle had run into him by chance or design. Was she going to make another pitch for the 'Mech company? "What about you? Home Guard not providing cover?"

"Armor corps only. They wanted to get out to the site as quickly as possible." Danielle took a bite of her fish and chewed slowly. "Turned out to be a good decision. A battalion of Canopian Fusiliers walked in before they were half done and secured the area for the Confederation."

That got his attention. He pushed his tray away. "Fusiliers? I thought they were on Milos?" Fitz had been following reported troop movements, as if his knowledge of them might somehow make a difference. He was almost trying to handicap the war like some giant Solaris match, and the odds didn't engender much hope.

Danielle shrugged. "Who can follow all the players anymore? Rumor mill has it that the Lyrans have been pulled offworld, and the Fusiliers are here to take their place." She glanced meaningfully at his tray. "Why aren't you eating, Fitz?"

"Not hungry," he said, thinking to leave it at that, but then relenting. If there was anyone he could talk to, it was Danielle. "The battlefield," he said simply. "It's bothering me." He stared at her hard then, no longer wondering if her presence here was an accident. "You came looking for me."

She nodded. "I ran into Chi Kung. She said the scene was disturbing, and that you'd begged off a dinner in Hazlet with the three of them." Danielle looked him over carefully. "I never thought of you having a weak stomach."

No brains, yes. Weak stomach, no. Fitzgerald shook his head. "It made me a little queasy, sure. But that passed. It was something else. Driving that light tank around a field where BattleMechs had fallen." He shook his head again. "Makes me wonder what I can hope to accomplish in recon." *What* we *can hope to accomplish against the Confederation.*

Danielle set her fork down and pushed her own tray toward the middle of the table. "They managed to remove five salvageable machines from the field out there before the Canopians ran them off. We'll be needing MechWarriors. You thinking about accepting Nevarr's offer?" She sounded genuinely hopeful.

"I haven't stopped thinking about it, Danielle." He exhaled sharply. "But I don't think I'm ready yet. I glitched up bad in the sims. I won't let that happen again."

"Sure you will."

Fitzgerald snapped his head around. After the meeting with Danielle and Nevarr, he was surprised to hear her say that.

"I'm not saying you will make the same mistake," Danielle said quickly. "I think you've solved that little problem of yours. But you *will* make mistakes out there. We all do. And they'll cost lives sometimes." Her brown eyes sought out his green. "The Seventh RCT and the Arcadians can only do so much for us, Fitz. We need more MechWarriors."

"We *need* Group W, but they were set down on Taga just in case the fighting spreads deeper into the Compact." *Or in case Kai Allard-Liao and his First St. Ives Lancers can turn this around, once he makes it back. If he makes it back in time.* Fitzgerald swallowed against the knot of anger tightening his throat. "One MechWarrior isn't going to make the difference here on Nashuar."

Startled, Danielle sounded worried all of a sudden. "You sound like you're ready to bet against us."

Fitz calmed down, and even managed a stab at a smile. "I don't think I'm that bad. Not yet. We'll hold out here, and with the new support from the Arcadian mercenary battalion we can hope to chew up the Canopians and even House Hiritsu. But don't forget, they chew back."

"Just remember," Danielle said as she stood, picking up her tray, "we don't hold BattleMechs while waiting on any one MechWarrior to make up his mind. We have openings now. Who knows when that will happen again."

He watched her walk off, dumping her tray and then passing through the door. *Sooner than any of us want,* he told her silently. *And that is a safe bet.*

30

Poyang Hu
Wanzai Province, Nashuar
St. Ives Compact
8 May 3061

The lakeside resort in Nashuar's remote Wanzai Province resembled an ancient Chinese village, laid out around the green waters of Poyang Hu. The buildings, from the large resort hall to the far-flung individual cottages, were all styled in graceful, flowing lines, sweeping roofs with peaked corners, wide steps—all the classic architecture for which China had once been known and that Japan later stole. Meticulously maintained trees and shrubbery landscaped the entire resort and screened cottages for some privacy. The midday sun sparkled on the water, in a setting meant to suggest the tranquillity of an earlier era and to promote peace of mind and rest.

Still in House Hiritsu field uniform, Aris Sung sat cross-legged out on the resort's floating dock, his back against one of the rough-hewn pilings that anchored the dock as he stared out over the lake. Every so often he dipped his hand into the cool waters, stirring the reflections. He was not seeking tranquillity, or rest. With his company back from the field and Li Wynn away in the support of another operation, he had hoped to sort out the thoughts plaguing him of late. But the Asian setting somehow disturbed him all the more, distracting him from his thoughts.

House Master Non had selected this place as their base of operations because of its ties to their heritage, he was sure. But as a personal reward for the Warrior House? Or a reminder that this world had once belonged to the Confederation and that its people, though misguided, were still Capellan?

Both, he finally decided. Following the death of previous House Master Virginia York, Aris had been very critical—but silently critical, of course—of Ty Wu Non's performance in the position. But over the last few years Non had grown into his role as Master of House Hiritsu. His orders were often based on reasoning that eluded the common warrior but, more often than not, in the end were seen to be full of a wisdom that Aris had simply been unable to fathom.

He felt the vibrations through the dock's planking of someone approaching from behind before he heard the gentle footfalls. He chose to ignore them, wrapped up in his own reflections.

"Brooding is not something I admire in my warriors." Ty Wu Non's voice was quiet but matter-of-fact. "Especially in a House *Sifu*."

Startled, twisting about violently and trying to uncoil from his relaxed posture, Aris nearly fell off the dock and into the lake's cool waters. In one quick motion, House Master Non stepped forward and laid a steadying hand on Aris' shoulder. "Remain seated, Aris Sung. I will join you." The House Master knelt on the dock, careful of his wide-shouldered robe, and swept his gaze out over the lake's green surface, which reflected the wooded shore. "Quite a view you have selected here."

Many House Warriors had taken to informal dress while between missions. Going native, Aris had thought of it, keeping to his field uniform though he knew he was being uncharitable. In actuality, they were simply wearing their in-House dress, rarely seen outside the House Hiritsu stronghold but which Ty Wu Non had authorized. Suddenly Aris felt very standoffish, sitting next to his House Master, who had chosen such simple garb for enjoying a beautiful day. He tugged uncomfortably at his collar.

"Not brooding, House Master," he said in response to Non's earlier statement. "Reflecting."

"Na dui ma?" Is that so? "There is a difference?" The House Master smiled thinly. "The occupation of Nashuar has

been hard on us all, Aris Sung. I would never go so far as to say that House Hiritsu was wrong for this assignment, but Master Kung's teachings do weigh heavy on us. We want to give our family, even extended family related only by the thinnest Capellan blood, our respect and courtesy. That is difficult when our duty here requires of us to defeat them."

That is probably as close as any House Master ever came to criticizing the Chancellor. Aris nodded his understanding, nearly struck dumb with shock. The teachings of Kung-fu-tzu—Confucius to those of the House not quite as heavily learned in the older forms of address—were central to House Hiritsu philosophies. Noble sentiments, and engendering a strong sense of familial loyalty within the House. Perhaps Master Non was correct, and it should be House Imarra, with their political leanings, or Daidachi and its drive toward excellence in combat that should be here.

After a moment of silent thought, Aris decided that perhaps the House Master expected some response from him. *But something oblique. Not polite conversation, but as close as we can manage.* "I studied the ROMs of the Khingan battle," he said carefully, the slight shift in Ty Wu Non's posture telling him that he had his House Master's attention. "Supplied by the Lyrans before Chancellor Liao ordered their return to Alliance space." He shook his head. "That was not duty, that was personal. I doubt House Hiritsu could ever turn on another Capellan with that kind of ferocity."

Ty Wu Non looked straight at Aris, their dark gazes meeting. "Which could be the very reason we *were* selected. Interesting viewpoint. Hold onto that thought, Aris Sung, and you will do fine."

No, Aris thought. *Not fine. But I will do my duty. And when I can, I will take some pride in the execution of my responsibilities.* But he nodded, and said, "Of course, House Master."

In one fluid motion, Non levered himself up from the dock and rose to his feet. "I did not mean to interrupt your . . . *reflection.* I actually came out here to simply enjoy the view, and to let you know that I am pleased with the progress of your charge. Infantryman Wynn has proved himself very resourceful. I would almost go so far as to say an asset to the House." And with that, the House Master retreated from the dock.

Aris agreed, feeling a brief touch of pride. For a moment he remembered the young warrior of last year who had been so eager for glory and the chance to serve his House. Aris believed Li had become what he had dreamed of, though he still had much to learn.

"As do I," Aris whispered to his reflection in the lake. He swiped his hand through it, dissolving it in a splash of water. *As do I.*

Li Wynn wrestled against the unconscious body of another infantryman, dragging it off his legs. *Someone is going to pay for this.*

The interior of the brand new Blizzard hover transport was chaos, with bodies and weapons thrown around during the crash. The transport rested against something, throwing the vehicle's floor into a strange angle. The left-side armor was more memory than fact, with large holes punched into it and the red-hot edge where a laser had burned partially through. A few luckless infantrymen had caught pieces of the penetrating damage, and their blood slowly pooled in the lowermost corner. Li checked himself over, finding bruises and aching joints but otherwise whole.

"They're banking around," the driver yelled back from the forward compartment. "A Harasser and a J. Edgar." Overhead came the roar of long-ranged missiles from the turret launcher.

Li put about as much faith in the LRMs protecting them as he did in the light armor that had already failed its job. The Blizzard relied on speed, and now even that had been lost to it. Slinging his assault rifle over one shoulder, he grabbed a loose grapple rod and a satchel charge and was already at the rear door before anyone yelled, "Evac!" As the other House infantrymen grabbed up whatever weapons they could, Li punched the controls that lowered the entire back wall as a ramp. He hit dirt first, and moved immediately for some cover behind a small cluster of boulders at the foot of a small rise.

Flanked by two long, low hills, the main battle raged at fairly close quarters. The BattleMechs under Company Leader James held one pass while the Nashuar Home Guard supported by armor held the other. The Blizzard had been attempting to sneak around, where the infantry could come in close and try to plant satchel charges on the BattleMechs, when the light screening tanks of the Home Guard caught them.

You don't take Hiritsu infantry out of a fight so easy. Li spotted the two enemy hovercraft, wisely making a long sweeping turn to avoid Warrior House BattleMechs. He tried to gauge their next run against the Blizzard, then set off on a sprint for a point a hundred meters out onto the open plains.

"Li, get back here," Infantryman Mikhail Chess called out as Li broke cover. "What are you doing?"

"Payback!" Li yelled back. Then he concentrated on nothing except placing one foot after the other in an all-out run for his goal.

A small and scraggly bush offered the only cover nearby and Li slid down behind it. It was only then that he became aware of other footsteps, and then a body flopping down to the ground next to him.

"I didn't want you to get lonely," Chess said. Then both of them buried their heads under their arms as a flight of missiles that had missed its intended target slammed into the earth and detonated not twenty meters away, throwing up a cloud of dirt and scorched vegetation that rained down over the two infantry. "What are we doing here?"

"I'm going after one of those tanks," Li said simply.

Grapple rods were invented to match infantry against Battle-Mechs. A foot strap attached to one end of the meter-long shaft and a special adhesive ball fired from the other on a thin cable. The idea being that the ball would affix itself to the lower torso of a 'Mech and then the infantryman would ride up when the winding mechanism reeled the shaft up toward the ball. With a bit of luck, the infantryman could plant a satchel of explosives into the BattleMech's vulnerable knee or hip joint.

Well, hovercraft have their own vulnerabilities. Li unfastened one of the straps on the satchel charge, looping it through the grapple rod's foot strap before fastening it again. *With no one to thumb the activation button, this won't reel in.*

"Li, they're coming in."

And thirty meters off my estimation! Li hurried, readying the explosive charge. "I'll never make the first one, but when I yell you spray some laserfire over the windshield of the Harasser." And with that simple instruction, Li was off and running again to intercept the hovercrafts' line of attack.

As he expected, he missed the J. Edgar, which flew by at better than a hundred kilometers per hour. For the Harasser, though, he was dead on target.

"Now!" Li yelled, crouching in the open and aiming the grapple rod at the tank. He wanted the driver distracted, so as not to notice him. It worked too well. The Harasser, with bright laser bolts splashing into its window, swerved hard to throw off the unseen gunner and pointed the speeding craft directly at Li Wynn.

Li barely had time to fire off the grapple-rod ball, point blank, and then hit the ground as the hovercraft skimmed right over him. The roar of the fans was deafening, and Li felt as if he'd been thrown into a giant air compressor. He could feel his hair snapping against the side of his neck, stinging, as dirt ground into his eyes and ears. He also heard yelling, almost drowned out at first by the fans, but then growing louder in his ears as the hovercraft passed on.

It took Li a few seconds to realize the yelling was coming from him, then he stopped yelling and started counting while he watched the retreating Harasser. At the count of six the explosive charge, which had been dangling at the end of the grapple rod cable right near the lip of the hovercraft's skirt, detonated with a fiery explosion. One quarter of the skirt ruptured, spilling the cushion of air it had trapped beneath the light tank. The Harasser plowed into the ground at better than a hundred-fifty kph, nose crumpling, then flipped end over end as it continued to disintegrate.

Li stood up slowly and brushed off his uniform, as if he had all the time he could ever want. Ignoring the near-deafening sound of the 'Mech battle that still raged between the hills, he unslung his rifle and advanced on the Harasser. *I have a prisoner to acquire or a body-count to confirm.*

And it mattered little to Li Wynn which it would be.

31

Hai Fen-ling
Xin Singapore Province, Indicass
St. Ives Compact
28 May 3061

Cassandra cracked the hatch on her *Cestus* and climbed out onto the BattleMech's shoulder, welcoming the fresh air and a view of Indicass that did not involve staring at a monitor or out through her pitted and scored cockpit viewscreen. Sunlight filtered down through a canopy of vines and broad leaves, muted to a green tint, the perpetual shade responsible for the name Hai Fen-ling, the Black Forest.

There the peaceful scene ended, however. Any soothing forest sounds Cassandra might have heard if out for a nature walk were replaced by the gunshot-cracks of snapping tree limbs and splintering trunks as her battalion closed in around her position and then also shut down. Several of them carried salvaged parts from their recent battle—BattleMech limbs and even three fairly complete machines of Free Worlds League manufacture including a near-perfect *Apollo*.

Tamas Rubinsky waited for her at the *Cestus'* foot. His own Enforcer stood thirty meters distant, the 'Mech holding a silent vigil at the head of its company. The other Light Horse MechWarriors sat or, more often, slept on blankets thrown onto the forest floor. *Looks good to me,* she thought, knowing herself to be several hours away from anything remotely resembling sleep. Her joints ached from too many hours spent in her

'Mech. Sweat from the latest battle had dried, leaving a gritty residue in the folds of her eyes, which she rubbed away. Her mouth was pasty and she felt weary from lack of fluids, but there was no help for that.

She rolled out her chain-link ladder and then climbed down as Tamas held the lower end from swinging free. "Thanks," she said, reaching the ground and leaning back against *Cestus*. An awkward moment built up between them, as Cassandra remembered the first time she'd met Tamas and the way she'd been forced to part company with the Light Horse on her last visit to Indicass. *My actions were later vindicated. Sun-Tzu was coming, no matter what, but twenty-twenty hindsight rarely helps excuse an error in judgment.*

One hand mysteriously held behind his back and the hint of a smile tilting his mouth, Tamas remained stoic throughout the awkward moment. Then he nodded a simple greeting. "Is good to see you again, Major Allard-Liao."

Cassandra rubbed her hands briskly over her face for a few seconds, waking herself up, then glanced suspiciously at the Light Horse captain. "Don't tell me you're holding a bottle and two shot glasses behind you, Tamas?"

Laughing, Tamas shook his head. "Not vodka, no." He brought out a VitaOrange sports drink, condensation dripping off it. "But still good for what ails you."

"What's it going to cost me?" Cassandra asked, enjoying the banter almost as much as she yearned for the drink. *Has it been so long since I've been able to relax with someone?*

"Trade you straight," he offered, his Slavic accent warm in her ears. "Drink for the salvage you just bring in."

"Deal," Cassandra said, accepting the plastic bottle as he laughed again, deep and rich. She like his laugh, full of life and energy like his accent. "If I weren't so tired," she said after her first deep drink of the orange beverage, "I could kiss you for this." Then she turned serious again. "Really, Tamas, how much do you need? Take it all if necessary. My Lancers have nearly a full company of replacement 'Mechs already."

Tamas gestured her toward a nearby blanket, and she nodded

gratefully. "What you bring us from Milos was most appreciated. The colonel sends his regards and thanks." The two of them settled onto the blanket, Tamas sitting cross-legged and Cassandra lying back to stare up into the forest canopy. "So the question is, how much do *you* need, Major?"

"I think we've known each other long enough that you should call me Cassandra," she told him. "And I got away light. One 'Mech down and two with major damage, but no warriors lost." She took another long pull at her drink. "They weren't expecting a full battalion to hit them."

Tamas regarded her silently for a moment. "Every warrior in the Light Horse has a 'Mech. Perhaps you should take this salvage yourself, or for another unit."

"Giving away free equipment?" Cassandra allowed her surprise to show. That wasn't quite the mercenary way. "Colonel Rubinsky might take exception to that."

"He said to extend you every courtesy." Tamas shrugged, though mention of his father obviously did seem to sit uneasily with him. "I think you have more worries than just Indicass."

Cassandra sat up, feeling more energetic. "Maybe not. I have a plan that will allow us to reclaim Indicass. At the very least we'll retake Ceres Metals. But I need Light Horse support before I put it before my mother." She moved over to the edge of the blanket and sketched a rough outline of the province on the forest floor. "If we can lure the Second Hussars away from the facility with a diversion—"

"The Second Oriente Hussars no longer guard Ceres Metals, Cassandra," Tamas said softly, interrupting her. "I talked to my father before you arrive. Warrior House Daidachi has claimed the facility."

"House Daidachi? Here?" Cassandra lay back with a groan, her aches returned with a vengeance. She tried to puzzle out a new solution. Daidachi was one of her cousin's best Warrior Houses. She could match her Lancers against them, but she knew her mother would never allow her to risk the battalion to such a plan. Cassandra struck the ground with her fist. "Then it can't be done," she said quietly.

"It can't be done *right now*," Tamas offered. "But the Light Horse will continue to oppose the Confederation. Sooner or later, you get the break you want." He was silent a moment, then said, "Cassandra, for what it is worth, you were right before, when the Second Hussars landed on Indicass. It would have been better to drive them back early."

She smiled wearily. "Thank you, Tamas. That means a lot to me. But I'm finding out that being right doesn't help without the resources to act on it." She exhaled in a long sigh. *And today Sun-Tzu outbid me.* "I'm afraid I'll have to take you up on your offer. What salvage I don't need I'll take to another unit on another world." *Sooner or later, I'll find the chink in my cousin's armored juggernaut.* "So long as the offer stands."

Tamas regarded her through narrowed eyes. "I do not know," he said, drawing out every word which exaggerated his accent. "As you say, my father could get unhappy, and that is not pleasant sight."

"I remember," Cassandra said, sitting up to lean on her elbow. A true smile flickered at the corners of her mouth, but failed to fully materialize. "What is it going to cost me, Tamas?"

"Your Lancers will join my Light Horse for a terrible dinner of field rations, before we head back to new camp and you head for DropShip." He smiled roguishly. "Maybe I scrounge a bottle and some glasses."

Sitting up, Cassandra pushed aside her other problems for the moment. She told herself to enjoy the good company while she could. "You drive a hard bargain, Tamas. But you have a deal."

Celestial Palace
Zi-jin Cheng (Forbidden City), Sian
Sian Commonality, Capellan Confederation

Once again Sun-Tzu had shunned the robes of Chancellorship, this time to fully present himself as First Lord. He wore an embroidered gold silk Han jacket over silk trousers, green dragons chasing up the jacket sleeves. *Gold, the color only emperors were allowed in the old dynasties.* The same outfit he had worn at the beginning of the Star League conference on Tharkad, the conference where he had been elected to the post. Fitting, if Talon Zahn did not exaggerate the situation.

The bronze-faced doors leading into the Celestial Palace's throne room stood open, awaiting him. Conspicuously absent were the two members of the Death Commandos who normally would have stood guard. He passed through the doors and into the formal reception. Isis Marik, Talon Zahn, and *Sang-shao* Hyung-Tsei of the Death Commandos all awaited him at the far side of the throne room, gathered near the Celestial Throne.

And flanking the red-carpeted path between the small committee and the door stood the twenty-four members of the Black Watch, one company to each side.

The old guardians of the First Lord!

Every member stood at ramrod-straight attention, resplendent in a dress uniform the Inner Sphere had not seen for over three hundred years. Tartan sashes and kilts, the arrangement of colors within the plaid unique to the Black Watch since the days of pre-space flight Terra. Heavy, forest-green jackets cut along the lines of the old Star League Defense Force uniform, with a high collar and deep hem. Sporran with large cream-colored tassels backing four smaller tassels in black. Rank devices worn on the shoulder, and on the cap the ancient Black Watch insignia.

Ghosts from the past. That was Sun-Tzu's first thought. Once a proud regiment devoted to the protection of the First Lord of the Star League, the Black Watch had ceased to exist when the old Star League fell. Sun-Tzu walked slowly down the double-rank of men, his intense gaze boring into the soul of each man. As he passed between each pair of the Watch, they turned inward with crisp military precision and a sharp crack as the heels of their dress shoes snapped together. In every pair of eyes the First Lord saw a ruthless, unforgiving edge—the same fanatical gleam he knew from his Death Commandos.

His review complete, Sun-Tzu approached Talon Zahn first.

"I was not sure whether to believe it possible." He smoothed out the front of his jacket. "Can the Black Watch really have survived over three hundred years in secret?"

Zahn, also back in dress uniform for the occasion, nodded toward the last man in the right-hand receiving line. "I believe that Colonel Neil Campbell can better answer your question, First Lord."

Turning to face the Black Watch commander, Sun-Tzu silently chastised himself for his lack of attention. The officer wore the rank insignia of a Star League colonel, though by Zahn's initial report only two companies of the Watch currently existed. But who—except perhaps the First Lord— would dare tell this unit that they had to obey strict ranking conventions? Sun-Tzu looked the colonel over, and was forced to admit that he liked what he saw. *This could be just what I have been looking for.* "Well, Colonel? Is it true?"

Released from his parade-grounds posture with the First Lord's recognition, the Black Watch commander took a crisp step forward. "Very true, First Lord Liao. Some members of th' Northwind Highlanders long believed that they were still a part of th' Black Watch in spirit, bein' fierce upholders of the traditions of the Star League. They formed an 'order' within the Highlanders, secretly waiting for the rebirth of th' Star League."

Sang-shao Hyung-Tsei frowned his disbelief. "Then why didn't you come forward two years ago?" Sun-Tzu read both jealousy and suspicion in the Death Commando's voice, but it was a fair question. He also noticed the tense ripple of frustration that played over the augmented muscles under Hyung-Tsei's uniform. The Death Commando was a dangerous man, and Sun-Tzu would have to make sure that he did not alienate his realm's prestige unit or its commander.

"We felt it necessary t' prove our worth," Campbell said simply, as if the statement explained everything, "to ourselves, if nothin' else." After a few seconds' pause, he picked up his thread. "Th' Black Watch failed in its duty only once, two hundred years ago, when Amaris the Usurper staged the coup that ultimately sundered th' first Star League. We have suffered our own penance, but before we would ask a new First Lord t' trust our service, we decided to test ourselves against the Clans, who represented a threat at least as great as th' Usurper."

Sun-Tzu hid his elation behind half-veiled eyes, thinking this was too good to be true. "Well spoken, Colonel. So your two companies have defeated the Clans on their homeworlds, have they?"

"Just one company, First Lord." The colonel's voice was strong and vibrant, and showed no hesitation in answering with complete honesty. *A quaint mannerism,* Sun-Tzu thought. "We traveled by th' fastest possible route to Sian upon return. A second reinforced company from Northwind, some of the best th' Highlanders had to offer, joined up with us en route. And we expect t' keep growing, until we are as we once were."

"And you hope to replace my Death Commandos?" Sun-Tzu asked, letting just a trace of hesitation slip into his voice for Hyung-Tsei's sake.

"Until a new First Lord is elected," the colonel answered promptly, "we would pledge our lives and honor t' your defense and t' the defense of your homeworld."

Walking into the next Tharkad conference with a Black Watch escort would turn some heads. Perhaps earn me the extra political weight I've been wanting for the meetings. I will placate Hyung-Tsei's ruffled pride in private, later. Sun-Tzu drew himself up proudly, as if struck by Campbell's words.

"Colonel," he said, "welcome to Sian." And he actually meant it.

Colonel Campbell personally set two Black Watch guards at their permanent posts outside the bronze-faced throne room doors and then went to set two more at the main entrance to the Celestial Palace. Only Isis Marik remained behind with her fiancée, her features shining with the pride she felt as Sun-Tzu half-sat, half-leaned against the seat on the Celestial Throne. *How far he has come. And with my help, he will go farther still.*

"I suppose you would now advise me to withdraw from the St. Ives Compact," Sun-Tzu said, extending legs and arms in a cat-like stretch, "in order to prove my deserving of the Black Watch."

Isis recoiled at his mocking tone, a warm flush rising to her cheeks. *He is under a lot of stress now,* she thought, trying to excuse him. Still, she allowed a bit of her hurt to tell in her voice. "That is unkind, Sun-Tzu. Because I suggested you treat St. Ives with more compassion than you have does not mean I think you undeserving. In three short years, you have done more for the Inner Sphere and for your own nation than anyone would have thought possible." She smiled her support. "Allowing the Black Watch to escort you into the conference will be a strong end to your term."

A hooded look crossed Sun-Tzu's features. "So now you support my efforts to reclaim St. Ives?" The mocking tone faded but not entirely.

"The day you declared Denbar a Confederation world, it became too late for any other course of action." She shrugged, seeing in Sun-Tzu's attitude a dangerous undercurrent on the subject. "Perhaps I was wrong, and it *is* time to reunite the Confederation."

That seemed to mollify Sun-Tzu, who reclined back in comfort. "See if you can't impress that thought on your father, next time you send him a message. If he will not allow us to marry, he might at least offer some more military support."

Put so bluntly, Isis felt like a bargaining chip. *But Sun-Tzu is not totally without justification for his cynicism. Nine years is too long an engagement, regardless of any political considerations.* "Of course, beloved. I shall do so at once."

"At once is not necessary," Sun-Tzu said with a wave of his hand. "Tomorrow will do just fine." He rose from the throne. "You will excuse me, Isis, but there are some matters that require my attention."

Isis read her summary dismissal in his tone. She nodded once. "As you desire, Sun-Tzu." She bit her lower lip, holding back a sigh. She would certainly press her father, asking for more support. He might even send it. *Anything to keep her at a distance, anything except the marriage I desire. And when we show up on Tharkad, escorted by the Black Watch, maybe it will be time for us both to confront him and force a marriage date.*

And by the time Isis left the throne room, she had convinced herself that this was exactly how it would happen.

32

Yasu
Wanzai Province, Nashuar
St. Ives Compact
3 June 3061

Lance Sergeant Fitzgerald raced his hovercraft through Yasu's merchant district, dividing his attention between his head's up display and the main ferroglass viewscreen. A city far south of Hazlet, Yasu's only claim to strategic value was that, at this moment, it served as Nashuar's latest battlefield and one of the most deadly mazes Fitz had ever encountered. Buildings on either side of the narrow, meandering streets rarely rose above three stories, but they pressed in uncomfortably close. His hands ached from several hours at the J. Edgar's controls, and a light tremble threatened to betray him during any one of the high-speed turns.

Ignoring the danger inherent in brick and steel flashing by at close proximity and at better than a hundred kilometers per hour, Fitz stuck to the tail of Karen Simmons in Prowler Three's Harasser just as the Arcadian mercenary in the *Hussar* 'Mech stayed glued to his rear. The three had formed an interim partnership after being separated from the main battle, where the company of Arcadians had shattered into its component lances under House Hiritsu's pressure. They had scattered like dry leaves before a storm. Now these three searched through the twisting streets for a return route.

Three blind mice, see how we run. The line from the old

nursery rhyme swam up from the depths of Fitz' mind. Actually this wasn't so hard. All they had to do was follow the smoke.

Occasionally, over the lower buildings, Fitzgerald saw the black-gray smoke column of a large fire. It reached into the sky to feed the growing haze over the village, and by all observations it appeared to be spreading. Wood was used primarily for residences around here, and that fire was too far away to be within the merchant district. Those had to be homes on fire. And until his group cleared out of the city, any emergency vehicles would stay safely out of their way and the fire would spread. Fitz damned the Arcadian's company commander, who had decided to fall back into the small city and then damned the Hiritsu officer who had followed.

While you're at it, you can damn yourself. You were serving as recon, and could have led them off in another direction. Fitz shoved aside the self-reproach. In three other directions had been lake country and heavy forest, not the type of terrain he wanted to be caught in by the Warrior House. He knew his job. *Right now, my job is to help the Arcadians regroup.* Another turn, and another. They had to be getting close.

How close, Fitzgerald learned not five seconds later as an enemy *Wraith* fell from the sky to land ninety meters back from the *Hussar*. He doubted, however, that the ambush had been planned. The 'Mech would have come down firing if it had. Before he could think the action through, Fitzgerald spun his J. Edgar one hundred eighty degrees, now gliding backward along his former path of travel but slowing as the drive fans countered his momentum. The *Hussar* raced by, stepping over the small hovercraft as Fitz fired his medium laser and then backed up the short lance of energy with a full spread of the hovercraft's missiles. *Draw his fire and then evade.* Wasn't much of a plan, but it was the best he could come up with on the fly.

The medium laser struck the *Wraith* in the lower left leg, carving into the BattleMech's bellbottom-flared armor. The energy weapon drew a ragged scar against the blued-steel finish, splattering the streets with a quarter-ton of the *Wraith*'s armor protection. Two of the four missiles also scored against the Hiritsu BattleMech, one blasting a chunk of ferro-fibrous armor from the left elbow and another clipping the head, snapping off one of the *Wraith*'s two whip antennae and doubtless giving the MechWarrior inside a good shaking.

Rattled by the head concussion or not, the Hiritsu pilot did not seem to lose consciousness or sense of target priority. The pulse lasers on either arm spat out scarlet pulses that flew after the retreating *Hussar,* all of them tracking in on the light armor that protected the mercenary's back. What little armor there was evaporated under the intense energy barrage, which then chewed deeply into the *Hussar*'s internal skeleton. The light 'Mech faltered on its next step, but then regained its balance and raced onward.

"We're cutting left," was Prowler Three's only communication as Karen's Harasser and then the *Hussar* took the next corner open to them.

Time for me to be making my escape as well. Fitz powered up his drive fans and threw a violent twist into his tank's controls. The J. Edgar swung hard right and dove into a nearby alleyway, knocking aside a few large plastic trash cans and then speeding down the back street with little more than a meter to spare on either side. The roar of the fans reverberated off the brick walls. Dirt and old papers billowed up, raising a small storm of light debris behind him. *That will make me harder to follow.* Then, in the next instant, he remembered. *The* Wraith *jumps!*

"Prowler Three," he shouted, opening a channel to his remaining lancemate, "break away. That *Wraith* can clear the buildings and come down in your six again. Break away!" He burst out of the alley just long enough to cross a new street, and then plunged back into another dim back street as he waited for a response.

"Too late," the reply came back softly. "The *Hussar* is down. Where away, Fitz?"

Fitz punched the padded wall of his hovercraft cockpit. *"Ma de dan!"* he yelled, cursing the situation as much as himself. *I*

*asked for mercenaries, and we were actually sent some merce-
naries, and now we're losing mercenaries. Nice, neat little
package. Just like I lost Chi Kung in Prowler Two to Hiritsu
infantry last month, and last week David in Prowler Four, still
alive but being fitted for a prosthetic leg.* Fitz ground his teeth
together in a mixture of frustration and raw anger. *By bits and
pieces they're taking my unit apart.*

"I'm in an alley, running parallel to your course," he finally
told his lancemate, cutting across another street. "Take your
next left, and we should meet back up." That was all guess-
work. With Yasu's meandering streets, the two hovercraft
could be speeding apart at ninety degrees by now. Fitzgerald
could only hope he was right.

"Copy, Prowler One. Tracking in." A brief pause, and then,
"It's opening up. And we have a firefight."

A blur near the end of the alley was Karen's Harasser gliding
by at flank speed. Fitz pulled out and wheeled in a hard bank
that put him in her six and speeding along a lakeside street. The
lake was narrow but long—dividing the merchant district from
a residential area. Counting the bordering grounds and streets
along each side, it provided the kind of open area inside a city
where BattleMechs tended to converge. No exception here.
Fitz looked to his tactical screen to read one lance of Hiritsu
BattleMechs playing a deadly game of tag with a like number
of Arcadians.

Correlating his tactical display with the view through his
ferroglass shield, it looked as if most of the 'Mechs had
grabbed a defensive location and were holding it—jousting
with heavy weapons at medium or even long range. The smoke
Fitzgerald had been trying to track in on earlier rose from a
group of burning houses on the lake's other side. A *Centurion*
belonging to the Arcadians still prowled that area, taking partial cover behind other homes as it fired its medium-bore autocannon at a House Hiritsu *Huron Warrior.* The emerald lance
from the *Huron Warrior*'s large laser stabbed in after the *Centurion,* but gouged into the roof of the house instead. Shingles
blew off and rafters shattered under the hammer of raw energy,
and several pieces caught fire to start that home burning as well.

Stabbing angrily at his comm panel, Fitzgerald opened a channel to the mercenaries. "Striker Two," he said, reading the *Centurion*'s designation off his tactical screen, "clear out of there." He threw his J. Edgar into some light serpentine twists as a Capellan *Catapult* tried to bracket him in with a flight of long-ranged missiles. A few clipped his left side, gouging armor, but Fitz rode out the damage and kept transmitting. "Those homes can't stand up to heavy weapons."

"Neither can I," came back the response. "I've lost over sixty percent of my armor, and there's no more defensive positions to fall back to."

"Then fall back and evade," Fitzgerald ordered, though he possessed no authority to do so. *But dammit, at some point someone has to take responsibility for these people.*

"This is Striker One," the commander of the Arcadian support lance broke in. "We're holding this position until we regain communications with our command lance or even our scouts. Prowler Recon, can you at least confirm scout lance location?"

If you won't move, then I've got to convince that Huron Warrior *to turn its weapons in another direction.* Fitzgerald overtook the Harasser and then plunged his J. Edgar down the bank of the lake toward the water, followed by his lancemate. Riding on a jet of air, he skimmed across the water as easily as gliding over a grassy field. Easier.

"Scout Lance was scattered," he informed the Arcadian officer. "You're down a *Hussar* for sure." He raced up the opposite bank, throttling up to flank speed.

Their first pass against the *Huron Warrior,* Fitzgerald scored with a pair of missiles that Karen made look weak by connecting with four of her own. The *Catapult* threw another flight of LRMs at the two hovercraft, the missiles plowing into the ground in front of them and throwing up a heavy curtain of dirt and sod, which the J. Edgar and Harasser flew through. The *Huron Warrior* ignored them, striking out again with its laser and Gauss rifle, this time connecting with the Gauss rifle while the laser missed high. The slug slammed into the *Centurion*'s right shoulder, crushing the joint and then tearing the entire arm away—robbing the 'Mech of its primary weapon.

Swinging around to line up for another run, Fitzgerald cursed as the *Centurion* responded with its long-ranged missiles, and the *Huron Warrior* stabbed into the house again with another errant laser shot. He doubted the hovercraft could draw off the *Huron Warrior. Those two are locked onto each other hard, and we're too small. We can't do enough damage to these BattleMechs.*

"Our command lance was heading into the industrial district," someone said. Fitzgerald thought it would be Striker One, but wasn't able to tell for sure by voice alone. "They were followed by a *Wraith* and a *Thunder*. Seen any of them?"

Opening his mouth to ask for a description of the *Wraith*— the blued-steel look of the 'Mech that had taken out the *Hussar* was fairly unique—Fitz closed it quickly as some thoughts came together. *I'm asking for trouble again,* he thought as the two light hovercraft strafed the *Huron Warrior.* They managed slightly better against it this time, between the two of them connecting with a medium laser and seven missiles, but still nowhere near the level of damage necessary to threaten the medium-weight BattleMech.

"Your command lance is either down or pushed out of the city then," Fitzgerald informed the Arcadians. "It was the *Wraith* that crushed your *Hussar* not five blocks from here. Which means it will be leading a new Hiritsu lance against this position any moment." A slight exaggeration, but plausible.

"Then we fall back and try to circle in toward the industrial district. Pick up survivors or regroup as possible."

Fighting through the residential areas the entire way, Fitzgerald figured. "If you fall back straight for the edge of the city," he transmitted, "Prowler Three and I will take the back alleys over to the industrial sector. We can get in and out faster than you." *And without drawing a 'Mech firefight into the middle of the residential district.* "If they're in there, we'll lead them out. If not, we'll scout the countryside beyond and then guide them in on your path of retreat."

Fitzgerald ignored the incredulous "We'll what?" from Karen and waited for the support lance commander to respond. *Take the deal. All you can hope to do here is lose more people.*

Apparently the Arcadian officer came to the same decision. "The battle is lost today, sure enough. All right, Prowler One, we're pulling back. Good hunting."

Good. Fitzgerald dialed back over to the private frequency he shared with Karen. "Back the way we came, Three, and no stopping unless we see Arcadians hitching a ride."

"Copy that."

He appreciated that Karen made no more of the order. They were diving back into a deadly maze of twisting streets and enemy 'Mechs, but their duty as Home Guards was to place themselves on the danger line, and that meant protecting Nashu-ar citizens as much as it did running light hovercraft against BattleMechs on the field. Neither of them would ever shirk that duty.

He frowned, recalling his last conversation with Danielle that touched on the same ideas. *We don't shirk, no matter what it calls us to do.*

Lance Sergeant Maurice Fitzgerald stood easy in Nevarr's office, his padded helmet held loosely by the strap in his left hand. He'd come straight here from the maintenance bay, after helping to load new ammunition for his missile launchers, hoping to find Nevarr in. He still wore the padded field uniform of the Home Guard armor corps and was in desperate need of a shower. Fitz raked fingers back through his brush-cut hair, combing through where his helmet had matted it down.

"You could have showered," Nevarr said, not looking up from the work spread over his desk.

Fitz remembered that Nevarr had spoken exactly the same words to him nearly a year ago. "Yes, Captain," he answered, noticing the new rank insignia on Nevarr's collar. *Because of the expansion of Home Guard BattleMech Forces?* Fitzgerald hoped it was so. "Sir, I wish to reconsider your offer to join the Home Guard MechWarrior forces."

Nevarr did not look surprised. Glancing up he studied Fitzgerald with his cool stare. "I read the report you radioed in an hour ago," he said quietly, returning to his work, dividing his attention between a thin pile of papers and a noteputer. "Exceeded your authority again, didn't you?" Nevarr did not wait for an answer. "That's becoming a habit, Fitz."

Fitzgerald stiffened, the mild rebuke still scoring deeply. Nevarr always knew where to cut. "Yes, sir," he said simply.

"This time, *maybe* you saved what was left of the Arcadians. As well as numerous civilian lives." Nevarr shoved aside the noteputer and papers. "So was the situation lost at the lake? Could the Arcadians have beaten back House Hiritsu?"

Was there anything Nevarr didn't know? Between helping to reload his missile racks and the walk over, he couldn't have had more than forty-five minutes to check into the situation. "They *might* have been able to win at the lake," Fitzgerald admitted, "yes sir. But the entire situation was unstable. A victory isn't any good if you can't make use of it." He paused, then, "And there were the civilians to consider."

Nevarr evidenced no reaction. "So why do you want to be a MechWarrior? You turned it down last time it was offered."

"I said that I would be back when I thought I was right again." Fitz knew that sounded odd but didn't know how else to explain it. "I stayed with my armor lance out of a sense of responsibility, even though I wanted the MechWarrior position more than I can say. Today I pushed the limits of what I can do in the armor corps, and it was lacking."

Frustrated, he exhaled sharply and searched for better words. "I am responsible for my people, to my unit, and mostly to the citizens of Nashuar, Captain Nevarr. I can better serve everyone in a BattleMech. I can make a bigger difference."

"That sounds fairly egotistical, sergeant." Nevarr's tone bordered on complete neutrality, as if it mattered not to him one way or the other. "So tell me this. Do you think we can stop the Confederation?"

A chill raced along Fitzgerald's spine as he considered the loaded question. *A year ago, even a month ago, I might have said yes regardless of the odds, thinking I could make the difference in a BattleMech. And I would have been lying, to Nevarr and myself.* "No sir," Fitz said, his voice slightly subdued. "We can only delay the inevitable here. If there is a solution to this war, it will come from outside Nashaur. Our job is to give them that time."

Nevarr reached into the thin stack of papers he had shoved aside. Thumbing through it, he selected a sheet and glanced over it quickly. "Group W's third battalion has been sent here from Taga. They escorted in a supply ship, which carried two more BattleMechs for the Home Guard, a BJ-3 *Blackjack* and a new assault-class *Emperor*." The captain's face betrayed none of his thoughts. "Which would you prefer?"

"If it pleases the captain," Fitzgerald said at once, "I would prefer the *Blackjack*."

"Not the assault 'Mech?" Now Nevarr frowned. "Couldn't you make an even bigger difference in the *Emperor*?"

Fitz shook his head. "I honestly think that's a bit much for me right now. I'm well-trained for medium 'Mechs, and that's where I should start." He gave Nevarr an even gaze. "If nothing else, I hope I've learned when to limit my ambition to a practical level."

Nevarr smiled, and his eyes gave away his satisfaction. "So do I, *Subcommander* Fitzgerald," he said, immediately promoting his newest warrior.

"Welcome back to the unit."

33

Hé-Mí-Lù Canyons
Yuling Territory, Denbar
Xin Sheng Commonality, Capellan Confederation
13 June 3061

Sang-shao Ni Tehn Dho hated canyons, and Denbar's Hé-Mí-Lù were among the worst he'd ever seen. Literally translating to Box Mazes, the fractured landscape split and rejoined in so many places that getting lost was a real danger. Sheer cliffs measuring forty meters and higher pinned all but the best jumpers to the canyon floors, which ran anywhere from two hundred meters at the widest point to narrow, rubble-filled passages barely wide enough for a 'Mech to pass through. The rock was so unstable in certain areas that a heavy footfall could bring down a massive slide, and hiding places so numerous that to check every one would slow any unit down to a crawl. An ideal site for ambushes.

Just like the one my Hustaing Warriors walked into.

A missile-lock warning screamed for attention even as the enemy *Apollo* appeared on the *sang-shao's* head's up display, near the left edge of the band and so one hundred-sixty degrees to his rear. He wrenched on his control sticks, knowing that he could not make the turn in time but muscles straining anyway as he tried to pull the *Victor* around faster by force of strength. Two flights of missiles from the enemy *Apollo* peppered his left side, blasting chunks of armor from his leg, arm, and rear torso. Minor scratches to the assault 'Mech's thick armor plating, but sill something he would rather have avoided. *Too many surprises already, too many unknowns.*

Like the very appearance of the Blackwind Lancers, finally out of hiding and returned to the field like avenging spirits. And who had equipped them with Free Worlds League designs?

From first contact, when two enemy lances had stepped from concealment to savage the Warriors' front line, there had been little doubt whom they faced. Paint schemes varied, but each 'Mech proudly displayed the insignia of the Blackwind Lancers—blue ax head on yellow field. And in case there might be some doubt as to which battalion, the MechWarriors had added the Chinese ideogram for the number *two* into the ax head. That at least solved his earlier questions as to what happened to the Dispossessed Lancers. But not where they received BattleMechs.

Squeezing down on the right control stick's main trigger, Dho launched a single Gauss shot off at the *Apollo* as the Earthwerks-designed BattleMech stepped back into the cover of a narrow defile. The nickel-ferrous slug slammed into the canyon wall, shattering a large section into shards and dust and triggering a large slide of unstable rock from the cliff face. The rubble piled up against the canyon wall along a sixty-meter stretch, and the large cloud of dust it raised worked to further obscure the retreating Lancer 'Mech. *Last I heard, Earthwerks was under strict orders not to sell to the Compact. When did that change?*

Victorious shouts suddenly bled over each other on the Warriors' general frequency, followed by *Sao-shao* Evans' report. "*Sang-shao* Dho, we finally dropped that *Tempest* up front. It lost a leg, but is currently being shielded by a *Marshal* and a *JagerMech*. Request permission to push forward."

"Negative," the Hustaing Warriors' commander ordered, "hold position." *We're scattered enough as it is, and we've seen only a company of the Blackwind Lancers. If the entire battalion is somehow out here, they'll take us piecemeal the moment we split up further.* "That *Tempest* was the best we've seen, so heads up, everyone. If it was their commander, its loss should start something."

It did, though not in the way *Sang-shao* Dho expected. The *Apollo* was peeking back out of the defile again, just far enough for its LRM launchers to loose another spread of missiles. Facing it this time, Dho easily floated his own targeting reticule over the enemy machine. This time his Guass rifle scored, like a marksman slamming its one-hundred kilogram slug into the *Apollo*'s sternum right over the Lancer's insignia and crushing roughly a full ton of armor. The *Apollo* responded with another two flights from its LRM launchers, and Dho set himself to ride out the buffeting.

What he did not anticipate was the sudden appearance of eight enemy machines, medium to heavy, along the left-hand cliff rim and the intense fire that suddenly fell down on him.

"A trap! A second trap," the *sang-shao* had time to warn his command as two PPCs and a number of lasers cut into his *Victor*, followed immediately by a hail of autocannon and missile fire and one Gauss slug from a *Cestus*. Dho's assault machine, normally a stalwart fixture on any battlefield, shook mercilessly under the onslaught. He did not even try to stand up against such an attack, and abandoned the *Victor* to gravity while working to lessen any damage from the fall.

"We have multiple contacts," *Sao-shao* Evans transmitted, voice showing strain. "At least four lances of St. Ives Lancers. Repeat, *St. Ives* Lancers. Two 'Mechs down. Falling back."

And right into the concentrated fire of two more lances, Dho thought, rolling the *Victor* to its front and working to stand. The fall had shaken him, and he could feel the bruises forming where his safety harness straps crossed his body. *There must be a back way onto the ridge for them to put larger machines above us like that. With that kind of concentrated firepower, one out of every three Hustaing Warriors will die right here in this part of the canyon. A trap within an ambush, and the St. Ives Lancers holding the ax over our heads.*

"All units retreat," the *sang-shao* ordered as the *Victor* rose to its feet. His damage schematic showed the loss of over seven tons of armor, more than half his total protection. His right side and leg were especially vulnerable, damage already penetrating to the skeleton but no critical equipment touched as yet.

Their next salvo will finish me, but maybe I can buy time for a few Warriors to escape. Standing in the middle of the canyon, enemy machines above him, Ni Tehn Dho prepared himself for a glorious last stand. *Nothing like going out in true Capellan fashion, fighting in a hopeless situation.*

Then he noticed three Warrior 'Mechs, rising on jump jets toward the ridge. *Vindicator, Blackjack,* and a new *Snake. The Arcade Rangers!*

But only the Snake *can reach the edge of the cliff,* Dho thought with some amount of amazement, until he saw the fourth Ranger in a *Hunchback* standing toe to toe with the *Apollo* near the massive rockslide Dho's errant Gauss shot had brought down earlier. The *Vindicator* and *Blackjack* must have crawled up onto the pile, using it as the little boost they needed to reach the top of the ridge. And if they could divert just enough firepower from the canyon floor . . .

Targeting the *Cestus,* its low-heat Gauss rifle the greatest danger to him, *San-shao* Dho struck out with every weapon at his disposal. Medium pulse lasers stuttered emerald energy darts into the *Cestus'* left arm and side, while the *Victor*'s own Gauss rifle placed a large slug directly into its center torso. Three of four short-ranged missiles connected next, one slamming into the *Cestus'* head and the other two worrying more armor on the front chest. The *Cestus* managed to return fire only with its two large lasers, its Gauss rifle missing high, burning more armor from the *Victor*'s right arm and central torso.

As he had hoped, the Arcade Rangers managed to redirect the firepower of several St. Ives Lancers' BattleMechs. While their lancemate in the *Hunchback* tore into the *Apollo*'s armor with its Kali Yama big bore autocannon, the rest of the Rangers targeted another four 'Mechs, with the *Blackjack* splitting its weapons fire between two targets. The *Snake,* having foregone the use of its arm-mounted LB-X autocannon, shoved a *Gallowglas* and sent it plummeting off the backside of the ridge.

Their formation disrupted, only three of the ambushing 'Mechs fired in concert with the *Cestus* in an attempt to savage the *Victor.* The blue-white lightning of a single PPC scored the

Victor's left side, cutting into the internal structure and slagging Dho's short-ranged missile launcher. A quartet of lasers, mixed staccato pulses and energy lances, cut across his arms and chest but failed to damage any more equipment.

Dho worked his control sticks, keeping his balance as one of the Hustaing Warriors' forward lances retreated back through the canyon to regroup at his side. That evened out the odds, even if they took down his *Victor*. So until the enemy's own forward-placed elements could catch up, and so long as he could stay alive, it gave the Warriors the advantage. *Care to continue?* he silently challenged the opposing commander, whichever 'Mech it was.

The *Cestus* answered, regardless of command structure. With a parting Gauss rifle shot, the 'Mech retreated off the ridge. Singly and then in pairs, the other Lancers also vacated the area.

"Rangers, get back down here," Dho ordered, not about to leave his people sitting up there as targets. Communications from his forward elements warned him that the enemy was still advancing against them, but more cautiously than before. The *Snake* and *Blackjack* made safe landings, but the *Vindicator* came down hard in the rubble and left shattered armor behind amidst the boulders and dirt. Still, it regained its feet quickly enough.

"Sir, this is *Sao-shao* Evans. Shall we form a new offensive line back here?" A pause, and then, "We lost three 'Mechs, and we only have one warrior pickup."

Dho shook his head. It hurt, having to leave behind good men, but the Lancers owned the day regardless of any last minute reversal to the trap. "No. This round goes to the Lancers, Blackwind and St. Ives both. They obviously know the Hé-Mí-Lù Canyons, and we're getting out before we learn any more hard lessons today. Rangers, you earned yourselves point duty, lead us out of here. Evans, take rearguard.

"We hurt them," he reminded his people, wanting to get them thinking on this as a tactical retreat, not a rout. "Maybe not as bad as they hurt us, but it could have been much worse. Two months ago, I doubt any of us would've walked out of the canyons alive. Take what you can from that, Hustaing Warriors. And don't worry. We'll get another shot at them."

Dho closed the commline and piloted the *Victor* out from the canyons. *Yes, we'll get another shot at them. And another,* he told himself. *And another.*

The war is far from over.

Near sunset, the shadow of the Hé-Mí-Lù Canyon walls already falling over the St. Ives Lancers' DropShip, Cassandra Liao shook hands with Brevet-Major Warner Doles of the resurrected Blackwind Lancers second battalion. "Your people did good today, Major Doles," she said, having already confirmed his new rank before the battle. "Sorry we couldn't grab you an entire company."

"You tried, Major Allard-Liao." Doles broke his grip and stepped back, then snapped Cassandra a crisp salute, which she answered. "No one can ask for more."

Cassandra shook her head. "I can," she said. "Good hunting." The she turned away sharply and moved up the ramp into the ship. The *Overlord*'s 'Mech bay was a flurry of activity as technicians secured the Lancers' BattleMechs into their stalls, preparing for space travel. No one approached her or called out, and Cassandra was glad for the privacy.

My plan could have worked. Should have worked. Not that she expected to turn the tide of the war on one raid's success. But if the Lancers could've taken down a company of the Hustaing Warriors, threatened the Confederation hold on this planet, it might have forced Sun-Tzu to tie up more forces in garrisoning Denbar. *To be thwarted by a rockslide!*

Cassandra forced a calm on herself. The Blackwind Lancers were running back at company strength at least, plus three more machines acquired from the Hustaing Warriors. With any luck, they could now mount a successful guerrilla warfare campaign.

Not that Denbar was such a major priority now. Even before landing, the ship had picked up on local news that told of fighting also on St. Loris and Ambergrist, two nearby worlds. *No telling what is happening up near Nashuar and Brighton.* Cassandra pursed her lips in thought. *If nothing else, though, the*

Cossacks on St. Loris will give my cousin's forces a welcome they will not soon forget.

Thinking of the Cossacks, Cassandra wondered how Tamas was getting by on Indicass. The planet was considered Confederation-controlled, like Denbar a part of Sun-Tzu's Xin Sheng Commonality, but not completely pacified. Until some priority reports caught up to her, she could only assume that meant Rubinsky's Light Horse retained a strong presence there. *Good luck, Tamas. I'll get back to you when I can.*

Cassandra found an empty crate and dragged it over next to a stanchion, where she could sit with her back to the cool metal and watch techs work on her *Cestus'* damaged armor. Her mother would be off for Tharkad soon, to the next Star League conference, leaving Caroline Seng behind in charge of the ongoing resistance. Cassandra would remain in the field. *The St. Ives Lancers go to Ambergrist next, to assist in its defense. Then perhaps back to Indicass. And somewhere along the way I can hope to find a fatal flaw in my cousin's armor.* She offered thanks once again at not having been dragged from her unit, from the fighting, to accompany Candace. *I am not needed on Tharkad. Mother and Kai can handle that. I'm needed here. I can see what needs doing, and I can get the job done.*

I can!

Epilogue

Candace Liao walked slowly through the Hall of Treasures, paced by Senior Colonel Caroline Seng. Comfortable in the museum setting but not taking the time to enjoy any of the exhibits, Candace's bearing remained almost military in nature, back straight and hands clasped behind her. Even with the strain of the last six months, the weight that often settled on her when no one was around, she refused to give in to the effects of age. *While I live, I owe my people more than frailty or weakness. I owe them hope, and whatever possibilities I may wring from the situation.*

"Indicass is confirmed?" she asked, more to ease Seng's growing discomfort at her own silence than any hope for a denial.

"It is," Seng answered. "Indicass, Denbar, and Vestallas are all under direct Confederation authority now. Part of this so-called Xin Sheng Commonality." She sneered the words, her opinion obvious. "We still have resisting forces on each world, mostly thanks to Cassandra's efforts, but the civilian populations are suffering under the prolonged struggle." She paused in thought. "Could we present the growing civilian problems as a charge against Sun-Tzu's efforts? That his Xin Sheng program is failing?"

"In the Star League chambers in November, perhaps. But for

the common masses . . ." Candace considered the idea a moment as the two walked in silence, their footfalls against the polished wood floor echoing in the stillness. "No, he could too easily reverse that against us." *And he might anyway.* "See what he has done with Kuan Yin's humanitarian efforts, presenting them as proof that we hold ourselves responsible for the devastation even though I'm sure her efforts keep him frustrated.

"Xin Sheng means new birth. It would be very Capellan to argue that deteriorating conditions in the Xin Sheng Commonality are due to the bad karma earned from the Compact's *previous life*. For our abandonment of the Confederation during the Fourth Succession War." *Yes, that would be just his way. And the sad thing is, such an idea would find a reception in my realm as well as his.*

Caroline Seng was not put off so easily. "Well we must do something, Duchess, or we will lose Brighton next. Our forces were making progress with noncompliance against the Star League occupation units present, but reports now place a regiment of McCarron's Armored Cavalry on the world. Nashuar is a mess, and Milos . . ." She shook her head. ". . . Milos we've heard nothing from, good or bad. And that worries me." The Compact's Senior Colonel clenched her hands into fists. "We must *do* something," she repeated.

"We are, Caroline," Candace said, placing one slim hand on the arm of her aide and friend. "We have slowed the Confederation's advance, and now we must be patient." But patience, Candace knew, was a trait hard-learned and one that atrophied quickly if not practiced. *Dear Justin taught it to me so long ago, and I have never had cause to put it aside in favor of impulsiveness. Caroline has spent her career reacting, and so cannot be expected to take such waiting easily.*

"Are you saying there is nothing left to do, Duchess?" Caroline Seng's frustration colored her voice with just a touch of resignation.

Candace smiled grimly, and shook her head. "There never was anything to *do,* Caroline. Nothing to prevent this, and certainly nothing to contain it now. Sun-Tzu made up his mind to come after the Compact, and would have found his support somewhere to do so. But," and Candace heard the confidence in her own voice as she explained her plans, "he relies heavily on the political weight of the First Lord office, as well as the SLDF troops placed at his disposal, and there we can attack him. It is just a matter of when, not whether."

"The Tharkad conference in November," Caroline said, nodding her understanding.

"Yes. My brother Tormano's recent messages have hinted at a pledge of support by Katrina, in return for my vote toward her candidacy, I am sure, which could be used to reverse the failure of my vote six months ago. And even if not, I believe Thomas Marik may be persuadable. He has to be considering his chance for the First Lord office, and this would present an opportune moment to reinforce his image as a facilitator for peace." Candace's eyes narrowed and her voice hardened. "And Kai will be there. If anyone can give Sun-Tzu pause for thought, it will be my son."

Caroline smiled at the thought. "Kai is enough to give anyone pause, Candace. He's the best warrior anyone has ever seen. You are right to be proud of him." She clasped her hands together, rubbing them gently while analyzing the situation. "So we undercut Sun-Tzu's support, and then force a recall of the Star League Defense Forces, which will leave his positions in the Compact vulnerable. Better still if we can shift the SLDF troops over to our side and immediately put them back into use."

"That is the ideal," Candace agreed, "but we must beware. I will not have the Compact becoming a Star League protectorate. Katrina Steiner-Davion is too near, sitting on her throne on New Avalon. We could easily trade one conqueror, hiding behind the title of First Lord, for another." *One I might have to vote into office, whatever my personal feelings are toward her. I am sorry, Victor.*

"A tough decision, choosing between Katrina or Sun-Tzu," Seng said, attempting a light touch of humor but failing.

Candace gazed off with a far-away look in her eyes. "No," she said softly, "it wouldn't be. Not for the people of the Compact, and I doubt even for you, Caroline. *That* is the danger.

And *that* is the power we must not allow to fall into my nephew's hands, at any cost."

Not if the Compact is going to live.

Celestial Palace
Zi-jin Cheng (Forbidden City), Sian
Sian Commonality, Capellan Confederation

Sun-Tzu Liao sat on the carved mahogany throne of the Capellan Confederation, left hand cradling a small glass of light plum wine while the right traced the smooth back of one long fingernail down his jawline. *We've come such a long way in the last twelve months, so close now to restoring to the Capellan Confederation a large measure of its former strength and glory.* He leveled a cool, jade gaze at his chief advisors, who carried their own drinks and stood just below the dais awaiting his recognition.

Jiang-jun Zahn bore up under the scrutiny well, secure as always in his competency. A far-off glaze to his eyes suggested that he might be looking in on another scene. *Perhaps reviewing a recent battle in the Compact, or orchestrating a future one?* Only a flicker of unease showed on Sasha Wanli's face, the remnants of her failures in the past year. But the Maskirovka reform was coming along well, and so Sun-Tzu did not begrudge her a slight sense of well-being. Ion Rush, fully recovered from his ordeal and operations, waited off to one side as if distancing himself from the meeting. Burn scars peeked out from his collar and left cuff. *They all deserve a word of recognition, if not praise, but also a reminder that we have yet to finish what we have started. The threads begun last year will see 3062 with certainty before the design is finished.*

Sun-Tzu raised his crystal goblet. "To the rebirth of the Capellan Confederation," he toasted, voice soft yet full of its own strength. He sipped at the sweet wine, noticing the slight tartness for which the year was known.

On the floor, all three raised glasses in salute and then sipped at their own wine, poured by the Chancellor's hand. Sun-Tzu noticed Sasha's hesitation, as if considering whether the wine had been poisoned. Ion Rush moved slowly, with great deliberation as if the slightest muscle twitch required great concentration of effort. The Chancellor and First Lord could see the Imarra Master's myomer muscles bulging under his uniform, even in their relaxed state. *I left the choice to him. He will adjust.*

"*Jiang-jun* Zahn, I saw by your initial report that the Death Commandos have put an end to the situation on Wei." Sun-Tzu controlled his eagerness by speaking slowly. "We now have possession of the nerve agent they used against McCarron's Armored Cavalry and others?"

Zahn's self-assured expression faded just slightly. "Not yet, Chancellor Liao. Wei is pacified, yes." He glanced toward the door, on the other side of which two members of the Black Watch stood guard. "Using the Watch to free up your Death Commandos allowed me to put an end to the rebellion, but *Sang-shao* Hertzog reports that the chemical graveyard was already raided and the nerve agent gone." Zahn glanced at Sasha Wanli. "Though the rebellion leaders deny ever having removed more than a small percentage, I feel fairly confident that the Maskirovka *investigation* will find that they moved it to a new storage center."

Unfortunate. Not that Sun-Tzu had immediate uses for such deadly material. *But better I have control of it than anyone else.* "And you have read Naomi Centrella's report on the situation on Detroit? You are satisfied with the outcome?"

Zahn settled a politically neutral mask over his face. Only Sun-Tzu's sharp gaze picked out that his *jiang-jun's* dark eyes lost some of their normal animation. "I do not grieve for the loss of Jeffrey Calderon, Chancellor, that is true. He was a hindrance to Confederation goals. His death during the final battle for Detroit is most convenient, from a military viewpoint." Now Zahn's gaze sought out Sun-Tzu, and he raised his glass slightly in a silent salute. "Perhaps we will find assistance from the Taurian Concordat after all."

Sasha Wanli cleared her throat, edging in on the conversation. "If I may. The Maskirovka has noted an increase in anti-FedCom sentiment coming out of the Taurian Concordat. While it does not constitute proof, the Taurians, at least, seem to believe that the FedCom was behind Maltin's coup *and* Calderon's death." She paused, considering, before speaking again. "The Maskirovka can find no trace of intentional assassination," she said, though her expression hinted that she might have said more in other company.

Not even back to me, is that what you left unsaid, Sasha? And you are consumed with curiosity to know whether, and how, I might have arranged it. Sun-Tzu awarded her a tight-lipped smile. *Do you know how many people can keep a secret? I do.* The Chancellor then spared a few seconds for Naomi, liberator of Detriot and now Emma Centrella's heir. *The thread that pulls all final knots free? Perhaps.*

Sun-Tzu sipped again at the purple-tinted wine. "Ion, what about the SLDF troops in the Compact? Are you prepared?"

The Imarra Master again nodded, only his head and neck moving. The rest of his body remained motionless, like an immovable slab of rock. *Or steel,* the Chancellor thought. "The Lyran troops were already pulled back to Brighton, abandoning Nashuar to *Jiang-jun* Zahn's forces alone. We control Indicass through Vestallas, so no troubles there. On your order, Chancellor, I will move them out. Security will hold."

"I trust that it will," Sun-Tzu said. "Begin operations, then. I want no SLDF troops left in the Compact by the time of the conference." *And won't that ruin Katrina's plans? Promise my Uncle Tormano that as First Lord you would order the SLDF occupation troops out, will you?* He glanced to his Maskirovka Director, who for once had pulled off a fair intelligence coup, intercepting Tormano's messages to Candace. *That might have hurt, losing a standing garrison force such as that so quickly. I must find a way to remind Katrina that I am a better ally than enemy. In case she has forgotten.*

He glanced between his ranking general and intelligence chief. "Step up activity in the Tikonov area," he ordered. *That is a start, but I still have a personal score with her. One that can be settled on Tharkad, though.*

Tharkad. "I leave very soon for the Star League conference," he said. "I expect to return to Sian with matters further advanced than when I leave them." His three advisors all nodded with a degree of solemnity. *Though it has been my office, they too have enjoyed some additional power from my carrying the title of First Lord. And when I return, that will be gone.* He sympathized, not that it mattered so much to him personally. *Up until the final vote is cast, I am First Lord. No one can take that away from me, just as I will not let anyone ever again take away my Capellan Confederation.*

"Our renewed Capellan effort has been a success," he reminded them, "so far. We have our paths to travel, and threads to collect, but what was once ours will be again. Do not lose faith." He let a trace of threat creep into his voice. "But do not ever think to relax our vigil." *Just in case they are inclined to forget what complacency once cost us.* "We will protect our victories, and we will grow stronger yet.

"The Xin Sheng has only begun."

Glossary

Officer Ranks

Capellan (Han)	Old Ranking	Equivalent
Sao-wei	Subcommander	Lieutenant
Sang-wei	Commander	Captain
Sao-shao	Captain	Major
Zhong-shao	Major	Lieutenant Colonel
Sang-shao	Colonel	Colonel
Jiang-jun	Senior Colonel	General
Sang-jiang-jun	Nonexistent	Senior General

Warrior House Ranks

Zhang-si	Infantryman	Lance Corporal
Ban-zhang	Squad Leader	Lieutenant
Pai-zhang	Lance/Platoon Leader	Captain
Lien-zhang	Company Leader	Major
Ying-zhang	Battalion Leader (infantry)	Lieutenant Colonel
Shiao-zhang	House Master	Lord Colonel

About the Author

Loren L. Coleman has lived most of his life in the Pacific Northwest, an on-again off-again resident of Longview, Washington. He wrote fiction in high school, but it was during his five years as a member of the United States Navy, Nuclear Power Field, that he began to write seriously.

His first year out of the military, Loren joined the Eugene Professional Writers Workshop, and within a few months sold his first story. He has spent the last four years working as a professional freelancer, writing source material and fiction for game companies such as FASA Corporation and TSR. For FASA, he has written for both the BattleTech and Earthdawn games. His first two novels, *Double-Blind* and *Binding Force,* were also set in the BattleTech universe and published by Roc Books.

Loren Coleman now lives in Washington State with his wife, Heather Joy, two sons, Talon LaRon and Conner Rhys Monroe, a new daughter, Alexia Joy, and the usual troublesome cats.

Yu Huang

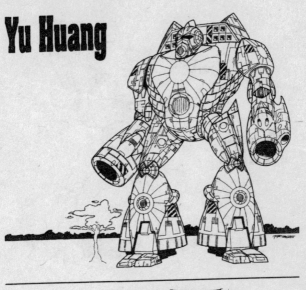

JagerMech

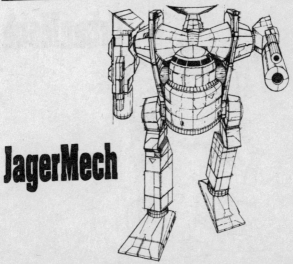

Wraith

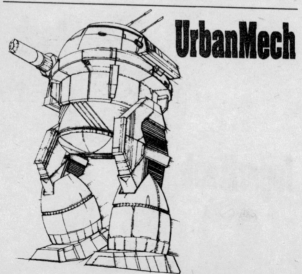

UrbanMech

Cataphract

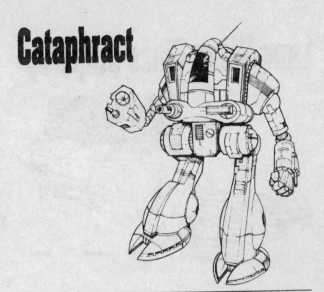

Hunchback

Lung Wang Class DropShip

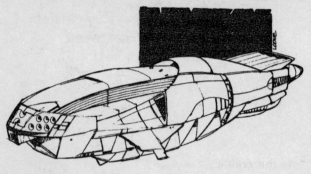

Invader Class JumpShip

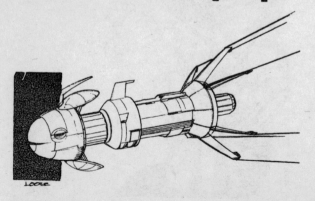